THE HOLLOW GODS

Smiler's Fair

About the Author

Rebecca Levene is an experienced author of fiction and non-fiction and has written scripts for TV and video games. She began her career writing media tie-ins for properties ranging from *Doctor Who* to the *Final Destination* movies. More recently, she's had published two original supernatural thrillers and a short story which the *Guardian* said, ". . . combines thwarted ambition and a gallery of fascinating secondary characters to wonderfully readable effect". She is also a writer for the hit app *Zombies, Run!* You can follow her on Twitter @BexLevene.

REBECCA LEVENE

Smiler's Fair

THE HOLLOW GODS
BOOK I

HODDER &
STOUGHTON

First published in Great Britain in 2014 by
Hodder & Stoughton
An Hachette UK company

I

Copyright © Rebecca Levene 2014

Maps by Clifford Webb

A CIP catalogue record for this title is
available from the British Library

Hardback ISBN 978 1 444 75368 4
Trade Paperback ISBN 978 1 444 75369 1
Ebook ISBN 978 1 444 75370 7

Typeset in Plantin by Palimpsest Book Production Limited,
Falkirk, Stirlingshire

Printed and bound by Clays Ltd, St Ives plc

Hodder & Stoughton policy is to use papers that are natural,
renewable and recyclable products and made from wood grown
in sustainable forests. The logging and manufacturing processes
are expected to conform to the environmental regulations
of the country of origin.

Hodder & Stoughton Ltd
338 Euston Road
London NW1 3BH

www.hodder.co.uk

For Muriel Levene
for everything

THE
MOON
FOREST

Aethelgas
⊚
Ivarholme

EOM
territory

SALT ROAD

THE
MOON
FOREST

MAENG
territory

The
Spiral

Birdview ✷ ✷

Little Bird

BEZDONY
SEA

WILDERNESS

THE FOUR
TOGETHER
territory

Rune
Waste

THE BLADE PASS

RAH
territory

New Misa River

Winter's
Hammer

Misa Delta

BADLANDS

CHUN
territory

DAE
territory

NORTH

THE
SILENT
SANDS
territory of
the Ahn

✷	Shipforts
⊚	Twin Cities
⊙	The Spiral
▭	Path of Smiler's Fair

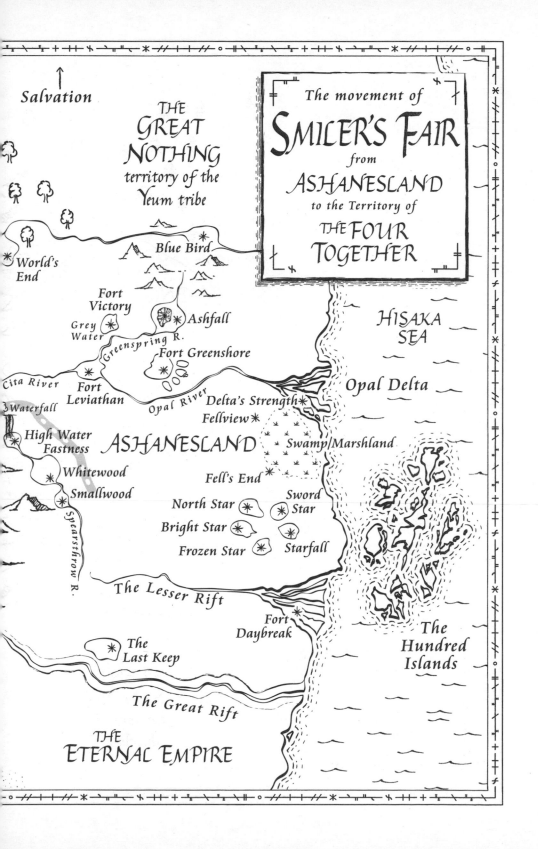

Smiler's Fair

Prologue

Samadara felt the baby kick and shift, a sudden pressure against her bladder. He was nearly ready to leave her and she had run out of time to save him.

The room didn't look like a prison. Her royal husband had been generous when he'd chosen her quarters and her chambers were in the oldest part of Ashfall, its ancient heart. The wooden walls were stained purple-red with grassweed and the tapestries over them showed scenes of the great ocean crossing, the smiling faces of their ancestors looking out from their ships towards the new lands. A thick rug covered the floor, giving her feet a sure grip as it rocked beneath her with the motion of the water. The windows were wide, letting in the weak winter sun and the not-quite-fresh smell of the lake.

The guards were out of sight outside the door, the door itself unlocked. But the guards were there and they wouldn't let her leave, not while the baby remained inside her. She'd have her freedom again when her husband had taken his child's life.

Athula huddled in the rocking chair opposite, a string of drool connecting her lips to her stained woollen dress. Samadara could see the meat knife at her belt. It was unremarkable and unthreatening, something the guards wouldn't have thought to question. But if her maid had done as she'd asked, it would be sharp enough for the job.

'Athula,' she said, and again when the old woman's eyes blinked open, 'Athula, it's time.'

The wrinkled face was hard to read. Was it pity Samadara saw there? Fear? Or perhaps those were her own feelings.

'Are you sure, my lovely?' Athula asked.

Samadara nodded. 'The babe stirs – he's eager for freedom. Soon Nayan will have his guards inside the room and there'll be no saving him.'

'Do you have to save him?' Athula held up a hand when she would have protested. 'Babies die every day, my duck. If your little mite comes into the world this way, he might live but an hour. It's a high price for such a short time.'

'I'll pay it. Your man's waiting outside as we arranged?'

'And the guard has no eyes below, I've checked it myself. We're ready, if you mean to go through with it.'

Samadara nodded. 'Well then.'

Her body was ungainly, barely within her command in these last weeks of her pregnancy. She struggled with the front ties of her dress, her swollen fingers clumsy on the ribbons, but she batted Athula's hands aside when the old woman tried to assist. She wanted her dignity now, or as much of it as her husband had left her. She let the servant help with her slippers, the barrier of her belly hiding even her own feet from her. She felt, more strongly than ever, that her body had been stolen from her, boarded like a river barge by brigands and forced to carry a cargo she had never sought. But though it wasn't of her choosing, it had become more precious to her than she could have imagined.

Soon she was in nothing but her underdress. She hitched it over her hips and then sat on the edge of the bed to pull it over her head.

'Here.' Athula drew a flask from her apron pocket and offered it to Samadara.

'You're sure this won't harm the baby?'

'It might, my sweeting. It might. But screaming will harm him more, when the guards hear your cries and come to dash his head against the wall. Drink.'

The concoction was so sweet it almost gagged her, but she tipped the flask and drank it all. Its effects took only moments, a syrupy lethargy that was perilously pleasant. She nodded at

Athula, fighting against her drooping eyelids. She wanted to be awake to see her son, at least once.

'Ready?' Athula asked.

She nodded again and her maid drew the knife. The blade was pitted but the edge was keen. Samadara watched as that gnarled hand rested it against the tight skin of her stomach. Her belly button protruded comically in its centre. She remembered the day it had inverted and how she'd thought about this moment and chosen it for her future. 'Show me where you'll cut,' she said, suddenly desperate to delay.

Athula's finger was cold as it traced an arc like the Smiler's wicked grin the length of Samadara's belly. 'Here. It must be deep, but not too deep – I don't want to be injuring the babe, now do I?'

Her touch tickled and Samadara squirmed away from it. 'Yes. I see.'

There was no sound except the old woman's harsh breathing as she pressed the blade more firmly against Samadara's skin. The cut stung immediately and blood gathered into droplets along its length.

'Finish it,' Samadara said.

Athula grunted, clamped her hand across Samadara's mouth and slashed the knife across her from hip to hip. Even with the sorghum juice inside her, the pain was deeper than she could have guessed and she screamed, her maid's hand muffling the sound to a desperate whimper.

For a moment the cut was just a red line on her stomach. She watched with wet, shocked eyes as the line widened and then split, and the fat that lay beneath gleamed greasily for a moment before blood coated and hid it.

Athula smiled at her, perhaps encouragingly. Her broken teeth looked like old bones as she pressed her fingers against the gaping wound. The brown of her hand and the brown of Samadara's stomach blurred together as tears misted her eyes and she realised that she was close to passing out.

Athula's fingers clawed into the raw wound and pulled. Samadara tried to scream again and felt the horrible ripping as something tore. When she looked down, though, she saw that it had only been her skin. The cut was deep, but not deep enough. The welling blood was already beginning to clot and her babe still curled inside her, under a sentence of death.

She forced her eyes to remain open as Athula slashed the knife again, deep and hard. She was expecting the pain but it was less this time. Her mind seemed to overlook it, floating above her own body.

Her belly folded open and back. It looked like the flowers Lord Rajvir of Delta's Strength had once sent her husband, the ones that smelled like rotted meat and trapped flies in their sticky petals. An evil mix of blood and darker fluids seeped from her stomach until Athula slashed the knife a third time and there was a gush of water, washing it all temporarily clean. And there he was, her son, his dark hair stringy and sparse.

The baby's head poked grotesquely from her mutilated stomach. Her fingers tingled with fading sensation as she ran them over his soft scalp. She could see his little mouth, pursed like a rosebud. There was a smear of something over it and she realised that he wasn't breathing and that this might all have been for nothing. 'Help him,' she gasped. 'Please, Athula. Save him.'

Athula nodded, but her fingers fumbled against the slick blood coating Samadara's son and his face grew bluer with every second.

'Hurry, please. He's dying.'

'These old bones have lost their strength, my duck.' But Athula's grip tightened, and then she was lifting the babe clear of the wreckage of Samadara's body and wiping his face clean with expert fingers

Samadara smiled to see his mouth open in a sudden, shocked gasp as he drew air into his body. Then his eyes blinked open and she was the one who gasped. His irises were silver, the unlucky colour of the moon, the pupils a vertical crescent within them that swelled into a dark sphere as her son looked at his mother for the first and last time.

'He has the mark of evil,' she whispered. 'The prophecy was true.'

★

Athula walked the spiral corridors of the palace. She swayed with its gentle rocking and winced as the strain of staying upright set her knees to aching. The purple-red of the walls reminded her of her mistress's body, spilling its insides out on to the bed. Her hands were still damp from washing the gore away and every time she passed a guard, she felt the sluggish beat of her heart quicken. But the alarm had not been raised and shouldn't be for another hour; the guards only checked in on Samadara twice a night.

She thought of the woman she'd left behind, broken on bloody sheets. The death grieved her, of course it did, but the pain was a dull one. She'd done her mourning already, back when Samadara had first spoken of her plan. For the last few weeks when she'd looked at her mistress she'd seen a woman already dead.

The babe was what mattered now and he was safe, lowered in a basket to her son waiting below. They were to meet in the fallow barley fields beyond the rookery and then away, to the mountains and out of Ashanesland entirely. The heavy bag of gold wheels hidden beneath her dress would keep them as they raised King Nayan's stolen son.

The spiral corridor opened into a broader one and to her left she saw the open space of the wheel room. The Oak Wheel sat at its head, the symbol of her sovereign's power. She hurried past as quickly as she could, dropping her eyes from the carrion riders who slouched on guard outside the double doors.

The sanctuary was next, and she lingered there a moment to stare at the prow gods of the nation. She might offer a prayer for her success, but which of them would help her now? Lord Lust concerned himself with the making of babies, not their raising, and the Crooked Man healed the sick, not the newborn. There was the Fierce Child, perhaps, but he cared only for his beasts, and neither the Lady nor the Smiler had time for the life of one small child. Well, in some things the gods could help a woman, in all else a woman must help herself.

She sighed and shuffled on, through the painted library and the great dining hall lined with portraits of the little babe's illustrious ancestors. Then there was daylight ahead and she was through the gates and at the foot of the bridge.

The 500-foot-long wooden span perched on top of the chains that linked the floating palace to the lakeshore. They were near the rookery now, as chance would have it, so she'd have to walk through the home of the carrion riders to reach freedom.

It did look a terrible long way. The inner bridge was shorter, but it led only to the island in the lake's centre and the pleasure gardens that covered its conical peak. As a lass she'd often climbed its slopes to pick wild flowers with her swains.

The guards watched her incuriously as she began crossing the outer bridge. The musky odour of the mammoths reached her, the six hairy giants labouring in their traces to pull the weight of Ashfall along. The chains creaked and wavelets slapped against them as they moved, dragging the palace on its endless circuit of the lake. The walk was slow on her weak legs, but soon enough the shore came into sharper focus.

She turned for one last look at her home. Its wooden spires rose above the platform on which it floated, the paint that had once brightened them flaking and dull, as worn as her body. The pictures of lilies had decayed into leprous white splotches and the figures she remembered as proud guardsmen were faded to shades of themselves. They'd paint Ashfall again soon, as they'd last done in her twenty-third year, but she wouldn't be there to see it.

The mammoth-masters smiled at her as she passed, touching their fingers to their foreheads. She smiled back and walked on. If all had gone to plan, her son was waiting for her. She looked for him, but the lake was littered with the craft of the landborn and it was hard to pick out his little skiff among them.

As she walked through the rookery, the cries of the carrion mounts sounded like warnings of ill-fortune, but when she finally reached the fields beyond, her son was there. The babe was tucked in a sling across his chest and her gut clenched as she thought of how many people must have seen him. They'd be certain to remember Janaka, who'd fathered no child but was carrying one on the very day the King's cursed son was stolen from his mother's womb.

It was too late now for such fears. She took Janaka's hand and they walked together, along the bank of the river that gushed seaward from the lake.

'He lives, then?' She nodded at the bundle in her son's arms.

'He breathes. I gave him a drop of sorghum juice. I couldn't have him cry out when I was on the boat.'

'He seemed sickly to me. Too long without air, I've seen it before. Jamula's lad never spoke more than five words, never grew in his mind more than a three-year-old, and he was blue at birth just like this one.'

'I doubt he'll live,' Janaka said. 'Even without the King's men after him.'

Athula nodded and was surprised to find that they'd both stopped on the riverbank. The lively water rushed past beneath their feet. The purse felt heavy between her breasts, her skin warming the gold inside. She drew it out to show her son, and his eyes glittered as bright as the coins.

Janaka dropped to his knees and plucked a rounded rock from the mud, then another. 'It's hardly killing,' he said. 'The child was never meant to live.'

She stared at the bundle in his arms as he fixed the heavy rocks inside the swaddling clothes. It didn't even really look like a baby. She'd only had one brief glimpse of the boy's face and his strange eyes. Samadara was dead, and the child *did* have the mark of misfortune on him.

'Well, Mama?' Janaka asked. He was looking for her to take responsibility, and so she should. That was what a mother did for her son. It was what Samadara had done for hers, but Samadara was gone. This babe had killed her: he might as well have held the knife himself. Athula found that it was easy to hate him when she remembered her mistress's mutilated, lifeless body.

She nodded. 'He's sickly – he'll never live. Better to end it quick.'

She turned as the water swallowed the small, silent bundle and followed her son when he walked away.

PART I

Partings

I

If there had been just one thief, Krish might have tried running. But the moment he noticed the man ahead, lounging against a rock with his knife drawn and a stony look on his face, he heard the crunch of boots in shale behind him and turned to see the second.

The headman's donkey, hired for the journey, raised his shaggy muzzle and brayed. Krish would have liked to do the same. He'd come all this way, three days down the mountain, along high, narrow tracks and through snowdrifts, and he hadn't lost a single one of the hides and herbs and bone carvings his da had sent him to sell. And now this.

'Going to Frogsing Village?' asked the man in front, while the man behind sidled closer.

Krish nodded, lowering his head but not his eyes.

'Trading?'

'Hides.' Krish saw no need to mention the other things, perhaps too small for the thieves to spot in the donkey's saddlebags.

There was a moist hawking sound as the man behind spat. Krish realised his face was still pimpled and that he was no older than Krish; but they both outweighed him, and the second youth held an axe with loose strength. 'We've no use for hides,' he said. His voice was thick, as if his tongue was too large for his mouth. 'It's coin we want.'

'I don't have any money,' Krish told him. 'Not yet.'

'Really?' The first man closed his meaty hand around Krish's left forearm and his friend took the other. They startled a little when they got a close look at Krish's eyes but didn't loosen their grip.

Krish knew he was shaking. He gritted his teeth so they wouldn't chatter and said, 'It's true. I haven't been to market.'

That seemed to give the thieves pause. The first released Krish to scratch a finger through his short hair. 'Well,' he said to his companion. 'He is heading *into* the village.'

The doubt on their faces slowed Krish's pounding heart a little. They were young and their weapons were flint like his own belt knife. They hadn't managed to steal the coin to buy metal, which made them either inexperienced or inept.

'I can tell you where you need to wait for other traders,' Krish said. He pointed at a rock formation on the shoulder of the mountain, a twisted heart inside a brown ring. 'See there, the grey boulder – another path runs beside it. This way is slow, for when the donkey's carrying. That's steeper but quicker. We take it when we're going home.' It might even be true. This was the first year his da had sent Krish down the mountain rather than going himself. Krish hadn't yet figured out his route back, but he'd spotted the goat track he was pointing to and thought it hopeful.

The first thief was looking where Krish pointed, but the second's gaze shifted over his shoulder, into the valley far below.

'What is it?' his companion asked.

'It's . . . I think . . .' He walked forward, towards the lip of the escarpment. The other thief followed, his captive seemingly forgotten, and Krish thought he might stand a chance of slipping away. But now he could see what they'd spotted: a vast, complex collection of shapes in the distance, out of place against the brown mud and scattered trees of the valley. A dirty haze rose above it, circled by birds.

'Is that Ashfall?' Krish asked. He moved forward to stare between the two thieves.

'Ashfall?' the thick-voiced man scoffed. 'We're a thousand miles from Ashfall. Don't you know nothing?'

'That's no shipfort,' the other agreed. 'It's too big. And it weren't here last week. You *don't* know nothing, do you?'

'Then what is it?'

'That's Smiler's Fair,' the thief said.

*

Nethmi paused fifty paces in front of the gates and grasped Lahiru's arm tighter. His two guardsmen shuffled to a halt behind them, so close she could feel their garlicky breath against her neck. She knew they were gawping over her shoulder. She was gawping too. She'd heard of Smiler's Fair, of course, but hearing and seeing were two different things. Now she was here, her uncle's orders to stay away didn't seem quite so unreasonable.

The gates were wood and twice as tall as a man. Through them she could see a broad street surfaced with straw and lined with buildings three, four and even five storeys tall, leaning perilously above the crowds. Further in there were taller spires yet, brightly tiled and hung with pennants whose designs she didn't know: a fat, laughing man, dice and – she blushed and turned away – a naked breast. It was impossible to think that none of this had been here two days before. And the *people*. Tall, short, fat, thin, with skin and hair of every shade, a babble of languages and faces eager for the entertainments of the fair. It was hard to imagine herself a part of that crowd, swept along in its dangerous currents.

'What's that stink?' one of Lahiru's armsmen asked.

'It's the smell of everything,' Lahiru said. 'They say the fair holds one example of all that there is in the world – every food, every spice, every pleasure and every vice.'

'And the virtues?' Nethmi asked.

He grinned, not seeming to share her fear. 'The fair's only interested in what it can buy and sell. There's no profit in virtue. Come, you'll see when you're inside.'

He pulled on her arm and she let herself be led. This might be the last day she ever spent with Lahiru, and she was determined to enjoy it. So what if her uncle had forbidden her to come here? Last night he'd told her of the marriage he'd arranged for her, a match to Lord Thilak of Winter's Hammer in the distant and cold west. It was just three weeks until she went from her home to that lonely place.

Her uncle had given her no choice, only a portrait of her betrothed so she could grow accustomed to his face. Lord Thilak looked handsome enough, with thick hair and smiling eyes, but shipborn painters were paid to flatter. She'd seen her own portrait and while it had captured her doll-like prettiness with reasonable accuracy, she knew her nose wasn't quite so straight nor her lips so full and red. And Thilak was old, approaching fifty. What kind of husband could he be to her? But there was no use dwelling on her situation. There was nothing she could do about it – only this petty act of rebellion, which would have to be enough.

The entryway to the fair was thronged with the landborn, but Lahiru's men shouldered a way through so they soon came to the gate and those guarding it. Nethmi couldn't help but stare. She'd seen Wanderers before, with their strange pale skin, but these men were odder yet. Their hair was gold and silk-fine, their limbs were wrapped tight in cloth of the same colour and they were as tall and slender as the spears they held crossed to bar the way.

'Halt, stranger,' one said, 'and speak your name.'

Lahiru stepped forward confidently. 'I am Lahiru, lord of Smallwood, and this is the Lady Nethmi of Whitewood.'

'And those?' the man asked, nodding at the guards.

'Saman and Janith, also of Smallwood.'

Nethmi saw the other pale man carefully writing the names on his tablet, and then the spears were uncrossed and they were waved through. The smell was stronger and ranker inside, and the noise almost overwhelming. She held fast to Lahiru, an anchor in the tide of people washing down the thoroughfare. A goose honked at her and chickens flapped their wings from the doorway of one house while their brethren boiled in great tureens opposite. White-coated men ladled the broth into bowls and passed them out to anyone with the coin.

'Why do they need our names? Will they report us?' she asked Lahiru.

He shook his head. 'It's for their own use, not to be passed on. They keep a record so they can tell if anyone is missing. You'll be asked again at each gate between districts, if I recall. Each company keeps its own records of who's come and gone and a roll-call is taken every morning.'

'But why?'

'Well . . . So they know if the worm men have eaten anyone in the night.'

'The worm men?' She stared at him to see if he was teasing.

'They believe so, yes. It's how the fair knows when it's time to move on. The worm men fear the sun—'

'In children's stories!'

'The citizens of the fair believe them to be true,' Lahiru replied, herding her away from a donkey cart and into the path of a juggler, who cursed as his batons and balls dropped all around him. 'They believe the sun poisons the land against the worm men so they can't emerge from their lairs below. But as the weeks pass and the fair keeps the soil in permanent shadow, the influence of the sun fades until the monsters are able to dig to the surface and snatch a victim. And when the first death comes, Smiler's Fair breaks its pitch and travels on.'

'But . . .' Nethmi looked around. They'd moved deeper into the fair as they talked, into a region of narrow alleys and houses open on their lower floors to reveal stalls selling jewellery and cloth and spices and weapons and other objects whose use she couldn't guess. They passed a tall, narrow house whose walls were covered in slippers of every shade, another filled with silver teapots and delicate glasses and a third whose walls of empty-eyed masks made Nethmi turn away uneasily. The stalls' owners were of every race and people but their faces shared a knowing, cynical cast. 'They can't believe in the worm men here, can they?' she asked Lahiru.

'And why not? Haven't you ever wondered why the shipforts always circle their lakes and the wagons of the landborn move once a week?'

'That's to remind us of our origins. We're shipfolk – to move brings us luck. I learned that from my nursemaid.'

'Maybe.' Lahiru grinned, shaking off his unaccustomed thoughtfulness. Nethmi knew his light-heartedness irritated her uncle, but she'd always found it appealing. He'd been the same as a boy, back when her father was still alive and she'd imagined herself destined to be his wife, uniting the neighbouring shipforts in one family. But her father was dead and her uncle had chosen his own daughter Babi for Lahiru. He'd given her three children but little happiness, nor she him. And soon Nethmi was to be married to old Lord Thilak, an even less joyous union.

'So, what shall we do now we're here?' she asked.

He pointed above her, to a pennant hanging from a roof beam, showing a rayed sun. 'See that – it marks the company whose territory we're in. Journey's End, I think. Traders. And those others—' he pointed over the roofs to distant regions of the fair '—the raven is Jaspal, so that's the Fierce Children's district. They're in charge of the Menagerie, filled with animals from all over the world.'

'I'd like to see that.'

'I think it's near the centre. And that–' He blushed and froze with his hand pointing at a banner showing two dice with a strange bulbous-ended rod between them.

'That there's Smiler's Mile,' a high voice piped up and a girl no more than ten insinuated herself between them. She smiled, gap-toothed, and swung her arm in a wide circle over the roofs of the fair. 'The fat man with a spoon, that's the Merry Cooks. It's them what serves the food, though I ain't saying it's good. The horse is the Drovers, no need to worry yourself about them – they ain't for visitors. The snowflake's the Snow Dancers. See, it's simple. Queen Kaur's face, that's the Queen's Men. You don't want to go near them. They don't do nothing but rob.'

Lahiru smiled and ruffled the urchin's hair, though it was filthy with grease. 'And the winged mammoth? I confess I don't find that one so simple.'

The girl squirmed away from his touch. 'The King's Men. They put on plays. Boring. But that one—' she pointed to the simplest banner of all, the black silhouette of a figure against a white ground '—that's us Worshippers. We're the best of all the companies, because we keep company with the gods.'

'So we should go there, I suppose?' Nethmi said. 'That's your impartial advice?'

'No,' the girl said. 'Winelake Square in the Fine Fellows' quarter. That's where Jinn's preaching today and he's the best of all the Worshippers. You ought to go there.'

Nethmi pulled out a glass feather, but Lahiru took the coin from her and held it out of the girl's reach.

'Jinn, you say? The boy preacher who teaches disrespect for the Five and sedition against our King?'

The girl shrugged, seeming more annoyed than alarmed. 'Some people think so, but he keeps the fair's peace and the fair keeps him safe. Why not hear him out?'

Lahiru held the coin a moment longer, then tossed it to the girl and watched her catch it, bite it, slip it somewhere beneath her cloak and melt back into the crowd.

'Well?' Lahiru asked, turning back to Nethmi. 'Shall we hear sedition being preached? Your uncle would be furious if he learned of it.'

She thought of her upcoming marriage, unwanted and inevitable, and returned his sly smile. 'Yes,' she said. 'He would.'

Eric didn't have many strong opinions, but he felt strongly that if a boy was about to be replaced, it was kinder not to let him know. It didn't seem Madam Aeronwen shared the sentiment, though. Not with the way she was fawning all over Kenric while the rest of her sellcocks and dollymops gobbled their lunch in the kitchen paying customers weren't invited to.

The room was cramped and rough, nothing like the public areas of the house. The wooden ceiling was low, the walls unpainted and the smell of stew made from tainted meat lingered. Eric liked it here, or he always had. But that had been when he was the one being smiled at and slipped little treats. Now it was Kenric.

Kenric was lapping it all up, the way he always did. He picked at pieces of fruit and put them in his mouth one at a time, being sure to lick his lips and his fingers of the juice after each. It was shameless, even for a whore of Smiler's Fair, but Eric knew he only had himself to blame.

Six months ago, Kenric had been a stable boy with the Drovers, miserable and with many years of shovelling shit left ahead of him before he bought out his debt bond and earned full membership in the company. Eric had shared a few small beers with the thirteen-year-old, and maybe he'd boasted a little about his life in the Fine Fellows and how he was near halfway to buying out his own bond.

But he hadn't known that Kenric would go to his master and beg him to sell his bond on to Madam Aeronwen. Nor that she'd shell out so many gold wheels for the boy, who was pretty enough to be a girl and young enough to have no hair on him and skin as smooth as a baby's.

The lad seemed to feel Eric's eyes on him. He grinned and rose, oozing over towards him until he was sitting in Eric's lap with his thin arms around his neck.

'Tell you what, mate,' Kenric said. 'I'm out of lotion, and you got that palm oil what your clients go crazy for. Lend me it, will you?'

'It's mine,' Eric protested. 'I paid for it.'

Kenric batted his long lashes and looked up through his curly honey-coloured hair. 'But you ain't using it. You ain't got no gentlemen booked today, and I got three.'

'Give it him, Eric,' Aeronwen said, her square face stern. 'I'll drop you five glass feathers, if you're begrudging the cost.'

And that, of course, was that. Kenric left Eric's lap as soon as he had what he wanted and they all went back to eating. Except Eric didn't have much of an appetite any longer. He put down his knife and stood.

'Off to drum up some custom?' Kenric asked in that sweetly poisonous way of his.

'Going for some air, ain't I?' Eric said. 'It's close in here.'

'Not much fresh air to be had out there,' Madam Aeronwen said. 'The Worshippers sent to ask leave for their boy Jinn to set up shop in the square. He'll be preaching to the cullies and there won't be room to swing your balls.'

'Then I'll listen to Jinn.'

Madam Aeronwen laughed, a sound like hard cheese being grated. 'You turning cully, my Eric? You've been in the fair five years now, you know how it goes. You pay the Worshippers' coin and they see you right with all the gods a person needs to bother with. There's no call to go believing any of it.'

'Ain't no harm in listening,' Eric muttered. 'Might be entertaining.'

She frowned at him, face fierce beneath her short grey hair, then waved a hand. 'Go then, but keep a keen eye out while you do. Your takings are down this pitch and your room and board ain't cheap. Find yourself an old man with a fat purse, my lad. That's better than any god.'

The air wasn't any fresher outside, but then he'd hardly expected it to be. The square was filling already. There were the usual cullies scurrying into drinking dens and the arms of other whores, and the citizens of the fair getting ready to relieve them of their coin in any way that presented itself. But another crowd was building in the centre around a small stage.

Eric strolled towards it, not actually that interested in hearing what the preacher boy had to say, but too proud to go back inside. And maybe Madam Aeronwen was right. Perhaps there was trade to be picked up here. The folk who came to the fair weren't generally looking for religion and he could provide something a lot more fun than praying, couldn't he?

The preacher himself was heading for the stage now, a slight thing younger even than Kenric. He didn't look like much, but Eric knew he had a big name among the Worshippers, and they weren't the sort to be easily impressed. Maybe he would have a listen after all. He eased himself closer just as the man next to him did the same. They bumped into each other and it wouldn't have mattered, only the cully tripped over his own legs and fell against a man seated at a table outside the Blessed Dice.

It was remarkable how quickly it went off after that. The man the first had fallen against lashed out, hit the wrong fellow, he in turn thumped the wrong man and soon a general brawl had broken out. Eric didn't get the impression anyone involved had been much averse to the idea of a fight in the first place. He wasn't too keen on it, though, and he scrambled aside.

He wasn't the only one making himself scarce. He saw Thin Pushpindar and Fat Pushpindar laughing as they hopped out of the way of a falling tribesman, and the cullies were scattering all around. One woman was almost squashed before her companion grabbed her hand and dragged her clear while the two bruisers with them scowled and pushed the fighters away. The woman's friend looked round, scanning for more trouble, and his eyes hooked Eric's.

The man was handsome enough to be a whore himself. His skin was the pleasing brown of the Ashane, with wavy hair a shade darker, while his trousers hugged his trim legs. Eric's prick twitched appreciatively and he felt something in his gut, or maybe higher, that made him stop and stare. He didn't even remember to pout prettily the way Madam Aeronwen had taught him.

The other man was staring too and Eric knew that expression. He used to see it a lot, and now he was sixteen and not such a pretty boy as some others, he saw it less. This man wanted him. But then the woman he was with touched his arm and he glanced down at her and smiled. Maybe he was wed to her and couldn't have what he lusted for. Maybe not, though, and so when the man looked back over, Eric pointed to Madam Aeronwen's and winked and even remembered to pout this time. And it seemed like the man winked back, but a group of brawlers fell between them, more and more cullies piled into the square and Eric lost sight of them.

He sighed and turned back to the stage, where Jinn was getting ready. He might as well listen to the preacher talk about his god. Perhaps if he had a word afterwards, Jinn could pray a little for him and get the man to remember Eric's wink. Perhaps he could get things back to the way they were before Kenric came along and made his sweet life a little more sour.

Dae Hyo had found himself in many fights over the years, but he'd never before woken up in the middle of one. The tankard he'd half drunk was knocked into his lap and he leapt to his feet with his trousers soaked and his head fogged with beer.

As fortune would have it, his leap took him into the path of a flying fist and he fell back into his chair, clutching his bruised temple as the man who'd hit him yelled and shook his hand in pain.

'I tell you what,' Dae Hyo bellowed. 'That's no way to wake a man.'

His attacker wasn't listening. He'd turned to the man on his left, a lanky, ginger-haired thegn from the Moon Forest, and was busy trying to grind his face into the nearest table. Beyond him, a Maeng warrior was kicking the belly of a downed Ashaneman while his brother drew his knife on another. It was more of a general brawl than a specific grudge, it seemed. There were at least a dozen men involved that Dae Hyo could see and he could think of no reason he shouldn't join in too, just for the fun of it.

The nearest man available for a beating was a broad-shouldered Gyo with a squint and fists the size of boulders. Dae Hyo let one brush past his head and then returned one of his own, watching in satisfaction as a bloom of blood burst from the other man's nose. After that it was hard to keep track. He sweated as he fought and a brief rain shower turned the ground to mud, which soon coated them both. Dae Hyo smiled, though most of the rest looked grim and the knife-wielder was grimacing at a slash in his own side. But what did he expect if he was going to come armed to a friendly little fight?

Dae Hyo had his hand around the ginger thegn's neck and his knee in the man's back when someone shouted 'Stop!' in such a loud, high voice that he let go in surprise and his opponent fell into the mud and shit below them.

The other fighters seemed equally frozen as the shout came again. Fists dropped to sides and they all swivelled to face the source of the noise, which turned out to be a boy not old enough for his balls to have dropped. He stood on a small stage, a woman beside him, the two so alike she could only be his mother. They both shared the high, sharp cheekbones of the people of the far savannah, though his skin had the darker tint of the tribes about it. He smiled at the startled fighters and more broadly around the square, where Dae Hyo saw quite a crowd had gathered.

'Friends,' the boy said. 'Will you sit and listen? I promise I ain't gonna keep you from your fighting long. There'll be time enough before sundown to beat each other bloody if you choose.'

'It's Jinn,' said the man Dae Hyo had been in the process of strangling, as friendly as if they'd just been sharing a beer. 'Jinn the preacher boy. You'll want to hear this.'

Dae Hyo stared at the strange boy a moment longer, then sat in one of the few remaining chairs.

Jinn nodded across the crowd, seemingly at Dae Hyo himself. 'Thanks to all for the attention. It ain't for me, I promise.'

'It's you what's talking!' a woman shouted.

The boy Jinn laughed. 'That's true, I ain't denying it. But I ain't come to talk about myself.'

'The moon! The moon!' other voices yelled from the crowd.

'The moon it is,' Jinn agreed. 'I see there's some here have heard me before. I'll speak of the moon and plenty else besides. Will you listen? I promise it's a good tale, one you all need to hear – one that's for you all.'

His face was suddenly solemn and the crowd quietened.

'Thank you,' Jinn said in a soft voice that somehow filled the crowded, muddy square. Dae Hyo looked round to see a good three hundred people watching the preacher. Even those outside the gambling dens and whorehouses had turned their chairs to listen. The air was so still, Dae Hyo could hear the rattle of dice echoing through one window and the low grunts and high yelps of fucking from another.

'Let me tell you all a story,' the preacher boy said. 'It's about the moon, like you guessed, and the sun, and the war they fought many years ago, before the Moon Forest folk, or the Ashane, or any of the tribes came over the sea to these lands. It all happened so long ago that no one but the mages remember, and they told it to me true. For centuries the Ashane and the tribes and the folk of the forest have looked up in the sky at night and all they've seen is a dead rock. And that's all it was for centuries, but it wasn't always so. The moon was a god once, who was called Yron, and he and his sister the sun, who was called Mizhara, studied the world together, when the world was young.

'See, Mizhara, she wanted to know how things worked, orderly things, and she made up the numbers to describe them: one, two, three, four, five and all the rest. But Yron saw that her numbers were only good for talking about circles and squares. He wanted to know how waves worked, and what was less than nothing and what happened after the end of eternity, so he invented a new type of number to describe all those things.

'While they were busy arguing over that, they looked down on the world below and saw things neither of them could explain, not with all their numbers. There were animals and people, which couldn't either of them be pinned down that way, and so together Yron and Mizhara devised the runes to explain them. But animals and people ain't like rocks or waves. They're alive, and so were the runes. They had the power to make things as well as describe them, and that scared the sun, but the moon loved it. He made new life, and that's when his sister turned against him, because she only liked order and life is always messy, especially the type he made.'

'The worm men!' a woman shouted. 'He made the worm men!'

'He did, it ain't false,' Jinn said, and there was a murmur of disgust. 'He made them as his servants. The worm men loved the living, because Yron made them to understand life. They were ugly-looking, though, and Mizhara hated them for that. She only cared for what was perfect. But nobody's perfect, not truly. We all got our faults and our scars and the ways in which we're different from each other.

'When Mizhara said she hated the worm men, she really meant she hated us. Not all people, maybe, but all you gathered here. I ain't met each individual one of you, but I know this about you: you ain't come to Smiler's Fair to be like normal and live a normal life. You want what you ain't supposed to want, and that's what Yron understood. Mizhara, though, she couldn't let folk be as they wanted, only as she ordered them to be. So she and Yron fought a great war, and the sun won and blotted out the moon.'

This time the silence was complete, and Dae Hyo couldn't help noticing that the moon itself had risen white in the blue sky, as if summoned by the boy preacher's words.

'She killed him,' Jinn said, 'and his death made his servants crazy and sent them beneath the ground, where they're a blight on us all to this day. We're afraid of the shadows, friends. We run into the light and we move. We always move, not because we want, but because that's what the sun ordered. Wouldn't you like to bide in one place, just for a while? Don't you want not to be afraid? Don't you want to sit in the shade and not feel your heart thumping but only the cool and comfort of it? Don't you want to be who you are, and not who people say you should be?

'Friends, you can sit in the shade and you can sit still and you can be who you want one day very soon. You can do all those things because the moon ain't just a dead rock any more. The moon's god has returned. He's been born again, right in this very kingdom, and though he was cast out, he'll come back to claim his inheritance. He'll change things, but he ain't gonna do it alone. You've gotta change too. You gotta be ready. Some of you here, you feel it in your hearts, you're the moon's men and the moon's women. Yron's speaking to you, you just gotta listen. Because the moon is rising. And all those who don't rise with him will fall.'

When the speech was over, Dae Hyo sat in a daze as the square emptied around him. He'd intended to stay the night in the fair, renting a room in one of the lodging houses or – he'd be honest with himself – in the company of one of the whores. Jinn's words kept circling round his head, though, and those words told him he had to go.

Leaving seemed quicker than making his way in, as if the fair couldn't wait to spit him out now it had sucked all the profit from him. They'd put the place near a sluggish, muddy river and he followed it back up its course for two hours until its waters had grown a little livelier and Smiler's Fair was lost to sight. Only a smudge of smoke in the sky showed its location. A black cloud of birds circled within it, like a hungry whirlwind.

Dae Hyo found a good rock to sit on and dropped his pack on the ground beside him. The bottles clinked as it landed: whisky from the Fine Fellows' quarter and the vodka he'd found an old Yeum woman selling from a stall beside the Menagerie. The stall had smelled of animal shit, but when he'd sampled the drink he'd found it pure and strong as a stallion's kick. Between them, the bottles had cost him a full third of what he'd earned in the mines since the first frosts fell this winter. It had seemed easy to justify the expense. The work was dangerous, often lethal. A man didn't go down to face his death without something fortifying inside him.

Now, though, he wasn't so sure. That gold he'd spent had a purpose. *He* had a purpose and he could see that he'd been letting the drink wear away at it, like a river eating out its bank. It was as that boy Jinn had said – he needed to change the way he went about things.

The water in the stream was bubbling nicely over the rocks. Dae Hyo stared at it for a while, as the sun slipped away and the moon took over lighting up the sky, though it didn't do such a good job of it. Its reflection wobbled in the water until Dae Hyo threw in a pebble and shattered it entirely.

It was hard to change, that was the thing. A man grew used to the way he was and the way he went about his business. He knew it worked, or to be fair, that it didn't fail frequently enough to be a problem. Change was dangerous. He'd already faced one so monumental it had broken his world as completely as the reflection of the moon had shivered into pieces on the surface of the water.

Dae Hyo flexed his arms and felt the strength in them and he knew the power in his legs. But he patted his belly and felt the wobble of fat that hadn't been there five years ago. He was more than he had been, and not in a good way. It was the drink, he knew that. He could almost see it sloshing beneath his skin.

When he kicked his pack, the bottles tinkled. It was a pleasing noise. He savoured it a moment and then opened the ties and drew them out, all seven of them. He didn't let himself hesitate long before pulling the stoppers and pouring the contents of each into the river. Their smell was soon stolen by the water.

After that, all that remained was to throw the bottles to float away on the surface. The moon suddenly emerged from behind a cloud, a pretty sphere of silver, and he knew it was a sign. He'd become the warrior he was meant to be. The moon god wanted the world changed, and he was ready to change it.

Krish decided it would be safest to return to the mountains in the dead hours of the night. He'd sold the goatskins and herbs and carvings for a good price. There was coin rattling in his purse and he couldn't risk meeting the thieves.

He travelled by the same path that had brought him to Frogsing village. If the thieves were still waiting, he hoped they'd be doing it on the route he'd shown them on the opposite shoulder of the mountain. The one he'd taken was broad and easy to pick out even in the pale moonlight. His footsteps crunched against the pebbles, far too loudly. There were few other noises. A night bird hooted. Something unseen splashed in a stream and a hunting cat yowled nearer than he would have liked. But there was nothing that sounded like other men.

Still, he could feel the tension making his back ache as he led the donkey on. When the beast brayed he almost cried out himself. He halted, heart pounding, and stared into the darkness. He could see nothing, and after a few moments the donkey dropped its head and started cropping the grass, unconcerned.

Krish stroked its warm back to calm himself and then led it round the next bend and onto the escarpment where the thieves had confronted him. His muscles knotted as he walked past the spot where the knife had been waved at him, but no new attack came. He crept to the edge of the path to look down into the valley below.

Everything was in darkness aside from one blaze of light, a great sprawl of it near the horizon. It was mostly the yellow of flame, but there were stranger blues and purples too. The village men had told him about Smiler's Fair. They said it was a place of great excitement and awful activities they'd been coy about describing. He wondered if they really knew.

Some of them had spoken of travelling there and one young man had asked if Krish wanted to join them. He *had* wanted to. But his ma needed him back in the village and his da would be angry if he was late. This was the only occasion he'd ever left home, and it was time he returned. What would he do in Smiler's Fair anyway, in a place so big and foreign? He'd be lost. He looked at it a little longer, then turned his back on the light and began the long climb back into the mountains.

2

Nethmi felt the muscles in the bird's back shift beneath her thighs. Its claws dangled beneath them, each talon longer than her hand, while the stench of rotten meat wafted around her with every beat of its great grey wings. Her legs were burning after a full day of riding and she groaned as one wing tipped and they veered towards a narrow pass between jagged peaks. The rider behind her clucked sympathetically, but she wasn't sure if it was for her discomfort or the carrion mount's effort.

She'd wanted to travel by land, but Puneet had insisted that only the birds would be fast enough. So she'd hidden her distress and remained proudly silent as she took to the air above Whitewood and watched the ancient, ossified trees and the half-frozen lake and the winter-brown fields and everything that was her home pass away beneath her. She'd hoped for one last look at Smiler's Fair, but their route hadn't overflown it. She saw nothing but sheep on the foothills of the White Heights.

Then High Water Fastness was beneath her, its squat towers dwarfed by the frothing waters of the falls. And here the true mountains were. There were no more shipforts, only an occasional cluster of tents beneath her, landborn settlements. She spotted wolves too, and once a yellow blur that might have been a mountain lion.

It was so strange to be back. She'd been born in the Black Heights, and when her mother had died delivering her, her father kept her with him on campaign as he fought to subdue the mountain savages for his king. Nethmi's earliest memories were of this pure white landscape, the army's encampment spread like a pox across it and herself seated in her father's lap beside the fire as he discussed strategy with his lieutenants. Those were happy memories – the best she had. But though she could remember the snow, she'd never remembered the cold. The past had a warm glow to it that the present was sorely lacking.

This high, the sun still blazed in the blue sky, but dusk had already come to the valleys. The carrion mount's head dipped and her stomach lurched as it dropped towards the gloomy ground. Minutes later, it landed in a three-foot-high drift and she sighed as she dismounted, then yelped as her muscles seized and she nearly toppled sideways into the snow.

The carrion rider was too busy fussing with his mount to notice, ruffling its feathers and murmuring softly to it like a lover, but one of the household guard stopped her fall. She nodded her thanks and he blushed to the roots of his brown hair. He looked like he meant to speak until he saw Captain Mahesh watching him and scurried away to attend to his duties. Mahesh was her uncle's right hand, his eyes and ears on this journey, and he'd not like his men growing close to her. They were all too young to remember her father and the way Whitewood had been run before his death. She believed they'd been chosen for that reason.

Her own tent was larger than the rest, but it was still a tent. And she would sleep on furs, but there was rocky ground beneath them. She watched as her servants put it all in place, shifting from foot to foot impatiently. It had been like this on campaign all those years ago, but then her father's soldiers had competed to make her comfortable, to bring her the choicest treats.

'Whisky, milady?' one of Mahesh's men asked, holding out a flask. 'Helps to ward off the chill.'

She took the drink and smiled at him, grateful for the small kindness. 'How much further?' she asked.

'Five days, milady.'

Five days until she reached Winter's Hammer and the beginning of her exile – though no one called it that. She sighed and stooped to enter her tent.

★

The next morning dawned even colder. She could feel the icy bite of the air from beneath her sleeping furs, and the thought of rising from them was unbearable.

'Ayesha, a fire please,' she called.

Her maid entered quickly and Nethmi guessed she'd been waiting outside. She moved stiffly as she laid the logs in the sooty brazier. 'Breakfast, milady?'

'Yes, breakfast, and for you too. You look like you need unfreezing.'

The girl smiled. 'Aye, 'tis bitter cold out and them carrion riders ain't no use. All they do is groom them awful birds, which don't make them smell no better, let me tell you. But you've a good heart, Little Blade.'

Little Blade. Not many people used that name now. Her father's soldiers had chosen it, when he made her a miniature copy of their own uniforms to wear, complete with a tiny sword. The sword had been blunt, so a six-year-old couldn't hurt herself with it. Later, when the war had been won and the lordship of Whitewood awarded for the victory, her father had sharpened the blade.

Ambitious men need fear only failure, he'd told her as he handed her the weapon. *Successful men must fear everyone. I'll be happier knowing we're both armed.* But a sword hadn't saved him from the snake venom that carried him away in screaming agony only six years later. Oh, they all said it was a terrible accident, the creature somehow escaped from its cage beneath the Fierce Child's shrine, but Nethmi knew the truth. Puneet had worn a mask of grief no different from the animal masks the landborn wore to honour the Fierce Child on Deep Winter Day. His real face, the real feelings, were hidden beneath.

She quickly washed her armpits and face in the hot water Ayesha had supplied, shivering as it cooled on her skin. After that there was nothing to do but go out and face the men.

It took Nethmi a second to notice what was different about the camp. It seemed empty, and then she realised: the carrion mounts were gone. Mahesh caught her gaze and hurried over, smiling insincerely.

'We're not at Winter's Hammer yet, are we?' she asked. 'I thought Lord Thilak's shipfort was in the highest peaks.'

'It is, milady. But the air's too thin up there for the birds; they can't stay awing. I've seen a mount sicken and die just for lack of breath. We'll be taking a different transport the rest of the way. They should be meeting us – ah yes, here they are now.'

Nethmi heard the jingle of harness and turned to see a train of mules being led towards the camp by a man who appeared as rough and unwashed as his animals. 'Could we not ride horses, Captain Mahesh? Those poor creatures look as if they'd break under the weight of some of your men.' The beasts looked mean-tempered and foul-smelling too.

'You'd be surprised, milady. The mules are stronger than they appear, and they can climb the rocks where a horse would break its leg and send you both plummeting to your deaths. The mountains don't breed them pretty, but they breed them tough. You'll see for yourself.'

It wasn't an entirely encouraging thought, and judging by Mahesh's expression, it wasn't meant to be.

Up close, the landscape was no more appealing than it had been from the air. The rocks grew sharper as they climbed higher and what plants did claw their way through the snow looked thorny and desiccated. Her mule didn't seem to mind, stooping its head at unpredictable intervals to take a mouthful of thistles and jarring her already bruised flesh.

To one side of the path there was a landslide of scree stretching down to the valley, now many hundreds of paces below. To the other was a sheer cliff. She had always remembered the peaks as majestic, even beautiful, but now there seemed nothing romantic about them. This was a harsh, ugly land.

She fell into a sort of brooding daze as she rode. *Damn Puneet*, she thought, round and round and over and over. *Damn him*. Lord Nalin of North Star had sought her hand for his son. Nalin Nine Eggs they called him, a miserable old man forever harping on the raw deal his ancestors had negotiated for the shipfort in the New Covenant: 'Nine eggs, only nine carrion eggs, and we the largest fort on the five lakes.' But Arjan was a promising youth and not terrible to look at. Her uncle could have made the match. Instead, he'd sent her to be married on the outer edge of the civilised world.

The path had flattened as it reached a high plain before the next range of peaks, and she saw heaps of rocks tumbled over the grass to their right. When they drew closer, she began to discern forms in the rubble, sharp right angles that must surely be man-made, and then the glint of sunlight on something polished. She realised with a start what these must be: the ruins of Manveer's Folly, the palace which, legend said, had killed its creator.

Captain Mahesh had seen it too. He hesitated a moment, then raised his arm and waved it left. 'Away,' he shouted. 'Let's skirt them wide.'

'No,' she said. 'No, stop.'

He turned to frown at her. 'Milady, it's not safe.'

She yanked on her mule's reins and slid from the saddle, grimacing as her cramped legs took her weight. 'Why isn't it safe?'

'You know full well why, Lady Nethmi. Every child learns the tale.'

He meant the worm men. Lahiru had spoken of them too in Smiler's Fair. But even if they were real, the boy preacher Jinn had said they weren't to be feared. They were the moon's servants, and the moon was the god of change. She needed his power now more than ever.

'I'm a grown woman,' she said. 'I no longer believe cradle-tales. I tire of riding and must stretch my legs.'

'Stretch them later, then. A darkness lives below. King Manveer was a fool to build this place, everyone knows it, and he paid the price with his kin's blood and his own. There's a reason they call it Manveer's Folly and not Manveer's Pride.'

'My father said it was treachery, not folly, which put the knife in Manveer's back. It's not unheard of, is it, for a jealous man to kill one greater?'

If Mahesh felt the point of her barb he chose not to show it. He wore a mask too; it was the Whitewood way.

'Besides,' she said, 'it was nearly two hundred years ago. Memories fail in a generation; how much less reliable must they be after ten?'

'Ten generations or a hundred, it makes no matter,' Mahesh snapped. 'There's death beneath the ground here as much as in the lowlands. The shipfolk sail on and it can't touch us. But those rocks have been here far too long.'

'My father said–'

'Your father said a great many things, milady. Perhaps if he'd listened more and spoken less he'd be here to advise you himself. But he's not, and I say it isn't safe.'

'Do as you will, Captain Mahesh, but I choose to trust my father's word. He led his men to victory after victory. Where has Lord Puneet led you?'

She turned her back on any reply he might have given and slipped off her mule. The walk was difficult, over frozen and broken ground, but pride kept her spine straight. After a few seconds she heard the clatter of boots and the rattle of scabbards against leather-clad thighs and knew that Mahesh and one of his men had accompanied her, as duty dictated. Her uncle wanted her gone but he couldn't afford for her to die on the journey. He needed this alliance to strengthen his hand at home.

The ruins were further than she'd realised, because they were far larger than she'd guessed. When she finally drew near, she saw the monumental shadow of a watchtower laid across the snow ahead. She shivered as she crossed it, not just from the lack of sun.

'Milady–' Mahesh pleaded.

She ignored him. She'd hung her father's honour on her actions now. A hundred more paces and she was in the ruins themselves, an intact wall to one side and broken wreckage on the other.

'And what do your children's tales say destroyed this place?' she asked Mahesh. 'Did the worm men eat marble as well as people?'

The captain looked around uneasily. 'Perhaps. Or perhaps it's naught but time. The years leave the same wounds as war, if there are enough of them.'

Ahead of her she could see the gleam she'd spotted from a distance. She jogged towards it, then stumbled as her foot twisted in a hidden pothole.

'Careful, milady.' Mahesh took her elbow to support her, but he was no longer suggesting that they leave. He'd seen the glitter too, and they could both tell what it was: metal.

'Gods,' the other guardsman muttered. 'So much of it.'

There was a very great deal of it indeed, huge beaten sheets pressed on to the sides of a jumble of marble slabs. She thought the rounded bumps on its surface might once have been the figures of horses, with the smaller lumps above them their riders. It was more metal than Nethmi had ever seen in one place.

'Enough to outfit the King's whole carrion flock,' Mahesh said. 'They called Manveer's mother the Iron Queen, but I never thought . . . Such a waste for it to lie here.' He was leading *her* now, pulling at her elbow to urge her on.

As they drew closer, though, his expression fell. The metal was . . . wrong. It gleamed, but more dully than iron. Nethmi approached a sheet of it and ran her fingers over the faint whorls and lines etched into its surface. It was icy cold beneath her touch.

'What is it?' she asked.

Mahesh shrugged. 'Lead, I think.' He drew his knife and gouged the tip into the metal. It gave, far softer than she had expected. 'Useless. And heavy, too.'

'But Manveer didn't think it useless,' Nethmi said. 'He built up here, so far from Ashfall, because he'd heard the mountain savages lived below the ground and took no harm from it. Maybe he'd learned that lead was what kept them safe.'

High walls blocked her way to either side, but ahead there was a clear space that might once have been a park, and beyond it an almost intact building. It was larger by far than Whitewood, larger even than Ashfall, and constructed of solid blocks of white marble veined with red and orange. She tried to imagine what it would be like to live in a place that never moved. She'd come this far; it could do no harm to investigate a little further.

She hesitated only a moment before striding across the overgrown park towards it. Mahesh huffed but followed, with the soldier beside him.

The park had seemed green from a distance, brushed clean of snow by the relentless wind. As they walked through it, she saw that the grass was filled with flowers: yellow sunbursts, and tiny blue jewels, and red bells suspended from slender stems. She'd never seen their like, not even in the royal pleasure gardens, and she didn't understand how they could bloom so brilliantly in the depths of winter. She plucked one of the blossoms and placed it in her hair.

'Perhaps you should take some back to my uncle,' she said to Mahesh. 'A gift for his gardens even the King would envy.'

She'd thought the idea would appeal to his ambition, but he frowned and shook his head. 'Unnatural things. We should leave, milady. The sun sinks and we've further to go before day's end.'

'Not yet. Where there's lead there might also be iron. Wouldn't Puneet want you to find out what treasures lie hidden inside?' She nodded at the building, now only fifty paces before them. Its roof was supported by great pillars of marble, with intricately carved vines twining from earth to sky. The marble had been cunningly worked so that the yellow vein shone out as sunflowers along its length. The wall was studded with windows, small shards of glass still glittering in their corners. The entranceway was wide enough to accommodate two horses but the door itself must have been wood and had long since rotted away, leaving only a dark hole.

'Men were never meant to stay in one place,' Mahesh said. 'This is cursed, I feel it. Don't go inside.'

'Are you *ordering* me, captain?'

'Lord Puneet's command was to protect you.'

'He isn't here,' she said and strode towards the doorway.

She'd almost reached it when he grabbed her arm. His face

was implacable. 'Let Saman scout ahead, then. If you won't admit the dangers of the past then at least have a care for those of the present. It's wild country here and many still disdain to call themselves Ashane or bow to the King's law. Bandits or worse could be using this as their base.'

She nodded reluctantly and he released her and gestured to the guardsman trailing behind them. The young man's throat bobbed as he swallowed. His hair was cut very short, a new fashion that had crept down to their lands from Ashfall, and he ran his hand nervously through it before lifting his lantern and striking flint to light it. He paused and looked at her a little pleadingly, but when Mahesh waved him on he raised the lantern and turned to the doorway.

Nethmi stepped forward, ignoring Mahesh's protest, to watch Saman's progress. His face glowed in the lamplight and the beads of sweat on his upper lip and brow looked like crystal. The circle of illumination that surrounded him was little more than ten paces across, and beyond that utter darkness.

As he walked, the building revealed itself in tantalising flashes. There, for a moment, a mosaic face stared up from the floor beneath his boots. Nethmi recognised the Smiler's lunatic grin picked out in ruby-red glass before the circle of light moved on. Then the young man stumbled and she saw that a fallen statue had tripped him. It was of a man encased in plate armour, an outfit so grand only the King himself could afford it. A huge green jewel gleamed in its helmet, then, as the light shifted away, was gone.

Saman paused a moment, ringed by the circle of light. Seventy paces distant his face was a brown blur, his eyes and mouth dark slashes across it. The room must be vast, vaster than any she'd known, if he'd not reached the end of it. 'Further?' he called. His voice trembled, the trembles echoing in the huge emptiness.

'Yes,' Mahesh said. 'Check every corner.'

'Nonsense,' Nethmi cut across him. 'It's clear there's no one here. The place has been deserted since Manveer's day. Wait there and we'll join you.'

Even at that distance, the young soldier's relief was clear. He smiled as she took a step into the room towards him. She smiled back, and was still smiling when something reached for him from the darkness. Even at seventy paces, she could see that the hand that closed around his throat was viciously clawed. Something black and liquid bloomed beneath its fingers. For a moment another face hung in the circle of light beside the soldier's, grey and inhuman, as the young man's smile twisted into a wide 'O' of shock. And then she heard the clang of the lamp dropping, and the light was gone.

The screaming sliced through the darkness, high and desperate. Without a thought she took a step forward, and then another, and a third, towards the creature that could only be a servant of the moon, and then a hand closed on her arm and jerked her away.

'Let me go!' she said as she was dragged back towards daylight.

'Don't be a fool,' Mahesh snarled. 'You've killed him. You'll not kill us as well.'

And then they were out and running, back through the ruins and towards the safety of the camp.

3

Dae Hyo often dreamed about the dead. The drink used to chase away the phantoms, but now he went to bed sober they came nearly every night and he woke smiling. The smile disappeared as he saw the red of dawn on the horizon. Could it really be morning? If he closed his eyes he could sleep just a few minutes longer. But he knew minutes would become hours. And there was a debt he owed the departed. And so, every morning, Dae Hyo got up with the sun.

This morning was no different. An expedition was setting out and he'd been told there was a place for him on it. He sighed, rolled on to his back and rose.

The walk back to the settlement felt long, maybe because the sun had risen fully now and the light jabbed into his eyes. He'd thought giving up the drink might make him feel better, but even weeks later he still had a headache he couldn't shift and a weakness in his limbs he didn't like. He pulled out his dwindling stock of purple sorghum and filled his pipe, taking a grateful pull of the scented smoke. The drug eased the ache in his temples and he was glad he'd thought to buy it when he'd decided to end his drinking. A man needed some consolation.

After a few minutes the village came into view, huddled between two hillocks of debris from the mines. The spoil heaps were brown, the plank houses of the village grey and a grim black dust hung over the whole place. The dust coated clothes and faces so that everyone looked to be of one people: a race that had grown from the earth and lived underground.

'Dae Hyo, you're late,' Maeng Lu called out as he passed his forge. 'They're going in without you.'

'Motherless scum – they wouldn't dare!' But he picked up his pace as he headed through the village towards the mine shaft. The buildings that loomed over him looked to be on the point of collapse, as they had since the day they were built. They'd been moved since he last saw them, slid along the wooden rails that ran the length of each street.

He splashed through the mud sink that always filled the central square, circled the well that, when it felt like it, gave them clean water, and then he was through and climbing the shallow slag heap that spilled from the nearest shaft.

He caught up with the others just as they'd paused at the entrance. There were nine of them as arranged: five miners and four other guards, with him making the fifth. The expressions they turned to him were a mixture of dislike, disdain and relief.

He barely spared them a glance, his attention focused on the mine entrance. They'd been working this shaft for a few months now. He'd been on his way back from Smiler's Fair when the last group went down, but he'd heard the haul had been slight. They seemed to be nearing the end of the vein of iron and they were perilously deep.

The sun threw its pale rays down the shaft. They caught the glitter of crystals in the walls and a few puddles of water on the floor. Early morning was the best time to go; the precious light would see them as deep as possible before the darkness took over. Dae Hyo remembered when they'd still been mining the west shaft and they'd had to set out in late evening, the ominous red glow of the setting sun lighting the tunnels the colour of blood. He loosened his sword in the sheath at his back, nicked two fingertips on his axe blades to check their sharpness, then nodded to his companions. 'Time to go.'

The miners looked sick with fear. Well, to be fair, Dae Hyo wouldn't have wanted to march into those tunnels with nothing but a pickaxe to defend himself. Still, they got two shares of the spoils to his one, so they were well paid for their risk-taking.

Two of the guards led the way into the tunnel. They were men of Ashanesland, dark-skinned and dark-haired. Though they were much shorter and more slender than Dae Hyo, he was reassured to see that they handled their swords like they knew how to use them. Dae Hyo had heard they'd served in their king's guard, before being discharged for reasons they were tight-lipped about. He didn't care why they'd been let go. If they could fight, they'd do.

The miners went next, huddled together as they pulled the empty cart they hoped to fill with ore and darting nervous glances at the rocks around them. Dae Hyo brought up the rear with Edmund and Edgar. The twins were two of the most unappealing men he'd ever seen. They'd been born ugly, with coarse red hair, bulbous noses, crooked teeth and arms and legs that seemed too long for their torsos. And they'd devoted their lives to growing uglier still, picking up a collection of scars that rivalled his own, some from blades and, in Edmund's case, a whole rash of them from the pox he'd caught the last time Smiler's Fair passed by.

'You're late,' Edgar said to him. 'Are you drunk?'

'Stone cold sober,' Dae Hyo said.

The other man didn't look convinced. 'You're shaking.'

Dae Hyo shrugged. 'And you're hideous, but you don't see me complaining.'

Both twins glared at him and Edmund snarled and tightened his grip on his sword, but Dae Hyo had his axes in his hands and besides, they knew it would be reckless to fight each other now. There were dangers enough here already.

Thirty paces in and the sunlight was beginning to fail. Ahead of them, the miners lit lanterns, but the guards would carry none. They needed their hands for their weapons. Besides, that flickering yellow light would provide no safety; the worm men didn't fear it.

As they went deeper, the tunnel grew narrow and Dae Hyo felt all the weight of the rock above them. They were walking into a grave, and it could be their own. To their right the wall was smooth, to their left ragged, scored by the marks of many picks prising out the iron ore that would make the whole expedition worthwhile.

Dae Hyo tried to figure how much his share might be. If they found the same as last time, he'd only have enough to make one blade and pay for the forging of it. But if they got lucky . . . His best haul ever had made him ten axes and a score of knives. He'd added them to his hoard, hidden in a small cave a mile from the village. He now had enough to outfit a war band stronger than any on the plains, but he could always use more. The murdering Chun could send a thousand warriors against him, even if most would be armed with flint. But he was sober and working hard. Maybe another year, and he could return to his home and his long-awaited revenge.

They were deep inside the mine now. Edmund and Edgar were wound as tight as a harp's string and the miners, who'd been humming to cheer themselves, fell silent. Twenty paces ahead stood the workface. The moment they began would be the moment of gravest danger, they all knew it. The worm men were vicious but they were no dumb beasts. They understood what the miners came for and often waited in ambush. The boy preacher had said the moon god would tame them when he came, but the moon god wasn't here yet and Dae Hyo would take no chances.

The miners' feet dragged the last few steps, stirring up the rock dust beneath their boots. Sound was amplified here and their footsteps echoed down the tunnels that branched off to either side. The drawn weapons glinted in the lamplight and the air was thick with dust and the smell of fear. The miners took two paces, three – and then they were at the workface. Nothing had happened. The vein of iron ore gleamed temptingly in the lamplight.

After a moment, the biggest of the miners, a broad-shouldered man with a face like a mouldy potato, shrugged and hefted his pick. The first blow rang out and the others followed. The guards grinned at each other and moved back from the miners to leave them room to swing.

Dae Hyo watched until it grew boring to idle as others laboured. The purple sorghum had left him pleasantly relaxed and he sighed and slid to his arse, setting his axes beside him.

'Get up, you lazy bastard,' Edgar said. 'You're not paid to sit.'

'I'm paid to fight. Do you see anything here worth fighting? No? Then piss off.'

The ringing of the picks was almost musical, he thought. A rhythm a man could dance to. A hazy memory floated forward, softened by time: himself in a ring of his brothers, dancing the Spring Dance with the horse masks on their faces and the meat of a sacrificed deer in their guts. Dae Sun had kissed him that night. He closed his eyes and tried to remember the flavour of her lips.

He'd fallen asleep when the attack came. It was the scream that woke him. He opened his eyes to see the glint of swinging steel and one miner's face contorted in agony as a grey hand pulled him through a crack in the rock.

Dae Hyo jerked to his feet, stumbled, then realised he'd left his axes on the ground and stooped to pick them up. He could see five more worm men surrounding their crew while the sixth dragged the unfortunate miner away.

The crack in the rock was too narrow to take a good swing, so he worked his axe blade in and sawed it against the bony fingers of the creature where they'd clawed into the miner's arm. The miner babbled, begging for help, perhaps too terrified to grasp that Dae Hyo was providing it.

The axe was sharp; it was the work of only a moment before two of the worm man's fingers fell free. They landed with a splatter – in a puddle of the miner's blood, he realised. The worm man had nearly torn the miner in half trying to force him through the crack. It was a waste of time trying to help him, then; there was no way the miner would survive. Dae Hyo spun round to look for another target. The trapped miner whined pitifully and Dae Hyo spared him a last glance before leaping across the tunnel to Edgar and the two worm men who'd cornered him.

The bastards were always tougher than they looked. Their bodies were almost skeletally thin and the dead colour of ash. They carried no swords or axes; their claws were weapon enough. Dae Hyo could see a jagged cut that ran from Edgar's forehead to the corner of his mouth: another scar to add to his collection, if he lived long enough for it to heal. Edgar was fighting back, of course, swinging his sword in short, choppy arcs. But the worm men were lethally fast. One dodged out of the way as another leapt forward, claws slashing. A gash opened in Edgar's side, and Dae Hyo could see gore and worse, glistening in the flickering lamplight.

Dae Hyo let out a cry of fury and panic and charged into the fight. The axe in his right hand caught one of the worm men in the spine and smashed through the creature, its guts slithering to the floor like greasy snakes. His left-hand axe swung at the head of the second, but it moved, lightning quick, and the weapon took only a sliver off its pointed ear before embedding, haft deep, in Edgar's neck. The other man's shocked expression met his for a moment before Edgar's head tipped halfway off his shoulders and his body toppled to the floor.

'Fuck,' Dae Hyo said as he yanked the axe from Edgar's body. He heard a roar behind him and turned just in time to raise the axe and block the sword blow from the dead man's brother. Edmund's face was red with rage and his eyes were half mad.

'It was an accident!' Dae Hyo yelled, but the other man didn't hear or didn't care.

Edmund was an expert swordsman. His first stroke forced Dae Hyo's axe back and his second opened a long gash across Dae Hyo's chest. Around them, the miners were fighting and falling, their picks no match for the swarming worm men. There were more than six of them now. A dozen maybe. Twenty. The other guards were somewhere in the melee, but if they were still alive they wouldn't be for long.

Edmund swung at Dae Hyo again, catching him across the cheek this time. 'You rat-fucking moron!' Dae Hyo shouted. 'You'll get us both killed.' But the other man didn't seem to care about that, either.

Dae Hyo had Edmund's rhythm now. Slash, slash, stab. Very predictable. There was an opening there, right inside his defences. Dae Hyo almost took it, but the worm men were all around and he didn't want to face them alone.

'I tell you what,' he yelled, 'why don't you stop fighting me and start fighting them?' He blocked a stroke to his kidneys and aimed one at Edmund's head, forcing the other man to duck and retreat.

Edmund's sweat trickled down his pockmarked cheeks. 'You killed my brother,' he gasped.

'I'll pay his blood price when we're out of here,' Dae Hyo said. 'Behind you!'

There was a flicker of distrust on the other man's face, a hesitation, and the worm man was nearly on him, its long, dirty claws stabbing towards his back.

Dae Hyo shouted 'Duck!' and flung his axe, not really caring if the other man listened to him. It would be one enemy less either way.

But Edmund threw himself down and the axe flew over his head to split the worm man's, showering the area with blood and brains. Behind that, another of the monsters finished with a miner, ripping out his throat with its sharp teeth. It followed the man to the ground, teeth still latched to his neck and chewing, eating through it until the head detached and rolled to lie beside Edgar. The worm man didn't notice. It turned its attention to the torso, hungry mouth at work on the soft flesh of the miner's belly. It must have bitten through his gut – the smell of shit wafted around them – but it just kept on eating, shit and flesh and bone all the same to it.

Other worm men had finished their meals and there were more all the time, oozing out of the rock and turning their glittering black-and-silver eyes on their prey. Only two men left now: Dae Hyo and Edmund.

'Run!' Dae Hyo shouted, turning toward the mine's entrance, and this time Edmund didn't hesitate. There were three worm men blocking the way out. Dae Hyo drew his sword from his back and held it out in front of him like a spear. One of the creatures reached for it with its bony hands. Its nails skittered against the metal as the blade plunged through its flesh and, for a moment, it was face to face with Dae Hyo. Its breath, strangely sweet, filled his nose. Then he yanked his blade from it and it fell before him. Dae Hyo sprinted over it, feet crushing the corpse beneath him.

The other two worm men grasped at him, slashing their claws across his scalp and flank. He kicked one but it unbalanced him and he fell against the other. It grinned wickedly at him, its teeth red with blood. Well, he wouldn't be its next meal. He pulled a knife from his boot and plunged it through the creature's eye. It twitched and jerked, falling away from him, and Dae Hyo let the knife go. Three weapons lost in this fight, and no metal to show for it.

It wasn't any way for a warrior to go, trapped in a mine. But he could hear Edmund's fleeing footsteps ahead of him, and he decided that if he was going to die, he'd at least die last. He tucked his head down and sprinted.

His legs burned and his wounds throbbed, but he pumped his arms and flexed his thighs and within twenty paces he'd overtaken Edmund. And then he realised that he recognised a rock formation, the one that looked like a tree. It was near the entrance, he was sure of it. He grinned and pushed harder, running to the frantic beat of his heart.

He heard the sound of metal hitting meat behind him and guessed Edmund must be engaging the creatures. Let the crazed fucker buy Dae Hyo time. He didn't look back. Arms reached for him from the walls and he used his last knife to hack at them as he passed, a rain of black blood spraying his face and splattering into his open mouth as he gasped for breath. And then there was light ahead, and though he thought his heart might burst from his chest he forced it to give him just a few beats more and threw himself out of the mine and into the sun.

A crowd waited outside. They always did when an expedition had gone down, ready to treat the injured for a share of their spoils. Dae Hyo barrelled into the first two men, knocking them to the ground, then fell to his knees beside them. Behind him, he heard more footsteps and guessed that Edmund must have made it out, too. There was a gabble of voices around him, but it took too much effort to attend to them and he didn't bother.

When he'd got his breath back, he pushed himself to his feet and through the people surrounding him, then staggered down the road. He wanted a drink. He wanted it so badly he could taste it, feel the fire as it burned a trail down his throat to his belly, but he was a changed man. He'd find a place to sleep and hope his dreams and a little more purple sorghum would soften the horrible memories of the morning instead.

He was woken by a kick to the gut. It hurt, but not as badly as the pounding in his head. His eyes were glued shut and he had to wipe them clean before he could open them. When he did he saw that he was surrounded by a ring of men. All had weapons drawn and one of them kicked him again. It was Edmund.

'What?' he croaked. 'Can't you see I'm sleeping?'

Edmund kicked him a third time, leaving him doubled up and retching. 'Get up,' the Moon Forest man said. 'And get out. You're not welcome here any more.'

That sounded serious. Dae Hyo pushed himself into a crouch and glanced around. Ten men and all of them angry. He'd been asleep for the gods knew how many hours, so how could he have done anything to annoy them? Then he saw the bundles all of them were holding – the oilskin bundles he'd sewn shut and buried with his own hands.

'You thieving bastards!' he yelled, leaping to his feet. The next instant, a ring of blades surrounded him. 'Those are my weapons,' he said more quietly. 'My spoils. They're mine.'

'Not any more,' Edmund said. 'You promised me blood price for my brother, remember?'

Dae Hyo's temper snapped. 'Yes – but a fair price! For Edgar that would be one rusty blade and a hairpin. Now give me back my weapons, curse you! I earned them.' He glared at the men surrounding him. He recognised all of them: a few miners, more guards, most of them men he'd fought beside on many occasions. Treacherous scum.

'Blood price for all the other men you've gotten killed, too,'

Sarv said. 'Edmund told us you were asleep when the attack came, drunk out of your mind.'

'I wasn't drunk! I've stopped drinking!' The unfairness of the accusation was like a sword through his chest but the gathered men just shook their heads.

'Even if you weren't drunk this morning, you've been drunk on a hundred expeditions before. We've had enough of it,' Sarv said. 'Enough of you. Take your things and get out.'

He threw a sack at Dae Hyo. It landed with a soft thud: clothes, not weapons.

'You can't do this to me!' Dae Hyo roared.

'Watch us.' Edmund reached into the sack he was carrying and pulled out a pair of axes, then tossed them to Dae Hyo. They arrived blade-first and he had to dance out of the way. 'There you go. You can't say we left you defenceless. And there's money enough in your purse to buy a whole crate of vodka. Why don't you go somewhere far away from here and drink yourself to death?'

None of them laughed. They didn't move, either, and their swords were steady as they pointed towards his chest. After a moment, Dae Hyo stooped to pick up the axes and slid them into his belt. Then he slung the bag over his shoulder and turned his back on them. Fuck them. Fuck them all. He'd find more weapons somewhere, and when he did, he'd pay a quick visit to this mine, these men – before he finally returned to the plains to serve justice on those who'd murdered his people.

4

Eric lit the final candle, then licked his fingers and snuffed out the taper. The room was filled with a warm glow and the smell of pears. The scented wax had cost him half of what he'd earn this evening, but it was worth it.

He turned to look at the man lounging on his bed. Lahiru had stripped off his trousers already and the candlelight was kind to his smooth brown skin and duellist's muscles. The other man waved a negligent hand around the room. 'Very nice, Eric – very *atmospheric.*'

Eric grinned. 'I done it up for you special. Kenric lent me them drapes. He says they come all the way from the Eternal Empire, though he says a lot of things that ain't precisely true.'

'Very nice,' Lahiru said again, but the words were absent and his eyes were tracing the pale skin of Eric's chest, visible through the V of his shirt-collar. He crooked a finger and Eric knew it was time to earn his keep. That was just fine. His cock had been hard in his breeches ever since he'd seen the other man laid out like that, just begging for a tongue to taste the exposed flesh of him.

Eric moved to take his shirt the rest of the way off, but Lahiru tutted at him. 'Now now, my lovely boy – let me do that. I've paid enough for the privilege.' He reached out and stroked the bone buttons before slipping them free one by one.

'And do I get to do the same for you?' Eric asked.

Lahiru smiled, exposing even white teeth. 'I don't know. Have you been a good boy?'

'I ain't never good. That's what the gentlemen like about me.'

After that, it wasn't time for talking any longer. Eric laid himself

across the other man's bigger body and enjoyed his mouth for a
while. But the kisses quickly grew impatient and so he moved
down and used his own mouth where it would do more good,
enjoying the musky taste of Lahiru and the way he grew so very
hard, like Eric was the best thing he'd ever felt. When Lahiru
was good and ready, Eric took him between his thighs, the way
he knew he liked, and brought him to the end.

Lahiru sprawled a moment, spent, then reached a hand round
and with quick, rough movements gave Eric his satisfaction too.

After, they lay side by side on their backs, breathing hard.
Then they turned to face one another and Lahiru twirled a lock
of Eric's hair between his fingers. 'Like spun gold,' he said wonder-
ingly. He said it every time, but Eric didn't mind. He knew his
pale hair and paler skin were what had caught Lahiru's eye, and the
thought that the other man found him beautiful tightened his chest
and brought a warm glow to his cheeks. He reached out in turn
to finger the brown curl that always dipped over Lahiru's eyes.

'You know,' he said, 'you could go inside if you wanted, the
next time. I don't mind.'

'Next time, is it?' Lahiru's eyes narrowed. 'You're very certain
I'll be returning.'

The glow faded as fast as it had come and Eric drew away,
but Lahiru laughed and grabbed his hand to pull him closer. 'I
will return, have no fear. Where else could I find such a beautiful
boy to please me? Not in my home, that's for certain.' His expression sank into a frown.

'Your wife ain't a sharp one, though. She can't be. Where did
you tell her you was today? Not out enjoying a grind with a
young sellcock like myself, I'd lay ten gold wheels on it.'

'No indeed. She believes I'm out hunting, and so I am: hunting
the finest boy flesh to be had for many miles.'

'Better than any what you got here in Ashanesland. You was
just lucky Smiler's Fair was passing through. Normally we go
round by the Five Stars, but the Merry Cooks had a bit of a
falling out with old Lord Nalin Nine Eggs, and so this time we
come the long way round.'

'And I was lucky that you did, you're right. It's been somewhat of a drought for me this past year. The last time I had so much fun was on a visit to Fell View, where a very pretty young serving boy seemed happy to spread his legs for a dashing young ship-born lord.'

He smiled, and Eric tried not to frown. So there'd been others before him, so what? He'd wager they didn't know how to please a fellow the way he did. And there was something special between him and Lahiru; he was sure the other man sensed it too. He'd known it the first time their eyes had met across Winelake Square, and the certainty hardened with every day Lahiru returned to him. Him and not Kenric, no matter how much the other boy had fluttered his lashes.

Lahiru rolled over, exposing his perfect flank to Eric. His expression was suddenly melancholy and Eric didn't know if it was the thought of his wife or just the low mood that often plagued a man right after he'd spent himself.

'How does a lovely young thing like you end up in a place like this, making his living on his back?' Lahiru muttered.

Eric grinned, to still be called young when he was sixteen now and other clients had begun to complain about the stubble beneath his rouge. But Lahiru turned to look at him, and Eric understood that his lover really did want an answer to the question.

'Well, I was born over the mountains and up in the north – in the Moon Forest what you probably ain't never seen. It's all right there, I suppose. But I was born Jorlith, and my mum had popped out ten before me and half of them already starving. I reckon she prayed I'd be born with the hawk mark, so I'd be the Hunter's problem, but no such luck.'

'The hawk mark?'

Eric shrugged. 'It don't matter. Point is, I wasn't wanted and they wanted me even less when they saw I'd never be a fighter. Among the Moon Forest folk, that's how the Jorlith make their living, from the wergeld for those they kill. So my dad, he took me by the hand and down to the nearest family of churls what needed cheap labour for the fields. I suppose you'd call them landborn – farmers, anyway, but rich enough to buy a new son what everyone knows will just be a servant to 'em. That's the folk's way. I don't know what price my dad got for me, but it can't have been much 'cause he sold my sister not two months after.'

'That's awful,' Lahiru said, his face grave. 'How old were you?'

'Seven winters. Well, the churls, they put me to work straight away, but I wasn't no better at farming than I'd been at fighting. And the other children, they knew I was a molly even when I didn't know it myself. If I wasn't stooped and sore from the planting and weeding I was black and blue from the beatings.'

'I know how that feels. Our kind aren't welcome in Ashanesland, either. I've hidden what I am my entire life.'

'But it ain't the same. Your Lord Lust, I've heard he don't approve of sticking your cock anywhere it can't make babies. You reckon being a molly makes you less of a man. My people say it's the opposite. The folk think men are wicked, see – filled with evil just waiting to spill out. So a man goes with a woman and she cools down the fire inside him. But two men together, that's a dangerous thing.'

'I see,' Lahiru said, though Eric wasn't sure he did.

'Anyway, I used to dream that one day a Janggok raider would come and carry me away to be his knife woman. Course, that was before I knew what the tribes do to turn boys into girls. And when I was getting towards my thirteenth winter and my cock started to stir I thought, 'You know what, young Eric? You ain't much of a fighter and you ain't much of a farmer and maybe you ain't no use to no one, but you deserve better than this.' So I run away to the edge of the forest, where I heard Smiler's Fair was stopped, and I joined right up.'

'Twelve years old when you became a whore?' Lahiru's voice was thick with horror, and Eric slipped his arms around him.

'Don't you go pitying me – I landed on my feet. Turns out I got a knack for it. I didn't take the first offer I got, even though I was hungry enough to eat my own hand by then. I took my time and asked around about what company I should join. If I'd been stupid I could have sold my bond to Smiler's Mile and ended up fucked out by the time I was fifteen, sick with pox and hooked on bliss pills to make the pain go away. I seen it happen plenty of times. You was lucky you didn't go for one of their boys. We say the dice on their standard's on account of the gamble you take every time you dip your wick in their merchandise.

'But Madam Aeronwen offered to buy me into the Fine Fellows, and I've already saved up nearly half of what I need to pay back my debt. It ain't a bad life. At least I ain't still grubbing in the dirt and married to some skirt who don't understand why my cock stays soft for her. And I get to meet great lords like yourself, don't I?' He smiled to show he meant it and wasn't just having a joke.

Lahiru nodded, his expression suddenly closed off. 'I suppose you're right. And if you hadn't come here, I would never have had the pleasure of your company.'

'Exactly. Like they say, the sun shines after every storm.'

Lahiru sighed and rolled from the bed to his feet.

'Oh,' Eric said. 'You ain't going already?'

'I fear I must. We have guests this evening, my father-by-vow and his household, and I must prepare. I shouldn't have come here at all, but –' he smiled that bright smile '– how could I resist you?' He pulled up his trousers and shrugged into his shiny blue jacket, which, unlike Kenric's drapes, probably *had* come from the Eternal Empire.

Eric sat up, splaying his legs to show everything he had. A boy used the weapons he had to hand. 'You'll be back tomorrow, though. You said you would.'

'If Smiler's Fair is still here then so shall I be. Do you know how much longer it's likely to remain?'

It wasn't a subject Eric wanted to think about. 'There's no telling for sure, but we've been here near a month already. We're bound to go soon.'

'I mourn that day already. I shall be bereft without you.'

Eric's heart sped up and his mouth felt dry, but he'd never get a better chance to say it. 'You don't have to be. That pretty young servant boy what you had your way with – what if he was me? What if I worked in your home? You're a lord, ain't you? You must have a hundred people at your beck and call. Can't I be one of 'em?' He pouted his lips to remind Lahiru of what he'd done with them before. 'I'd do *whatever* you asked.'

The other man was silent for a long moment and Eric felt light with hope. Then Lahiru shook his head. 'My wife may not be that bright, but she's not that dim, either. Carrying on right under her nose would be far too great a risk. And a lord I may be, but a poor and powerless one without her father's gold. No, it won't do I'm afraid. I wish it could, but it won't.'

'No, course not. Stupid idea anyway.' Eric realised that a tear was trembling at the corner of his eye and turned his head away.

Lahiru had seen it, though. He grabbed Eric's chin and lifted it to kiss him. 'Don't despair, beautiful. Perhaps we shall find another way. We still have tomorrow – and if we are lucky, the day after too.'

'Yeah, here's to tomorrow,' Eric said, but Lahiru had already closed the door behind him.

Marvan woke to see the glazed eye of a dead chicken staring back at him from his pillow. He yelped and Stalker, who had been sitting on his chest purring, hastily jumped down, offended that her gift hadn't been better received.

He groaned as he stretched and rose, the floor creaking beneath his feet. It always sounded on the point of collapse, and two storeys up it no doubt was, but he wouldn't abandon his high room. Let the fair's foolish visitors sleep off their beer on the lower floors. They'd been here nearly a month already and the worm men were bound to find them soon. The First Death would not be his own.

Stalker had returned to wind round his legs, leaving ginger and black hairs on his white silk hose. Fell's End, the home of his childhood, had been overrun with dogs: his brothers' hunting hounds and his mother's pampered little pets. He'd despised them all. He hated how they'd show their bellies in craven submission whenever a voice was raised to them, and the shameless way they'd beg for scraps. He couldn't respect an animal that so desperately needed to be loved. Cats were different, he'd discovered. Stalker did precisely as she liked and never once obeyed his commands. The gifts she brought him were for her own inscrutable reasons.

The chicken, now he looked at it more closely, seemed to be Ned's black and gold rooster, the one that woke the whole street with its crowing at sunrise every morning. He supposed he should take it to Ned but, old and scrawny though it was, it would make a decent soup, and his coin was running low. It always did towards the end of a pitch when no one had need of his mammoth's services.

He threw the bird on to the small bench he used for preparing his food, then walked to the chamber pot. His half-hearted erection wilted to let the piss come out and he breathed a sigh of relief. He hadn't the gold to hire himself one of Lord Lust's Girls and besides, he'd found his enthusiasm for the activity waning of late. He could barely keep himself hard with the thought of a woman these days, except when . . . Yes. Except then.

When he was done, he tossed the contents of the pot out of the window and ran a comb through his tangled hair. He was dressed already, so that was it: ready for the evening.

He'd been feeling it for a few days, the churning in his gut and the buzzing in his mind that seemed to come more frequently now: every few weeks where once the urgency had been separated by months, even years. Excess nervous energy, the apothecary had called it, and put leeches on him to suck it out. It hadn't worked, of course. When did the old quack's cures ever do what they promised? Marvan should have gone to the Worshippers instead. Their prayers might have proven equally useless, but at least had the virtue of being cheap.

He thought about ignoring the feeling and heading over to see the King's Men perform *The Innocent and the Rake* for a seventh time, but he knew he wouldn't be able to sit still for it. Or he could tend to his mammoth, which, after all, was his livelihood and guarantee of membership of the Drovers. But the boy he'd apprenticed looked after the great ugly thing well enough and it needn't do anything but eat and rest until it was time for Smiler's Fair to move on. No, the nervous energy needed working off and he knew just the place to do it. He pulled his good woollen coat from its hook, then opened his arms chest.

The weapons glittered in their velvet nests. He ran a gentle finger along the blade of a Jorlith hand axe, but that wouldn't be any use to him tonight. The sabre he'd had from a proud Ahn warrior lay in its jewelled scabbard and he smiled as a ruby winked up at him. He loved the feel of the blade, its speed and strength, and he felt a pang as he moved past it. The twin tridents were near the bottom, unused for many years.

He drew them out and found that they fit in his hands as comfortably as ever. They had no blades to keep keen, but there was no rust on the metal of each half-foot-long central prong or the shorter outer guards. He twirled them experimentally, changing his grip to rest each prong along his arm so that the pommel could be used to stun. The movement was a little hesitant, but long years of practice couldn't be entirely erased.

Yes. He'd use these, his very first weapons, the ones he'd taken from his brother half a lifetime ago. He seated them in the loops of a leather belt, bound it round his waist and turned to inspect himself in a square of glass the merchant had sworn came from Mirror Town itself. No need to shave. He looked well enough, as well as a man with nose and chin so long and sharp could hope. He straightened his shaggy brown hair, spat on his finger to wipe away the crusted sleep beneath his eyes and opened the door.

As he passed the second floor, he heard the scrabbling of claws across wood and guessed that one of Nae Kim's rabbits had escaped again, perhaps searching for her latest brood, which was no doubt already in the tribesman's stewpot. On the ground floor Ethelred's goose honked a warning at him. It reared up to flap its strong brown wings, but it knew him well enough to let him pass, and then he was out on the street.

The mud covered the top of his foot, watery and foul-smelling. When they'd first arrived the streets had been grassy, but that had soon been trampled away. Some of the Drovers had spread straw for better footing, until that too had sunk beneath the muck. Now there was no stopping the filthy tide.

A turd floated towards him, barely visible in the moonlight, and he jumped aside to avoid it. Something unidentified crunched beneath his foot as he landed, probably the carcass of an animal. Smiler's Fair was always welcome when it arrived – he'd known shiplords and elder mothers pay gold by the bucketload to tempt the fair and the trade it brought with it. But he wondered what they thought of their bargain when Smiler's Fair had moved on and left only a vile, rubbish-filled swamp behind. *Shit and piss and decaying meat, that's what we leave them,* he thought. *But then again, that's all anyone leaves behind when they go.*

It was quiet in the Drovers' quarter where people only slept and ate. The tall wooden houses were mostly dark, their residents out tending their animals or spending their earnings. But he could hear the sounds of revelry coming from ahead and soon enough he passed the crossed whips that marked the end of the Drovers' domain.

Two Jorlith guards stood stiffly under the arches, their gold hair bleached by the moonlight to the same white as their faces. They lowered the weapons and nodded at Marvan when they recognised him, putting a mark against his name on the census.

Beyond lay the territory of the Queen's Men. Queen Kaur's stern face flapped on banners to either side of the street. She looked disapproving, and who wouldn't, at the debauchery being undertaken below her? The bars were so crowded their occupants spilled into the street, bringing gusts of laughter and an aura of barely controlled violence with them. There were acrobats to entertain the drinkers, songbird sellers, men masked like animals and women with their breasts bare and their bodies painted silver. There were cutpurses, too. The Queen's Men was a haven for them, but the visitors didn't know that and stood oblivious as their coin was cut from their waists while they gawped at the performers. Marvan put a firm hand over his own purse and moved on.

He passed another two Jorlith guards and then the banners flapping above him showed a round breast squirting wine into a glass and he was in the Fine Fellows' streets. As he passed the first of the knocking shops a man walked out into his path, ship-born to judge by his embroidered blue silks. He was still doing up the last buttons on his jacket but his expression was blank, as if the pleasures he'd left behind were already forgotten, or he was already contemplating the next vice he'd sample.

Marvan's destination, the Two Cocks, was next door. Gurpreet always contrived to place his tavern next to one of the many houses of ill-repute, explaining both its name and the quality of the custom that crowded it. The faded wooden sign, a mangy bird pecking at a man's member, swayed in the breeze as Marvan elbowed aside the lollygaggers cramping the entranceway.

The smell of cheap ale and cheaper gin wafted over him. 'A small pint of beer, Jotti, and none of your barrel dregs,' he shouted across to the barmaid, then pushed his way through to pick up the tankard.

'Nothing but the best for you, Marvan, you know that,' Jotti said.

He pressed two clay anchors into her palm to ensure it remained true. When she smiled at him he saw that her plum lipstick had smeared on to her teeth. She'd caked powder on her face, turning the brown skin a dirty yellow, and stuck no fewer than three patches on it, but they did little to disguise the pox-marked skin beneath. She'd earned her membership in the Fine Fellows with her legs spread wide.

He scanned the room, nodding greetings to the sellcocks and dollymops and cutpurses who caught his eye as they searched for a suitable cully among the visitors huddled at the tables. The visitors, in turn, eyed the local colour with a mixture of horror and excitement. The pair in the corner were obviously female. Their long hair had been piled up under their hoods and one of them had even painted on a false moustache, but there was no mistaking the womanly waists beneath their jackets. No doubt they were shipborn girls out for some excitement and their fathers would have their hides if they were caught. They'd probably thought it worth the risk. Smiler's Fair might pass by only once in a person's life, and how could anyone resist the lure?

An old man sat alone at a table, already deep in his cups, his beard smeared with froth and his cheeks a feverish red. He was no use. The youth at the table beside him, however – but, no: he was bouncing a cheap dollymop on his knee and Marvan knew he'd soon be retreating somewhere private.

At a table near the back, talking to one of the whores but not yet paired with her, was a young man who seemed just perfect: well-dressed, proud-faced and far enough into his cups to take the lure. Marvan slid into the seat opposite him. He smiled at the whore, a new Ashane girl he didn't recognise with soft brown eyes not yet turned to hardness by her work. She smiled back, perhaps hoping for a double booking, but he shook his head and she slunk away to find fresh meat.

The man turned to look at Marvan. His round face held round eyes that made him seem perpetually startled. 'Do I know you?' he asked, irritated.

'Only you can answer that question,' Marvan said.

The man's eyes widened even further. 'By the Five – I *do* know you. That's not a nose a man forgets in a hurry. Marvan of Fell's End, am I right? Lord Parmvir's youngest.'

It wasn't the response Marvan was expecting. 'It *is* right,' he said after a moment. 'Or at least, it was. I'm simply Marvan, a Drover of Smiler's Fair, these days.'

'You don't remember me, do you?'

'I shouldn't take offence at it. I've travelled a long way and met a lot of people.'

'I'm Ishan.' He paused, clearly expecting recognition.

After a moment, it came. 'Ishan. Ishan of Fellview, Lord Isuru's nephew? But you're a child!' He remembered a tousle-headed boy with the same wide, startled eyes who'd often been a visitor to Fell's End. Ishan and he had been friendly once, both overlooked and insignificant within their families. They'd sailed the reed-clogged marshes and talked of a future that, in the end, had been very different than they'd imagined – at least for Marvan. He'd joined Smiler's Fair and left his past behind without a backward glance. But it seemed you could never entirely escape it. 'I'm twenty-four now, Marvan, a man and soon to be Lord Ishan. I'm wed to the eldest daughter of old Lord Bayya of High Water Fastness. He has no male heirs and little chance of getting any, so I'm to inherit the shipfort and its lands. There's no need for *me* to run off to live amongst whores and thieves.' Ishan relaxed against the wall and smiled smugly.

Marvan wondered for a moment if he should change his plans, but the child who'd been his friend was many years gone. He was as good as dead, killed to make way for this proud young lordling.

Marvan felt a curious mixture of tension and relaxation. He leaned back in his chair and rested his long legs on the table. 'No, indeed. You only visit such a place when the tedium of your life becomes too much for you.'

'Tedium?' Ishan's lips thinned with displeasure. 'Well, I suppose a third son's existence might have been dull, especially in a backwater like Fell's End. Nothing to do except impregnate the landborn and drink yourself into a stupor. Some of us have responsibilities, though.' He fingered the gold embroidered anchors at the collars of his jacket.

So, a thrust parried. But Marvan could already see the weakness in the other man's defence. He was aware of a growing silence in the tavern as its regulars turned their attention to his conversation. They knew his game; they'd seen him play it before.

'Naturally, you have responsibilities,' he said to Ishan. 'No doubt it's to shirk them that you've come here.'

'A hard-working man's entitled to a break.'

'So he is. And by the look of the conversation I interrupted between you and that charming young dollymop, you were planning on giving your wife a break this evening, as well. If I recall correctly, Lord Bayya's daughter bore a striking resemblance to her father. The girl had a face like a pig and manners to match. But then it wasn't her looks that got your father's cock hard for the match, and I suppose all cats look grey in the dark. You do quench the lamps, don't you?' He eyed Ishan's round face and slightly crooked teeth. 'No doubt she also prefers it that way.'

Ah – a hit. Ishan's hands clenched and unclenched at his side. He stuttered for a moment before managing an indignant if unoriginal, 'How dare you!'

Almost there. Almost, but not quite. Marvan shrugged. 'Perhaps during my years in this place I've forgotten how to varnish the truth until it shines more prettily. But as for your needs tonight, I recommend Beomia – she's a healthy young thing. Or there's Orson if you prefer the back door, and if I were married to your wife, that would certainly be my entrance of choice.'

Ishan's complexion darkened from beige to mauve as he rose to his feet. His chair fell backwards to clatter on the wooden floor. 'That's enough. Enough. You – you – I'll *kill* you.'

Marvan swung his feet down and leaned forward, arching a brow. 'Are you challenging me?'

Just for a second, Ishan hesitated. Then his hand fell to touch the hilt of one of his twin tridents. 'Yes, curse you!'

There were many indrawn breaths around the room and some laughter. Marvan stood and smiled. 'Your challenge has been witnessed. Very well, then. Who am I to refuse a friend satisfaction?'

The crowd followed them from the room to the street outside. The muck sucked at their boots and Ishan frowned. There'd be no fancy footwork here, no finesse. But Ishan was bigger than Marvan and that should give him an advantage. When they'd been boys, Ishan had excelled at duelling. Marvan felt a not-quite-pleasant chill of fear at the memory.

A hand grasped his arm as he took position, and nerves taut with anticipation almost caused Marvan to lash out. But it was only Lucan, a thin-faced clerk of the fair, and Marvan lowered his weapons and smiled pleasantly. 'Come to see all goes according to the rules, Lucan?'

'Come to tell you to stop,' the clerk whispered. 'We've looked the other way before, Marvan, but this is a shipborn lord. Don't be a fool.'

Marvan stared at the hand on his arm until the other man removed it and took a nervous step back. 'It's all legal and above board: a challenge was issued. Am I to prove my cowardice by refusing it?'

'You could prove your wisdom by apologising.'

'I'm sorry, Lucan. If I were a wise man, why would I ever have come here?'

Lucan frowned and shook his head, though he retreated. 'Be careful, Marvan. There are some vices even Smiler's Fair won't accommodate.'

Marvan understood the warning, but his gut was too tight with hunger to heed it. The street was busy, the full moon illuminating a ragged assemblage of the lowest Smiler's Fair had to offer and the outsiders who came to use them. Passers-by stopped to stare at the two armed men, but the customers from The Two Cocks pushed them roughly aside, clearing a duelling space twenty paces long and nearly ten wide. A ring of interested faces surrounded it, eyes bright with the hope of blood.

Marvan twirled his twin tridents, loosening his muscles. His heart was pounding and he felt something flowing through him, something that left him light-headed but alert, aware but dreaming. This moment. This feeling. It was the only time he ever felt alive.

Opposite him, Ishan was moving his own twins in a series of intricate forms. It was both a warm-up and a warning: *I am a formidable opponent*. Fear could defeat a man before a weapon came anywhere near his flesh. All the shipborn men of Ashanesland learned to use the tridents and Marvan had noted the broken shape of Ishan's cheekbone, probably the legacy of another duel. Perhaps his prowess with the twins was what had won his wealthy wife for him, when better-born men must have wooed her.

Ishan stood straight and still now, waiting for the duel to be formally opened. Well, no need to disappoint him. Marvan nodded over at fat old Gurpreet, who'd waddled out of his bar to watch the excitement.

'All right then, you sorry buggers,' Gurpreet said. 'Weapons at the ready. Let's get this over with so I can get back to selling beer.'

Ishan frowned, clearly expecting a more formal pronouncement. After a moment, when it didn't come, he said, 'I stand ready before the prow gods of my people.'

'Ready as I'll ever be,' Marvan said. 'Let's give the mob their entertainment.'

The mud squelched beneath their boots as they circled each other. Marvan shut the crowd out of his mind. They were just a wall to encircle the field of battle.

When Ishan struck it was swift and hard. The only warning came from his wide eyes, which narrowed a moment before he moved. He'd twisted the twins so that the prongs ran parallel to his arms and the pommel added weight to the fist he swung towards Marvan's cheek.

Marvan's instinct was to dance back. He lost a crucial moment as he fought it, knowing the mud would hold him fast, and when he finally ducked it was too late and the pommel powered into his temple. His vision greyed for a moment before the pain bloomed inside his head. He had no time to decide on his next move; his body did it for him, rolling through the muck and bringing him to his feet behind Ishan's back.

He couldn't take advantage of the position. Ishan spun to face him, smiling mockingly at the muck now covering Marvan and the blood trickling down one side of his face. 'Apologise abjectly enough and I might just end this while you're still conscious,'

Marvan managed a smirk, though his whole face ached. 'A more skilled man would have killed me. But you seem to have misunderstood. This won't end until one of us is dead.'

Ishan's moment of shock gave Marvan his opening. All the old training came back to him as he thrust forward, the trident's point flung towards Ishan's chest by the weight of his body. Ishan saw the danger and twisted aside, just fast enough to spare his heart, but he couldn't avoid the blow entirely. A trident's power is in its point. It met Ishan's skin and parted it easily, skimming a rib before sinking into the lung beneath.

The crowd shouted and some cheered but Marvan heard boos, too. They'd wanted a spectacle and the fight was ending almost as soon as it had begun.

Ishan's momentum pulled the trident free and a gout of blood sprayed after it. He gasped and staggered back, his face pale. Marvan understood the disbelief in his expression. The trident was a weapon meant to injure, to disarm and to defend. That was why the shipborn used it in their duels. Their noble lives were too valuable to waste on petty squabbles. But a trident *could* kill. And tonight it would.

Ishan staggered back a step. He must have known that he was in trouble. The blood flowed freely from the puncture in his chest. Each breath wheezed out of him and a red froth was beginning to form on his lips He didn't give up, though. Marvan supposed that was admirable. Slower than before, but still deadly quick, Ishan lunged forward – point-first this time, aiming for his own killing blow. It struck, but only a glancing impact, a scrape against Marvan's ribs that hurt but didn't wound.

Weakened, Ishan was no longer a danger. Now Marvan could give the crowd their show. He reversed the tridents in his hands and circled his opponent. Ishan stumbled round to keep him in sight. When Marvan darted forward to crash a metal-filled fist into his stomach, he did nothing to evade the blow.

Ishan bent, coughing, and a trickle of blood fell from his mouth to the darker mud below. Marvan took the opportunity to move behind him, and aimed a kick for his buttocks. The crowd roared as Ishan fell face-first into the muck. He struggled to rise as Marvan watched, finally dragging himself to his knees. He'd lost one of his twins and the other dangled limply from his right hand.

The fight was suddenly boring. Marvan's chest felt tight with the need to end it, the need to complete the act he'd been yearning towards for days. He kicked out again, knocking the other man on to his back. Ishan's face was empty of arrogance. His expression held only fear now.

Marvan licked his lips as he dropped to his knees beside Ishan, delaying the moment, savouring it. Ishan's hair felt coarse against his fingers as he grabbed a fistful and pulled back, exposing his vulnerable neck. The other man's eyes rolled wildly, trying to follow Marvan's hand and the trident that he moved to press against the apple of his throat.

'You show him, Marvan,' someone shouted. It was meaningless. This wasn't about anyone but him and Ishan.

'I yield,' Ishan croaked. He was sobbing, the tears mingling with and smearing the other filth on his face. 'I yield. You're right, I do take my wife from behind. She is a sow!'

'Is she?' Marvan said. 'I barely remember her.'

The metal hilt had warmed in his hand. It was a part of him, an extension of his own arm. He raised the spike above the other man's throat and then brought it down. The point pierced the thin skin and the thick tube of Ishan's windpipe, cleaving clear through the tendons and arteries of his neck until it hit the bones of his spine, where it stuck fast. But it had done its job. Blood spurted out on to Marvan's face and across bystanders who'd leaned too close to watch the end. The smell of it was rich and coppery, stronger even than the stench of shit.

Marvan watched the last breath shudder out of his childhood friend with a surge of pleasure. As Ishan's life drained away, a beautiful peace filled Marvan. It was done. He closed his eyes, enjoying the quiet in his mind. When he opened them he saw that Lucan was watching him, an expression of disgust on his face.

If only the feeling would last. If only it ever lasted.

Eric woke alone at dawn. There'd been no john willing to pay fifteen glass feathers to spend the whole night with him and he stretched luxuriously, enjoying the temporary solitude. It was very quiet, though. Too quiet, and there was a heaviness in the air that made him twitchy, like an animal growing restless at the approach of a storm. His stomach clenched as he rolled from the bed and inspected himself in the mirror above the dresser.

His make-up had rubbed away in the night, exposing the pale face beneath the gold hair. Awful. His eyes looked dull, and was that a line beside his mouth? No wonder no one had wanted him for the whole night.

No wonder Lahiru hadn't stayed.

He applied his new make-up carefully, lining his eyes to make them seem larger and rubbing colour on their lids to bring out their blue and rouge on his cheeks to highlight the bones. When he was dressed in his fine linen shirt and the silver chain that had been a gift from a besotted old man, he looked almost all right, almost like a boy someone might lose his heart to.

The morning muster for the Fine Fellows took place in Gamblers' Square. Its entrance led between the Nine Times Nine and the Lucky Knot, whose owners had been fast enough to secure themselves the prime location. Both establishments sprawled out on to the muddy ground. Tables tipped at angles where dead-eyed men tossed dice that had betrayed them all night long but might, just might come good for them on the next roll. The members of the company crowded around them. They leaned against the tables and upset the games, uncaring as they peered up towards the platform where the censor would take the muster.

Eric found himself sandwiched between Mad Mercy, one of the whores from Madam Sin's rival house, and a stranger with bruised eyes and a stubbled face who seemed barely conscious. And there was the censor now, his jowls wobbling beneath florid cheeks.

It would be today, Eric felt it in his gut. The names started being called and there was an 'Aye, present' or 'Still abed' for each, but he knew it couldn't last. When they came to Ishan of High Water Fastness, a moment's silence seemed to confirm his fears and then a laughing voice piped up 'No secret there, mates. Marvan of the Drovers done for that one' and Eric gasped in relief. But three names later another silence fell, and this time no one filled it.

'Ravi son of Ravith of Deep Lake village,' the censor said again. 'Not seen? Not known?'

'I kept him company last night.' The young girl blushed when the crowd turned to look at her. 'But the bugger snored like a rockfall so I told him he could sleep on the floor.'

'And he wasn't there when you woke?' the censor asked.

She shook her head and a murmur travelled through the crowd: 'Dead, dead, dead.'

'The First Death!' the censor confirmed. 'The soil has spoken – we've hidden it from the sun too long and the worm men have found us. Smiler's Fair must move again.' The cry was repeated down side streets and along alleys to quarters beyond theirs, so that soon the whole fair would know.

Eric stood frozen while everyone around him rushed into motion. Only the gamblers at their tables remained still, watching in confusion as figures climbed the walls of the building in which they'd spent their night and began to dismantle it. Eric thought it was like watching ants at work on a leaf. They swarmed over the wood, little things tearing apart something much larger than themselves.

His heart felt pulled apart too. Lahiru never came to him before noon. Smiler's Fair would be in pieces by then, maybe even gone. No one wanted to remain long on ground that had seen the First Death. Eric should already be breaking down Madam Aeronwen's establishment, helping to load it into their travel wagons, or helping the Drovers feed and hitch the ice mammoths that would draw them somewhere new, far away from Lahiru.

He didn't help; he just watched. He saw the panels of the Last Luck pulled apart and stacked on the backs of wagons higgledy-piggledy so that some showed their decaying outer surface and others the brightly painted interior, tessellations of dice and cards. The Aethelstan's Rest was so small there was no need to pull it apart. George, its hulking doorman, rolled the wheels to each of its corners so that they could be attached to the axles and tight-ened. Then four brown horses were brought up and the tavern was departing Gamblers' Square. It joined the procession of buildings, whole and broken, already heading down the valley and away.

It was so fast. They'd each done it a hundred times before. Smiler's Fair moved on and they with it; it was the way of things. Gamblers' Square was soon a muddy blank with only a few stragglers left in it, knee-deep in the muck. Madam Aeronwen's had gone already and Eric would need to run to catch up. Smiler's Fair didn't wait. He had to go.

But they were heading for the plains. The tribes didn't have much use for a boy like him. The last time they'd passed through the lands of the Four Together, there'd been so little work for him that Madam Aeronwen had lent his bond to the Merry Cooks. And this time there'd be Kenric to lure away what trade there was.

He knew where Lahiru's shipfort was. The Ashaneman hadn't told Eric himself, but it had been easy enough to find out. Eric could go there instead, to Smallwood. He pictured it: he'd ride the bridge across the lake to the gates and they'd be opened for him before he got to them. Lahiru would have seen him coming and rushed down to greet him. He'd fling his arms round Eric in full view of all his men, then draw him inside the shipfort and tell him that this was his home now.

You're such a dreamer, my Eric, Madam Aeronwen would say to him. *When will you learn to live in the waking world?* But he liked his dreams better. And Lahiru did love him, he was sure of it. He simply lacked the courage to act. Well, Eric would act for him. He'd be brave enough to find happiness for both of them.

Smallwood lay to the west. Eric turned his back on the sun and began to walk.

5

The mountain lion was hungry enough to be desperate, but not so weak it couldn't kill Krish if it caught him. The sky was the same grey as the rocks on which it crouched, the sparse grass shrivelled, and the world seemed leached of all colour except the hunter's yellow fur and fierce golden eyes. The animal was barely fifty feet away, its gaze flicking between him and the herd. It had approached the goats from downwind, and they had yet to smell their stalker. Oblivious to their danger, they must make the more tempting target, but Krish couldn't let them be taken. His da would be furious.

He shouted suddenly to scare the herd and then turned in the other direction from their panicked stampede. Instinct told him to run, but he fought it. He'd once seen a blue warbler lead a falcon away from its nestlings by feigning a broken wing. He forced his own left leg to drag as if it was injured and looked back at the lion to see if it had taken the bait, a terrified part of him hoping it wouldn't.

But the ruse worked. The lion's burning eyes fixed on him, its tail twitched and it slunk towards him as the goats bleated and made their escape. Rain froze as it fell, into darts of ice that struck them both, and Krish was sure he must be as sorry a sight as the lion, its fur lank and dripping and its thin body racked with shivers.

Limping was hard, almost as hard as running, and after a score of paces he was panting for breath and the lion had eased itself ten feet nearer. Soon, he knew, it would decide that it had him and substitute lethal speed for its cautious creeping. He'd seen great cats hunting before. He had only a few moments more, and he wasn't sure they were enough.

His whole body shook with the desire to hasten his pace, but he knew he couldn't. Only the belief that he was injured was slowing the lion, convinced it had as much time as it needed to take down its prey. He limped as fast as he could and turned a little left, his breath rasping and a sweat of fear on his skin despite the damp chill.

And then the lion leapt. Krish gasped and leapt too, forcing speed from his aching legs. The ravine was only twenty paces away. If he could just make it, if he could just take twelve more strides – but suddenly the lion was on him. Its great clawed paws reached out to grab and rend him and he flung himself desperately to one side, scraping his side raw on the rocks.

The lion missed him by inches and was already turning to try again. But in its hurry it missed its footing and Krish felt a hot rush of relief as the hunter skidded on to its side and growled in anger and pain.

In the seconds its fall had bought him he gathered the last of his strength and pushed himself to his feet. Only a dozen paces now and his heart pounded out every one of them. He heard the scrabble of the lion's claws as it righted itself and then its roar as it leapt for a second time and he flung himself to the ground, tucked his head beneath his arms and hoped.

Claws raked his shoulders, teeth snapped so near his head he heard their sharp *clack*, and then the lion was past him and it gave a desperate yowl as it realised there was nothing beneath it but air. Krish craned his neck over the lip of the ravine to watch the beast as it plummeted fifty feet to the jagged bottom. There was a splash of red as it landed and, though he saw its body move a little, he knew that it was finished.

He felt a sudden sorrow for the dying creature. It had only wanted to eat and Krish knew what it was to be hungry. Triumph quickly banished his pity, though. He peered at the distant body and wondered if he could climb down the rocks to strip the lion of its hide. He could take it to sell next time he went to market, and no thief who saw that clawed pelt on his donkey's back would dare to attack him.

He was just planning how to climb the cliff when he heard the plaintive bleating behind him and remembered Snowy. His mind on the immediate threat, he'd forgotten the nanny was so near to her time. He groaned as he forced himself to his feet; the cuts in his shoulder stung, but he could see that he didn't have the leisure to tend to them. Snowy was panting her distress and her eyes were wild with pain.

He walked to her and gently stroked her neck, then led her back towards a half-cave in the mountainside that he sometimes used when the weather was bad. The danger past, the scattered herd began to gather round as if they felt the need to witness the birth of their latest member. Their warm flanks pressed against him and the smell of the billies was almost choking in the confinement of the rock.

Krish bent over his own knees as a racking cough shook him. There was an ominous rattle to it, the sound of water building in his lungs. The winter always brought it on, and last year a fever came with it that had melted the flesh from his bones until he looked little more than a skeleton. Running through the cold and wet hadn't helped, but what choice had he had?

When the cough passed, he turned his attention back to the goats. He'd helped to birth enough kids before: Snowy's own mother, and her dam too. He'd looked after the herd since he was seven. But this was going to be a bad one, he could already tell. He felt the shape of the kid against Snowy's sides and it seemed twisted.

He pushed her into a corner, away from the other animals, and started to build a fire from the branches he'd left on another visit. He set water to boil in a clay pot above the fire and then drew out the parchment from its hiding place at the bottom of his pack.

The scroll showed a family tree of the whole herd going back nine years, as far as he'd been able to remember. He'd scratched little sketches of the goats, then made a careful note of their coat colour, their eye colour, their size and horns, everything about them that marked them out. He'd never been taught the proper way to turn words into marks on a page, so he'd made up his own: an empty circle for a white coat and a filled one for brown. It was easy enough. He wondered if the true writing the shipborn learned was as simple.

Snowy was white, of course. Her horns were short and her eyes were a very pale yellow, almost as strange as his own. At the moment they were wide with fear as her flanks heaved and sweated. Krish remembered when his cousin had given birth and how she'd screamed and begged her mother to make it end; how she had cursed her husband for planting his seed in her.

He wondered if Snowy guessed the risk of her labour. Did those pale eyes see things not yet come to pass, or did she live only in the present? He did what he could to ease her, rubbing her sides with a dry cloth to stop the cooling sweat from chilling her.

'Good girl,' he crooned. 'It will all be over soon, you'll see.' He ran his hand over her stomach, felt the misplaced shape of her kid, and knew that it was a lie. His hand fell to the knife at his belt, thinking to cut the kid free, but when he drew it and saw the wicked edge of the flint he hesitated. Snowy was still watching him, and what if she really could sense death coming? What if she knew what he intended for her?

He sheathed the blade, shrugged off his woollen coat and rolled up the sleeves of his shirt, shivering as the frigid air tore at his lungs and raised goosebumps on his arms. There was a trickle of blood seeping from Snowy already, a bad sign but useful for him. It would smooth his way in. The passage was tight and her strong muscles clamped down painfully on his fingers as he eased them inside her.

He'd seen other men attempt this, but had never done it himself. It was far harder than he'd imagined. Snowy was moaning her pain now, a distressingly human sound. He could feel nothing inside but wetness and tight muscle and he was afraid that if he moved he'd hurt her more.

He gritted his teeth and did it anyway, pressing his arm forward and feeling with his fingers. He almost jerked back when they met something hard, then realised it must be the kid's head. He probed it gently and felt the bud of its horns. And he'd been right. Its legs weren't there, where they needed to be.

Snowy had stopped making any sound at all except a desperate panting. Even that was slowing and he knew that she was weakening. If the kid didn't come out soon, it would kill her. Krish slid his fingers from the baby's head and felt along the shape of its jaw and then down its neck to its chest. After that his fingers traced a bony shoulder and he followed it down until he felt a tiny hoof. He hooked a finger beneath the kid's knee and raised it.

Snowy's head jerked up and she moaned again, but he kept moving, lifting her baby's leg to where it needed to be. He gave her a moment, then did the same with the other leg. They were as thin as twigs and he worried they'd break, but there was a deceptive strength in them. And in Snowy too, who was still breathing, her yellow eyes watching him almost as if she understood what he was doing for her.

He pulled the legs and Snowy jerked and bleated but nothing else happened. It wasn't working – the legs were too fragile a handhold. He shifted his fingers again until he felt the little animal's shoulder, took a breath, and then yanked with all his strength.

Snowy screeched and the herd shifted and stamped around him. Outside, the wind howled through the rocks. He almost gave up. He could still use the knife. But her eye was on him and they were so close. 'You need to help me, then,' he told her. 'Do what mothers do.'

She couldn't have understood him, but she had a mother's nature all the same and he felt all the muscles inside her clench and push. He gasped and tightened his grip, pulling when she pushed and stopping when she stopped. When it finished, it finished suddenly, in a slither of mucus and blood and delicate limbs.

Krish fell back, sitting on the hard rock as he watched Snowy lift an exhausted head to lick her son clean. The little creature

staggered to his feet, seeming to gain strength as he moved. His
head turned towards his mother, nuzzling at her flank until he
found what he was looking for and started to suck hungrily on
her udder.

The fire was beginning to burn down to embers and the
sky too was losing its brightness. Hidden behind churning
clouds, the sun must be close to setting and he needed to head
home. The herd could shelter here for the night. He'd tether
Dapple, their leader, and the other goats wouldn't wander far.
He looked back at the kid, feeding at his mother's tit, and for
the first time took real note of the colour of his coat: not white,
like both his sire and dam, but a pure brown almost the same
colour as Krish's own skin.

He smiled as he noted it down on his scroll. He was right. He
was definitely right. It wasn't just chance now; his idea had held
true for four generations. This was better even than the lion's
skin to take back as a trophy. When he got home he'd tell his
father and it would change everything.

It was twilight by the time he neared his family's encampment
at the edge of the village circle. The distant mountains were lost
to sight, but he could see their shapes in his memory: the jagged
saw of the Teeth, and the twin peaks that the adults called The
Sisters and the children The Breasts. He'd sit sometimes when
he was tending the herd and think of walking the long miles over
rock and scrubby grass to reach them, walking to them and not
walking back. But things here would get better now and there'd
be no need to leave.

The village fires lighted the way as he approached, more tightly
clustered than they would be in summer. The cold drew people
in, and on the last day of every ten, when tradition dictated that
the tents were moved, they weren't moved very far.

The grass on the slope leading to the village was more brown
than green. He reached the gnarled tree that marked the edge of
habitation and brushed his fingers against a knot in its trunk.
It was a ritual he'd performed since he could first walk, a

confirmation that he'd reached safety, and he had to stoop to do it now. He'd grown but the tree never did. Like all old things, it had lost the energy to change.

He passed Isuru's large tent, which seemed to shine silver under the rising moon. The headman had demanded the skins of his neighbours' white goats in tribute for his wife to stitch it. The menfolk had grumbled and done it anyway, afraid Isuru would increase their taxes if they didn't. Krish didn't see that it mattered. It was better to be like his own family's mottled tent, almost invisible in the shadows. The mountains were full of predators and standing out was never wise. He knew that better than most.

His mother smiled at him as he ducked through the goatskin flap. Her skin sagged with age and her lips were cracked with the winter chill. His father said that she'd never been beautiful, but Krish didn't believe it. He could see the shadow of fairness in her high cheekbones and the long hair that must once have been dark and glossy.

His father was working at the far side of the tent, chipping a new flint blade. He didn't look up as Krish entered.

'A good day?' his mother asked.

Krish grinned and she frowned in surprise. He didn't smile very often. 'A very good day, Ma. Snowy gave birth to a little billy.'

'Curse her,' his father said without turning. 'More useless meat.'

Krish thought about explaining his idea then, but the tone of his father's voice was harsh. Food in his belly would soften his mood. Krish went to the hearth instead and bent to kiss his mother's cheek. 'The kid was twisted. I put him right.'

She smiled and ruffled his hair, dropping both smile and hand when his father said, 'Just as well. I could afford to lose you more easily than another dam in her prime. The herd's thin enough already.'

'Enough of them to put food on our plates, and that's what matters,' his mother said.

His father grunted, looking through her rather than at her, the way he often did.

'Dinner smells good,' Krish said, though in truth the meat was too rank and the herbs too few to make an appetising meal.

His mother ladled out a large bowl for his father and smaller ones for herself and Krish. They settled at the hearthfire, pots and half-finished shoes and sides of cured meat hanging around their heads. The rough stone forms of their prow gods watched them from beside the flames: the Thunderer with the zigzag lightning bolt across his chest, who warded against ill weather, and the fertile Goat God with two little horns on his head.

When his fifteenth spring had come and he'd become a man, Krish should have brought his own god to add to the hearth. His father had denied him that. He often wondered what it meant to be without a god, to be unwatched and unprotected. He prayed to the Fierce Child sometimes to spare the goats, but he wasn't sure the shiplords' gods, kept so far away in distant Ashfall, would have a care for a landborn herder on the outer edge of the realm.

The meal was silent as usual. Krish felt confined in the tent, hemmed in by the musty-smelling skin. It was different in summer. He could sleep under the stars and away from the judging eyes of his father. They were on him now and he realised that he was shaking. He wasn't sure if it was fear or anticipation. What he'd discovered would change things, and for the seventeen years of his life, nothing else ever had.

'Speak then,' his father said. 'I know you're able.'

'Snowy's kid, he was brown.'

His father frowned, not understanding.

'His sire was Woody,' Krish said. 'Woody is white like her. And Woody doesn't have the double horns, nor Snowy neither, but the kid's got them.'

'Then you're wrong. The sire must be Dapple.'

'No, I saw the mating myself. Woody mounted her. I've been keeping –' he drew out his parchment, spreading it on the rug between them '– I've been keeping records of all the herd, all the births and matings.' He pointed out Snowy's place on the chart and her unnamed kid beneath her. 'The circles show what colour they were and there's lines for the horns and I've put their eyes, too. Hatched means blue like Titch had. You remember, Ma. You always liked her.'

His mother's brow creased with worry. 'What's this about, Krishanjit? These aren't the King's carrion mounts we have here. There's no need to keep track of their breeding.'

'But look here. See.' Krish pointed along the lines of the chart, to Snowy's sire and dam and their sires and dams before them. 'Two generations back and the brown colour is there. I've thought a lot and I have an idea of why it could be.'

'Then you've too much time on your hands and not enough work to fill them.' His da was using his forbidding tone, which meant the conversation was over, but Krish was too caught up in his excitement to care.

'It's the mother, she gives a bit of herself to her child, and the father gives something too. And these gifts, they can be weak or strong. The white coat is strong. If sire or dam gives the white gift, that's the colour of the kid. The strong gift overpowers the weak. But it isn't thrown away. And when that kid has kids of its own, it chooses: will I pass on my strong gift or my weak gift? And sometimes it passes on the weak. Do you see?'

'I see that you've gone crazed,' his father said.

'I understand,' his mother said. She seemed to have caught some of Krish's excitement. 'It's how a white dam and a white sire have a brown kid. The weak brown gift was passed on, and passed on, until it met a weak gift from the other side.'

'That's it!' Krish said. 'And it shows, Da, that even though my eyes are different, even though they're nothing like yours or Ma's, I *am* your son. It's just a weak gift passed down from your granddad, or your great-granddad. Ma was never unfaithful to you. Never. I've proved it.'

He smiled at her, triumphant. All these years, his father must have looked at Krish's moon-coloured eyes and thought himself a cuckold, but it wasn't true. Krish had known his mother wasn't a harlot, and now his father could stop hating her, and him.

For a moment, his father looked stunned. His jaw clenched beneath his grizzled stubble and his eyes widened. Then they narrowed again and he let out a bark of laughter. 'You're a fool, boy! And you're none of my get. Wherever you got those freakish eyes of yours, it wasn't my bloodline, nor your mother's neither. Tell him,' he ordered his wife. 'I've kept your secret long enough.'

Krish's mother seemed to shrink in on herself. He looked at her, but she wouldn't meet his eyes.

'Coward,' his father said, and for once Krish agreed with him. 'I'll tell him then, will I? How you were heading down to Lord Lust's shrine at Starfall to pray for your womb to bear fruit, and instead of getting a child in the proper fashion you found this one thrown away by some stream, and brought him home without asking leave. Five years I'd been wed to you and no child of my seed, but you brought that mewling thing home as if it would do instead. As if I'd be pleased. Now that was a weak gift!'

Krish could see the rage darkening his da's face as he brought his hand back and then forward, the movement looking almost slow but the crack of its impact against his ma's cheek horribly loud.

Krish clenched his own fist, but knew he wouldn't use it. His father was twice his size and interfering only made the beatings worse. He watched instead, as the man who had never been his father hit the woman who was not, it seemed, his mother.

6

On the third dawn after the ruins of Manveer's Folly, Captain Mahesh told Nethmi that they'd reach Winter's Hammer by noon. They were the first words he'd spoken to her since they'd fled together from his dead guardsman and the thing that had killed him.

The events in the ruins had brought back long-faded memories of her childhood. Her father had tried to keep her from the battles he fought, but it wasn't always possible. Once the mountain savages had attacked the army's camp itself and she remembered watching men fight and die. She'd found it exciting. To a six-year-old, it had seemed like an entertainment put on purely for her benefit.

The territory they passed through now was a part of Ashanesland only because of those battles and those deaths. They hardly seemed worth it. The mules had trudged past the snowline long ago, and now they laboured through waist-high drifts and the soldiers were forced to stop often to dig them out. There was little sign of life up here, only the occasional buzzard circling above and sometimes the tracks of what might have been foxes. She'd seen nothing green for two days, nothing but the pure white of the snow and the dirtier white of the sky, pregnant with more of the stuff.

Two of the servants had been frostbitten. Nethmi had stared, horrified, at the blackened stumps of their fingers and heard them sobbing at night when everyone else was asleep. Her robes were thick and her fur mittens kept her hands safe, but nothing could keep her warm. Each day the memory of heat would bleed out of her, and each evening the fire reminded her so that she could miss it all the more the next morning. But now all that was over.

Her body had grown accustomed to her mule's rocking gait. She tightened her legs around its waist as it scrambled to the top of yet another featureless rise. With her eyes half-closed against the white glare, it took her a moment to recognise what she was seeing: the climb had finally ended as their path spilled out onto a vast, snow-covered plain. Its only features were the monumental black rocks scattered across it, each ten times the height of a man. Their tops were dusted white but the smooth sides glittered in the feeble sunlight. Nethmi couldn't imagine how the huge boulders had been carried here, all the way to the top of the world.

As they drew closer she saw that the rocks had been carved, every one with the same image: a face, long and thin and male and subtly but terribly wrong. Her heart lurched as she realised what it reminded her of. The brief flash she'd seen of the worm man's face in the darkness had had the same hollow cheeks and long, up-tipped eyes. The plain was covered in the rocks. There were a dozen within reach, hundreds of them just black spots in the distance.

'Who is he?' she turned to ask the rider behind her, realising too late that it was Mahesh.

He shook his head. His hands were tight around the reins of his mount and she was sure he'd seen the resemblance too.

'Did the savages carve them?' she asked.

He shook his head again, still staring, then roused himself from his daze. The smile he gave her was unpleasant. 'You can ask them yourself, my lady, if you like. We're here.'

Ahead lay the shipfort that was to be her new home. Winter's Hammer wasn't large, perhaps a fourth the size of Whitewood. It squatted on its platform like a black toad, fashioned from the same rock that littered the plain. Its towers were jagged, as if the material was hard to carve. Now she looked, she could see that the face on some of the rocks was mutilated where blocks had been chipped away. The edges of the working were ragged, like unhealed wounds.

The waters of the lake were very blue. The colour made her

think of toothache. On its banks, the shaggy forms of hill mammoths drew the fort around. Like Winter's Hammer itself, they were squatter and uglier than anything she'd seen before, their coats curled and almost the same colour as the rock. As her company drew nearer, the stench of them hit her, like bedding that hadn't been washed for a year. It made her mule seem positively fragrant.

A crowd of men waited for them on the lakeshore. There was no bridge that she could see, but small boats bobbed on the water behind them. All the men were armoured and armed, glints of metal shining from beneath their heavy furs. They were clearly the household guard and Nethmi wondered if her husband was among them. Her head spun and her breath was suddenly short. It hadn't seemed quite real before. Now it felt inescapable.

No one made a move towards them and there were no shouts of greeting. Their group approached the other in an eerie, hostile silence. Even their footsteps were muffled by the snow. When they were within forty paces, she saw swords being loosened in scabbards. Mahesh raised an eyebrow and his lips thinned but he waved at his own men to be at ease.

The strangers' expressions seemed to relax a little, but they weren't gentle faces. Their skin was unpleasantly pale, a yellowish sort of beige, and their hair was straight and black. Their eyes were narrower and their noses smaller than any true Ashane's. Theirs were faces she remembered from her childhood. She'd seen them dead on battlefields and caged by her father's troops, ready to be ransomed back to their tribe when peace finally came.

Her own people crowded behind her and she heard a murmur of discontent from the servants that they should have travelled so far and suffered such hardship only to be treated thus. When the two companies were face to face, a man a little taller and older than the rest stepped forward. 'You are the Lady Nethmi, daughter of Lord Shaan of Whitewood?'

'I am.'

There was no change in his expression. His cold eyes shifted from her to Mahesh's men. 'You bring many people and many weapons. It looks as if you've come to make war.'

Mahesh stepped forward, quivering with rage. He seemed to have forgotten his anger at her in his fury at this affront. 'The Lady Nethmi has come to be married, and she was expecting to be welcomed to her new home, not questioned like a common brigand on a cold lakeshore. These men are for her protection and her honour. Lord Puneet does not send his beloved niece into your savage mountains unescorted.'

The other man bowed, a very tiny amount. 'Your forgiveness, Lady Nethmi. Many attacks may come under the cover of friendship, and we have long memories here.'

She felt quite as angry as Mahesh, but schooled her expression into a smile. She could wear a mask when she needed, and there was no profit in starting her new life by making an enemy. 'I understand, Captain . . .?'

'Seonu Lin.'

'Captain Lin. You've fulfilled your duty admirably. But now, I beg of you, my people are tired and cold. We'd welcome a warm hearth to sit by.'

If his expression softened, it wasn't perceptible. 'You may come, but your soldiers and servants do not stay.'

'Am I to understand you're denying us the hospitality of your house?' Mahesh asked, incredulous.

'This land is hard. Food is scarce and we have many mouths to feed. You are strangers to us, your servants owe us no fealty. There are none within our walls who have not sworn an oath of service to Lord Thilak. It is the Seonu way.'

'It's a cold, mannerless way!' Mahesh snapped.

'And this also,' Lin said. 'There are those within Winter's Hammer who remember the war, back when we were a free land. Men such as yours burned our tents and killed our children. Your father's men, Lady Nethmi. It is safer to stay apart, so that old grudges cannot turn blood hot and see it spilt.'

Suddenly, the tension that had dissipated was back. Lin's men had never moved their hands far from their sword hilts and now Mahesh did nothing to stop his own as they grasped their weapons. Nethmi realised they were an eye-blink away from lethal violence. A part of her wanted to let it happen and see her uncle's plans for this alliance turn to ash.

But her eyes shifted to the black walls of the shipfort and the high bow-slits within them. It wouldn't be a fight; it would be a slaughter and she'd be caught in the middle of it. She remembered her father, after the mountain campaign was won, when King Nayan had offered him lordship over the newly conquered lands. *I've had enough of fighting,* he'd told his liege, *and these people haven't. Send me somewhere my sword can stay in its scabbard.*

'Enough,' she said. 'If you cannot accommodate my people then we must be content with that. If you have some kindness in you, perhaps you'll send out fuel and food to warm them before they begin the long journey home.'

Mahesh scowled and his men muttered, but they didn't dare countermand her.

'Your people will be fed one meal,' Lin said. His lips twitched into the sketch of a smile. 'I will send to the kitchens. There was a hunt yesterday, so there is a little meat to spare. Now, Lady Nethmi, you come with me. Lord Thilak waits.'

She nodded stiffly. 'I'll need your men's help, if you won't let my own cross to Winter's Hammer.'

'Your clothes and bags will be brought.'

'And my prow god.' She gestured at the sled being drawn by two mules. The figure on it was draped in canvas to protect it from the snow, but the outline of its head and upraised arms was visible beneath the fabric.

Lin stared blankly at her, then abruptly crossed to the figure and raised the canvas to look beneath. There was a shocked gasp from her people and several moved to stop him. Only she was permitted to touch her own prow god, but it was already too late. The jewels embedded in the statue's torc glittered in the light. Its face, smooth and calm, neither male nor female, gazed benignly at Lin. He stared back. '*This* is your god.'

Nethmi yanked the cover back over the figure. 'Peacebringer, yes.' Her uncle hadn't stinted her on that, paying one of Bright Star's finest sculptors to make the piece according to the truthteller's god-dream on her fifteenth birthday. The prime family's prow gods reflected on the whole fort and Peacebringer had protected them all while he was under their roof. She had prayed that war and ruin would come to Whitewood with her god's departure.

'I understand,' Lin said after a moment. 'Your ways are not our ways.' He gestured to a group of his men, and they moved silently to grasp the four corners of the god's palanquin and lift it towards the largest boat. It dipped low in the water beneath Peacebringer's weight, and for a terrible moment Nethmi thought it might sink. But the boat stayed afloat and then she was being handed into the one beside it, a fur-wrapped tribesman taking his place facing her to pull the oars. She turned to watch the lakeshore as they moved away, lifting an arm to wave at Ayesha's retreating figure. She hadn't even had the chance to say goodbye to her maid.

Halfway across the water, the tribesman had begun to sweat beneath his furs, his face red with effort. She realised that it was a young face, only a few years out of boyhood. The tension in her muscles unwound a little as he smiled cautiously at her.

'Why isn't it frozen?' she asked him.

He frowned, and she wondered if he understood her at all, but continued, 'The lake. Why is there no ice on it?'

'Hot,' he said. His eyes met hers for a moment before dropping shyly back to his oars.

She laughed, surprising herself. 'I hardly think so. If it grows any colder than this, *I'm* going to freeze solid.'

'No, *water* hot. Feel.'

He nodded down at the very blue lake beneath them, and after a moment she pulled off her mitten and cautiously trailed her fingers in the wavelets. It *was* warm, as warm as a bath. She realised that the mist hovering in patches above the water was actually steam.

'Mountain burn,' he said. 'Make lake boil. Make tears of the moon.'

'The tears of the moon?'

He pointed behind her to one of the massive black rocks, then lapsed back into silence. The splash of the oars in the water was soothing, and the warm steam even more so. Nethmi's eyes had drifted shut by the time they reached Winter's Hammer and she jerked awake with a start as they bumped against the small dock. The oarsman jumped ashore to help her out of the boat as the others made their landing around her. She found herself reluctant to part from the young tribesman and his gentle face. Her future began as soon as she stepped through the doors of King's Landing, uncertain and unwanted.

She didn't know if the tribesman sensed her hesitation, but he touched two fingers to her chest, just above where her heart beat out its sudden fear. 'Welcome,' he said. 'May our tent always shelter you.'

Then Lin was beside her and the youthful tribesman faded into the mass of his fellows, leaving her stranded. She scanned the docks ahead of her, but they remained empty. 'Will I meet my betrothed soon?' she asked Lin. 'I'm . . . anxious to do so.'

'Of course, Lady Nethmi. Tonight, at the wedding. It is ill-luck to see his face before.'

And that seemed to be the end of the conversation. He turned away from her to shout orders at his men in their own language. Her goods were gathered and carried towards the gates of the shipfort, and she was left with no choice but to follow after.

The room they brought her to was big but austere. Its walls were covered by tapestries, which did little to keep out the chill radiating from the black stone beneath. Each tapestry showed a different view of the landscape outside the windowless shipfort. On the floor there were the hides of three bears, one black, one white and one the orange of gingerbread, the only colour in the place. Their heads had been left on and their glass eyes followed Nethmi as she crossed the room.

Her possessions had been dumped in one corner. There were wardrobes and drawers, but without Ayesha there was no one to fill them for her. Lin had told her a woman would come with her gown and Nethmi guessed she must be her new maid. She sat on one of her chests, chin resting on her fists, and waited. It didn't seem right that she'd woken in a cold tent this morning and would be lying in her wedding bed tonight. She'd thought she would have more time to prepare.

She heard footsteps outside the door and a woman entered without knocking. Nethmi had hoped she might be Ashane – her betrothed must surely have brought some of his own people with him when he came to rule here – but she had the untrusting eyes and pale skin of the mountain savages. Their thin mouths didn't seem to be made for smiling and the woman didn't try.

'Your gown, lady,' she said, mangling the title as if she didn't understand it. Perhaps she didn't. Her father had told her the tribes had neither nobility nor rank before the Ashane came. The woman laid the dress out on the bed, then stared at Nethmi.

After a few seconds, Nethmi realised that she was expected to dress herself. She ran her fingers over the material. It was grey and soft but thick, maybe woollen. She'd wanted to bring her own gown to wear. Wanderers often brought fine linen from the far west to Whitewood and Ayesha had known a woman who could sew a dress with seed pearls so that it shimmered wherever she walked. But her uncle had forbidden it. He'd told her Lord Thilak would be insulted by the suggestion that he couldn't clothe his bride.

Though the dress was clean, Nethmi could see the shadows of stains on it. She wondered how many women had worn it before her. There were no jewels, but the front had been heavily embroidered. The scene showed two warriors, two *female* warriors, engaged in a furious battle. The red thread of their wounds was vivid against the pale material.

Nethmi ran her fingers along the stitches. 'It's not the most romantic scene I've ever seen.'

'The first bride to wear this dress won her husband with her axe. The dress remembers.'

'Oh.'

The fireplace was filled with slabs of what looked like earth. They burned low, smelled terrible and seemed barely to heat the room. Nethmi shivered as she removed her travelling clothes. The buttons at the back were awkward to unclasp without help, but the woman didn't offer any. Her bright black eyes watched expressionless as Nethmi stripped down to her petticoats. They were grubby from the long journey and she could smell her own stale sweat trapped beneath.

'May I bathe first?' she asked. 'I'd like to go to my husband fresh.'

'Bathe? No. The flesh must not be washed in winter. Illness follows.'

'Oh,' Nethmi said again. So there was no choice but to pull the dress over her soiled undergarments. It felt gentle against her skin, but the embroidery made it heavy. Her shoulders were weighed down with it. The back gaped open, its ribbons out of her reach, and the woman finally moved forward to assist. The calluses on her fingers brushed Nethmi's skin as she tied them.

When she was done, Nethmi turned to the tall mirror in one corner. She looked . . . not like herself. The dress made her seem older and her brown skin looked ill against the grey.

'Very beautiful,' the woman said. 'Come now. Lord Thilak waits.'

'But –' Nethmi realised there were too many objections she wanted to make and no point to any of them. Where are my followers, my maids to strew flowers in front of me? Where is my honour guard? 'Where is my prow god?' she asked instead.

'It is in the hall, waiting. Come. Time to wed.'

The woman took her arm and Nethmi let herself be led through the door. The hallway outside was unadorned, though at intervals statues lurked in niches in the wall. They were of hard-faced men and stern women, carved from the same rough rock as everything else. Lanterns sat in brackets along the length of the hallway but did little to lighten the darkness. Winter's Hammer looked as if it had been built by savages trying to imitate the wondrous ship-forts of civilised folk they had only ever seen from a distance.

As they walked further down the corridor, she heard a low murmur that might have been water or voices and then more raucous laughter and a baying that sounded like a pack of hounds. They turned a corner and suddenly the source of the noise was in front of them. The hall was long and low, almost like a tunnel through the black rock. Two great fires blazed at each end, so that everyone within was lit with a golden glow. There *were* dogs here, scores of them, but the baying came from the men at whose feet they lay. She'd never heard talk so loud or so unrestrained. Her uncle kept a table far colder than this.

Lin had told her there was little food in Winter's Hammer but he'd said nothing of ale. She could see great vats of it on the tables and guessed that as much again already swirled in the men's guts. If this was the wedding party, it had started long before the bride arrived.

A table stood on a pedestal at the far end of the room and the dozen people seated along its length faced the other revellers. Nethmi's prow god had been brought on its palanquin to sit in front of them. The firelight cast odd, dancing shadows behind it, as if its arms were swaying in time to the wailing music coming from a group of players at one side of the room.

When she'd walked half the length of the hall, someone finally noticed her. There was a shout, which echoed from the rock walls, and in its wake a silence so total she heard the scrape of the chair as the man at the centre of the high table rose to his feet.

'Lady Nethmi!' he shouted. 'Come, come – no need to be shy.' Lord Thilak's portrait hadn't done him justice. It had shown a grey-haired, stern man, but this fox-fur wrapped figure was bright with drink and pleasure and his smile was welcoming.

She took a hesitant step closer. 'I . . . my lord, I don't know the mountain ways. What is my role in this wedding?'

'Role? Why to look pretty, say yes and later – well, a gentleman doesn't speak of such things, eh?'

There was a roar of laughter around the room. Nethmi blushed but forced herself to meet his eye. 'I hope, my lord, that you'll think I've fulfilled at least the first of those.'

'Indeed you have! Your portrait was a pale reflection of your true beauty.' He rose to his feet and, to her shock, vaulted over the table and then jumped from the platform until he was by her side. Up close, she could see that what she had taken for bulk was thick muscle. His face was finely sculpted and though he *was* old, there was no hint of infirmity about him.

'Come, let me greet my bride properly.' He leaned forward to kiss her cheek, and as he did whispered, 'Have no fear, Lady Nethmi. Smile and curtsy and follow where I lead and all will be well.'

Something that had been wound tight in her chest loosened a little and she ventured a smile. 'That too I can do, my lord.'

'Let's begin, then! You'll meet my companions and vassals soon enough, but first you must meet my god. This is Mistislav, lord of snow, and I'm sure he'll be happy to adopt Peacebringer as his son when he's made his acquaintance.'

He gestured to the pedestal in front of them. Her own prow god glittered in the torchlight. Beside him was what she had taken for an unformed lump of white rock. Now she saw that it held the hint of some not-quite-human form. The rock didn't appear carved; some other force had shaped it. She understood now why Lin had seemed shocked by Peacebringer. Her prow god looked a safe and man-made thing beside this primitive, unknowable figure.

Thilak didn't need to prod her for her to curtsy deeply before it.

'Good. Good,' he said quietly. 'He's an odd-looking fellow, I know, but he's served me well enough in my years here.'

The ceremony was a blur after that. She was garlanded with small, withered flowers and told to turn five times, first leftward, then rightward. Bites of food were given to her, some sweet, some sour, some so vile she had to fight not to spit them out. She drank from a gold-chased horn, feeling the burn of something strongly alcoholic down her throat, and through it all Thilak was there to guide her with a gentle hand or a soft word. Finally he bowed and handed her a metal ring jangling with heavy iron keys. 'I give you the keys to my home,' he said, 'along with the key to my heart.'

Then it was over, and she was seated beside her new husband at the high table. His men had returned to their merrymaking and the roar of conversation washed up and down the long, low hall. Thilak introduced her to their dozen tablemates but she forgot the names as soon as he spoke them, her head heavy with exhaustion and the drink they'd made her consume. She noticed a tribesman of around Thilak's age, thin-faced and solemn, and two Ashane who spent the whole meal arguing with each other, voices raised and cheeks flushed with displeasure.

At the far end of the table sat a young man who looked to be some mixed-blood relative of Thilak's. Though his skin was pale and his hair as yellow and coarse as straw, he shared her husband's sharp nose and crooked smile. But he was monstrously, improbably fat, rolls of it spilling from the sides of his chair to brush against his sour-faced neighbour. Only one other woman was present, a savage with greying hair and lined skin. She had laugh lines around her mouth but nothing about her behaviour during the meal suggested how she'd acquired them – she remained stony-faced throughout. She barely spoke, only watched Nethmi with thoughtful eyes.

Nethmi didn't mind. She had no energy for conversation and little appetite for food. She let the servants fill her plate and nibbled at its contents, willing the meal to end.

'Hold on a little longer,' Thilak whispered in her ear. 'It will all be over soon.'

Soon meant three toasts and then a speech that must have lasted an hour or more. She didn't understand the words but from the roars of laughter and leering glances thrown in her direction she could guess what they were. And then the speech was over and Thilak rose and offered her his hand. She took it and hoped he couldn't feel her shaking. She knew a wife's duty and she would do it, however much it hurt. At least her husband seemed a kind man.

He led her the length of the hall and she held her head high, meeting the assessing glances of his men with proud eyes. Outside the hall, the cold slammed into her. Thilak saw her shiver and put his arm around her shoulders. His body was furnace-warm and she made herself relax and lean into it.

'A difficult day, I know,' he said as he led her up a flight of stairs, then down a corridor carpeted with wolf pelts.

She shrugged. 'A long day, my lord.'

'Good, good.' He smiled at her abstractedly as he stopped before a wooden door. She expected him to open it, but he turned to face her. 'Tell me, when were your last courses?'

'I'm sorry?'

'Your courses, your monthlies – when did you last bleed?'

She blushed fiercely, a combination of shame and anger. 'Two weeks ago.'

'Ah.' He opened the door but set his back to it, blocking her way. 'You won't be fertile until you finish bleeding again. Well, there's no rush, I suppose.'

She was so shocked that he'd almost shut the door on her before she roused herself and shouted, 'Wait!'

The door creaked fully open again and his head poked round. 'What? Oh yes, of course. You don't know your way around yet, do you? Go to the end of this corridor, take the left turn then the second right and you'll find your room – the third on the left. Your woman will come in the morning to bring your breakfast.'

He shut the door again and from inside his room came a clattering that might have been him removing his sword. She stared at the door for a long while, but the corridor was chilly and dark and she was aching with exhaustion. He wasn't coming out. She drew a deep breath and began the walk to her room.

When she reached the end of the corridor she found herself face to face with the woman from the high table at dinner. The pale-skinned savage nodded curtly at Nethmi but didn't pause as she walked by.

Nethmi turned to watch as the woman went to Thilak's door and opened it without knocking. As minutes passed and she didn't emerge, Nethmi's incredulity slowly curdled into something sour. So much for any hope that her life could be better here, out of her uncle's shadow. So much for her belief that she had left the masks behind in Whitewood. People hid who they truly were everywhere, but now she understood exactly what mask she would be asked to wear in Winter's Hammer. Her chest felt hollow with anger as she continued on her way to her empty room.

7

The thick goatskin tent let in only a trickle of dawn light, but it always woke Krish. In the bleary uncertainty of returned consciousness he briefly thought it just another day and rolled to his feet to begin it. But when his eyes focused he saw his mother watching him from across the dead fire. His father – no, not his father. Now he was fully awake, his memory of the night before was cuttingly sharp. The man he'd thought his father had wrapped all the skins and furs around himself. The woman he'd thought was his mother shivered on the ground, one arm wrapped around her middle with the hand tucked beneath her armpit, the other flung out to the side at an unnatural angle. Krish could see the swelling and purple bruising around her twisted elbow.

He dropped to his knees beside her. 'Is it broken?'

She shook her head and looked uneasily at her husband, though he'd drunk himself into a stupor on bag after bag of fermented goat's milk and would be unlikely to wake before noon.

Krish touched the skin of her elbow and she flinched away. 'It *is* broken. Let me send a message for the healer.' He knew that his voice was strangely tight. He wasn't sure if he'd forgiven her for her lies, but he couldn't stop caring about her.

She shook her head. 'We don't have the coin to waste on a bruise. It will heal itself. A few days should see it right.'

'Then I'll stay and help you. The herd are safe enough. They don't need me, not today.'

'No! No. Go out and do your work. He'll be angry if you don't. And with me he'll be sorry this morning, he always is. It's just his way, he doesn't really mean it. He didn't mean what he said to you last night. You understand that, don't you, Krishanjit?'

He grunted, because he didn't understand. 'I'll be gone then. But you can send a boy to fetch me if you need me.' He bent down to kiss her on the forehead, then thought better of it. He gave her an awkward half smile instead and hurried from the tent.

The rest of the village had woken too. His neighbours nodded at him at he passed, the young men on the way to mind their own herds and the fathers to the hunt. The women would remain in the tents in this cold season; no gardens to tend and plenty of salting and smoking and weaving to be done. The girls had the worst of it, sent to the river to break the ice and wash their family's pots. Their hands would redden and chap and later in life they'd twist with arthritis from all that hard use.

Krish wondered how many of them had known about him. Every one of them, probably. They'd have asked how his mother had a child when her belly had never swelled. He felt like the butt of a secret joke and hurried away from them all to begin the long and wearying climb to the herd.

The goats were scattered across the hill outside the cave where Dapple was tied. The billy bleated as he approached, an indignant note in his voice. Krish reached out carefully, wary of his horns, but the animal let him untie the harness around his neck and chest before bounding over the rocks towards the rest. They were nosing through the frost to find the hardy plants that had survived it. There were few enough of them, and Krish knew he'd soon have to begin feeding them the grain they'd stored after the harvest. It was early in the season for that. It had been a hard year: a cold year and getting colder.

He scratched Shorty between the ears, then climbed the rise to begin his headcount. The goats' yellow eyes turned to watch as he walked among them. He found their impassive regard comforting. They didn't care who his mother and father were. But who *were* his mother and father? They'd thrown him away, he knew that much. Maybe he was better off with the people he'd thought his parents. His da might not have wanted him, but at least he'd *kept* him.

He was so lost in the maze of his own thoughts he almost didn't notice when the count came up short. Snowy was missing and her unnamed kid with her. Weak as she still was, he knew she couldn't have gone far, and it didn't take him long to find her. She'd crossed the next ridge in search of food, probably hungrier than her fellows because of her child. She'd found a whole bush, green and tempting, its shiny leaves and red berries stark against the white-rimed ground.

Snowy lay next to the bush. Her sides were heaving and he could see a pool of shit at her rear where she'd lost control of her bowels. She was still alive, though, and might stay that way if she hadn't eaten too many of the poisonous berries. He could crush some spinewort and mix it with water, force her to swallow it and hope it made her bring up the rest of her lethal meal.

It was too late for the kid. Its little body lay between her legs and chest, huddled against an udder from which it could no longer suckle. Snowy watched Krish with bloodshot eyes as she licked at the body and then nudged it with her nose. She bleated pitifully when it didn't move.

'It's no good,' he told her. 'You fed him the poison in your milk. You killed him, Snowy.'

He sat on the ground beside her and rested his hand on the kid. Its corpse was already cold; soon enough it would be frozen solid. There was enough meat on it for a meal or two in these lean times, but the flesh would be full of the berries' poison. The thought of eating the little creature turned his stomach anyway. There were rocks enough to build a cairn and no heat in the air to rot the flesh and sicken the herd. Snowy's kid would have a proper memorial.

He'd been crying since he saw Snowy by the bush and realised what it meant. He drew a shuddering breath to try to stop, but it hitched on another sob and he rested his head on his knees and let it out. Nothing was right. Nothing was fair.

He felt drained when it was over, as if something more than water had seeped out of him. His throat was raw as he drew icy

breaths through it, but his mind felt clearer. He looked at the
bush again, with its half-nibbled leaves and very red berries. Then
he rose to his feet and began to pick them.

His ma was surprised to see him back so early but his da was
gone, as he'd hoped, probably on the trail of that wild pig whose
tracks had been spotted around the village. His mother had been
trying to weave, but it was impossible with her injured arm and
she'd left her work tangled at her side and was instead chopping
the vegetables for dinner. That was awkward too with just one
hand. He could see blood smeared across the white bulb of the
turnip where she'd cut herself with the knife.

'Here, let me.' He prised the knife from her fingers and set
about chopping.

Her face was drawn, with dark circles under her eyes. His
probably looked the same. He doubted either of them had slept
well the night before.

She turned more fully into the light, revealing the ugly purple
swelling around her right eye. 'You're home early. Is all well with
the herd?'

'Well enough. Ma, you look ready to fall. Why don't you close
your eyes for a little while?'

The bedding was behind a screen on the other side of the tent.
She'd be out of sight if she went.

She shook her head. 'You don't need –'

'Go!' he said, more sharply than he intended. He made an
effort to gentle his voice. 'I hurt just looking at you, Ma. You'll
work better when you're a little rested, anyway.' He put a hand
against her uninjured arm, but his fingers were trembling and he
quickly snatched them back and clenched them into a fist.

She blinked up at him and he wasn't sure what she read in
his expression, but she sighed and nodded. 'Maybe a minute or
two. You don't need to do this, though.'

'I want to. Go sleep. I love you.' He was surprised to feel the
words slipping out and the way they choked up his throat.

There were tears in her eyes too as she gave him a hard,

one-armed hug. 'I love you too, Krishanjit, since the day . . . I always have.'

He waited until she was safely hidden behind the screen before he took up the knife and continued chopping the vegetables. She'd never taught him to cook – it was women's work – but he'd seen her do it a thousand times. He set the vegetables aside and fetched the meat. He took a large strip of smoked goat's meat and chopped it. He wanted this stew to be appetising.

He piled all the ingredients into the pot with a scoop of water and set it to boiling over the fire. When it was bubbling, he took out the berries. He'd counted the number on the untouched branches, then those on the branches Snowy had nibbled, and figured she'd eaten about ten of the things. That had been enough to kill her kid but had left her merely sick. He'd tended her after he buried the little body and he thought she'd survive.

Snowy was heavy, but not as heavy as a full-grown man; maybe a third his father's weight and no more than half his. Krish had reached his full height but long illness had kept him scrawny. So he could eat twenty berries and not die, his mother likewise. But his father – his father always took the headman's share of the food. Krish thought back to their last meal, when his mother had put three full ladles into his father's bowl and only one into each of theirs. That was five ladles altogether, five portions. Twenty berries each for him and his mother, sixty for his father. That was an awful lot – more than he'd reckoned. Had he picked that many?

He shot a look at the screen, but his mother remained behind it. Still, he kept his back to it to shield his hands as he counted out the berries from the pouch at his belt. There were eighty-nine. Fewer than he'd hoped, but they'd have to do the job. He scooped them up and dropped them in the stew. They mixed in easily, their red colour soon lost in the brown. He didn't know their flavour, though. Would it be too off-putting? His mother still had a good stock of herbs. Moss-flower had a strong taste and his father was partial to it. He threw in a half-handful and mixed that around too.

'Smells good,' his mother's voice said behind his shoulder.

He managed to squash his surprised start into a small twitch. 'Not as good as yours, Ma.'

She managed a tired smile. It sat badly on her bruised face. 'What a flatterer you're getting to be. You'll have the girls eating out of your hand.'

Silence descended as they waited for his father to return. The sun set outside in its slow winter way, the air chilled despite the fire and the stars were bright in the sky before he finally appeared.

Krish's heart lurched and he knew he'd paled, but his father wasn't looking at him. The older man's face was more grey than brown and the stubble on his cheeks looked like the symptom of a disease. When Krish's mother rose to greet him, he grunted a reply but didn't meet her eyes. She'd been right: he always felt ashamed the day after a beating. He often swore he'd never do it again – it was what Krish despised the most about him. *But he's not really my father*, he thought, and for the first time it made him happy. *There's no part of him in me. He gave me no gift, weak or strong, that will burden me for the rest of my life.*

'Dinner's ready, husband,' his ma said.

His da shook his head. 'Not for me. My guts are twisted tonight.'

Krish fought very hard not to react, mind racing as he wondered how he could get rid of the stew before his mother shared it out between them and killed them both. But then she laid her good hand on his father's cheek and said, 'Eat, please. There's nothing better for a sick man than food in his belly.'

'All right, then. If it'll please you.' His father's thumb rubbed gently against her knuckles as he smiled into her eyes. Krish had to look away from the tender gesture. But he looked back as his father sat and his mother put one, two, three, three ladles and another half of the food into her husband's bowl.

Krish sat cross-legged beside the fire with his own bowl in his lap. His mother had given him most of the rest, leaving only the dregs for herself. He put his spoon in, but stopped with it halfway to his mouth. He'd always been sickly and he could feel the winter illness gathering in his chest, shortening his breath and bringing a tight ache that followed him even into sleep. His body was weak and the poison might be enough to finish it off. He hesitated only a moment longer, then took his first mouthful.

The moss-flower had done its job and disguised the flavour of the berries. The stew tasted good and his father seemed to like it. After a tentative couple of bites he was wolfing it down. His mother saw and flashed a secret smile at Krish, a thanks for his help. He nodded back, his face too stiff to form into a smile.

The berries started to work far more quickly than he'd expected. He'd thought they might spread their poison while he and his family slept, that he'd wake to find his father gone. But Krish had barely finished his meal before he felt the first stab of pain in his stomach.

His father felt it too. He put a hand against his belly and frowned, looking up at Krish before doubling over in pain. A moment later Krish too was curled in a ball around the agony in his own gut. Sweet Lady! He hadn't thought it would hurt so much. He felt as if a burning ember was lodged inside him. If he'd had the strength to reach for a knife he might have used it to try to cut the poison from his stomach.

He was aware that his mother had crouched down between him and his father, but his eyes didn't want to focus on her face. She was speaking. He thought she might be asking if he was all right. He shook his head and then groaned as that movement sharpened the pain in his guts. Her hand rested against his shoulder, then was suddenly snatched away, and he wondered if the poison had hit her too.

He couldn't think about that. He couldn't think about anything. The agony consumed him. There was a blackness on the borders of it, fast approaching. He knew that if he let it, it would take the pain away. It would take him somewhere safe, but he wasn't sure if he'd ever be able to return. Though he hadn't thought he valued his life, he found himself desperately clinging to it. His feverish mind circled round and round, trying to figure out what it was he wanted to stay for, even as he fought with all his strength to stay.

Time had no meaning. There was only the pain, the darkness and the thin grey light he clung to. It could have been an hour or a week later when his eyes blinked open to the light of the real world and he realised that the pain was gone. There was a terrible smell around him, a mixture of vomit and shit, and he guessed he'd lost control of himself. His clothes felt sticky and foul but his fingers only twitched feebly when he commanded them to move.

'Krish! Krishanjit!' his mother said, and then she was leaning over him, a shadow blotting out the light.

'Ma,' he croaked.

'Oh, thank the gods.' A droplet of water fell on his cheek.

'Da?' he asked.

She didn't reply and he could hear that she was sobbing. He forced his arm to push him from his back to his side. His head flopped so that his cheek pressed against the goatskin rug. The musky smell of it was in his nose as his eyes focused on his father's body, lying on the opposite side of the rug. It was wrapped in a blanket. Maybe his mother had wanted to keep him warm, but why had she covered his eyes? Krish's mind fuzzily mulled over the puzzle as he felt his mother pressing something wet against his face.

Oh, he thought at last. *My father isn't breathing. She's covered his face because he's dead. It will stay covered until he's lying under the rocks of his cairn, so that his spirit can't escape to wander the world of the living.* Krish found that he had just enough strength left to smile.

8

Eric whistled as he walked. He hadn't realised how noisy Smiler's Fair was, or how much he missed the constant, comforting racket, until he was away from it. Here in the white forest there was only a haunted silence. The trees had been stunted in life and in death they were diminished even further, their leaves centuries gone and their branches dripping with the persistent rain. In places they'd been chopped down to clear land for farming, but Lahiru's lordship seemed sparsely populated. Here and there, the caravans of the landborn sat in their fields, and the few people stopped to stare as Eric passed. Travellers couldn't be common in these parts, near the western edge of the Ashane lowlands. Or perhaps it was his fair skin and golden hair that drew their eyes. He was a stranger here and he felt it.

He reckoned he was only an hour's travel from Smallwood itself if he kept up his earlier pace, but he found he'd been dawdling more and more as he approached his actual meeting with Lahiru. It had seemed such a fine idea when he'd set out from Smiler's Fair nearly two days ago. A night spent shivering under his coat as he tried to sleep through the long dark had lessened his enthusiasm somewhat. His home was travelling further and further away from him as he walked in the opposite direction. And what if Lahiru didn't want him? The other man had said as much, hadn't he? *It won't do*, he'd said. *I wish it could, but it won't.* Why hadn't Eric remembered that before he'd set out?

Well, he wasn't getting anywhere just standing around. Better to get the unpleasantness done with and then move on. His legs were stiff from the walking and they ached as he strode off. He wasn't made for heavy work and long trudging; it was why he'd run away from his own folk in the first place. He was more suited to bed-sports. A lovely memory of the last evening with Lahiru came to him, the other man's back arched as his pleasure crested, and Eric felt a little cheered. They'd had fun, hadn't they? Why wouldn't Lahiru want some more of that?

At first he took the bumps on the horizon for more caravans. But then he drew closer, they grew taller and he saw them for what they were: the towers of the shipfort. The lake on which it floated came into view soon after. Its waters looked murky and the shore was nothing but churned mud. He soon saw why when the ice mammoths came into view, straining in their traces as they pulled the shipfort on its circuit of the lake.

It seemed a terrible waste, those poor creatures trudging endlessly on a path that went nowhere. At least the mammoths and horses and whatnot that pulled Smiler's Fair were heading somewhere new and got a break when they reached it. The fair travelled a circle as big as the world. The Ashane gentry named themselves shipborn, but their ships only sailed back to the beginning. No wonder the Fourteen Tribes called them the sit-still people.

The lake was little more than a pond, only a couple of hundred paces across. It was amazing these particular mammoths didn't get dizzy. When Eric had pictured Lahiru's home, he'd imagined it bigger, more a palace than this little mansion huddled on its platform. Weren't toffs supposed to be grander than ordinary folk?

Eric was still gawping at the place like the worst sort of cully when the guard came up to him. He was a bald-headed man who seemed like he enjoyed frowning, and his leather armour didn't look as if it fitted him all that well. 'You have business here, boy?' he asked.

Eric sucked in his chest and raised his shoulders. 'Yeah.'

'Well, what is it?'

'I'm a mate of Lord Lahiru's, ain't I? His lordship invited me on a visit.' Behind his back, Eric spread his fingers in the sign for luck.

'A friend of Lord Lahiru's? I suppose you studied under the same swordmaster.'

Eric grinned. 'You could say that.' He saw the soldier's hand easing towards his own sword and added, 'Look at it this way: if I'm lying and you take me inside, you and your mates can rough me up proper. But if I'm telling the truth, it's you what's going to get a beating if you don't let me in.'

The soldier shook his head and Eric's heart sank, but then he sighed. 'All right, boy. But believe me, a beating will be the least of it if you're lying.'

'Fair play. Lead on then, mate.'

The mammoths turned their great hairy heads to watch him as he passed. Eric tipped them a wink and one of them huffed out a cloud of steamy breath. The bridge itself was narrow and it creaked when he stepped on it. He looked uneasily at the water below. It was too murky to see the bottom but no doubt it was deep enough. He'd never learned to swim and he wouldn't lay odds on the soldier diving in after him if he fell.

Smallwood was even more disappointing close up. He'd pictured bright banners snapping in the wind, high battlements and walls thicker than a man was tall. In reality it looked like someone had taken a few houses from Smiler's Fair and thrown them on a raft. The place was made from the dead white wood of the surrounding forest, and some of it looked in need of a good hammer and nailing. The rightmost tower listed perilously towards the water and he could see gaping holes where windows had been broken and never replaced. Lahiru had said he was poor but Eric had thought that noble modesty. Apparently not.

As they drew nearer to the gate, his heart began to pound. Well, it wasn't like he hadn't taken beatings before; some of his clients liked it rough. And at least he'd know. He looked at the bleached wood beneath him as the soldier pounded on the door.

There was a short wait and then it was flung open. Lahiru stood on the other side. He was flushed and short of breath, as if he'd run. He and Eric stared at each other for a moment, until the other man's face broke into a broad smile.

Eric smiled tentatively back. The expression felt as fragile as his hope. 'I told your bruiser here I was a mate of yours.'

'And so he is, Janith. You did well to check, but you may go about your duties now.' Lahiru clapped the guard on the shoulder. The man's expression had changed from dubious to baffled, but he nodded at his lord and turned on his heel to march back across the bridge.

There was another, longer silence as they looked at each other. Eric felt more eyes than Lahiru's on him. He knew curious gazes were studying him from the broken windows above, and he kept his voice low as he finally said, 'I know you told me not to come. I give it some thought, honest. But I reckoned I had to . . . I don't know. I had to see if you really meant it.'

'I did mean it.'

'Oh.' Eric started to turn away, until Lahiru's palm cupped his face and turned it back towards him.

'It won't be easy. But when I heard Smiler's Fair had moved on . . . With Nethmi gone I haven't a friend in the world. I can't lose you too, Eric. We'll just have to break the rules and write them fresh.'

Eric looked round his new room in wonder, then fell backwards on to the bed. It bounced him up and down twice before he came to rest in the centre of its softness. He spread his arms wide and looked at the ceiling, which was painted with a picture of the Ashane's Lady sitting in the centre of one of her storms. Was this real? He supposed it must be. He could have dreamed this last part, but he'd never have put sleeping under a tree or that nasty guard into his fantasy.

Before leaving him here to attend to some lordly business or other, Lahiru had said Eric was to prepare himself for supper, when he'd be introduced to the rest of the household. Reluctantly, he got back up from the mattress and did a circuit of the room. On the far wall, a window gave a view of the lake as the sun sank beyond it. Shadowed and tinted red by the dying light it looked a whole lot more romantic than it had earlier.

To one side of the window there was a large wardrobe. Wooden snakes curled round its door handles, ivory tongues pointing out of their mouths. Eric touched them a little gingerly as he pulled open the door.

Now that was more like it. The inside was stuffed with clothes: fine linens and silks from the Eternal Empire and wool as thin as the silk. He pulled out a delicate bone torc and snorted. It was all very fine and dandy, but he'd look as out of place wearing it as a goose in a cloak. He didn't want people thinking he was putting on airs.

He inspected himself in the mirror on the inside of the door. No, that wouldn't do either, would it? Apart from the fact that he was spattered in mud and worse, his shirt was covered in frills and the buttons only went to his navel, leaving it to gape open over his smooth chest. His fair, curly hair was sadly in need of a comb and a wash and his trousers were tight over his crotch. Got to advertise the wares, haven't you? He looked like a whore. 'And you are one, Eric,' he reminded his reflection. 'You don't get nowhere forgetting your place.'

'I beg your pardon, sir,' a voice said behind him.

Eric felt like his skin jumped a second behind the rest of him as he spun to face the intruder. He was a tiny man, with the usual brown skin and brown hair of Ashanesland, only the skin was somehow too tight over his bones and his hair was so thick it looked as if it was trying to swallow his head. He was holding a pile of cloth in his arms and bowed as Eric studied him.

'Lord Lahiru sent me to bring you some clothes, as I gather you've been travelling light.'

There was no hint of sarcasm in his tone and Eric could only nod dumbly as the clothes were laid out on the bed for him: a white, austere shirt, far less whorish, and nice embroidered blue and green trousers, colours he knew the Ashane favoured and which had always suited him. There was other stuff too that he'd need to figure out as he put it on.

'My lord thought you might also appreciate a chance to wash,' the little man said, then turned and snapped his fingers before

Eric could reply. The door swung open and four young men entered, bearing a huge bowl between them. As they set it down, a trickle of water sloshed over the side and a waft of steam rose above it. Madam Aeronwen had a bath to herself, but she never let her boys and girls use it.

'That'll be a proper treat,' Eric said. 'Thanks.'

The little man nodded and Eric expected him to withdraw but he and all four young men stayed.

'Would sir like some help undressing?' the servant asked after a moment.

'No! No. That'll be fine.'

They still didn't go, so he turned his back on them as he slipped out of his grubby clothes. It wasn't as if he was modest, but a boy didn't like to get naked with a whole bunch of strangers he wasn't going to shag.

It was worth it, though, for when he slipped into the water. He was a little nervous at first. What if he drowned? But the water wasn't that deep, and when the four young men moved to wash him with lavender-scented soap, even scrubbing the grubbiness out of his ears, he let them. So this was what it was to be pampered. He reckoned he could grow used to it.

After that, he let himself be dressed in the fine linen shirt and a silk jacket above it. They even tied his shoes for him, kneeling at his feet. He thought about making a lewd remark, but didn't. Lahiru would like him to act respectable, he was sure.

The clothes felt itchier and more uncomfortable than those he was used to. When he turned to inspect himself in the mirror, a stranger faced him, a right little nob. He smiled and the stranger smiled back.

'Are you ready, sir?' the little man asked as, somewhere outside the room, a bell rang.

'As I'll ever be, mate. Lead on.'

The little man bowed as he held the door open, then gestured to the left along the wooden corridor. A strong wind blew outside and Smallwood was bobbing violently on the water, making walking in a straight line a challenge. Eric wasn't sure he liked the motion, but he supposed he'd get used to it. Shame it made him feel so sick, though. He expected the dinner to come would be a lot better than he was used to.

He didn't need to ask which was the dining hall. He could hear the sound of voices and the clatter of crockery inside, but he hesitated at the door, suddenly shy. There seemed to be an awful lot of people, thirty at least. They were all dressed even more smartly than Eric and the babble of their conversation sounded like the ducks on the lake outside. Servants weaved among them dressed in plain navy with flasks of wine in their hands. Eric couldn't help feeling he should be joining them, not the diners.

'You're to sit beside Lord Lahiru,' the little man said, nodding to the furthest table, raised a little above the others on a pedestal.

Eric squared his shoulders and strode towards it, determined to act like he belonged. Still, the weight of all the glances that fell on him as he walked slumped his shoulders a little, until he caught Lahiru's eye and the other man smiled at him. Then he lifted his chin and crossed the rest of the distance as if he was being carried on a cloud.

'Eric,' Lahiru said. 'Let me introduce my family. In the corner there looking glum is my brother Chatura. Don't worry that you've offended him – he hates everyone equally. Beside him is his delightful wife Amanthi. Now the reason she looks so gloomy is that she's married to Chatura.'

There was a slightly manic tone to the other man's voice. Eric realised that Lahiru was nervous and that made his own doubts return full-force. He swallowed to moisten a suddenly dry throat as he nodded at the couple in question, who looked perfectly normal to him. They nodded cautiously back.

'And this is my lovely wife, Babi,' Lahiru continued. Eric could hear the slight quaver in his voice as he gestured at a pretty woman with plaited hair and a dainty nose. She looked puzzled but pleasant as she smiled a greeting at Eric. She wasn't at all what he'd expected. When Lahiru had talked about her . . . Well, he hadn't said much, but he'd left Eric with the impression she was a bit of a battleaxe.

After that Lahiru introduced Eric to his children. Eric forgot their names as soon as he was told them, but there were three of them. Three! There was a toddler, who could have been a girl or a boy, seated on a high chair beside Babi. The five-year-old was clearly a girl, as pretty as her mum, and the boy was in the awkward process of turning into a man, his voice warbling between high and low and the first hint of hair sprouting on his face.

'A pleasure to meet you all,' Eric said in his best posh voice, then slipped into the seat beside Lahiru.

The other man rested a hand against his thigh and Eric did his best not to jump at the unexpected contact. But he was glad it was there as the meal progressed. It was torture. There must have been about a thousand different knives, forks and spoons in front of him, and how was he supposed to know which to use?

He'd hoped Lahiru might give him some guidance, but the other man was busy talking to his kin. They were discussing the crop planting for next year and Eric had left his farming days far behind him. He kept quiet and watched those around him to see what he should do. The food was delicious – vegetables and roast meats, fresh not salted like he'd have had back home – but he was so nervous about doing the wrong thing he didn't get much of it inside him.

Through it all there was Lahiru's hand on his leg, warming the skin beneath his trousers. As the meal progressed, the other man's fingers began to tense and claw so that soon what had been a comfort became a painful distraction. Would he send Eric away as soon as the meal was over? It hardly seemed like he was enjoying having him around.

'So, Eric,' Babi said, 'how *did* you and my husband come to know each other?'

It was a polite enough question, but it made all thoughts flee from Eric's head. He had no answer prepared.

'Don't quiz the poor man,' Lahiru said. 'He's had a long journey to get here and you'll have plenty of time to question him once he's rested. He'll be staying a while.'

'Will I?' Eric asked. The hand on his leg was bruising now, but the smile Lahiru gave him was sweet and real.

'You may remain here as long as you wish, Eric.' Lahiru looked round the table as if daring anyone to contradict him.

It appeared as if several of them wanted to. His wife's expression had shifted from puzzlement to the beginnings of suspicion. His children seemed sulky, unwilling to entertain this stranger in their midst. And some of his relatives, the more worldly of them, looked purely horrified.

But Eric made himself not care. Lahiru wanted him, and that was enough. 'I'll stay then,' he said. 'I suppose you're stuck with me.'

9

Dae Hyo knew they were being hunted. He felt it as surely as a rabbit feels the shadow of the hawk before it strikes. There were eleven wagons in the train and seven men to guard them, counting him. A wagon train this size needed at least double that number to be safe, but the merchants had been reluctant to part with the coin. They might regret their meanness soon, but he'd regret it more. If the bandits attacked in force, the merchants could lose their livelihoods; Dae Hyo and his fellows would be expected to lay down their lives.

He particularly disliked the valley they were moving through now. It was green and pleasant enough, certainly greener than the mine, though the plants had a defeated quality. Their ragged stalks looked like they'd paused for breath after pushing through the stony soil and never bothered to start growing again.

The cliffs at either side, though – they made a nice little trap, if anyone cared to spring it. The merchants seemed happily oblivious, leading their horses and chattering as if they hadn't a care in the world. Their voices merged with the clatter of the wagon wheels into a constant meaningless rumble. But Dae Hyo could see the other guards darting uneasy glances all around.

He sidled up to the nearest man, a sour and entirely bald Ashane. 'You feel it too?' Dae Hyo asked.

The Ashaneman nodded.

'How many, do you think?'

He shrugged and Dae Hyo gave up on the conversation. They seemed a good bunch, though, the guards. A more promising outfit than the fucking miners, that was for sure. Despite the present danger, he'd made the right decision to earn an honest wage this way rather than searching for another mine. Only desperate men risked the hunt for metal underground.

The sun disappeared early in the valleys and, as the sky turned a pleasant violet, the merchants spotted a flattish field beside the river and decided to make their camp there. No attack had come, but Dae Hyo didn't find that reassuring. If he were in charge of the raiders, he'd strike at night.

The guards congregated as the merchants unhitched their horses and pitched their tents, while their wives boiled water for tea and the two babies wailed. The smell of manure spread as the horses unloaded their bowels and some of the other men wrinkled their noses, but Dae Hyo liked it. His youth had smelled just so.

'Three sleeping and four guards, one at each point,' said Balkaran, the leader of their little crew.

There were a few groans but no protest. Balkaran might be so young he looked like he shaved once a month, but he knew his trade. He chose three men to take the first rest and they began to set out their sleeping mats, swords laid carefully beside them. The merchants would rest under canvass but not the guards. They needed to be ready when trouble came. And it would, Dae Hyo was sure of it.

He found himself assigned the north-west corner until moonset. A drink would have been nice to warm him during his watch, but he'd been more than two months without. The shakes had gone and he felt good for it. He didn't even need the purple sorghum any more, which was just as well, since he had none left. He should have waited until this point to venture down the mine, he saw that now. A man changing himself was all well and good, but you had to allow the changes a chance to bed in. The boy preacher should have been clearer about that. Well, this wagon train was heading to intercept Smiler's Fair, which was now pulled to pieces and travelling through the Blade Pass. When they reached it, Dae Hyo might pay the boy a visit to tell him so.

Without booze, his attention failed to wander and the minutes passed very slowly. He spent a while admiring the shape of the wagons, silhouetted against the twilight sky. They looked like ships, as they were designed to. The Ashane fancied themselves sailors still, despite the many centuries since their ancestors had crossed the ocean to come here. They carved anchors on their wagons and wore them on chains round their necks. Anchors brought them luck, they said, and Dae Hyo supposed he could understand why. An anchor held you to your home. Without it you'd just drift away.

He looked at the wagons until the growing darkness took their shapes. The merchants had left a few glowing embers in their fires, and by that light Dae Hyo saw the glint of drawn swords to south and east. He wasn't so green, though. If he held his axes out for his whole watch, he'd be too tired to use them when needed.

The night was very noisy. There was hooting and water splashing over rocks and chittering insects and that baby again, which must be driving its poor mother to distraction.

And then there was another sound. He might not have heard it if he hadn't been paying attention, which just went to show the benefits of a clear head. It was the sound of a gentle tread on rock. He was certain it wasn't an animal. That foot was shod, or he was a Maeng knife woman.

The noise had come from his left, but if the attackers had any sense – and why wouldn't they? – the camp would be surrounded. Dae Hyo considered quietly alerting the others, waking the three sleeping guards and setting an ambush of their own, but there were too many ways the plan could go wrong. Besides, stealth wasn't his way.

'Attack!' he shouted, loud enough to scare the horses. They whinnied as merchants cried out in alarm. Lamps were lit, the three sleeping guards stumbled to their feet, the waking men turned to look at him in shock, and for a moment it seemed that was all that would happen.

Then the raiders did what they'd come to do. The kindled lamps and hastily poked fires shed little light, so it seemed as if a cluster of shadows detached themselves from the rocks all around to attack. It was impossible to tell how many, but there was no doubt the guards were outnumbered. It was clear to the merchants too and the brawniest among them grabbed their own weapons and threw themselves into the fray. Dae Hyo didn't rate their chances, but the more warm bodies between him and a blade, the better.

He took one final look behind him to check that the women were safe, the babies hidden, and then the first bandit was on him. The man overtopped Dae Hyo by a head and stank like an unbathed mammoth. A great waft of the stench came over Dae Hyo as the raider raised his sword over his head and swung it down.

The bandit was big but slow. There was more than enough time to dodge the blow, and when the sword missed and hit the rock below it snapped. The bandit had a moment to share a look of astonishment with Dae Hyo and then an axe cut through his throat and the smell of his blood overpowered the stink of his body.

The next man was shorter and swifter, but his axe was made of flint and his technique left much to be desired. One blow parried, another turned aside, and Dae Hyo had taken care of that one. He hopped over the two corpses and went in search of more foes.

A broad-shouldered Ashaneman had broken in as far as the wagons themselves and was dragging one of the younger women from them by her hair. The woman screamed and Dae Hyo did too as he grabbed the assailant by his own hair and threw him to the ground with the full strength of his fury. He hacked at the Ashaneman's neck, smiling in pleasure as the bandit's head separated from his shoulders even while his eyes pleaded for mercy.

The woman had gone by the time Dae Hyo was finished, hopefully fled to safety. Another bandit stood a few paces back, staring at Dae Hyo with wide eyes. Dae Hyo felt his foe's blood dripping from his face. He darted out his tongue to lick it from his lip and the bandit turned and ran.

They were all fleeing, leaving five of their number behind dead or dying. But they'd left behind other corpses too. Dae Hyo saw one of the merchants curled up on the ground, embracing the spilled tangle of his guts. His wife's head had rolled to lie beside him. Their six-year-old child stood above them, eyes uncomprehending.

Dae Hyo roared and set off in pursuit of the raiders. He heard yelling behind him, calls to come back, but he wouldn't let these rat-fuckers escape. He wouldn't give them the chance to do the same again to anyone else.

The night was very dark away from the fires, but fleeing, the raiders were far noisier than they had been stalking. Dae Hyo soon picked up the sound of footsteps crunching over the rocks. He grinned, gripped his axe and slipped after them.

The chase was as satisfying as the earlier waiting had been wearing. Dae Hyo was faster than the man he was pursuing, catching him up step by step, and he could hear his quarry's desperate gasping breaths. It felt good to be the hunter. Pretty soon he was close enough to make out the little whimper at the end of each exhale that suggested the other man was injured as well as terrified. And then his quarry was in front of him, his outline blotting out the stars above the crest of the hill. Dae Hyo yelled, raised his axe and flung himself forward.

The fucker was fast, though. He got his own axe in the way of the blow, Dae Hyo's body barrelled into his and then he was lying on his back with Dae Hyo on top of him. They were face to face, breathing in each other's stale air, and all Dae Hyo's went out of him. He *knew* this man.

'Min Ki,' he said.

He saw the moment when recognition replaced fear on Dae Min Ki's face. 'Tall Hyo,' he said.

They stared at each other awkwardly a moment before Dae Hyo shook his head, dropped his axe and rolled off the other man to sit beside it.

Min Ki sat up too, his arms wrapped tight round his legs as if he meant to make himself as small as possible. 'I'm sorry,' he said. 'I would never have – if I'd known you were one of the guards . . . I wouldn't – I would *never* have attacked you.'

'I tell you what, I don't care about that,' Dae Hyo said. 'I never thought to see you again, brother. We parted so long ago, and I heard nothing of you. I thought you must have died of grief.'

Min Ki had been out hunting with him and the others when the attack came. It had been his first hunt as a man. And Min Ki had been with their band when they returned to the camp and saw the slaughter. At thirteen, he had found the murdered corpses of his mother and his four sisters, the oldest with a baby killed inside her belly.

'I thought you were dead for sure,' Min Ki said. 'You were so angry, and you talked of nothing but revenge. I thought you'd thrown yourself against a Chun blade somewhere and ended it.'

There was another little silence after that. Of all the people Dae Hyo might have expected to meet in this way, Min Ki would have been the last. He'd been a gentle boy and not much suited to hunting. 'So,' he said eventually. 'Banditry? It's a low profession, brother. Hardly fit for a Dae.'

Min Ki shrugged. 'The world doesn't have much use for a warrior without a home or a tribe. And these Ashane, they have enough coin to spare us a little.'

'And the women? Did they have spare what your friends meant to take from them?'

Min Ki lowered his eyes and Dae Hyo felt a sudden dropping in his stomach and an awful doubt. 'Or did you mean to take it from them too?'

'No!' Min Ki looked up, fierce but still red with shame. 'I would never! I'm no Chun.'

'No Chun, yet you ride with men no better than the Brotherband.'

'I stop them when I can.'

'Let's leave it in the past, brother. You'll ride with me from now on. I should never have let you go off on your own. The fault was mine. When you and the others said to forget revenge, I was angry, but I understand now. You didn't see how revenge could be had. But I've been working all these years, getting us weapons, staying strong. We can pay back the Chun for what they did.'

Dae Hyo didn't understand Min Ki's expression. 'Weapons?' he asked.

'Well . . . There *were* weapons. I'll be honest with you, the rat-fuckers I mined with took them from me. But I mean to have them again. I just need to work a while, earn enough to buy *more* weapons and fight to get back the ones I already had.'

Min Ki smiled suddenly. 'I missed you, brother.'

'So you'll join me? Let's leave the merchants behind. The danger's past, since you *were* the danger. We can loot a few of your fellows and head back to the mine. They won't stand against two Dae warriors.'

'I can't. I have . . . I have a child. A daughter.'

'A daughter?' Dae Hyo felt joy as strong as vodka jolt through him. 'A girl. The first new Dae girl.'

Min Ki's smile was so bright it made him look like that untroubled thirteen-year-old again. 'You should see her, brother. She's beautiful. When she was born I couldn't believe it, that there could be a whole person that little. You've never seen fingernails so small! Her mother's Ashane, a cook at High Water Fastness. She's so pretty, it's no wonder her daughter turned out perfect. And her skin is dark – almost as dark as an Ashane's.'

'That doesn't matter. You're her father: she's still Dae.'

'No, you don't understand. Her skin is so dark she can pass for Ashane. No one would know her father is a foreigner, not just by looking at her. She's four now. Sometimes she asks why I look different from the other men. I tell her I caught a fever and it turned my skin pale.'

'But – but why?'

'Why would anyone want to be Dae? We were the unluckiest people on the plains. And the Chun are still out there, thousands, and more every day. Have you not heard how the Brotherband is growing? Don't you wonder if one day they'll decide to finish the job and come looking for the last few of us? Little Gursimrah is safer if she's never heard of the Dae.'

'You called your daughter Gursimrah? What kind of name is that?'

'An Ashane one.' Min Ki seized his arm, fingers tight and expression intent. 'The Dae are dead – let them rest. The spirits of our people haunt me. Why should they haunt her? Why shouldn't she live free of a past that brings nobody happiness?'

Dae Hyo pulled his arm away. 'Because it's a lie! She *is* Dae! She's our hope for the future and she needs to know who she is.'

For a moment they stared at each other and Dae Hyo thought the other man might bend. But then Min Ki shook his head and stood. 'There are no Dae, not any longer. You call me Min Ki. I haven't gone by that name in a long time. The Ashane call me Manvir, after their long-ago king.'

Dae Hyo stood too, shaking. 'That's you, then, if you want to forget who you are. What about Chin Ho and Kwan and Suk Chul and the others? There were seven of us in that hunting party and we weren't the only survivors.'

'I see Chin Ho sometimes. He married an Ashane too. Suk Chul was taken into the Butterfly Band of the Maeng and Kwan is dead. There are no Dae any longer.'

'There's me!'

'Then you're the last, brother.'

'You're no brother of mine!' Dae Hyo stooped to pick up his axe and Min Ki flinched back. 'Go. Get out of my sight,' Dae Hyo told him, before rage could make him do something it was possible he'd regret.

Min Ki didn't pick up his own weapon before turning and fleeing. His shape was soon lost in the darkness, as if he'd never been there. Dae Ho thought for a moment about running after him and telling Min Ki he was sorry. Wasn't any brother better than none? But the answer must be no, because his feet stayed rooted to the ground until the sound of the other man's footsteps was lost in the hush of the wind.

He couldn't face going back to the wagons, not now he knew one of his own had helped kill those he was guarding. He decided to finish off the rest of the bandits at least, in payment for the food he'd had while travelling with the caravan. But the first man he stumbled over was already dying, so Dae Hyo bent to finish the job with a knife across his throat.

Gouts of blood splattered the man's pack. Most of the clothes inside were ruined, but there were a few coins tucked among them, and at the bottom there was a bottle. Dae Hyo knew the instant he pulled out the stopper what it contained: whisky. The smell filled him with a longing he no longer saw any reason to resist, and the first swallow sent a fire through him he'd missed more than he knew. Let other men change. He'd stay exactly as he'd always been.

10

It felt good to be a man at last. Krish looked round the tent at the eleven others in the village who were permitted a voice in the council, and Isuru, the headman, who had the loudest voice of them all. He was speaking now about their choice of winter grazing for the goats, using that hectoring tone Krish's father hated. His father beat his mother sometimes, after a council meeting, because in his own tent he had power and here he must bow to Isuru. His father . . .

But his father was dead. It was odd how often he found himself forgetting it, even though they'd raised his cairn only yesterday. The entire village had turned out to watch Krish laying rocks on his father's corpse. Some had gagged at the smell of decaying flesh, but he hadn't been nauseated. How could he be, when he was the one who'd turned a living man into meat?

'Bored already, Krishanjit?' Isuru asked and the others laughed. The headman's face was almost perfectly round, skin tight over the fat beneath. He'd probably been handsome in his youth, but now he looked like an overstuffed sausage, with a mole on the side of his nose like a protruding lump of gristle.

Krish didn't mind being mocked. He was junior here, he knew it, but a man all the same. He smiled and shook his head. 'I want to listen and learn, that's all.'

'A wise answer,' Isuru said in his ponderous, patronising tone, which Krish's father had also hated. 'It seems sometimes the apple does fall a little way from the tree.'

Some of the men looked uncomfortable while others laughed. Krish wondered if he was supposed to defend his father's honour. But his da wouldn't have cared about his reputation in this place and this company. He'd had no time for any of the village men.

Krish remembered his father's dead eyes staring up at him from the floor of their own tent. His mother had wailed and wept. He'd been weak with the poison himself and he'd felt . . . nothing. Not the satisfaction he'd hoped for, or the guilt he'd dreaded. Maybe he'd sucked all the marrow from the act during the years he'd dreamed of it. The actual moment had been oddly flavourless.

Isuru was droning on again, about the next market and which of the men should go downriver to trade their goods. But he stopped at the sound of voices outside the tent flap: a boy's and a woman's, both high and excited. And then, in a terrible breach of tradition, the flap was thrown back and the pair entered. Krish felt a surge of indignation. He'd waited long enough for the privilege of sitting here, listening to Isuru tell them all what they should think and do. How dare someone else intrude without permission?

It was Amanthi and Bayya, a widow and her son who scraped a living by watching others' herds when illness or work kept them away. The boy seemed to realise where he was and shrank back into Amanthi's skirt, one eye blinking out at them from behind the material. Her gaze stuck on the floor as she shuffled forward.

'Well?' Isuru snapped. 'What is it, woman?'

She seemed struck speechless, and it was the boy who finally piped up. 'A man, a man, a man from the King on a big bird. A justice!'

A low murmur of surprise went round the room as Isuru nodded in satisfaction. 'Good. It was past time he showed up.'

Krish felt a sliver of ice pierce his gut. 'My da,' he croaked. He cleared his throat. 'Is it about my father?'

Amanthi nodded and finally looked up. 'Yes, sir. He's here to study the death.'

'He flew in on a bird!' the little boy said. 'I saw him!'

Krish scrambled to his feet. His whole body felt rigid with terror. He knew his face was flushed with it and was glad it was too dark inside the tent for the others to see. 'I need to tell my ma,' he said.

Isuru seemed like he might object, but Krish didn't give him time. He stumbled out of the tent and into daylight, looking frantically for the justice and his bird. They were further away than he'd feared, down at the bottom of the valley. Though the man's face was impossible to see at that distance, the carrion mount was unmistakable, its dingy grey feathers a shade lighter than the rocks on which it perched. It was a scrawny animal, far past its prime, but its long curved beak still looked capable of delivering a mortal blow.

If Krish went to his mother he'd have to pass close enough for the justice to see him. He couldn't let that happen; he knew his guilt was written all over his face. He turned away from the village instead and began to climb the hill that led towards his herd.

The walk took half an hour, not long enough to calm down but enough time to think. He'd been a fool to rush out of the council, he realised. It made him look guilty when nothing else had. He'd poisoned himself too; he'd nearly died and everyone knew it. If Isuru had summoned the justice to investigate his father's murder he should see Krish as another victim. Krish needed to make sure of that, and the most important thing was not to act like a guilty man.

Still, checking on his herd wasn't an unreasonable thing to do. The wind was picking up, filled with a cold moisture, and the goats would need leading to shelter when the storm the black clouds promised came. He could see the distant dots of the animals on the hillside ahead of him. They'd climbed high. His chest was tight with infection and following them would be difficult, but he didn't dread it as he once had. His belly had been full since his father's death. He was strong enough: a man.

Snowy bleated a greeting as he approached and he rubbed the nanny between her horns as the goat's eyes drooped in pleasure. Her udder was full and he'd need to milk her or it would turn bad inside her. 'You miss your little boy, don't you?' he said. 'It's all right. You'll have another soon and I'll take better care of him.'

He hadn't brought a churn with him, so he had to squeeze the milk out of her and straight on to the ground. It was a waste and he resented it more now that it was *his* milk, his herd. When he'd done with Snowy he led the rest of the goats into the shelter of an overhang and tethered Dapple to a stake he drove into the ground by the cliff face. The herd were a comforting presence around him, with the warmth of their bodies and the musky scent he'd known all his life.

They needed food, though, and they wouldn't be able to graze in the storm. He left them in their shelter and went out into the driving rain himself. The drops stung like summer insects. There was a grumble of distant thunder and he knew it wouldn't be safe to stay out much longer. He found one patch of greenish grass and plucked it, lifting his tunic to hold it, though it exposed his bare belly to the freezing air. In an hour he'd found enough to last the goats until the morning, and turned towards his real goal.

Stripped of its berries by him and its leaves by the goats, the bush was just the skeleton of a living thing. He'd brought flint and kindling, but it was too damp to burn. He took out his knife and cut it up instead, patiently breaking branches into twigs and twigs into fragments.

When he'd finished, only the stump remained, pointing up at him like an accusation. He left it where it was and threw the broken remnants of the bush into the nearest crevasse. He paused on the edge of the drop, looking down, and tried to think if there was any other evidence against him.

'Krishanjit?'

The voice, carried on a ragged gust of wind, made him jump so hard he almost tumbled down to fall on top of the evidence of his guilt. He gasped in a breath of cold air and made himself stop trembling, then turned round.

It was the justice. He stood ten paces away, his green and blue cloak flapping round his thin body. Krish knew that, like all justices, he'd once been a carrion rider for the King, but it was hard to imagine. The man had aged and diminished more than his mount. It wasn't surprising the pair of them had retired from fighting to serve the Oak Wheel in this distant place.

'I'm Krish,' he said at last, stepping towards the man and offering his hand.

The justice took it, his grip far stronger than Krish had expected. 'Good. Good. Your mother said I might find you here. I'm sorry indeed for your loss. My wife lost her own father last year. Devastating.'

Krish nodded, not knowing what to say. Should he pretend grief? But if the justice had spoken to anyone in the village, he'd know how things had stood between him and his father.

'A man of few words,' the justice said after a moment. 'I respect that. I was wondering, though, did you think your father's death unnatural? To be frank, I'm not sure why I'm here.'

'Isuru our headman summoned you,' Krish said as carefully as a man walking on a cliff edge. 'I suppose he wanted to be certain he kept the law. But it was just bad food. I ate it too.'

'So I heard. You don't think it could have been poison, then? Maybe whoever it was wanted to dispose of your whole family.'

'To steal our goats?' Krish laughed and the justice smiled a little uncertainly. 'I don't think so.'

'Well, better to be thorough. Better to be sure. Have you finished your work here for the day?' He looked up at the sky, dark with rain, as a jagged flash of lightning split it apart.

Krish nodded. 'Yes. I'm heading home.'

'Then I'll walk with you. You can tell me exactly what happened, and with the Lady's blessing I can be on my bird and away by sunset.'

Krish's head jerked up at another flash of lightning. When he looked back down the other man had stepped close to him and their gazes locked for a moment. The justice startled, as if in delayed reaction to the lightning, but Krish knew it was the sight of his strange eyes that had surprised the man. He'd seen that expression before. Then the thunder growled violently and the justice jumped again and swallowed nervously.

'Don't worry,' Krish said. 'We'll be safe from the storm down below.'

'Yes. Yes. Safe.' The man drew in a deep breath and seemed

to steady himself, giving Krish a wobbly smile. 'Safe indeed. Let us get down as soon as possible, then.'

But he stayed still and after a moment Krish realised the justice meant for him to lead. Maybe he was uncertain of his footing on the goat tracks. Even Krish struggled over the slippery wet ground. The gloom painted everything grey, so that he turned his ankle on unseen loose rocks more than once. After they'd been travelling a little while he heard the justice curse and the clatter of stones as he fell to his knees. But when Krish turned back to help, the man waved him on. 'No need. No need. Speed is of the utmost, is it not?'

The storm *was* blowing fiercely now. It prevented any talking and Krish used the time to consider what more he could say. He'd be truthful about his father, he decided. He'd say that he was a violent man, not well liked. He'd admit that his life was better without him. And he'd concede that someone might have tried to poison them both. He considered hinting at who it might be – Rahul was known to dislike his da – then decided that would be dangerous. He didn't want to look like he was trying to put blame elsewhere. No, he'd tell only the one, big lie and stick to it. Other little lies would just tangle him up.

He was smiling by the time the village came in sight. He could do this. He stopped to wait for the justice to catch up, offering him a hand to help him down the steep ridge that bounded the settlement on its western side. The other man's arm shook beneath his hand and he felt a stab of sympathy. Up close, he could see that the justice was an old man, his hair more grey than brown and his thin face seamed with wrinkles. It seemed cruel of the King to send him out to such distant parts in such bad weather.

'Almost there,' Krish said.

The justice nodded, his eyes scanning the village. 'I don't see any people.'

'They'll be sheltering from the rain. Who did you want to find?'

That seemed to stump the justice for a moment. 'Your headman, perhaps?' he said finally.

Krish led him towards Isuru's big, white tent. He found that he was shaking too, and he wasn't quite sure why, except that the justice kept shooting quick, sideways glances at him when he thought Krish wasn't looking.

Without having made a conscious decision, Krish found himself drawing away from the other man as they approached the headman's tent. He was bowing an awkward farewell when the tent flap was thrown back and Isuru strode out, followed by the rest of the council.

The moment he saw them, the justice spun to face Krish, one trembling finger pointed at his chest. 'Arrest him!' he screeched. 'You men, arrest him now!'

For a second everyone was too shocked to move. Krish began to run just as the others started to move towards him and in five strides he was thrown to the ground beneath a pile of bodies. The mud was sucked into his nostrils by his desperate breath until he panicked, thrashing and lashing out at the people over him. One body fell away, then a second, and he saw a flash of sky and a brief hope of freedom before both his arms were grabbed and twisted behind his back and he was dragged to his knees. Filth dripped from his face as he lifted it to stare at the justice.

'But I told you,' he gasped. 'The food was bad. I didn't kill him!'

The other man looked puzzled. Then he shook his head. 'I'm sure you didn't. It's no matter.'

'Then why . . .?'

'Yes, I think you need to answer that,' Isuru said. He was using his pompous tone and Krish didn't mind at all.

'You don't know?' the justice said. 'You really have no idea, do you?'

Isuru deflated a little. 'No, we don't. Why don't you tell us?'

'It's incredible. Here in this backwater, this village without even a name, you have living the most wanted man in all of Ashanesland.' The justice looked at Krish, smiling triumphantly. 'And I found him.'

They took Krish to the edge of the village and manacled him

to the old tree with loops of chain he knew he'd never break. He'd never seen so much metal in his life. It was heavy on his wrists and the tree's bare branches provided little shelter from the wind. He hoped he might be given food or at least a cloak, but the hidden sun sank towards the horizon and no one came. His throat was dry with fear and he raised his mouth to let the rain trickle down his throat. It dripped from the gnarled branches and tasted of wood.

The most wanted man in the kingdom.

It was ridiculous. They must have mistaken him for someone else. The only time he'd ever left the village was to go to Frogsing. Could the men who'd tried to rob him have accused him of a crime to cover their own? But why would anyone believe them? He told himself over and over that it would all be fine. They'd realise they had the wrong man and let him go.

But he remembered, with unforgiving clarity, the moment when the justice's friendliness had changed. It had been when the man saw his eyes for the first time: his strange, moon-silver eyes, which had always marked him as different – which proved he was a foundling. Those eyes were a gift from his parents, his real parents; his study of the goats had proven that. So who *were* his real parents? Were they enemies of the King? Was he being held to pay for their crimes?

Just before full dark, he saw a commotion at the far end of the village around the justice's carrion bird and then it took to the air. There was a figure on its back and he guessed it was the justice himself, gone to get help. The bird was probably too old to carry two, or perhaps the justice was afraid to share his ride with Krish. *Afraid I'd attack and overpower him*, Krish thought, *being this dangerous criminal that I apparently am.*

A little while after the justice left, Vidu separated from the other villagers and headed towards Krish. He was a squat, ugly man, about the same age as Krish's father but gentle and warm where his da had been cold and hard. He stopped a dozen paces away, then sighed and settled to the ground, wrapping his cloak round him and pulling it up to cover his head. His eyes settled on Krish, but he didn't say anything. His expression was hard to read. Maybe a little ashamed.

'I didn't do it,' Krish said. 'Whatever they say I did, I didn't.'

The other man didn't answer, but his eyes shifted away.

'What *does* the justice say I did?' Krish asked after a moment.

It didn't seem that Vidu would answer him. Then he sighed and said, 'I don't know, Krish, but he said there's a five hundred gold wheel reward for you. He'll split it with all of us if we'll just keep you safe until he brings more men.'

'Five hundred gold wheels,' Krish said. 'It's nice to know what I'm worth.'

'It's a fortune. Would you turn it down if it was me?'

'And you believe the justice? I'm the most wanted man in Ashanesland, he says. They're probably offering five *thousand* gold wheels for me. He'll be laughing at you as he gives you a few coins and keeps all the rest.'

'Maybe,' Vidu said, 'but a few gold wheels will keep food in my children's bellies for the next five years.'

They fell into silence as the rain dripped and the time passed. When the moon was high in the sky, shining white on the drenched world, Rahul approached and Vidu rose, nodding at the other man as he handed off the watch to him. Krish didn't even bother trying to speak to Rahul. He was as harsh as Vidu was kind, and he'd never liked Krish.

When the moon was leaving the sky, Krish saw another figure approaching. With a shock of mingled hope and distress, he realised it was his mother. His father's murder sat heavy in his gut, and knowing he'd done that, how could he tell her he was innocent of anything else?

He thought she'd come for him, but instead she stopped by Rahul to whisper in his ear. Krish could see the pale square shapes of her teeth as her mouth moved and he heard the hiss of Rahul's reply, like a snake. His mother spoke again, and then the pair of them turned together and walked into the darkness of the village.

Whatever his mother was doing, it had given him a little time unwatched. He could barely see his manacles or the chains that bound them to the tree, but he felt their contours with his fingers, searching for weak points. There was one: the links binding the manacles to the chains were thin. He'd need something hard to break them, though. He crawled on his knees through the mud, searching for a rock large enough. His fingers closed on something solid and his heart pounded once, very hard, before he realised it was only the old tree's root, exposed by the rain. Finally his hand closed around a flint barely big enough to fill his palm.

He ran his fingers along the chains again and felt the outline of the weak link. It might work – it *might* – but how many blows would it take? He took a deep breath, then another. What did he really have to lose? He raised the rock—

'No, Krish!' his mother said, and he dropped it into the mud, spinning to face her and tangling himself in his chains.

Stupid. He should have been listening for his guard to return. But after a moment he realised that his mother was alone. She dropped to her knees in front of him and put two packs into the mud beside her.

'It's not safe for you to be here, Ma,' he whispered. 'You need to go before Rahul comes back.'

'He won't be back, not for a while. He's asleep in his tent.'

'How do you know?'

She looked down, away, anywhere but at him. 'I've seen the way he stares at me, all these years. Your da noticed. Why do you think they hated each other so much? I told Rahul he could have what he wanted if he'd let me have a little time alone with you, and he fell asleep after. I knew he would. Your father did the same.'

Krish's stomach lurched queasily. 'With Rahul?'

Now she did look at him, her expression fierce. 'With anyone, Krish. I'd do anything for you.'

'Would you, Ma? The justice says I'm a wanted man. Don't you wonder what I've done?'

'It's not what you've done, Krishanjit, it's who you are. The justice didn't want to tell the others. He's afraid they'll realise how much you're worth. But he asked me questions: where I'd found you, when. He knew you weren't mine.'

'Then who am I? Why does the King's justice want me?'

'Because you're his son. The King's, I mean. He's been looking for you a long time.'

He stared at her, trying to see the joke, but she seemed in deadly earnest. 'You're saying . . . but then why have me arrested? Why treat me like an enemy?'

'There was a prophecy, before you were born. It said you'd kill your father.'

'Kill my father?' He laughed harshly at the awful irony.

'Yes. And so the King tried to kill you, but someone stole you from your mother's belly and got you away. They hid you on a riverbank, and that's where I found you, seventeen years ago.'

He studied her face closely and finally saw what should have been obvious all along. 'You knew. You've always known who I am.'

'It was the talk of the lowlands when I went there. I didn't want to stay with your da. I'd never planned to come back to him. You'd not think it now, but I was beautiful then. I'd meant to run away from him and find myself a new man down by the Five Stars. They say it's warm there, Krish, all the year. And the crops are tall and fruit grows on the trees sweeter than you could imagine. But then I found you. The King had it put around that your mother killed herself and you, but the moment I saw you I knew he must have lied. Anyone else who saw you would know it too. Everyone at the Five Stars would know it. They'd look at your eyes and know who you were. So I brought you back here, to the edge of the world. Back to your da. It was the only place you could be safe.'

'But why didn't you ever tell me?'

'I wanted to.' She sighed and touched his face. 'First you were too little. And then – you're so angry, Krishanjit. I was afraid of what you'd do.'

Angry? He'd always thought he was afraid, but as soon as she said it he understood that anger was the hard knot at the heart of all his feelings.

'And then you did it anyway. If only you hadn't killed him, Krishanjit, the justice would never have come. You could have lived your whole life in peace.'

Of course she'd known that too. She was his mother. 'I'm sorry,' he said, hanging his head. 'For everything. Now you'd better go. The next guard will be coming soon.'

'No, I'll not let you be sent away to die. I saved you once and I'll do it again. I don't care what they say, you're my son.' She fumbled in one of the packs, pulling out first a hammer and then a metal chisel she must have stolen from Isuru.

He stared at them, suddenly weak with relief. 'You can't, Ma. They'll know it was you. They'll kill you.'

She shook her head even as she gently took his hand and laid it flat against the ground so that she could reach the chain, awkward with her injured arm. 'We'll both run. My sister will put me up, and they won't follow me. It's you they want.'

'No, we'll go together. I won't leave you.'

'I can't get over the mountains. I'm not strong enough, and that's where you need to go. You have to leave Ashanesland. I looked at a map once, before I came down to the lowlands. The Fourteen Tribes live to the west, and they don't obey the Oak Wheel. I've packed food and warm clothes for you. There's your da's knife, and I'd saved a few anchors. You'll be all right, Krishanjit. You're stronger than you look. You always were.'

She raised the hammer and struck the first chain from his arm. Then she grabbed his other hand, placed the chisel on the chain and that one was gone too. Only the manacles remained around his wrists. He was free, but the sound of the blows had echoed loud in the midnight silence. He could already hear raised voices from the village.

'The goats!' he said in sudden panic. 'Who'll take care of Snowy?'

'They'll be taken in. Goats are valuable – they'll always find a home. It's people who don't get shown any kindness.' There was the memory of pain on her face.

'I'll find you again, Ma,' he promised her. 'I'll find you and take care of you.'

'Just take care of yourself' she said, thrusting one of the packs at him. 'But listen to me, Krish. You can't run for ever – the King will find you and kill you. He'll hunt the whole earth for you if he has to. That's how much he wants you dead.'

'Then what can I do?'

'You can fight back, find people who'll fight for you. There's many that hate King Nayan. When you were born I heard talk – shiplords who'd rather have followed you than your father. You need to find them, Krishanjit, and you need to raise yourself an army and you need to make yourself the king you were born to be. It's your only hope. Now go!'

This time he didn't hesitate. He pressed a kiss against his mother's grey hair and ran into the darkness and away from everything he knew.

II

Nethmi had taken to starting her mornings with a walk round the shipfort's battlements. The cold was profound, but wrapped in her new furs she found it bearable. And it kept anyone but the scattered sentries from joining her. They saluted her silently as she passed and left her to her thoughts.

At least her anger kept her hot. She tried to tell herself it didn't matter. She hadn't wanted this marriage, so why should she care if Thilak didn't want her? But she did. She'd accepted that he might think of her as a prize to be displayed, but that she wasn't even that to him . . . How dare he! Her father had tamed the tribes who called him lord, and now he treated Shaan's only daughter as nothing, as less than the savage who warmed his bed!

The rage felt like a physical thing inside her, a burning ember in her belly, and she made herself breathe evenly as she studied the landscape around Winter's Hammer. It was bleak beyond belief. The view was the same in every direction, the rock-strewn plain surrendering in the far distance to mountains and the sky above a pure and unforgiving blue. Snow covered everything but the lee of the great black rocks. How could she have longed to return to this place? Her eyes wept with the cold and she shuddered.

On her third circuit of the battlements she realised that the eyes of one of the sentries were following her, and on the fourth she recognised him and stopped. It was the young man who'd rowed her across the lake when she first arrived at Winter's Hammer. Even swathed in furs she knew his face, the gentlest she'd seen among the tribesmen.

He smiled tentatively at her approach.

She hadn't meant to speak, but she realised suddenly how starved she was of conversation and smiled back and said, 'I didn't learn your name.'

His gaze dropped to his hand, which tightened on his sword hilt before he looked up and said, 'Seonu In Su, lady.'

'In Su. And I imagine you know mine.'

'Yes. Nethmi.' He blushed suddenly and surprisingly. She hadn't known the tribesmen's pale skin could colour so brightly. 'Sorry, lady.'

'There's no need to be sorry – that is my name. Tell me, In Su, whose is the face on those rocks? None of my own people seemed to know.'

He seemed glad to look away from her and out onto the endless snow, his eyes narrowing to slits at the glare of the whiteness. 'He is the moon.'

'The god of the moon?'

'Yes.'

She stared at that long, strange face. So this was the god the preacher had spoken of back in Smiler's Fair, unknown and unworshipped among the Ashane. He'd sounded like a more reassuring being then. And now she knew how much that face resembled the worm men's. Perhaps they really *were* his servants, as the boy had claimed.

In Su turned back to her, a little bolder. 'But dead now, lady. So they say.'

'It seems strange that gods should die.'

He shrugged. 'All things die.'

She supposed living here, in this icy wasteland, that was an easy thing to believe. Nothing could be impervious to the ravages of wind and snow and the terrible cold that cracked the rocks and year by year turned them to pebbles.

'I heard the moon god has returned,' she told him.

'Not here. This is the last place that any come. Who would choose this of all the world?'

It was a gloomy thought and she nodded to In Su and turned away, knowing that her duties awaited her. The brightness faded but the air heated as she reluctantly descended the stairs into the fort, the strange waters of the lake heating the lowest floors.

Thilak waited for her at the bottom. He smiled his big, friendly smile. 'Good morning, my lady. I'd feared you might have fallen to your death, you'd been gone so long.'

She ignored the implied criticism and smiled politely as at a weak joke. 'I find the fresh air helps me wake, my lord.' He hadn't yet come to her bed. She was dreading the moment when he would. She knew she'd smell another woman's scent on him as he lay on top of her.

There was a moment's pause and his smile froze as he studied her. She wondered what he read in her face. The years in her uncle's court had taught her to wear a mask of unconcern, but Thilak's eyes saw a lot. 'Well,' he said finally. 'You'll be wanting to head down to the kitchens now. We've a patrol reporting in this evening and they'll need feeding in the great hall. Your assistance will be invaluable.'

'I shall try to be helpful,' she said and, with another fake smile, walked down the corridor past him.

The kitchens were unbearably hot, the air solid with smoke and the smell of rosemary and meat. Nethmi had shucked off her furs by the door, but the material of her plain dress was soaked through with perspiration. She felt filthy and useless.

'This, or this?' the head cook asked in her broken Ashane, pointing at two huge carcasses. Skinned and bloody, they could have been anything.

'That one,' Nethmi said, pointing randomly to the left-hand carcass.

'Very good, lady.' The cook bowed, but her expression suggested Nethmi had made the wrong choice.

She'd already learned that she'd be expected to stay in the kitchens until lunch. After that, her time was her own as long as she used it for sewing. The hours crept past until the cook nodded at her, almost a dismissal, and she knew she could go. There'd be food in the great hall but her spirits sank at the thought of it.

Thilak's men would all be there, babbling incomprehensibly, and maybe *that woman* too, watching Nethmi with smug, scheming eyes.

Instead, she grabbed a withered apple and hunks of bread and cheese and ate them as she walked, exploring the maze of the shipfort. From the outside, it had looked quite small; far smaller than Whitewood. But the corridors there were wide and grand, the rooms high-ceilinged and painted all over with murals of flowers and trees. Here everything was cramped, twisted and dark. She doubted she'd seen half of it yet. She set off to her left, towards what she knew were Thilak's own rooms. But she was his wife, wasn't she? She had the right to go there. When a guard half-raised his axe at her approach, she raised her eyebrow back at him and he stepped aside.

The corridor beyond looked no different from the others. Lanterns hung from brackets on the wall, only every third lit. The floor was clean, the rock still rough. Unlike the ancient lowland shipforts, Thilak's stronghold was newly built in this newly conquered land.

She wondered if his soldiers, when they walked these corridors and saw the green wood, the rough stone and the unworn rugs, remembered that they'd been free men less than twenty years before. She imagined the silent, loyal guards rioting. She pictured them setting fire to all the wood, which would burn smoky and hot, and the fantasy made her smile.

There were several doors off the corridor. The first led to an armoury. She spent a few moments studying the swords and bows and halberds. She touched the dagger that hung at her waist, the one which her father had given to her all those years ago. She preferred it to all the weapons here.

The next room was just an empty chamber with scratch marks on the floor where something heavy had been removed. A bed? Perhaps this was where *that woman* had stayed before Nethmi had arrived. She shut the door quickly and moved on.

The next led to a library. Aside from the great hall, it was the biggest room she'd yet seen in Thilak's shipfort. She entered and shut the door behind her, smiling. This was a place she could while away her afternoons. It even had windows lining the far wall. The sunlight shone through them, scattered and warped by the uneven panes. A rainbow fell across the floor and Nethmi stood in it for a moment before moving to examine the nearest shelf.

Some of the scrolls were so old she was afraid to unroll them. Others looked like their ink was barely dry. She scanned a few and found that they were accounts of the leading noble houses in the realm: their holdings, their wealth, the conflicts between their scions, who might be induced to turn against whom. It occurred to her that these were a spy's reports and she hurriedly put them back.

Another shelf held big black books whose vellum pages were filled with the incomprehensible symbols of the Moon Forest folk. She flicked through them and found that many of the pages were covered with illustrations. One showed a group of children smiling up at a tall, golden-skinned woman with pointed ears who handed them daisies. Another depicted the same woman thrusting her spear through a monstrous, lizard-like creature a hundred times her size. There were pictures of boats on the high seas sailing through mountains of ice, of orchards, a device that trapped the sun. It was impossible to know what any of them meant and she put the book back and thumbed through another.

It took her a surprising amount of time to realise that she wasn't alone. There was an armchair in the far corner of the room, turned to face the windows and the lake. What she'd taken for a cushion was really a man's head. Her breath caught and she told herself to be calm. She had every right to be in her husband's library. Besides, she guessed the man must be asleep, lulled to it by the rocking motion of the shipfort on the waves.

But when she circled the chair to get a better look at him she found two bright brown eyes staring at her. 'Hello,' he said. 'I haven't seen you since your nuptials. A bad shrimp kept me abed, I'm afraid. You will forgive me, won't you?'

She recognised him immediately: he'd been sitting at the far end of the table on her wedding day. She'd noticed he was fat then, but he was even more grotesque than she'd realised, the biggest man she'd ever seen. Folds of flesh stretched his shirt round his waist and bulged from his thighs where the armchair squeezed his massive legs together. He seemed to have no neck, just the ball of his head connected directly to the bulk of his body. His face was round and innocent and it was impossible to tell his age, but she guessed he might be younger than her.

'I'm sorry to hear you've been unwell,' she said stiffly. 'But you have the advantage of me, I'm afraid.'

'I do, don't I?' His grin was far less innocent than his face. 'I'm Seonu Sang Ki. And you're Lady Nethmi, of course. My father's told me all about his bride. He's absolutely delighted with you, but I'm sure you know that.'

'Your father,' she said carefully. 'Thilak?'

'Naturally. I'm told I look a lot like him.'

He was right. She'd thought exactly that at the wedding feast. His eyes had the same sharpness and if the fat were melted from his face she was sure his father's strong bones would lie beneath.

But Thilak had never been married before, and this man's name belonged to a savage, not a shipborn Ashane. She saw the sickly pale tint to his skin, the way his odd, oat-coloured hair hugged the contours of his ears and the assessing, sly look in his eye, and she guessed who his mother must be. Her stomach churned with a nauseous sort of anger.

'It seems there's a great deal Thilak has chosen not to tell me,' she said, her voice shaking.

Her obvious anger didn't seem to worry him. He shifted his bulk into a more comfortable position in the armchair, then said, 'My father can be close-mouthed when it suits him. But he has it all planned out, you see. Sadly, he couldn't marry my mother. I was born on the wrong side of the sheets, as perhaps you've guessed and are too polite to point out.'

'A bastard,' she said coldly.

His lips thinned a little, but then he laughed. 'Well said. You've got spirit. I like that, even if my father doesn't. And you'll be mine after you're his. He's an old man, after all, and I'm still in the flower of my youth. Once you've whelped him an heir and he's moved on to whatever life awaits us after this one, I'm to wed you. I'll raise his heir as his regent. Do you see? That way both his sons get to be lord here. And I get –' His covetous eyes looked her up and down. 'Well, I get some recompense for my inability to inherit. Is that all clear now? Do you feel adequately informed?'

He was baiting her, so she made herself bite back her words and simply nodded her head. 'It's entirely clear,' she said when she could trust herself to speak. 'Thank you for your honesty.'

Back in her room she sat on her bed in silence. It would be time for dinner soon and she was expected to attend, but she couldn't face it. She imagined Thilak, charming and uncaring, and his woman, looking at her with eyes that she now understood held triumph, not resentment. Before Nethmi had even arrived in Winter's Hammer, her rival had won every battle they might fight. And then there was Seonu Sang Ki, who looked at her the way a woman caressed fabrics at market. No, she couldn't do it.

After an hour or so there was a knock on the door, then a rattling of the handle when she didn't answer. But she'd locked it when she entered and after a few moments whoever it was went away. She couldn't believe she'd been so stupid. She'd let herself hope for . . . She wasn't sure what. A loving husband? A new ally she could persuade to join her in revenge against her uncle? A man she could trust at last? Yes. And why had she ever thought her uncle would arrange for her to have any of those?

A little while later there was another knock on the door. She ignored this too, but the doorknob rattled again and then there was the grate of a key turning in the lock. When the door opened, Thilak was framed in the light of the entrance and Nethmi realised she'd allowed the lamps in her room to burn themselves out.

'I'm not hungry,' she said.

'Which would explain why you've missed dinner. However, I can't allow you to miss meeting my new guests – I think you'll find them entertaining.'

She could hardly stand to look at him. 'Why? You don't need me for anything except the bearing of a son, it seems. Just leave me in peace and I'll do my duty when I must.'

'Ah.' He frowned and leaned against the doorframe. 'Would I be correct to think that my son has been speaking to you?'

'You would,' she said flatly. But she found she couldn't keep up the mask of controlled disdain and hissed, 'Why didn't you just marry your whore? Why drag me into this?'

The slap against her cheek echoed in her dark chamber. It hurt, it hurt terribly, but she put her hand against the burning skin and glared at him, refusing to give in to tears. After a moment he sighed and resumed his previous pose, leaning against the doorframe.

'You mustn't speak of Seonu Hana that way. She's a fine woman and as noble as they come in the Fourteen Tribes – her parents lead the Flint Band. But unfortunately, the mountain honours mean nothing in the lowlands, and I need an heir who'll be able to inherit Winter's Hammer and not have it challenged. That's where you come in.'

'You've bought a thoroughbred for your breeding stables.'

'If you want to look at it that way. There are other ways. I know how things stood between you and your uncle. That's why I chose you, of course: no family at home you might complain to about the arrangement. But think of this as an opportunity. Here you're far away from him. You can make your own life and your own place. You'll be honoured; all that's required is for you to behave with honour. Do you think you can manage that? I can see that you're spoilt and selfish, but that's to be expected. You're also clearly intelligent – and very beautiful. Your future is yours to shape. What will it be?'

She wanted to throw his words back in his face. *Behave with honour?* As if there was any honour in a man breaking his vows on the night of his wedding and every night after. But he was right about one thing: she would make her own fate here. And she couldn't afford to have Thilak as her enemy.

She smiled. It was tense and false, but then that's what he must expect. He wasn't asking for affection, only submission. 'As you say, my lord. Now, who was it you wished me to meet?'

He flashed a delighted grin with the same suddenness with which he'd struck her. His expressions shifted like the surface of a lake when a gust of wind ruffled it. It was as if none of his emotions ran very deep, or as if the real feelings beneath them were never revealed.

'Oh yes – our prisoners!' he said. 'These two have been a thorn in the Oak Wheel's foot for quite some time. They had the gall to speak treason in Ashanesland itself, because they travelled under the protection of Smiler's Fair and thought themselves safe. No shipfort lord wants to anger the fair, you see, or it won't visit again. All that trade lost. But Smiler's Fair never journeys here and the arrogant fools didn't post a guard as they travelled through the Blade Pass. My men took them in the night and brought them here this morning. I thought you might like to join me as I question them.'

The jail was on the lowest level of Winter's Hammer. It was the same in Whitewood. Down here, captives were below the waterline. They could listen to the slap of the waves against the wall high above their heads and know that the only escape was death by drowning.

Nethmi felt herself shaking with tension as she descended the stairs. Speaking treason in Smiler's Fair? It didn't seem possible Thilak could mean the boy preacher. It felt too much like a sign, mere hours after she'd been staring at his moon god's face. She told herself it must be some other traitor, a rebel tribal leader. But when the guard unlocked the thick wooden door and gestured them inside, she saw instead a middle-aged woman and a boy.

They seemed less impressive close up than they'd looked striding about so confidently in front of the crowds. Both were white-skinned, paler even than the mountain savages, and had the same brown hair, curled on her and straight on him, and the same pronounced cheekbones and narrow nose. Their eyes were different, though, hers a muddy brown and his almond-shaped like those of a tribesman and almost the same green as spring grass.

The boy watched them calmly, but the woman's gaze skittered nervously away from hers. Nethmi saw that she had a large bruise on her left cheek and held herself as if there were more under her clothes. She was shivering and an unhealthy sheen of sweat stood out on her skin. The cell was filthy. The straw on the floor smelt of urine and something – a rat, a cockroach – scuttled beneath it. The boy hardly seemed to notice his surroundings. He held himself as if he'd been granted an audience in the great hall.

She felt a sudden jolt of terror. What if he'd seen her face in the crowd? What if he told her husband that she'd listened to his treasonous talk? With the right words, this boy could ensure that she ended up in the cell beside him. 'Who are they?' she asked Thilak with studied innocence.

'They are Vordanna and Jinn,' he said. 'Formerly of the company of Worshippers of Smiler's Fair. And their crime is sedition: fomenting rebellion against King Nayan.'

'Sedition?' She stared at the boy, willing him to remain silent.

He smiled a little, as if he knew very well who she was. But then he moved his gaze to Thilak. 'I *did* preach against your false king. Someone's gotta speak, even if it's just a boy – even if I'm the only one. I'd rather speak the truth than live a lie.'

His mother cringed and reached out towards him, but the boy gently brushed away her hand.

Thilak just laughed. 'They've been at this for years. I'm told they're very popular out on the plains. But my tribesmen aren't impressed by their nonsense.'

'*Your* tribesmen?' the boy said. 'People can't be owned, not in their hearts. Do you know what's in these people's hearts, Lord Thilak? Have you ever asked?'

Remembering In Su's talk of the moon god, Nethmi thought he had a point. Had Thilak ever asked about the face on the rocks? Or had he thought it too unimportant, a part of this conquered people's superstitious ways? He certainly didn't seem troubled by Jinn's words now. 'You see,' Thilak said to her, 'they incriminate themselves from their own mouths.'

Nethmi couldn't tear her gaze away from the boy. Up close, his eyes were the most compelling she'd ever seen. 'If King Nayan is false, then who do you say is the true king?'

'Yron's heir, the risen moon.'

'The moon is dead,' one of Thilak's guards said sharply.

Thilak snapped him an irritated look and the man shut his mouth and looked away.

'You're right,' Jinn said. 'Yron the moon god died, but now he's reborn in the false king's son. His human father wanted to kill him, but his mother sacrificed her life to save him. He'll return one day to claim his birthright. He'll change everything.' His green eyes studied her, seeming to see inside her. 'He'll change *your* life. I know it's bad now, but it can be better.'

She heard Thilak shift behind her, and then his hand was on her shoulder. 'I think we've heard enough, don't you?'

He started pulling her towards the door, but she kept her eyes on Jinn even as she was forced to leave the cell. 'Yron's heir will change everything,' he said, as the door was slammed shut. 'You'll meet him soon. I know it.'

12

Marvan's legs felt as weak as water and he had to pause in his climb. He dumped his victim on a rock and sat beside the body, panting and looking at the view below.

Smiler's Fair was on the move at its usual sluggish pace. From up here, the massive carts and the beasts pulling them looked like children's toys. If he reached out he should be able to lift and rearrange them. The red rectangle he knew held the House of Ill-Repute could be swapped with the long white string of wagons that carried the Gambler's Paradise. The dots of people clustered around the furry black lump of an ice mammoth might like to ride on the horses that were drawing the Jolly Maid through the mountain pass. He could shift the Queen's Men behind the King's and watch the perennially squabbling companies fight. He'd be god of them all, deciding their fates.

He sighed, looked up briefly at the cloudless blue sky and then down to the corpse at his side. Its eyes stared back at him, as blank and empty as the sky. He'd caused himself enough trouble deciding just one person's fate. It was foolish – insanity really. The Blade Pass was long, it was true, and Smiler's Fair wouldn't stop on the ancient road. Too few people lived nearby and the local Seonu were known for neither their dissipation nor their wealth. But the broad grasslands lay only a few days away now and they'd make their pitch there, drawing others of the Fourteen Tribes to lose their gold and their morals for the pleasures the fair offered.

He could have waited five days and found strangers aplenty to choose from, but the urge had come upon him, stronger than ever, and he'd found he had to act on it. He'd strangled Jaquim as the apprentice left camp to piss and spent the rest of the night dragging his scrawny body up the mountain. Marvan knew the folk of the fair wouldn't have taken the same delight in watching him kill one of their own. But Lucan the clerk had warned him to stop killing strangers, and what choice did that leave him? Only to stop killing altogether, the one thing he seemed incapable of doing.

Jaquim's corpse was beginning to stiffen and Marvan didn't know how much further he could carry it. The thin, pimply face stared at him, no more attractive in death than it had been in life. Marvan looked back down at the valley and the slow procession of animals and men. A little further, he decided.

He groaned as he hoisted the corpse on to his shoulders. It rested awkwardly, one leg sticking out at an oblique angle and an arm stretched in front, reaching for something it would never catch. Marvan's back cracked as he rose to his feet and his legs almost collapsed under him. Just the next ridge, he told himself, and forced his body into motion.

There was snow on the ground up here, fallen several days ago and frozen into an icy crust. It crunched beneath his boots. The vegetation crunched too, skeletal plants that looked barely alive. Everything up here was brittle. Even the air felt fragile, as if it might shatter in his lungs.

He had to use his hands to clamber over a pile of rocks, scraping his palms and almost pulling his shoulders out of joint as Jaquim's corpse was caught by one of the spindly, ugly bushes. When he'd topped the rocks he looked up and saw only another ridge ahead of him, more rocks and an abundance of snow.

This would have to do. He released Jaquim's arm and shrugged the corpse off his shoulders. It fell to the ground and landed awkwardly, one leg bent at the knee and an arm reaching out to him in pointless pleading.

No one ever came up here. He could probably leave the body to the buzzards and the wolves. But . . . He looked back down and could still see Smiler's Fair, winding its way through the pass. What if *they'd* seen *him*? Someone might have watched him carry his burden up here. They might think he was hiding some prize and come to seek it for themselves. The people of Smiler's Fair were known for many vices, and greed was one of them.

He sighed, rubbed at the small of his back and then stooped to begin collecting rocks to pile over the body. They made a dismal cairn, a monument no one would see for a boy nobody had much liked. Marvan felt melancholy envelop him as he worked, stooping, lifting, dropping, the kind of manual labour Jaquim himself had probably once done before he'd run away to Smiler's Fair to find a better life.

It was several minutes before he realised someone was watching him. When he did, the figure seemed to coalesce suddenly out of the mountain, grass becoming hair and pebbles eyes. Marvan cried out and took a startled step backwards. But the man made no threatening move, just stood and stared at the rocks barely covering Jaquim's body.

Marvan wasn't sure if he should be relieved that the man seemed to be a local, with the light skin, almond eyes and straight, jet-black hair of the Fourteen Tribes. It was definitely a relief to see that the man held a bottle of whisky in one hand, and that it was nearly empty. Marvan could smell it from ten paces away and, now he looked more closely, the man did seem to be wavering a little on his feet.

On the other hand, if Marvan had brought all his weapons with him today, he'd still have had a considerably smaller arsenal than was hanging from the tribesman's body. He saw two hand axes, a bow slung over his back along with a sword and more knives than he could count. It must take immense strength to carry them all and he was a large fellow, a roundness at his belly that was clearly fat but a breadth to his shoulders and thighs that spoke of muscle.

Marvan had only brought his twin tridents with him, and he let his hands rest casually on their hilts. 'How can I help you, friend?'

'I tell you what, I think you're the one who needs help.' The man spoke Ashane with only a slight accent, but the words were heavily slurred. He must be very far into his cups. 'I'm happy to lend a hand.'

Marvan was careful not to look towards the body. 'No need to trouble yourself.'

'No trouble.' Before Marvan could move to stop him, he'd lifted a rock in each hand and thrown them onto the half-built cairn.

Marvan watched him in silence. The tribesman whistled as he searched for the rocks, tipping forward drunkenly when he reached for them and laughing a little when he dropped them on Jaquim's corpse. After only a little while, the body was completely hidden beneath stone.

'Did you want a marker?' the stranger asked, standing back to admire his work. 'Something with his name. You know. The kind of thing you people put on graves.'

Marvan let out a slow breath. So the man thought he was burying a loved one. 'No need. The rain would only wash it away, and I know who lies here – that's what matters.'

'If you say so.' The tribesman dropped a few more rocks on the pile, then seemed to lose his enthusiasm for the work and flopped gracelessly on to a larger boulder, wiping his hands clean against his leather trousers.

'So . . .' Marvan gestured vaguely over his shoulder. 'I suppose I should go before my home gets too far away from me.'

The tribesman frowned. 'You don't want to say some words over the grave? Make a prayer or an offering?'

'I've spoken the words in my heart,' Marvan said weakly.

The other man nodded. 'Your ways are not our ways. We don't bother to bury our enemies – we let them fall and rot where they are. But your people care even for those you kill. I say that's admirable.'

'He wasn't –' Marvan began, and then saw the sly expression on the other man's face and the glint of amusement in his eyes. 'Thank you for your help, friend, whyever you gave it.'

The tribesman raised the bottle of whisky in salute, then poured its dregs down his throat. 'The world is full of reasons – who can know them all? Good journey to you.'

Dae Hyo watched the man from Smiler's Fair walk away. His spine was stiff and Dae Hyo knew he was fighting not to turn around. Well, that had certainly made the morning more entertaining than he'd expected. He'd woken at dawn with a pounding head and no interesting prospects on the horizon. The way he felt, the whisky was medicinal, truly. *Poison for an antidote*, like the elder mothers always said. He took another swallow and his vision, which had begun to clear, became pleasantly fuzzy again. The world looked better this way. He didn't understand why anyone would choose to spend any time sober. Life was shit. Anything that made it seem less so was a gift from the ancestors.

But Smiler's Fair was here at last and he could move on with his plan. Min Ki might be a coward and a traitor, but he was right about one thing: raiding was the last refuge of a man who had nowhere else to go. Dae Hyo had no people to fight for any longer but he still had his own mouth to fill with food. And raiding could be honourable, if you conducted it honourably.

He tossed the empty bottle at the cairn, watching the glass shatter on the stranger's grave. 'May your ancestors welcome you,' he said, then turned away.

The Wanderers he'd been tracking were camped beside an energetic mountain stream. They'd been following its course for three days now, no doubt hoping they'd find habitation and a market for their wares somewhere along it. Probably they were right, but they'd been disappointed so far and, even packed up in carts as it was right now, Smiler's Fair should prove too tempting for them to resist. The important thing was making sure they knew it was there.

Dae Hyo could move silently when he wanted, a hunter's skill he'd never forgotten. He crept to the edge of a hillock that overlooked the Wanderers' wagon and peered down at them. There were four in their party: two freckle-faced men too alike to be anything but brothers, a plump, stern woman and her child. He'd yet to figure out which of the men she was married to. Maybe it was both – who knew how foreigners lived their lives? All four of them were clustered round a small fire where a pot bubbled, their conversation too low for him to hear. He caught a faint whiff of porridge and his stomach twisted. When he drank, he didn't remember to eat as often as he should.

He'd been careful to stay hidden and he knew they hadn't seen him. Wanderers were careless, anyway. Everyone knew they travelled under their Hunter's hawk pact and that it was death to hurt any of the Hunter's folk. That was no problem: he didn't have harm in mind, just a bit of robbery.

He had to admit, theft sat a little ill with him, but everyone knew the Wanderers had gold rather than blood in their veins and a locked box where their hearts ought to be. He'd never forgotten the three who'd passed through Dae lands when the great murrain was sweeping the plains and his brothers and sisters were starving. They'd sold grain and cheese to the tribe for ten times what it was worth. These bastards had money to spare. He wouldn't even take it all, just enough to keep him in whisky for a good long time.

Nothing would happen, though, until they could be made to leave their wagon unattended. It was clear they'd not heard the fair's passing. Sometimes a horse needed to be led to water. He touched each of his blades for luck and then stood up, smiled and strode towards them.

The woman noticed him first. She seemed almost insultingly unalarmed, shading her eyes against the morning sun to watch him approach.

'I tell you what, you seem to be lost,' Dae Hyo said when he was only a few paces away.

The woman frowned and one of the freckled men strode up to sling an arm around her shoulder. Probably her husband, then. 'What makes you think that?' he asked.

'Because Smiler's Fair is that way, and you're here.'

Oh yes, the hook was in their cheeks, no doubt of it. Husband and wife exchanged startled looks and the other man strode hurriedly up and said, 'Smiler's Fair?'

'You didn't know?' Dae Hyo asked, as if he didn't much care. 'I was hoping to buy something there myself. Let's be honest, probably a whore. But when I went down to see them in the Blade Pass, all the interesting parts were packed up and they told me they weren't stopping. You're not with them, then? I thought all you Moon Forest folk loved the fair.'

'Smiler's Fair isn't our home,' the first man said, 'though we have friends there.'

Dae Hyo peered blearily at him. 'I don't suppose *you* have a whore for sale?'

The man flinched away from the whisky on Dae Hyo's breath and Dae Hyo knew he had them for certain. People feared the violence of the drunk, but not their cunning tricks.

'No?' Dae Hyo said when the man didn't reply. 'Well, good travels to you then.' He smiled round at the whole group and sauntered past their wagon and along the river's course, as if that had been his route all along. A bright green frog leapt out of his path to splash in the water and he looked at that and not behind him, walking on until he was out of sight of the camp.

When he felt certain he wasn't being followed, he stopped. The snow-dusted landscape didn't give him much to look at, so he sat on a rock and picked at the scabrous grey moss as he made himself wait. The time seemed to trickle away with impossible slowness, but when he judged enough had passed, he stood.

He knew it was best not to return by the same path. If the Wanderers had chosen to remain, it was sure to rouse their suspicions, so he turned away from the river instead and took to the low hills. It was a difficult route, keeping to the shadows and muffling his footsteps in the scattered patches of grass, but eventually he'd circled himself back round to the campsite. He wriggled the last few feet on his belly and peered over the crown of the hill as a chill breeze picked at his topknot.

It had worked. The wagon still sat there, plump and inviting with the haughty golden Hunter painted on its side, but the people were gone. The only sound was the stream, its chuckle echoing Dae Hyo's own feelings.

The campsite was a little disorderly. The Wanderers had left plates scattered about in their hurry to visit the fair, and half their porridge in the pot. It was congealed and burnt on the bottom but Dae Hyo paused to scrape it out and lick it from his fingers. Then he'd run out of things to do except rob the wagon and he took a breath to stiffen his resolve before climbing in.

The interior was gloomy, even with the canvas flaps flung wide. It was thick with the clashing smells of the spices that were these Wanderers' trade, and he could see pots and pans and scales and knives and dried flowers and a big cured ham cluttering the space. Everything but what he wanted. He pushed aside a string of rosebuds and moved deeper in.

It was even darker here and he was forced to feel his way round. His fingers found a greasy solidity he thought might be a cheese and the rough weave of linen thrown on top of the softness of wool. He groped deeper into the material, sensing something harder beneath, and then the cloth moved, a hand clawed into his and there was a hoarse scream of shock.

He shouted as well, too surprised to be stealthy. For a frozen moment he did nothing else, until his wits returned and he drew his knife from its sheath and slashed downward. He'd mis-aimed the blow, though, and he felt the blade tangle in cloth. The figure below him squirmed and shrieked and he'd torn the knife free and raised it for a killing strike when his target twisted and turned her face to the dim light. He had only a moment to register the wrinkled skin, the rheumy eyes and the thin lips before he stopped his blade an inch away from her throat and fled the wagon.

He meant to run far away, but all the strength had gone from his legs. He fell to his knees on the stony ground instead, gasping as if he'd been in a real fight rather than about to slaughter a helpless woman. He'd come so close to killing her. If she hadn't turned towards the light, if he'd moved the knife aside just a little more slowly . . . He sat on the ground shivering with the horror of an almost done thing.

After a little while, though, it occurred to him that there was no noise coming from inside the wagon. Shouldn't the old woman have been shouting an alarm? But he'd given her a terrible shock and everyone knew the heart weakened as the body aged.

He had the strength to stand now and he wanted to flee the campsite and the murder he'd so nearly committed. But he was a Dae warrior and Dae warriors didn't run. He picked his knife up from the ground where he'd let it drop, sheathed it and then climbed back into the wagon. There was more daylight now and he could see the figure under the blankets quite clearly. When he stepped closer he realised that the cloudy blue eyes were open, and he sagged in relief as they blinked.

'I tell you what, I didn't mean to surprise you,' he said in the Moon Forest tongue he'd learned from Edgar and Edmund.

The old woman coughed, an awful gurgling sound that told him why she'd been staying in the wagon. Then she whispered, 'What do you want, warrior?'

'Oh well,' he said, 'they told me to look after you while they went to the fair.'

Her face was so leathery with age it was hard to read the expression on it, but when she smiled to show a few teeth and mostly gums, he thought that was a good sign.

'So you've been in here all these days?' He stepped a little closer. 'You people don't know how to look after the sick. All these bad airs trapped in here with you, and darkness, anyone can see that's no good. You need sun.'

They'd wrapped her up in the cloth so tightly she looked like a caterpillar in its cocoon. It made it easy to stoop and pick her up. The blankets weighed more than she did and she leaned trustingly against his chest as he took her outside and laid her on a soft piece of ground where she could smell the green things winter had left living and see the fish in the stream.

'That's better,' Dae Hyo said. He'd meant to leave her then, but it occurred to him there might be wolves about or other men with fewer morals than him, so he sank cross-legged to the ground beside her.

For a little while the old woman seemed to drift into dreams, her body twitching in its covers and her eyeballs rolling beneath their lids. But when her eyes opened they were clear. 'Still here?' she asked.

That didn't seem to require any answer, so instead he said, 'I'm Dae Hyo.'

'Dae Hyo. Dae Hyo, is it? I'm Mayda Maysdochter.'

'It's a pretty name.'

She gave a laugh, which turned into a rasping cough. 'A flatterer, aren't you? A charmer. I thought all you savages cared about was war?'

'The Dae aren't war-makers.'

'Not like those Janggok, eh? A child carried off in raids from each village we passed in the forest, and the Hunter nowhere to be seen. We tithe our bairns to her for hawks and still our children are taken and sold as slaves in foreign lands. My own Rheda stolen when she was still suckling at my tit. Oh, but that was many moons ago.' Her gaze sharpened as she looked at him. 'Before you were born, warrior.'

'Dae Hyo,' he reminded her.

'Oh aye, the Dae.' Then her eyes slipped shut and he thought she slept. He'd half risen to carry her back into the wagon when her shrivelled hand reached out to grasp his. 'The Dae are dead, you know. Their lands are empty.'

He gently loosened her fingers with his. 'My brothers and sisters are dead, but the Chun took our land. They live on what they don't own.'

'No,' she said. 'All gone.'

He nodded, not willing to argue with her on a topic he preferred to look away from when he could, but she tightened her grip against his resistance.

'The hunting grounds are empty. We rode through them, oh, five weeks past. The Chun – but they call themselves the Brotherband now, don't they? The Brotherband headed north, to harry the Four Together. The plains were full of talk of their murder and their rape. Maybe now the tribes will know what we suffer with the Janggok. Yes, maybe they will.'

There was more, but he hardly heard it. He let her talk herself to sleep, then lifted her gently and carried her inside the wagon to her bed. He washed the cooking pot clean of its porridge, which seemed the least he could do, and then turned his back on the camp.

The Dae hunting grounds were empty. The grasslands and the hills, the reed-fringed lake where Dae Sun had taught him to swim, the scattered ash trees the youngest boys had raced to climb, the river called the Snake because of the way the water hissed over the jagged rocks of its bottom, the camp where a thousand of his brothers and sisters and the elder mothers had been made into skeletons and bleached in the sun. Every place that held every memory of his childhood. For the first time in seven years, he was free to return home. The last Dae could live and hunt on Dae lands.

The whisky he'd drunk had vanished and taken its warmth with it, but now he felt a new sensation course through him, every bit as intense. It had been so long since he'd felt it, it took him a few moments to realise what it was: joy. It filled him to overflowing as he turned his back on the mountains and picked his path west towards the plains.

13

Olufemi passed the graveyard first. The dead lay on wooden platforms resting on piles of rocks. The recent thaw had melted the snow, at least for a while, and the bones were exposed to the chilly air. They'd long ago been picked clean by vultures, but she could see that some had teeth marks in them, too wide to belong to one of the mountain's many predators. There were hands missing here and there, and on one corpse the entire left leg was gone. Yron's servants had killed them, she felt certain, which meant she was probably approaching a mining community. Miners seldom buried their dead. Having lived their lives in darkness, they preferred to spend the aftermath in the light of the sun.

By the time she saw the settlement itself, her pack was digging into her shoulders, Adofo's sling weighed her down at the front and her bones felt as brittle as those in the graveyard. She sighed, slid the pack from her back and sat on a rock to examine her destination. She found it better if she prepared herself before speaking to new people, to decide which story she'd tell them, which shading of the truth. It should have been easy after all this time, but instead it seemed to grow harder with every month, every wasted year.

She didn't imagine her fortunes changing in this place. She'd visited its like before: a charmless collection of bars and brothels and boarding houses catering to the miners and mercenaries desperate enough to enter the earth in search of a few scraps of iron. Many of them seemed to be in town today, leading a motley collection of horses and donkeys. The men were hitching the mounts to the wooden bars that protruded from the side of each building. Then, as she watched, the beasts moved and so did the buildings themselves.

Olufemi smiled a little. Now that was different. She couldn't see any wheels beneath the houses and guessed they must be gliding on tracks of some kind. There was always something new to be discovered in the world, she needed to remember that.

She heaved herself up and moved a little closer. Then she drew out her notebook and began to write down what she saw in the script she'd been taught in her distant youth in Mirror Town. The rails were a complex network, with sidings that allowed one house to be shunted aside so that others could pass it. There were 112 buildings in the settlement and they all seemed to be on the move. The grunts of effort drifted up to her.

It didn't seem possible that order would emerge out of all that chaos. But after a surprisingly short time, a three-storey bar had been shuttled past a long, thin whorehouse and locked into place at the end of a row of tenements, and the job seemed to be done. The people dispersed, some clearly struggling to find their destination in the town's new configuration, and Olufemi sighed. She'd secure some lodgings and then she'd get started.

The lodging house was filthy. The walls were covered in a combination of soot and what appeared to be blood; Olufemi took one look at the bed and then stripped the sheets and blankets from it and piled them in a corner, hoping their collection of fleas wouldn't migrate to her in the night. She placed her own bedroll on the bare straw mattress and sat on it. She could remember a time when her slaves would have performed all these tasks for her. But there was no bedroom this dismal in Mirror Town, not even the slaves' own.

The place was warm, at least. They'd lit a fire in the grate when they brought her in here, and the floor itself radiated heat. She suspected she might be above the kitchens. It would explain the smell of overcooked cabbage.

The warmth was already waking Adofo from his hibernation. Olufemi removed the lizard monkey from his sling and placed him gently on the bed as the nictitating membranes over the creature's eyes blinked open. She took a moment, as she always did, to admire them: the silver irises and the black crescent of the pupil within them. His red scales glittered in the firelight. His claws looked wickedly sharp and his teeth too when he yawned widely. Then he rubbed his paws along each side of his face and peered mournfully at Olufemi. He seemed reproachful, as well he might. He'd been in the deep rest only five days since Olufemi had last awakened him. No doubt he'd been hoping to sleep the winter through.

Olufemi pulled an apple from her pack and carefully divided it, giving the bigger portion to her pet. 'Here, maybe this will make waking up worthwhile.'

Adofo's movements were still a little sluggish as he took the offering. He turned it round to inspect it from every angle before eating it. He always did that, as if he was afraid that one day Olufemi might try to poison him. When he was finished looking he took a delicate nibble, chittered in pleasure, then hurriedly scoffed the whole thing. After that he rolled on to his back beside the fire, half-closed his eyes and settled down to enjoy the heat.

'There are people I need to speak to, Adofo. Would you like to meet them?'

The little lizard monkey made a gesture that might have been a shrug and Olufemi smiled wearily. 'Better not, I suppose. They're not fond of the moon's servants here, and your eyes will make them think of nothing good.'

Vordanna laughed at her for talking to the monkey, but she hadn't been there at the beginning. She didn't know what it meant that he seemed to understand. Olufemi did. She remembered the day she'd heard that Samadara had killed herself and her unborn child with her. She remembered the despair she'd felt – and the rage.

'Even after those wretched truthtellers spread their poison, I had it all arranged, didn't I, Adofo?' she said. 'I had guards bribed and servants paid to spirit that baby out of there the moment he was born. It never occurred to me the queen might take things into her own hands.'

But she had, and everything Olufemi had planned had been for nothing. King Nayan had announced that his cursed son had been slain by his own mother and Olufemi had returned to Mirror Town and to Adofo, only two years old then and so wild that he had to be caged.

She'd meant to end the creature's life. He seemed like nothing but a symbol of her failure: a mocking echo of the dead baby and her dead ambitions. But when she'd walked to Adofo's cage – though he hadn't had a name then: he'd seemed too wild to own one – the lizard monkey had sat up and regarded her with something other than mindless violence in his strange eyes. Olufemi had reached a hand into the cage, not really caring if she lost it, and when Adofo had sniffed and then gently licked it she'd thought that maybe, just maybe, the King had lied and the baby had lived after all. For what, other than the entry of Yron's heir into the world, could explain such a change in one of his creatures?

The rumours had emerged a little while after that: that the queen had cut the babe from her own body, that it had clawed its own way out, that buzzards had swooped down to snatch the infant away. And so Olufemi had begun her long, long search. But eleven years passed with not even a trace of the child and her despair had grown once again, until it was a monstrous thing turning the world grey and all her hopes to dust.

But in the twelfth year of her futile hunt, when she'd retreated to Smiler's Fair to live with all the other fakes and failures, Adofo had changed again.

She remembered the day with a clarity that time hadn't dulled. She'd been discharging her duty in the Temple with Vordanna, taking coin from those gullible enough to believe their empty prayers were listened to. When she'd returned to their rooms she'd expected to find Adofo where she'd left him, lounging in front of the fire. But the little creature must have grown bored, because he'd opened the door, crept downstairs to the kitchen, pried open the pantry and used a knife to carve himself a hunk of cheese, which he'd always inexplicably loved.

Olufemi had stared dumbstruck at the lizard monkey sitting at the kitchen table and nibbling on his snack. Adofo shouldn't have known how to open a door or how to use a knife. He never had before. In the past, Olufemi had seen him throw himself against a locked door, frustrated that it wouldn't open and failing to understand that he simply needed to reach up and turn the key. Now something had changed again. Yron's heir, she had thought and still did, was growing into manhood and his creature was changing with him. Olufemi had always spoken to Adofo, her only constant companion, but from that day five years ago, she suspected that he understood her.

'Best for you to stay here, I think,' she told him. 'I'll bring you back some food. We'll remain the night and then move on somewhere more hopeful. And cleaner.'

She found the biggest crowd at a nameless bar that was currently opposite a whorehouse. When Olufemi looked through the bar's front door she judged that there must be thirty men present along with the two barmaids and a tall, scarred bruiser, who eyed her assessingly then stepped aside to let her pass. Word of her presence had spread, as it usually did, and a hush fell as she entered.

It wasn't an entirely friendly silence, but she was used to that too. With her skin darker than any Ashane's, her broad nose and the small, tight curls of her hair, once brown but now silver, she looked like what she was: a mage of Mirror Town. The other nations had always feared more than they knew of her people.

'What's your business here, milady?' someone asked, as someone usually did. The tone wasn't disrespectful – it didn't dare to be – but it implied that she was less than welcome.

'I'm admiring the sights,' she said.

'In the arse end of Ashanesland?' asked a pockmarked youth. 'There's prettier latrines elsewhere.'

So, they still counted themselves part of the kingdom here. That would make the story she told them a little different. She smiled and sat, facing the inhabitants of the room like a lecturer addressing her students in the Great Library of Mirror Town.

'There's magic in the bones of the earth here. You should know it better than most.'

The pockmarked youth seemed to have been elected their spokesman. He spat and sneered. 'No magic we want any part of. And what use has your magic been to us? My uncle bought a rune-marked blade when Smiler's Fair came past the last time. It shattered and the worm men had him.'

'You question the power of my runes?'

'The only power we know is the sun. Can you make it shine underground?'

There was laughter this time and she knew she was losing the crowd's respect. A few had turned back to their drinks.

'You doubt me,' Olufemi said. 'It's your prerogative, of course.' She walked to the fire as if to warm her hands, but when she was still two feet distant she made a complex gesture, a drawing of runes in the air, and the flames leapt towards her in seeming obedience, flaring a lurid green as they followed the path of her hands. The rune – Yay-Sat, the rune of fury, had these yokels but known it – hung in the air for a moment before fading to nothing. Olufemi's back was to the room but she heard the shocked gasp behind her.

When she turned back round, all eyes were on her once again. She smiled with kind condescension at the pockmarked youth. 'The runes are more subtle than the sun, but no less powerful.'

He nodded, stuttering too hard to get out the obsequious agreement he no doubt intended.

You're an idiot, she wanted to tell him. *Can't you see it's all just a trick, a mixture of sulphur and black powder cached in a purse beneath my sleeve? I'm nothing but a fraud and the runes are worthless and dead and have stayed that way for seventeen years, despite all my scheming, all my hope.*

'I've studied the runes my entire life,' she said grandly. 'Do you doubt that I've mastered them?'

There were murmurs of 'no' around the room. *But you should. You should. Yron's heir is in the world, Adofo proves it, and yet the runes haven't wakened as I'd hoped. If I'd truly mastered them, I could make them work for me as they worked for the mages of old.*

'What service can we give you then, milady?' the pockmarked youth asked diffidently.

'I'm searching for someone I lost many years ago.'

'Who is he?' an older man asked, and they were back to the customary script.

'He's the most important person in the world. So important, King Nayan himself has sent me to hunt him. I have his authorisation and orders in his own hand.' She drew out the letter from her pocket, its ink so faded with age that it could barely be read. But the imprint of an oak wheel in the sealing wax was still clear.

She didn't mention the reward Nayan had added and raised over the years: 10,000 gold wheels, the last she'd heard. She wanted these men's help; she didn't want them to keep the knowledge to themselves so that they could pocket the coin and she none the wiser.

Some of the men in the room rose to crowd round her and peer at the letter. A few reached out to run their fingers over the wax. She let them. She knew none of them could read it and besides, the letter was genuine enough. It was typical, she'd found, for people to doubt absolutely the wrong things.

'Who is this man King Nayan is hunting?' the old man asked.

'The King's own son, stolen from his mother's womb before he was born. The child with the unlucky eyes.'

And this was the part where the real questions came, and the answers always differed, depending on which would serve her best. *Why was the son taken?* Because he was marked for death by the King and saved by his mother. Because the moon's servants stole him, knowing the future that lay ahead of him. Because the King sent him away for his own safety. *What's so special about the boy?* A prophecy foretold he'd kill his father and bring evil to the world. A prophecy foretold he'd save the world from the evil of his father. *Why do you want him?* To save him. To kill him.

Except that, for the first time in seventeen years, no one asked those questions.

'The boy with moon eyes?' the pockmarked youth asked. 'The one with that big reward on him?'

Olufemi felt a bolt of something down her spine, as shocking as a lightning strike. 'There is a reward,' she said cautiously.

'And you claim you work for the King,' the old man said. There was new suspicion in his voice and in the faces of many around him.

'I travel the world for him,' Olufemi said. 'We don't speak every day.'

'You've been out of the country?'

'For a very long time.'

The old man grinned, showing the broken nubs of his teeth. 'Well then, you won't have heard. Your boy's been found. East of here a ways, in a mountain village. He ran, but King Nayan's soldiers are after him, and so are half the men of this town, eyes shining with all that gold.'

'He was – he was found?' Olufemi had pictured this moment for so long, and yet it was nothing like she'd imagined. The search had been her whole life and what should have been a long-awaited beginning felt oddly like an ending.

'Like I said, not far from here. You'll join the hunt too? Your runes might come in handy, I reckon, though they don't seem to have done you too much good these last years. I hear it was pure chance the boy was found. A justice went to this piss-poor village for some other crime and there he was. Didn't even know he was a wanted man, they say.'

And now he was on the run and likely to be caught at any moment – caught and killed. Her prize had appeared, only to be snatched away from her. No. No, she couldn't let it happen. 'I'll hunt for him,' she said.

And what if you find him, she thought, *and he isn't what you hope? What if he's just a boy?*

Krish stopped in the lee of the rocks to study the graveyard. He could see no one living, only the bare bones on their wooden platforms. What kind of people left their dead out for the birds to pick apart? He guessed the village itself lay somewhere beyond and he yearned to go there. He wanted to be among people like those he'd grown up with, to eat a hot cooked meal, sleep in a tent, talk. He thought that perhaps he could finally risk it.

The sky had been black with carrion mounts in the first days of his flight. He'd been forced to travel at night, risking his life on mountain paths he didn't know. He thought he'd broken a rib in one fall and his legs were dark with bruises. His chest was tight, too. He hadn't dared build himself a fire, and the cold had bred illness in his lungs so that his breath crackled like the flames he couldn't chance. But one night, when the soldiers had almost caught him and he'd crept past their camp, he'd heard them talking. They hoped they'd find him soon, they'd said. They were reaching the height beyond which the birds couldn't fly.

After that, he'd headed upward. The cold grew bitter, seeping through his mittens and goatskin jacket, and the strain of the climb hurt and then strengthened the muscles in his calves and thighs. His chest grew tighter and tighter and his breath shorter and shorter, but he kept going. At least now he could travel during the day.

He took a last look around the graveyard and a white glint caught his eye. He thought it was a fallen bone at first, but when he looked closer he saw that it was rock, twisted into a shape almost like a naked woman with wide hips and generous breasts. He stroked it with his finger and found that it was pleasingly smooth.

His da was dead, and his ma was . . . she was safe with her sister. She must be. But he was seventeen and head of his household. He was a man and a man needed his own god. He touched the rock to his forehead and then to his lips. He'd sleep with her in his hands until his dreams brought him her name, and she would watch over him. He'd whisper his quest to her, the instructions his mother had given him, perhaps the last she ever would. He'd tell her of his plan to raise an army and fight his true father, and she'd help him achieve it. That's what gods were for.

He slipped the prow god into his pack and then stood. Finding her here must surely be a sign that events were leaning in his favour at last. He *would* go to the village.

The path that led from the graveyard was clear, as if it was followed often. Krish felt himself smiling as he walked it. The landscape around him was almost like his home: grey and brown fractured hills, mountains in the distance and ragged vegetation clinging to the rocks. On the crest of a nearby rise, he could see two goats cropping at the grass.

The path curved round one hill and then climbed to the top of another. The footing was treacherous, loose stones and earth, and when he reached the other side he saw why. A wide tunnel had been bored into the rockface opposite. Its interior was dark and, if the mound Krish had just climbed was its innards, it must go very deep. He knew that metal lived beneath the ground but he'd never truly realised the cost of its retrieval. No wonder only Isuru had been able to afford an iron knife.

As he drew closer he saw that there was a man kneeling at the tunnel entrance. At first Krish thought he was wearing a red hood, but then he realised it was the stranger's own hair. There was a wild shock of it, brighter than fox fur, and when he turned at the sound of Krish's steps he revealed a pale face ridged with ugly scars. He was holding a wreath of leaves in his hand and he set it down gently on the ground before rising.

'I'm sorry,' Krish said. 'I didn't mean to interrupt. I'm looking for the village.'

The stranger scowled. 'You're wasting your time. He's not here.'

'I'm not looking for anyone. I just want food. I have coin.'

'Don't bother, lad. Do you really think you're the first? We've had a dozen through here in the last week, and we told them all the same thing. If we find him, he's *ours*. You can't go hunting in another man's woods.'

The stranger was armed. A sword hung from his belt with a knife beside it, and some of the scars on his face were clearly from battle. Krish knew he should retreat from the man's unfounded hostility, but he'd been so long without company and his food was all but gone. He took a hesitant step closer and said, 'Really, it's only a meal I want. I don't even need shelter. I'll move on after I've bought it if you'd prefer.'

The other man stepped nearer too, until only ten paces separated them. He studied Krish and smiled abruptly. Several of his teeth were missing and the smile twisted as his tongue flicked out to lick along his empty gums. 'Perhaps I was too hasty, lad. I apologise for my rough manners. I'm Edmund Aikensson.'

He was waiting for Krish to say his own name, to confirm it. Krish felt a jolt of terror as he realised what Edmund's earlier words had meant. He eased back a pace, trying a smile of his own, which was brittle where the other man's had merely been false. 'You're right. I was coming here to hunt him. But I'll move on. I won't take your prize.'

Edmund eased forward, his longer stride eating up more ground than Krish's. 'No, you won't.'

Krish backed away another pace, and in the moment when Edmund was preparing to follow, he turned and fled.

The other man was only a little surprised. There was no more than a heartbeat's pause before the pounding of footsteps followed Krish. He had no chance on the ground, he knew that already. Edmund was bigger, stronger and armed. But he *was* armed, and armoured, and weighed down by it all, while Krish had lived in the mountains all his life.

The cliff face was rough enough that when Krish leapt and clasped, his hands found purchase. His legs kicked frantically before his boots hooked into a crack in the rock and he pushed himself up. He was already gasping for breath, but he made himself do it again, and then again. His hands grew slick with sweat and his heart lurched when one slipped from its hold. He tore three nails in their desperate scrabble at the rock and the blood trickled down his hand, making it slicker still as he grasped and pulled again.

After long moments of labour, feeling sick with fatigue, he allowed himself to look down. Edmund was far closer than he'd hoped, only five paces below and climbing fast, but Krish had reached a ledge. He knocked out what breath remained in him as he flopped on to it and rested his head against the rock. He knew he had no time to waste, though, and he forced himself to his knees and tore his pack from his back.

His new prow god rested on top of his blanket. She slid smoothly into his palm and he raised her and knelt on the edge of the rock.

Edmund had reached him. As his hand grasped for the ledge, his eyes locked with Krish's and there was a moment when it was clear he knew what was going to happen. But he had no time to prevent it and Krish brought the rock down on his fingers.

The blow was too weak, too half-hearted. Edmund shouted in anger and brought his other hand up to join the first. Krish tightened his fist as he brought the rock down for a second time, and now there was blood when he struck, but Edmund only cursed and began to push his weight into his hands, levering himself up. His head was at the lip of the ledge and Krish raised his god a third time, closed his eyes and brought her down with all his force.

He heard the crunch as Edmund's nose broke and opened his eyes to see it flattened and blood pouring out of it. There was more pain than rage in the other man's eyes now, but he clung on and Krish brought the rock down seven more times, until Edmund's face had lost its shape and his hands finally loosened their grip.

The sound of his landing a hundred feet below was muted by the earth and Krish sobbed in mingled relief and horror. When he looked down he saw that Edmund's body wasn't moving and he knew that he'd killed a second time.

He dragged his eyes away and forced himself into motion, following the ledge as it wound to the top of the hill. He couldn't go to the village now. If word had reached this far, he couldn't risk any contact. His ma had been right: he must leave Ashanesland entirely to be safe, at least until he had soldiers of his own. And as for food, he didn't have much appetite for it after what he'd just done.

When the ledge spilled him out on to the top of the hill, he spent longer than he should looking at the corpse below. *He could have called for help*, Krish reminded himself. Edmund could have summoned the rest of the village and then Krish would have had no chance to escape, but greed had guided him. He'd been willing to sell Krish for a few gold wheels and Krish owed him no pity. Krish's prow god was still clenched in his hand and he wiped the worst of the blood from the white rock, stowed her in his pack and walked on.

14

Lahiru slipped out of Eric's bed at sunrise to return to his wife's. He pressed a kiss against Eric's cheek, a slower one to his throat, and then he was gone. The door shut behind him and Eric had only his posh clothes and soft furnishings for company. He sighed and rolled to his side, hoping for a little more sleep, but it wouldn't come.

An hour later the first servant entered. Eric had been trying his very best smile on him every day for the last seven, but couldn't tempt a return smile. The lad was as grim-faced as ever today. It was hard to enjoy his morning bath when the person soaping his back looked like he wanted to stick a knife through it. He climbed out as soon as he was clean and took the towel from the servant when he would have dried Eric. There were parts of himself he only wanted his lover to touch.

When he'd finished, a sour-faced girl brought Eric his breakfast. He didn't understand what their problem was. He didn't eat much and he'd overheard two of the grooms yesterday saying they'd never seen their lord in such a good mood. Shouldn't they be grateful to Eric for that? He knew Lahiru was smiling because of him. The soft ache in his arse and the love bruises on his neck and chest proved he'd been more than doing his duty on that front, and enjoying every moment of it too.

He wished he could take one of the gold wheels lying casually around the shipfort, as if money wasn't worth as much as his spit, and pay it to the Worshippers to pray to Lord Lust for him. They'd set him right with the Ashane god, make sure he didn't get in a dudgeon about what Eric and Lahiru did in their bed, and maybe they could put in a word with the Hunter too, who guarded all the Moon Forest folk. But the Worshippers were far away and over the mountains by now, lost to him with Smiler's Fair.

There was no point brooding about it, though. It would only give him frown lines. He slipped on his favourite green trousers and shirt, then headed out of Smallwood, across the bridge to Lahiru's gardens. He loved it here, even though it was the middle of winter and nothing was in flower. He could still see the potential for colour in the ranks of poles where, in a few months, jasmines would be twining. The trees were bare of leaves but buds had formed, waiting for their moment to burst. In the spring there would be flowers and in the summer fruit. They were still eating the dried remains of last year's crop, wonderfully sweet, especially dipped in honey. And there was grass underfoot, and quiet. Wherever Smiler's Fair went it brought the mud, but he could be happy here.

Just when he'd lost all feeling in his nose from the chill and was starting to think of going in, he heard the clatter of footsteps over the bridge and then a high, piping voice shouting his name.

'Over here, lovely!' he called.

It was Lahiru's little daughter, whose name he now knew was Liyoni, but everyone called her Yo-Yo. Someone had tied her long hair back in bunches and they flapped as she ran, the red ribbons already half undone.

'You're a little terror, ain't you?' Eric said, kneeling to redo the bows.

'I'm very naughty,' Yo-Yo agreed happily.

'So what we gonna do today, little Yo-Yo?'

'Bake a cake!'

He laughed. 'Maybe, but you ain't gonna do that with me. How about a swim?'

'Brrr!' She made an exaggerated shivering motion.

'Oh, you don't mean that.' Eric scooped her up, giggling and screaming, and ran towards the lake.

'I don't wanna swim!' she screeched.

'Bollocks! It's time for a dip, shorty!' He'd reached the water's edge now and he swung her backwards and forwards as if he really was going to throw her in.

'Stop it! Stop it!' she yelled delightedly.

'What do you think you're doing!' a much louder adult voice said behind him.

Eric spun round – almost dropping Yo-Yo into the water as she wriggled in his arms – and found himself facing Lahiru's wife, Babi. The woman looked furious. Her pretty face was flushed and her eyes snapping. Eric carefully placed Yo-Yo on the ground in front of him, partly to placate Babi and partly as a tiny shield.

'We was just playing,' he said.

'Eric says I'm a little terror!' Yo-Yo said and he couldn't help smiling down at her, though he suspected she was making it worse.

'Come here, Liyoni.' Babi held out an imperious hand. Yo-Yo stamped her foot in annoyance, then sighed and moved away from Eric to take it. 'Now go inside,' her mother said. 'It's far too cold out here for you.'

She waited while her daughter had crossed the bridge, the patter of her feet and the sighing of the wind through the bare trees the only sounds. Her silence was almost as cold as the weather and Eric felt compelled to break it. 'She's a proper little madam, ain't she? A real heartbreaker.'

Babi stared at him a long moment. He noticed for the first time the lines of tension on her face and the shadows under her eyes. He wondered if she found it as hard to sleep without her husband in her bed as he did.

'Listen to me,' she said eventually. 'I can't keep you away from Lahiru, but you stay away from my children. I don't want you speaking to them and I don't want you playing with them. Do you understand?'

And what could you reply to that? 'I understand,' Eric said.

Later that day, when he knew Lahiru was due back from his inspection of the far pastures, Eric went to his lover's room. He guessed that the morning's incident would get reported and he wanted to get his explaining in first. When he reached the door, though, it was shut and he heard voices coming from inside.

It was Babi, of course, who wasn't stupid and must have been waiting here for her husband all along. Eric checked the corridor for servants, then pressed his ear against the door.

'– absurd,' Lahiru was saying. 'Eric loves children.'

'He *is* a child!' Babi's voice was high and tight and Eric could absolutely imagine her expression, and Lahiru's too: pained and apologetic and infuriatingly stubborn.

'Hardly, my darling.'

'He's barely older than your own son, Lahiru! It's disgusting.'

'What –'

'Don't. Don't insult me by pretending I don't know exactly what you get up to when you creep out of our room at night. For the love of the gods, there isn't a person in Smallwood who doesn't know!'

And now Eric realised she was crying. It was muffled suddenly and he guessed Lahiru must have taken her into his arms, pressing her face against his broad shoulder. When he spoke, his voice was choked as well. 'I can't help myself. I've tried. But I simply . . . I love him, Babi. I do.'

When she spoke again it was from the other side of the room, as if she'd abruptly pulled away from her husband. 'You *can* help yourself, you just choose not to. You bring shame on your family – disgrace to your children if it's ever learned of beyond these waters. And for what? Because you can't control where you stick your – your – Because you refuse to control yourself!'

Eric moved away from the door. He didn't really want to hear any more. The conversation sounded like it had been going on a while and would continue for longer. The sun was near setting anyway, so he retreated to his room, asking a passing servant to have his dinner sent there.

He lay back on his bed and watched the light in the window change from orange to red and then fade to black. He didn't like the dark, so he lit all the lamps in the room. Then he took the clothes from his wardrobe and spread them on his bed. Back at the whorehouse, Madam Aeronwen had only ever given him three outfits at a time: one for relaxing, one for wearing with his current john, and the other to be in readiness for the next. Here he had a blue shirt, threaded with silver, nine pairs of trousers: five black, three grey and one a lovely grass green. He had suede boots, hats with feathers and hats without, and he had a string of pearls that looked very fine indeed with his blue and silver jacket.

And Lahiru loved him. He'd said so, hadn't he? Even though he'd said it to his wife and not to Eric, which hadn't been his most tactful moment.

Lahiru loved him and he loved Lahiru. He ran his fingers across the bruises on his chest and felt a twitch in his cock as he remembered how he got them. Lahiru set him aflame. And his lover was kind too, and clever. He was better than Eric deserved and yet he'd asked Eric to live here among his family, not caring what it did to his reputation.

Eric blinked and was surprised to feel the trickle of a tear down his cheek. He'd always known it was too good to last, hadn't he? Smiler's Fair wouldn't have gone that far and though he'd broken his bond with Madam Aeronwen he reckoned she'd take him back. The citizens of the fair tended to be forgiving that way. If Lahiru would give him a horse, he could catch up before they'd reached the great plains beyond the mountains. He realised he felt guilt about Babi crying because her husband was humiliating her and Lahiru didn't even seem to care. At least at the whorehouse Eric had only brought people pleasure.

He'd tell Lahiru he was leaving when he came to him tonight, after they'd had a tumble. He wanted one final warm memory to take away with him.

He woke up as the bed shifted beneath him, and smiled. But the smile faltered when he felt the press of cold metal against his neck, and he opened his eyes to see a stranger looking down at him. The man's face was scarred beneath his rough stubble. One eye was gone and the other looked a lot less friendly than Eric would have liked.

'Get up and keep quiet,' the man said, pressing the knife down harder to make his point.

'Gag him.' It was another voice, deeper and harsher, and Eric realised there was a second man in the room, lurking by the door.

The first man rooted around in the wardrobe until he found a pair of Eric's smalls and shoved them in his mouth. He was dragged to his feet and his hands bound, then a blindfold was tied round his head and after that he had only his ears, his nose being full of the rank smell of his kidnappers and unable to pick out anything else.

They pushed him through the corridors of the shipfort, the knife pressed against his back to keep him well-behaved. Even this late at night, Eric hoped they might pass a servant or two, but if they did, no one challenged them and no one raised the alarm. He felt the change in the air as they went outside and the swaying beneath his feet as they crossed the bridge to shore. And then the men threw him over a horse's flank, his arms and head dangling one side and his feet the other, and rode away.

It had all happened so quickly, he was still struggling to take it in when they stopped and pulled him from the horse as roughly as they'd thrown him on it. They couldn't have gone very far, a mile or two at most. He lay shivering on the hard ground and told himself that if they'd wanted him dead they'd just have stabbed him in his bed.

They left him lying there a long time while the cold seeped through his thin nightshirt and raised goosebumps all over him. He heard a rumble of conversation, then footsteps approached and the blindfold was lifted from his eyes.

He blinked up into the moonlight, seeing the silhouette of a head against it. It was only when she moved into profile that he recognised her face.

'I suppose you didn't think I had it in me,' Babi said. 'But my father's a powerful man, the lord of Whitewood. When I was a girl, he used to call Smallwood his little caravan. I borrowed his men for this evening.'

Eric tried to speak, but his own smalls were still gagging his mouth and he managed only an undignified mumble. Babi watched him struggle for a while, then reached down and removed the gag.

'I was going to leave anyway,' Eric said. 'Honest, I was. Just let me go and I'll be on my merry back to Smiler's Fair.'

'And I'm to trust you, am I?'

'I'm a trustworthy boy, and I ain't never done nothing to you.'

'Aside from corrupting my husband.'

I didn't do nothing he didn't want, Eric thought, but he didn't see much point saying it. It seemed unlikely to win her over.

She looked as if she was waiting for him to say something more, like she wanted to give him a fair hearing. After a few moments, when it became clear he wouldn't, she turned her head to the side and called out, 'Well? Don't you want to examine the merchandise?'

Another figure approached out of the darkness, but this one Eric didn't recognise. He was a tall man with a blunt nose and crafty eyes.

'Well?' Babi said again as the stranger leaned over Eric.

'Almost as pretty as you described,' the man said grudgingly. He hooked a finger inside Eric's lips and lifted them up, inspecting his teeth as Eric squirmed futilely in his bonds. 'Hmm . . . not bad. Disease?'

Babi paled. The thought obviously hadn't occurred to her. 'I don't know.'

'Easy enough to tell,' the man said. Then his fingers were at the ties of Eric's nightgown, undoing them and pulling it open. He slid gloves over his hands before picking up Eric's cock, which had shrivelled to the size of a baby carrot with cold and fear. 'Yes, he seems clean. I don't suppose you can get it up proud for me, boy, so I can see the size?'

Eric glared at him and the man laughed.

'I suppose not. Still, big enough, I'm sure. Very well then, I'll have him. One hundred and twenty gold wheels, did we agree?'

Babi shrugged. 'That will do. Just so long as you take him and he never comes back.'

'Oh, he won't be coming back from where he's going, you can be sure of that. Come then, boy. We've a long journey and we may as well get started.' He threw a heavy purse to Babi, then pulled Eric to his feet by the ropes binding his hands.

'Where are you taking me?' Eric whispered to him, too scared to be defiant. 'Why are you doing this to me?' he asked Babi.

'You know why. As for where you're going, I didn't ask. Just when I had a problem I needed to be rid of, this man appeared, hoping to catch your filthy fair as it passed by and purchase a suitable boy whore. I told him he could spare himself a further journey as we happened to have one of its finest with us. And so here we are – and there you're going. I'll tell Lahiru you ran away; it won't be hard to believe, especially with the missing money. He can return to my bed and everyone can forget this ever happened.' Her voice was brittle and too fast. Eric guessed it was a speech she'd been rehearsing.

'You're no better than me,' he muttered. 'I didn't do nothing evil. I just made him happy.'

'I know. That's what makes it so much worse. Now I think it's time for you to be leaving. I gather you have a very long way to go.'

15

After he'd finished with her, Thilak rose from Nethmi's bed to return to his. She suspected it wouldn't be empty. *That woman* would be waiting for him there.

She felt . . . numb. She'd been dreading their first night together but it hadn't been as painful as she'd expected. He'd been kind, in his way, trying to ensure she was ready when he entered her. But his caresses made her skin freeze and when he'd tried to kiss her she'd turned her head aside. After that he just got on with it. She could still feel the product of their coupling dripping out of her.

A baby might already be growing inside her. The thought horrified her more than the memory of his hands on her body and the dispassionate way he'd taken her. If she had his child it would bind her here for ever. The only hope she had was that she might prove barren and he'd be forced to set her aside.

Suddenly, the thought of spending another second in that bed, surrounded by the smell of their congress, was more than she could bear. There were no windows in her room, and he'd come to her when she'd been sleeping, but she guessed it must be the middle of the night. It didn't matter; she wouldn't be sleeping again.

It was freezing outside the bed. She slipped on her fur-lined boots and wrapped two of her blankets around herself, then took one of the lanterns from the wall to light her way. She caught her own reflection as she passed her wardrobe, hair tangled and shoulder red where Thilak had bitten her as he spent himself.

The corridors weren't entirely deserted. Thilak seemed always to be expecting trouble, and guards stood at every junction. They looked dazed with tiredness in this dead hour of the night and only watched her through bleary eyes as she walked past. She didn't pay them any mind. She was the lady of this place. They owed her their obedience and she knew that Thilak would see that she got it. His own reputation and the security of his heir were dependent on a recognition of her legitimacy.

She didn't know where she was going until she found herself walking down the narrow wooden stairs. The stench of the place brought bile to the back of her throat, and she knew that the guard here wouldn't be half asleep.

'Lady Nethmi,' he said, smiling guilelessly at her approach.

It was In Su. She clutched the blankets tighter around herself, unable to bear the thought of him seeing the mark Thilak had left on her shoulder.

'You are well, lady?' His gentle face studied her with concern.

'I'm unable to sleep,' she told him stiffly.

He nodded. 'It is hard, away from home, away from friends. It will be easier.'

She wondered suddenly if he was talking as much about himself as her. Thilak's men must come from somewhere, of course, must have homes that weren't Winter's Hammer. She hadn't thought that In Su might feel as lonely as she.

'You're probably right,' she told him. 'And I have one friend here, don't I?'

He blushed, lowered his eyes and nodded and she felt only a little shame at her manipulation. If he wasn't her friend, he was the nearest she had in this place.

'Why are you here, lady?' he asked.

'I want to talk to the prisoners.' She only realised it was true as she said it.

She thought he would deny her – he was still Thilak's man, after all – but he nodded as if her request made perfect sense. 'Jinn said you would come.'

'He did?'

'He wants to speak to you, lady. You should listen.'

'Has he been speaking with *you*?' she asked.

He hesitated, and she realised that he feared she'd drawn him into self-incrimination. She smiled to reassure him as he remained silent, shuffling from foot to foot in the filthy straw. Then he looked up and said, 'You should hear his words,' before stepping aside to let her pass.

'Is it safe?' She'd meant to question whether the prisoners might attack her, but perhaps she was also asking about the mere act of listening.

'I will be watching,' In Su said.

The cell door creaked as she opened it. It had been pitch dark inside and the two prisoners blinked at the light of her lantern when she hung it on its hook. They'd been given no seats and no beds. The boy was sitting against the wall while the mother had laid herself out on the floor, face staring blankly at the ceiling as she shivered. They looked thinner than when she'd last seen them, and she wondered if they'd been fed. The woman's eyes were dull and uninterested as they swept over her. Hopeless, she supposed.

But Jinn smiled and pushed himself to his feet. There was a clatter of metal and she realised that both he and his mother had been chained to the wall. The wide manacles looked obscene against his narrow young wrists. His cheeks were sunken and the dark shadows under his green eyes suggested he hadn't slept much, but there wasn't a hint of fear or uncertainty in his face.

'I knew you'd visit me, Lady Nethmi. You saw me preach at Smiler's Fair. You know I spoke the truth.'

Her stomach quivered with alarm. 'How could you possibly know I was there? There were – I mean there must have been – thousands who came to see you.'

'He has powers,' the woman, Vordanna, said. 'Yron gives him visions.' She rolled to a sitting position, arms clasped round her knees. Her eyes were more alert but her face was pouring with sweat despite the chill and Nethmi wondered just how sick she was.

'I guessed,' Jinn said. 'You seemed like a curious woman.'

His mother shot him a dismayed look, but Nethmi laughed

with relief. 'I see. It's all just a trick then, a way to charm coin out of the gullible.'

'I didn't say that. Yron's heir gave me the gift of understanding. I read your face when your husband brought you here, and I knew it wasn't the first time you'd seen me. Are you gonna deny it?'

She thought it safest not to answer at all. 'You call him Yron's heir,' she said instead, 'but you claimed he was King Nayan's child. You do know that King Nayan has no son, don't you? He has no children at all. His wife died years ago and he never took another. Prince Gayan, his sister's son, is to inherit the Oak Wheel, if the shiplords let him. There's already talk of a succession battle if the boy's too young when Nayan dies.' She snapped her mouth shut, suddenly aware of how much she was saying. Her words would sound like treason in the wrong ears, but there was something about Jinn that invited confidence.

'Nayan does have a son,' he said. 'He was told the boy would grow into the man who'd kill him. So he ordered his own child murdered the moment he was born.'

'Yes, I've heard that kind of story before: the self-fulfilling prophecy. It's just a cautionary tale told to children. Don't try to wriggle your way out of your destiny, you'll only wedge yourself tighter into the hole you're trying to escape.'

Jinn cocked his head, studying her. 'Why have you come to see me?'

'You tell me. You're the one with mystical powers. Or so you say.'

'The power's not mine, Lady Nethmi. I'm just a servant. But there's one coming who's greater than all of us. I reckon that's why you're here, because you *want* to believe he's out there. You want to believe there's someone who can help you. I can see you ain't happy. That's as plain as the day. And people who ain't happy, they often hope there'll be help along for them. But that's nonsense. It's foolish nonsense, because you'll just keep on believing it and keep on letting your life pass, one miserable hour at a time.'

'If you're trying to sell this lost prince to me, you need to work on your patter.' She chuckled, but it was forced.

His face remained solemn, his green eyes intense. 'You need to help yourself. Yron's heir ain't gonna come riding across that snow out there, swerving round them black rocks to your rescue. We've gotta serve *him*. And before we can do that, we've gotta get our own wagons in order.'

He slumped back, resting against the wall as if the speech had exhausted him. It was ridiculous, of course. He hadn't said anything she didn't already know. She needed to help herself? Of course she did. No one else would do it. And yet, maybe she *had* been waiting for something to happen, rather than being the one to *make* it happen.

She leaned forward, suddenly full of questions, only to see Jinn's eyes flick over her shoulder and belatedly remind her that In Su might not be the only guard outside. 'That's all I needed to hear,' she said instead, keeping her tone neutral, almost cold.

He nodded wearily, as if in response to the thanks she hadn't given him.

The next evening she returned to the library. She was displeased to find Sang Ki there, still sitting in the same chair, his rolls of fat spilling over its edges. She wondered if he ever moved.

'A fellow intellectual!' he said with apparent delight when he saw her. 'I hoped as much when I first saw you here. How marvellous. What nugget of knowledge are you seeking today?'

'Nothing in particular,' she told him.

His clever eyes watched her as she scanned the shelves. She looked at the scrolls from the Fourteen Tribes first, unrolling some to read. But the text was incomprehensible and the few pictures she found pedestrian and dull: an illustration of the workings of a crossbow, pictures of the leaves of a selection of flowers, a diagram showing how iron ore was smelted.

She put the scroll back and heard Sang Ki clearing his throat behind her. 'A scholar too, I see. I had no idea you could read the tongue of my mother's people.'

'I can't.' She didn't bother to turn and see his smirk. The next shelf along contained books in teetering piles. When she opened them she saw that they were marked with a series of lines, horizontal and vertical, broader at the tip, like no letters she knew. She assumed it must be writing but it wasn't a language she'd ever seen before. She put them back and moved on.

The next shelf held more familiar books, their names written on their spines.

'My father's collection is impressive, is it not?' Sang Ki said. 'It was the work of a lifetime. Several of them, in fact. He inherited it from his father, who had it from his. I imagine your own father's library was not as extensive, being a second son as he was.'

Nethmi turned to face him. 'Indeed, my father inherited nothing. Everything he had he won for himself.'

She hoped her words would sting, but Sang Ki just smiled and touched his finger to his forehead as if acknowledging a point in a duel. She frowned and turned back to the books.

It *was* an impressive collection. She pulled out a volume called *The Histories* and found that it described the rise of Ashane the Founder from a petty warlord to ruler of his own realm in the thirty-ninth year of the new calendar. The ink was faded and the pages smelled faintly of mould, but the few illustrations were jewel-bright. She smiled to see one of them showing the legend she'd been told as a child: that Ashane had made his armsmen sit on the carrion eggs he'd stolen from the Great Nothing to keep them warm on the long journey south.

'If you're looking for information on our current monarch, you'll find the biography by Calil at the far right of the second shelf very useful.'

'Why would I be looking for that?' Nethmi asked stiffly.

'Because you've been speaking to our guests down in the prison, of course.' She couldn't control her guilty start and Sang Ki laughed. 'My father's soldiers are very loyal, Lady Nethmi. But even if they hadn't told me, I could have guessed. Our prisoners are just too wonderfully fascinating. And now you want to know if anything that remarkable boy told you is true.'

She turned away from the bookshelf and took the armchair opposite him. It was too large for her, leaving her feet dangling above the floor and her body sunk into its cushions. They looked an absurd pair, she felt sure: she so small she was swallowed by her chair and he appearing to be in the process of absorbing his. 'So,' she said. 'Is what Jinn told me true?'

'That King Nayan has a lost son?'

She nodded.

'As a matter of fact, it is.' He grinned at her surprised expression, his brown eyes bright with pleasure. 'It's a rather lurid tale. Would you like to hear it?'

In that moment she almost liked him. It occurred to her that if they'd met in other circumstances, they might have been friends. 'Please,' she said. 'The more lurid the better.'

'Very well, then. A long time ago, in the year 323, when I was barely walking and you were but a young girl, a mage came to see our King, as mages are wont to do in such tales. She'd travelled all the way from Mirror Town, through the Silent Sands, across the Rune Waste and over the mountains to reach us. And do you know why she came?'

'If I knew, I wouldn't have asked you to tell me the story.'

He laughed. 'She had a prophesy for our King, you see. She told him his wife would soon be with child, and that the child would grow into a great man.'

'He was a king's heir. Of course he'd be a great man. He'd be a king.'

'You have uncovered the very kernel of the matter. King Nayan thought little of the prophecy, but it was only the first. One by one, all the truthtellers of the realm came to him. They'd been sent dreams, they told him, god-dreams that left them pale and shaking. The dreams foretold that King Nayan's unborn son would grow into the man who'd kill him.'

'And Nayan believed them?'

Sang Ki shrugged. 'King Tanvir didn't believe the truthtellers who warned him he must wear black to conquer the Black Heights, and he died in the mountains your father eventually won for the

Oak Wheel. Is it any wonder his son gave a prophecy of his own death the benefit of the doubt? And he did travel to the Feathered Lake to check the omens for himself.'

'They agreed, I suppose?'

'It was hard to tell. Every single bird on the lake had died. They say you could smell the stench of rotting flesh for miles around. The mage was the only opposing voice. She insisted the King's son would be a god made flesh, and that he'd do wonderful things. But naturally Nayan didn't care how wonderful his son's deeds might be, if one of them included killing him. So he locked his wife up and gave his most loyal carrion riders orders to kill the child the instant it popped out. The queen, of course, was less than keen on this plan. She cut the child out of her own body a month before it was due to be born, and sent it away from Ashfall clasped in the trunk of a flying mammoth.'

'A flying mammoth? And this is a tale I'm supposed to believe?'

'Well, it may have grown in the telling. But it's certainly true that Nayan put it about that his son was dead. He must have suspected the infant had survived, though. He sent out troops and spies to look for the baby, in his own lands and elsewhere, but the child was never found. And that, it seemed, was that. Except that certain people, our prisoners among them, built up a little legend around the boy. The lost prince, Yron's heir: a very convenient object for veneration, as he was never likely to be found or to tell his followers what he wanted them to do. The best kind of deity, I imagine – a god who leaves one entirely alone.'

It seemed extraordinary to Nethmi that King Nayan could have fathered a child she'd never heard of, and not only fathered him but condemned him to die. Why hadn't her own father told her? He must have known. But she supposed by the time she was old enough to be told, the boy must have been presumed dead. Except . . . there was something about the smug expression on Sang Ki's face. 'He's been found, hasn't he?'

'He has indeed. Less than a month past in a tiny village in the White Heights, not terribly far from here.'

'But Jinn didn't mention that,' Nethmi said slowly. 'He doesn't know.'

'Interesting, isn't it, that our little preacher should be ignorant of perhaps the most important fact about his god?'

So Jinn was a charlatan. Of course he was a charlatan. But Nethmi still felt a tug of doubt. She remembered the boy's bright green eyes, and the compassionate way he'd looked at her. She *wanted* to believe him. Because if he was right, there was some hope for her.

'Your fate is bound up with his,' Sang Ki said mockingly. He'd made his voice high and melodic, an almost perfect imitation of Jinn's. 'Yron's heir is your destiny. Don't look so surprised, he told me exactly the same thing. No doubt he tells everyone. But our lost prince is currently being pursued by half King Nayan's army and will shortly be hanging from a gallows for the crows to eat. If I were you, I'd make very certain that your fate *isn't* bound up with his.'

Later that night, she woke to a light tapping on her bedroom door. At first she thought it must be Thilak claiming his conjugal privileges. But of course her husband would never be so tentative. The knock came again and before she could answer it, the door swung open and a small shadow slipped inside. Some instinct stopped her calling out and instead she fumbled for a flint and struck a light in the wick of her bedside lamp.

It was Jinn. It troubled her that she'd known it would be. As he shut the door carefully behind him she sat up, clutching the bedclothes round her.

'I'm sorry,' he said. 'I wouldn't normally enter a lady's bedchamber without permission.'

It was so absurd she couldn't help laughing, but the laughter quickly withered in her throat as she rose from the bed. 'What are you doing here? How did you get out?'

'In Su freed me. I told him that's what you would have wanted.'

His brazenness almost surprised another laugh from her, but she kept her face stern as she said, 'You were wrong. Now I suggest you leave before anyone realises you're gone or before I come to my senses and raise the alarm. And you'd best take your mother with you. Where is she?'

'Waiting with In Su by the door.'

'Then use it and get out.'

'I wish we could, Lady Nethmi. We've found the entrance to your husband's private dock, but it's locked and I don't have the key. Nor does In Su.'

'Neither do I –' she started. Then a memory of her wedding returned to her. *I give you the keys to my home as I give you the keys to my heart.* Jinn knew that, of course he did – that's why he'd come to her. That was probably why he'd said all those things he said to her.

She distrusted the helpless look he gave her. 'Please, we need your help. You were meant to help us. I've seen it.'

'Really? And how clear are your visions? How clear *can* they be, if you didn't even see that this lost prince of yours has finally been found?'

She enjoyed the expression of unfeigned shock on his face. There was a long pause before he asked, 'Who found him, Lady Nethmi?'

'I don't know, but Sang Ki assures me the King's men are on his trail. Shouldn't *you* know? I would have thought you'd be the first person Yron's heir would contact, as you're such an admirer of his.'

'I don't know why I didn't know. Maybe you were *meant* to be the one to give me the news. I told you: your fate is bound with his.'

'Really? The way that Sang Ki's is?'

She expected at least a flicker of guilt, but he was calm again, certainty restored. 'Both of you. When they locked me and Mamma up, I knew there had to be a reason for it. Please. If he's been found I *have* to go to him. He needs me and I need you.'

'No, I can't risk it. And I don't trust you. How can I? You're sentenced to death. You'd say whatever it took to escape.'

'You're wrong.' He reached out to clasp her hands, his own fingers warm and a little damp against hers. They froze that way for a moment, then jumped apart as a loud knock rattled the door on its hinges. There was no hesitation this time; this was someone who knew he had the right to enter.

'Under the bed!' Nethmi hissed. 'Don't argue – it's my husband.'

Jinn obeyed her, but his legs were still visible as Thilak entered.

'My lord,' she said loudly, and caught his eyes before he could look downward while Jinn wriggled out of sight.

Thilak was wearing a fur-trimmed gown and, as he strode towards her, the fabric parted and she saw his naked legs beneath. To her disgust, his member already stood proud, tenting the material. She knew why he'd come. If she listened very closely, she could hear Jinn's soft breathing from beneath the bed. The thought of having congress with Thilak while he lay below them horrified her. Worse, it humiliated her. She couldn't bear the boy to know how her husband used her.

She took a step back and reached out her hand, pushing against Thilak's broad chest to hold him back. 'I'm . . . I'm unwell tonight, my lord. I fear I cannot fulfil my duty.'

He frowned, not pushing forward but not pulling back either. His weight rested against her hand, a reminder of his strength and power. 'You look well enough. What's wrong with you?'

'My chest is tight. I think I may have a fever coming on.'

He put a hand against her forehead. 'You feel cool to me.'

'My lord, I'm afraid I might infect you with an ague. Surely you can wait? There will be other nights.'

'Few enough when you're fertile. I don't want this process to go on for ever. I'm sure you don't either.'

She stepped back again, but the wall stopped her and there was nowhere further to retreat to. They stared at each other in silence for a moment.

'Can't you allow me one night to myself?' she said. 'Will you really force yourself on me?'

Even in the low light she could see his expression darken. 'A man does not need to force himself on his wife. A wife is always willing to fulfil her duty, and I thought you understood yours.'

He stepped forward, reaching for her. She couldn't endure the thought of him touching her, not with Jinn listening – not at all – and she lashed out without thinking. She was shorter and far weaker than he, but he wasn't expecting it and when she hit his chest to push him back he tangled himself in his own feet and fell backwards against her wardrobe.

The thud as his head hit the wood sounded wrong: too wet. She expected him to yell in anger and leap to his feet to beat her, but he only whimpered and collapsed to the floor. She stood frozen a moment, shocked. Then she sank to her knees beside him.

His eyes were open but he seemed unable to focus on her. He was shivering, and when she brushed the dark shadow pooling around him she realised it was blood. She didn't want to touch him, but she made herself lift his head. The back of his skull was too soft beneath her fingers. She could feel the indentation where he'd struck a corner of the wardrobe. He groaned and she dropped him, too quickly.

When his head hit the floor his eyes flickered with life, then focused on her, full of rage. 'You whore!' he said and pressed his hands against the stone to push himself up.

She thought, very clearly: *I've hurt him and made a fool of him and he'll never forgive me. He'll probably kill me.*

He was still weak. Even the light weight of her body, kneeling on his chest, was enough to hold him down. His hands scrabbled at her, trying to push her off, but he was clumsy and couldn't seem to get any purchase. Then he bucked beneath her and she knew that his strength was returning.

She pressed her forearm against his throat, gently at first and then with more and more force as he fought against her. His mouth worked but he could only croak as blood dribbled from his lips. The body trapped under hers spasmed. His face was reddening and a tiny vessel burst in his left eye.

She hadn't realised it would be so easy to kill someone. Her father must have killed a hundred men in his life. Had it been the same for him? She felt connected to him now, as if this act could bridge all the years between them and the gulf of death. He'd be proud of her, she was sure. He'd given her a sword; he wanted her to fight.

And she was winning. Thilak knew that too, and he was terrified. There was no pretence about him now, no charm masking the calculation beneath. In this moment he was entirely honest. As his body twisted beneath her she experienced a surge of warmth towards him. He seemed so vulnerable now. He was just a man, not much different from her, and her hatred gave way to a profound sympathy. She'd feared his strength, but look how weak he was. Weaker than she'd ever been. His mouth moved again, only a little now. Most of his strength was gone. She watched his lips and thought that he was saying 'please'.

'I'm sorry,' she whispered. 'I'm sorry.'

His eyes were wild, flickering here and there. He was probably looking for help, but none would come. Why would his men interrupt him at his pleasure? The skin of his throat was warm beneath her arm. It felt oddly intimate – far more intimate than their coupling.

She watched as his eyes drifted shut and his body shuddered and then stilled. The heart beneath her knee pounded once, very hard, and then no more. She sat back and looked down at him, experiencing a strange kind of peace. Was this how her father had felt in his moments of victory?

There was a clattering from the far side of the room as Jinn crawled from beneath the bed. He stared at her and the corpse beneath her for a moment and she realised that she'd murdered a man in front of a young boy. She'd wanted to spare him the knowledge of their congress and had shown him something far worse instead.

Jinn's normally expressive face was blank. Then he nodded once, sharply, in confirmation of something she didn't know. 'Well,' he said. 'I guess you're gonna *have* to help us now.'

16

They were closing in on him. Yesterday Krish had seen them, crawling up the mountain behind him. Today he'd found a region of undulating hills covered in vegetation that looked like grass from a distance but up close revealed itself to be a sort of soggy moss. His pursuers were hidden behind the green hillocks, but he knew they were still there and there was nowhere to run in this empty landscape.

The moss wasn't edible. He'd already tried and vomited it back up a few minutes later. He wasn't sure when he'd last eaten real food. Had he caught that rabbit two days ago, or three? Occasionally, the smooth surface of the moss was broken by a scrawny plant with narrow yellow leaves and seed pods as hard as metal. He'd found, when he pulled one from the ground, that its root was bulbous and white. He thought that boiling might make them edible, but he couldn't light a fire, not here in the open where it would reveal his position for miles in every direction. Only water wasn't a problem. It fell from the sky almost constantly, sometimes as a chilling drizzle and more often as snow. His lungs were filling with liquid too. He'd begun to avoid sleep, afraid he wouldn't wake. The image of the man he'd killed hovered on the borders of his dreams, the orange hair and the red bloody mess of his face beneath it.

Krish's thoughts were the only thing that warmed him. He'd had a lot of time to consider what it meant to be the King's son. His ma was right: it meant he was the King's heir, whether his da wanted him or not. He'd thought that in time he might inherit a tent and a herd of goats, but he was due far more than that: the whole of Ashanesland. And King Nayan had enemies, his mother had said. Once Krish was away from his pursuers, he'd find his father's enemies and they'd help him take the Oak Wheel so he could be a friend to them. He wouldn't be caught; he wouldn't die now. He had a plan for his future.

At first, the buildings looked like nothing more than a tumble of boulders, humped beneath the moss. It was only as he drew closer that he saw angles where nature would have made only curves and the glint of what might have been metal. Where the moss had been scraped from the ground there was a layer of black ash, as if the whole area had once been consumed by fire. And there were footprints in the ash. People had been here within the last day. He wondered where they were now – if hidden eyes watched him from behind the black and green hills.

His own villagers would have told him to avoid the place. *Ill-omened,* they would have said. *Never trust a place that never moves.*

The shape of the ruins became clearer as he drew closer. He'd thought it just one tumbled-down building, but now he could see the remains of at least a dozen. Most were little more than huts. The blocks of rock had fallen apart into ragged piles and ash had blown into the gaps. There'd be no shelter there. But further away was a much larger structure: a dome at least twenty paces high and fifty across, which seemed almost entirely intact. It looked like a miniature model of the hills that surrounded it.

He found himself reluctant to draw closer. The stillness and silence felt suddenly threatening. There seemed to be a presence in the ruins, something waiting with the patience of a hunter for him to approach. He'd been told that monsters lurked where there were shadows, but he'd been told many things that weren't true. Still he hesitated, until hail began to fall around him. The sky had been white moments before but now it was a metallic grey. The hail would be followed by snow and probably a storm. He shifted his pack on his aching shoulders and headed for the dome, head bowed to keep the hailstones from his face.

He'd been right. The dome was perfectly preserved, not a single break visible across it – and no entrance either. The ground was treacherous, with rocks and roots hidden beneath the moss.

He twisted his ankle twice and fell painfully on already bruised knees as he circled the structure, searching for a way in.

He found it at the back, in the lee of the hill behind. Here the structure had been sheltered from the elements and he saw that what he had taken for rock was really metal. In the diffuse light it looked almost like water, a dull and unreflective grey. He guessed that it stretched across the entire dome and he wondered why no looters had come to rip it free. But maybe they'd been wiser than him. Maybe they'd listened to their feelings of unease about this place and left.

The doorway was very clear, a yawning black emptiness in the grey. Daylight penetrated only a few feet into the darkness within and Krish realised he'd need to build a fire to see his way. There was a little dry, scrubby vegetation against the metal and he wearily stooped to pile it inside the doorway. His flint was buried at the bottom of his pack, unused since he'd started his flight. His numb fingers fumbled for several moments before he was able to strike a spark and coax his kindling to ignite.

He knew the fire wouldn't last long, but he couldn't resist the lure of the heat. He crouched beside the flames, warming his fingers back to life and filling his lungs with air that didn't feel as if it would freeze them solid. It was tempting to stay where he was, to curl up and sleep beside the flames, but after a while he made himself stand and fashion a crude torch from rags wrapped round the thickest branch he could find. He held it aloft as he headed deeper into the building.

The floor was perfectly smooth beneath his feet. It was rock rather than metal, patterned with unknown symbols. They seemed to be part of the rock itself, swirls of sparkling crystal or ebony against the pale marble. Their meaning nagged at the edge of his consciousness. His mind strained to understand them but no sense emerged.

He'd expected the building to be empty, yet it was clear that someone had been living here very recently. There was a long wooden table to his left. The flowers in the vase at the table's centre were wilting but not yet dead. They couldn't be much more than a week old. He could smell the sweet decay of them even from this distance, and his stomach clenched with fear as he took a step back towards the doorway. But if he ran from here there was nowhere else to shelter. And the people had gone – they seemed to have fled in a hurry. Perhaps they were as afraid of his pursuers as he was.

He squared his shoulders and walked on, only to jerk to a halt as something else loomed out of the shadows. It was a vast statue of a man, its head lost in the darkness. When Krish brought the torch down to study its feet he saw toes that were long, their nails clawed. Scales had been carved in its marble legs but it was impossible to tell if they were meant to represent armour or something else.

It was as he studied the statue that he heard the sound. He took it for wind, until he realised that it was coming from deeper inside, where no gust of air could stir. Something was breathing, but it wasn't a healthy sound. It occurred to him that whatever was making it might have heard him and thought the same of his own wheezing inhalations. He held his breath and stilled but the sound continued. He should run back to the entrance, enjoy the last of his fire and then leave. But after a moment he took another rattling breath and walked on.

He saw the blood splashed against the marble floor before he found its source. A step further and he nearly tripped over a foot, viciously clawed as the great statue had been. Whatever lay there was no man. Krish knew he should run, but this close he could hear the pitiful whimpers of the creature and when he raised the torch and saw its face, he had to stay.

Its grey cheeks were sunken and its skin stretched tight over the misshapen skull beneath. He'd seen such a face once, an illustration in the only book Ishan owned. This was the monster in the dark, a worm man. But its eyes were bright and alive – and exactly like his own. The swollen pupils narrowed to crescents as the light drew nearer and then Krish knew that it was looking at him, and the same shock he felt at seeing his mirror image seemed to be echoed in the creature.

It made a sound that might have been speech: a high, musical murmur.

'I don't understand,' Krish said.

It spoke again, faster and more desperate, and one of its clawed hands reached towards him. The palm was smeared with red and when he studied it more closely he saw that its chest was too. A ragged tear ran across its ribs and down to its stomach. The creature stared at him unblinking and he thought he understood what it was asking.

'I don't know if I can help,' he said. 'You're . . . you're hurt bad.'

When he knelt beside it, it looked up at him with what seemed like trust in its eyes. Up close, he realised that the darkness to its left wasn't a shadow, but a crack in the floor more than three paces across. The trail of blood led from the rift, as if the creature had emerged from that absolute darkness.

His mother had packed some healing supplies for him. He dug out bandages and an ointment she'd always sworn prevented infection and began to smear it across the creature's wound. It flinched and whimpered and for a moment Krish thought it meant to rake him with its claws. Then it seemed to relax, turning its head aside as if it couldn't bear to watch. It was such a human reaction that Krish felt a swell of empathy and murmured reassurance as he bound the bandage around the creature's chest.

When he was finished he patted its shoulder awkwardly. 'My fire's at the entrance. You can join me there, if you like. I've no food, but it would do you good to be warm.' He turned back towards the doorway – and froze.

Two men were silhouetted against the flames. He couldn't see their faces, but the shape of their armour was clear, as were the outlines of their drawn swords. It could only be the King's soldiers. They were walking towards him and he knew that his torch had given him away. He doused the flame against the marble floor, then stumbled back into the darkness. There was a desperate scrabbling beside him and he guessed the creature was doing the same, dragging its injured body away as best it could.

There was no other way out. He'd circled the building; he knew that. And more soldiers were entering, at least a dozen of them, their lanterns spreading into a line as they advanced towards him. He retreated a step, then another, then found his back pressed against what he guessed must be another statue. How could he have cornered himself in a room with only one door? Maybe he deserved to die. Being a king's son was no use if you were also a fool.

The soldiers were near enough now that he could see their faces. Many seemed so tight with terror it almost made him smile. What was it they expected him to do? But as they drew closer he saw the way their eyes darted around the room and guessed it was something other than him they feared.

They advanced still further, until the light from their lanterns was licking against his feet and they'd reached the place where the creature had lain. He saw three of them gather to inspect the bloodstain on the floor and another lower his lantern to peer into the rift in the marble. 'Injured,' one of them muttered.

The attack was so sudden, two soldiers had been pulled into the rift before the others realised their danger. The second screamed as he fell and the King's men spun, swords drawn, to see a swarm of ash-skinned creatures emerging from the darkness. It was hard to judge their number. A dozen? A hundred? They bore no weapons, but their claws dripped blood as they slashed and Krish saw one sink its teeth into a soldier's neck and rip free a gobbet of flesh and all his life with it.

He wanted to run, but there was nowhere to run to. There was nothing to do but press his back against the statue and hope that neither the soldiers nor the creatures saw him. And for a few seconds, none of them did.

It couldn't last. As a soldier sliced his sword through one creature, severing its head from its spindly neck, he spun to face Krish. His startled look quickly transmuted into avarice when he saw Krish's eyes. Krish remembered the gold that had been offered for his capture. There must be a very great deal of it for the man to think of it now, surrounded by all this death.

'Come with me, boy.' His sword point poked Krish's chest. 'You'll be safer outside.'

'That's not true.' Krish kept his eyes on the soldier as the shadowy form crept up behind him. Then its hands were on his throat and the sword clattered to the marble as it clawed through his throat and blood splattered across Krish and round the soldier's thrashing body in a wide arc.

Krish stooped to pick up the sword from the floor. It was far heavier than he'd expected and he had no idea how to use it, but it made him feel a little safer. He looked to his side and saw the creature crouched on top of the man it had killed, its mouth chewing at his flank. Krish felt his gorge rising and swallowed it back. That thing had saved his life. And predators must eat their kill; it was the point of the hunt.

The soldier had been right, though. Krish would be far safer outside. The battle had slowed a little. At least half of the men were dead and little groups of the creatures had clustered to feast on their corpses. The remaining soldiers had gathered into three groups, one large and two of only a pair of men, back to back and frantically fighting off the monsters that swarmed around them. They wouldn't last long, but they'd hold the creatures' attention for now. Krish hefted the blade in his hand, then regretfully dropped it. It was better if he didn't seem like a threat. He took a last look at the battle, turned his back on it and ran towards the distant door.

He made it halfway before the first creature appeared, its claws extended and teeth glittering in a wide grin.

He slowed but didn't stop, hands held in front of him to ward it off. 'Please. I helped your friend. I just want to get out.'

He didn't know if it could understand him. Its head cocked and its claws retracted and then re-emerged as it flexed the muscles in its forearms. It looked at him for a long moment, then stepped back into the darkness.

He gasped in a half-sob of relief and ran on. No more creatures appeared and the only soldier he passed was dead, body twisted and half-eaten on the floor. Then Krish was at the door, where he turned for one last look at the room. One of the creatures peered back at him. He thought it might regret letting him go, but its next step took it into the weak daylight radiating from the doorway and it hissed and turned back. Where its foot had been it left behind a black footprint and a wisp of steam.

Sunlight hurts them, Krish realised. *The old tales were right all along.*

But sunlight wouldn't drive back the soldiers and he could hear that some were still alive. Voices yelled in terror and there was the screech of iron against rock as a blade must have missed its mark. He half expected more of the soldiers to be waiting outside, but they'd left only their mounts, a string of sorry-looking donkeys. He used his belt knife to cut through the animals' tethers, slapping them on their rumps to send them ambling off. That should slow down any soldiers who survived.

When he was sure the others were well away, he mounted the last remaining mule and pointed its head away from the ruins and towards the setting sun. The hill was steep but his mount was built to climb it. He clung to its neck as it scrambled over the rocks, and wondered if this journey would ever end.

The donkey reached the top of the hill and Krish looked up wearily for the next rise. But there was none. Beyond the brow of the hill was only grey sky, as if he'd reached the end of the world. He kicked his mount on and then the land opened out below him, a great green plain spreading in all directions towards the horizon. Beneath the donkey's feet, a cliff led down and down and down, thousands of paces to the endless plain. He'd reached the border of Ashanesland. The King's reach ended here and freedom lay beyond.

PART II

Meetings

17

On the first day of their journey, Radek clipped a Rah slave collar round Eric's neck and then untied him. Until the moment he'd been sold, Eric had believed slavery wasn't allowed in Ashanesland. But then again, he didn't think it mattered. If he ran away, Radek would have him back. The other man had made very sure that Eric was aware of the two knives hanging at his belt and how wickedly sharp they were. Eric had no friends here and Smiler's Fair grew more and more unreachable with every mile they travelled east. He'd given up thoughts of escape many miles and days before.

Besides, Radek wasn't cruel. He wasn't kind either, just demanding and short-tempered and not a man you'd sit and laugh and have a beer with. He was a mix, Eric had realised, Ashane and part something else, maybe even the folk of the far savannah. That made Eric feel a little warmer towards him. He was a misfit too, in his own way, and the people they passed cast distrusting glances at them both.

Radek did think the day should start too bloody early, though. As far as Eric was concerned, if the sun hadn't risen it was still night. Radek had other ideas. Eric grunted as the taller man kicked him in the stomach. 'Up, boy. We'll reach the coast today and you're nowhere near ready.'

That was the other thing about Radek: he insisted on trying to educate Eric. Eric had lived sixteen happy years as ignorant as a rabbit. Now Radek was forcing him to learn about history and other lands and, worst of all, giving him lessons on how to speak proper. *Properly*, Eric corrected himself as he rolled from his sleeping mat and went to the creek to splash his face with icy water and fill the pot for their morning tea.

Radek had already pulled on his fur-trimmed robe and was sitting hunched beside their fire, feeding it logs and prodding it back to life. 'Bring that water here, boy. I'm gasping for a warm drink.'

Eric did as he was asked and then waited in silence as the water boiled. Radek dropped in the tea leaves and watched them swirl in invisible currents. They'd camped in a small clearing in a patch of woodland, its branches winter-naked and the brambles that twined round them nothing but stick and thorns. It was a mellow day, though, and Eric thought he felt the first hint of spring. There was a cluster of snow blooms under one of the trees and now he looked more closely he could see ripening buds along its limbs. The world was coming back to life.

'Well,' Radek said, 'I'll be rid of you by sunset. And you'll be rid of me, which no doubt will swell your heart.'

Eric didn't bother to deny it. 'You said the coast? Am I going on by boat, then?'

Radek laughed. 'Not quite. Now listen. I've got a very good price for you and that's because they think you're better than you are. Where you're going, you don't ever admit to being a whore, you understand me? You're a young shiplord or whatever you forest savages call it, picked especially for this great honour.'

'What great honour?'

'You'll see. And make certain you speak properly, the way I've been teaching you. And for the sake of my ancestors, don't let them know you can't read. I've shown you your letters, though the gods know it hasn't been easy with your slow wits. Find some books when you're there and practise till you can read without disgracing yourself.'

'Right,' Eric said. 'And I'm to do all this so you don't lose no money. Pardon me if I don't feel much inclined to help you.'

Radek lashed out in that horribly fast way of his, slapping Eric's face before grabbing his wooden collar to pull him close. 'I'm sure you don't feel inclined to help me, but if you've any sense at all you'll help yourself and do as I've said. Things will go much better for you if the people I'm selling you to think you're what I'm telling them you are. Understood?'

The grip on his collar was cutting off Eric's breath, so he just nodded sullenly.

'Good boy.' Radek sat back to fumble in his pack, coming out with a book in his hand, the same bloody book he'd been torturing Eric with for near on a month. He flipped halfway through and held it out. 'Now tell me, what letter is this?'

Eric had wanted to stop for lunch two hours ago, but Radek kept pressing on despite his complaints and now he saw why. He'd been smelling the sea for a while, only not realising it, and suddenly here it was, bashing itself silly against the rocks forty paces below them. There were clouds towards the horizon, a boiling mass of them that seemed to be moving closer. It didn't look like good sailing weather, but then there was no boat in sight and no way to climb down the cliffs either.

'We're a little north of where I planned,' Radek said, frowning.

Eric prodded the ground with his foot and saw a chunk of it fall away to be lost in the waves below. 'I ain't climbing down here.'

Radek tutted. 'I'm *not* climbing down here.'

'That makes two of us, then.'

Radek ignored him, turning a circle in place as he scanned the surroundings. There wasn't much to look at. This portion of Ashanesland was sparsely populated, with nothing but heather and thistles over rolling hills and the occasional wild pony cropping at it. 'This will do well enough,' Radek said. 'Get a fire started, boy. We need to send a signal so she can find us.'

Eric thought about refusing, but what was the point, now he was about to be rid of Radek for good? He looked at the restless sea and imagined travelling across it. Where would he be heading? Would they sail to the Hundred Islands where the purple sorghum grew that the mages bought and turned into bliss pills? Or he'd heard there was a place to the south of the Eternal Empire where the trees hung heavy with fruit and no one had to work, only needing to reach up to pluck their day's food. That might not be so bad.

'Stop daydreaming! I don't want to waste any more time.'

Eric sighed and went to pull up some of the nearest bushes. He tossed them in an untidy pile at Radek's feet.

'I need foliage too. That pine over there will do.'

Eric looked at the tree, a good hundred paces away. 'But that'll just make it smoke.'

'That,' Radek said with heavy patience, 'is the idea.'

It was a long trudge to the tree and back and Radek made him do it three times, but when he was done the wood and pine needles were piled as high as his head. Radek took some time striking a spark to the kindling. The fire was reluctant to take hold, crawling up the lower logs and lapping uncertainly at the pine, until finally it decided to catch and a gush of smoke poured upward.

'That should do it,' Radek said, folding his arms and standing back.

'How long till they're here?' Eric asked.

'Hard to judge.' Radek gazed along the shore, then shrugged. 'Not long, I think.'

'And are you ready to tell me where I'm going? Seeing as I'm about to get there.'

The other man looked back at him, hard eyes assessing. 'There's no harm in it, I suppose. You're going north. Far north, beyond the edge of the known world. There are . . . people there who have need of men and pay well for them.'

'Men like me?' Eric asked doubtfully.

'Close enough. Here – you won't be needing that any more.' Radek unclipped the slave collar from his neck and then turned away from him to study the coastline, his mouth back to being as tight shut as a clam.

North. Well, that was something he'd learned, he supposed. *Beyond the edge of the known world.* Outside the borders of Ashanesland and beyond the Moon Forest, then. Beyond even the Great Nothing, maybe. Smiler's Fair never travelled that way. Eric had always assumed it was just ice and wolves in the far north, but maybe there were people. There must be, or else why would Radek send him there?

'Ah, there she is!' Radek said.

Eric squinted out to sea, but there were no sails on the water from horizon to horizon.

Radek laughed and added, 'Look up.'

Eric craned his neck to follow the direction of the other man's gaze and froze. There was a black blot in the sky, heading down. He hoped it might be close already, otherwise it was frightful large. But as time passed it and it kept on winging towards them, he knew that it must be vast indeed, as big as a house. Bigger. Almost the size of Lahiru's shipfort.

He'd thought it a bird; now he saw that it was something else. There was fur on its legs and its wings looked like leather, but there seemed to be metal plated across its back and chest. As for its face – he preferred not to dwell on that. Its nose was blunt like a cat's and its mouth was horribly fanged. After he'd seen that he looked away.

He knew more of monsters than the Ashani or any other peoples of the south. The Moon Forest was full of them, or why would his folk tithe their children to the Hunter for the killing of them? He'd even seen one once, a blue-scaled lizard as tall as him peering out from between the branches of an ice oak. But he'd never seen, never heard of anything like *this*.

When it was almost upon them, the air churned with the beats of its huge wings and the overpowering smell of mouldy cinnamon washed over them. Their horses screamed and bucked against their tethers, and Eric would have liked to do the same.

'Sweet Hunter, what *is* that thing?' he yelled.

'*I am Rii.*' The voice boomed out from the creature itself, distorted by a mouth that hadn't truly been designed to form words.

The beast – Rii – hovered above them a moment longer, so that Eric was able to see the double row of teats in the matted fur of her chest. Then she landed and he had no choice but to look at the huge head with its large, pointed ears, its filthy fur and its misshapen, massively toothed mouth. It was a bat's face, he realised, expanded to a thousand times its natural size.

'You took your time,' Radek said, speaking to the creature with the same casual disdain he showed Eric.

Rii huffed out a breath that nearly blew Eric from his feet and he grabbed Radek's arm. 'You can't . . . You sold me to *that?*'

'I did not buy thee,' Rii said.

Eric dropped Radek's arm and backed away, wide-eyed with fear.

'What use have I for a morsel such as thee?'

'I . . . I don't know.' For the first time he noticed her eyes, each barely bigger than his closed fist. She was blinking at him as if she found it difficult to focus on his face. It made her seem – well, not pretty, obviously. But not quite so frightening either. 'If you didn't buy me, who did?'

'My masters. I am to carry thee to them.'

Eric swallowed, wondering what thing this monster might call its master. 'You're saying I'm supposed to ride on you.'

'There is a saddle upon me,' she said, and he saw it was true. It had been strapped to the dull grey armour on her back, tufts of greasy fur poking out around it.

'Is it safe?'

'I will not drop thee,' Rii said, which he couldn't help noticing wasn't really an answer.

'But first,' Radek said, 'my payment.'

'Thy chest is upon my back. Take it and be gone.'

Radek smiled and scrambled up her flank without fear. It reassured Eric a little that Rii didn't immediately attempt to eat him. When he climbed down again he was cradling a chest in both arms, large enough to contain at least a thousand gold wheels.

'You got me off Babi cheap,' Eric muttered.

Radek shrugged. 'We both got what we wanted. Now it's time for goodbye, young Eric. No need to look so glum. If you remember your lessons you won't find it so very awful. You can get what you want out of it too, if you're clever about it.'

Eric flinched away as Radek pinched his cheek and then the other man was striding towards his horse and Eric was left alone with Rii.

'*Thou must climb to my back if I am to carry thee,*' the monster said.

Eric nodded, his eyes still turned to watch Radek as he fastened the chest of gold behind his horse's saddle. The slave dealer dumped the bags from Eric's horse on to the ground, then drew the two nervously prancing animals along the path that led inland. Eric watched him all the way to its end, where it dipped downhill and out of sight, and Radek didn't look back at Eric once.

When he couldn't even hear the jingle of the harness any longer, Eric trudged over to the tree and the saddlebags, then turned back to face Rii. 'Can you carry these? It's just a few clothes and a bit of grub.'

'*I am strong enough,*' Rii said, and when Eric still didn't move, '*Thou must bring them to me. I am not thy beast of burden.*'

'I'm afraid of heights,' Eric told her, still unmoving.

'*Then thou wilt not enjoy this journey.*'

Eric laughed a little wildly, though he didn't really think the creature had been joking. 'Don't suppose you'd consider just letting me go, would you?'

Rii seemed to have realised that he wouldn't be moving closer. Her great leathery wings flapped and she hopped-flew nearer to him, squashing a bush and a terrified rabbit beneath her as she landed. '*I have been commanded to bring thee to my masters. I must obey.*'

Eric nodded. He hefted his bags, then gazed uncertainly at Rii's back. There was a tangle of ropes hanging from the leather saddle. He guessed that some were intended to secure her rider, but he could probably use the rest to tie on his bags.

There was no getting out of it. He really was going to climb up on this creature and she really was going to carry him over the sea to who knew where. His stomach had knotted itself with fear and he wasn't altogether sure it wouldn't empty its contents all down Rii's furry back as soon as they took off. He turned for a last look at the land he was leaving. It wasn't much, if he had to be honest – scrubby and unloved. But it was familiar, and everyone he'd ever met or cared about was on it somewhere. He'd be leaving them all behind, too.

But then again, none of them had ever done him much good, had they? Not even Lahiru. 'All right then,' he said. 'I suppose we'd better get going.'

He was forced to take handfuls of her greasy fur to climb her side. It must have been painful, but she didn't complain, and then he'd reached her armour, which, he was horrified to see, seemed to have been melded to her skin. He was glad he'd been horse-riding this last month, at least. His muscles had strengthened and it shouldn't be murder on his arse like his first few days on Radek's old nag.

'*Secure thyself,*' Rii said.

Some things Eric didn't need to be told. He fastened at least five ropes around himself, using his teeth to tighten the knots, before tying on his saddlebags. And then, before he'd had any time to prepare himself, he felt her muscles bunching beneath his thighs. With one powerful downstroke, she was airborne.

His stomach felt like it had been left behind. The air was ripe with Rii's sweet-rank smell, and the wind threatened to tear him from his seat despite the thick ropes around him. His ears were filled with a high, thin, horrible sound. When he realised it was his own scream, he snapped his mouth shut.

'*I have been told that the ascent is the most difficult,*' Rii said, her huge voice vibrating through him.

Her wings flung the air away from them and they rose towards the clouds. Once Eric's stomach had reunited with his body, it wanted very much to empty itself, but he swallowed back the spit that rose in his throat and concentrated on looking straight ahead, where there was nothing to see but blue.

After a length of time he couldn't measure, they stopped climbing and the feeling that he was about to fall to his death receded, though the air felt almost too thin to breathe. It was bitingly cold, but Radek had at least been thoughtful enough to leave him furs, and he fumbled them from his bags and clutched them round him.

The motion of Rii's flight became gentler, a bobbing up and down as if there were waves in the air to match those he could see crawling far beneath him on the sea. Looking down made him feel most peculiar, but he couldn't stop himself. When he looked back at the shoreline he spotted three black dots that he realised must be Radek and his horses. Further out there were the blue splotches of lakes and a scattered patchwork of cultivated land. It was beautiful.

It was beautiful, but he was leaving it behind. He turned his eyes away from it and watched the endless sea ahead as Rii took him north, wherever north might turn out to be.

Sunset at sea was spectacular. The perfect sphere of the sun sank through the blue of the sky to plunge into the deeper blue of the ocean. Eric expected to hear it sizzle as it struck, but apart from the *hush-hush-hush* of Rii's wings and the occasional lonely cry of a seabird, they flew in silence. He watched the red disk become a semicircle and then just a sliver, and still they didn't stop. Rii flew on through the darkness, guiding herself by the stars perhaps. He wouldn't have thought it possible, but the exhaustion that follows intense fear and the rocking motion of the flight lulled him into sleep.

He woke to the feeling of his guts being pushed up towards his throat and bit back another scream as the wind scoured his face and he realised they must be descending. The landing rattled his bones and he sat and shivered after all motion had ceased.

'Dismount,' Rii said. *'I cannot sleep with thee upon me.'*

He fumbled to undo the knotted ropes until both he and his saddlebags were free. He threw them down and then slid after, groaning as cramped muscles stretched. The moment his feet touched the ground, he was knocked to his knees by a blast of air as Rii's wings drove her upwards.

'Don't leave me here!' he shouted, but she'd already disappeared into the blackness of the night. He waited a moment longer to see if she'd return and then sighed and felt around him for kindling for a fire. The ground was rocky, though, and he found no wood, nor even grass, just a slimy sort of leaf blanketing the stone. After a while he gave up and lay down, pulling his furs round him. He was bone weary and if there was danger here, there was nothing he could do about it. He turned on his side and was asleep almost the moment he shut his eyes.

When he woke it was light and he was very cold. The furs had come unwrapped in the night and a heavy dew had settled over him. He did his best to brush it off, then pulled his heaviest coat from his pack and slipped it on.

It was lucky he hadn't tried to go exploring last night. Rii had stopped on an island, really little more than a rock. If he'd walked fifty paces to his left, he'd have tumbled down the jagged stones into the sea. Forty paces to his left, a sheer cliff would have thrown him to the same death. The rock was grey and smeared with bird shit. There was some of it on his sleeping furs and probably more on his face. He scraped a hand down his cheek. Yes, there it was, brown and foul.

He didn't fancy using seawater to wash it off. The waves looked vicious as they pounded against the shore, and who knew what lived beneath them? He used a little drinking water instead, then chewed a strip of jerky for his breakfast, standing so he didn't get any more muck on him.

There was absolutely no sign of Rii, and when he'd finished eating he could no longer ignore the gnawing worry that she'd just left him here. It wasn't as if the island had many places something that large could hide. If she was anywhere, it must be beneath the far cliffs. He walked carefully over the rocks towards them, cursing as cruelly beaked seabirds cawed and swirled and spattered more of their shit about him.

The cliff wasn't as steep as it had looked from a distance. There was something like a path down and he didn't think he had much choice but to follow it, shielding his face from the salt spray of the sea as it dashed itself against the rocks below. There were creatures here, too: massive ones. He couldn't imagine how they moved. They had no arms or legs that he could see and only the stubs of flippers on their long, grey bodies. One of them rolled on to its back and groaned as it scratched itself against the rock. Its face was quite the ugliest thing he'd ever seen, like a mammoth's only whiskery and even more squashed-up.

'*An adequate repast,*' Rii's voice said behind him.

He turned to see a brief glimpse of the giant creature suspended upside down by her feet from the roof of a deep cave. Then she dropped and spun to grab one of the grey creatures between her claws. The others barked and flung themselves into the sea, but there was no escape for the one she'd chosen. Eric saw its wrinkly head twisting from side to side in desperation until Rii sank her fangs deep into its neck. There was a horrible gurgling, slurping noise and she dropped the creature's limp body and licked the gore from her teeth.

'Ain't you gonna eat the poor bugger now you killed him?' Eric asked.

'*Thou art welcome to the meat.*' She widened her grotesque mouth in what might have been a smile. '*Only the blood pleaseth me.*'

'I ain't hungry.' Eric stared at the steaming corpse. The hook-beaked seabirds were already hovering above it, waiting for Rii to go so they could scavenge what she'd left. She was eyeing the sea, probably hoping for another of the creatures, but Eric didn't reckon there was much chance of them getting within a hundred paces of her after that little display.

'Where are you taking me?' he asked her. 'I know you don't have to tell me, but can you anyway?'

Her small, unfocused eyes studied him for a moment, then she launched herself into the air and flew back to her perch in the cave. Her claws hooked into a crack in the ceiling and she hung suspended, her wings wrapped round her like a cloak. '*I am to take thee to the servants of the sun.*'

'The sun? I suppose that don't sound too terrible.'

'*They are terrible indeed.*' She bared her fangs. '*They slaughtered my people and bound me to obey them.*'

'But what do they want with *me*?'

'*They have a purpose for thee, but it is not the true reason for thy journey.*'

'It ain't?'

She reached out one of her legs and made a gesture with her long claws that he realised was meant to summon him. He swallowed hard and thought of ignoring it, but it wasn't like he had anywhere to run if she chose to fetch him herself. His legs wobbled as he walked to stand beneath her.

'Thou needst not fear me, morsel.' As if to instantly undermine her point, she reached out with her furred leg until her claw rested against his cheek. He clenched his arse tight to make sure nothing leaked out of it, but he couldn't stop himself letting out a small whimper.

'I dreamed of thee last night. The moon fell into the sea and was quenched, but thou didst leap in after at great peril to thyself and lift it out.' She ran her claw gently down his cheek. He thought she might have meant it as a caress, but it left a trickle of blood behind.

'Right,' he said, his voice shaking. 'Two nights ago I dreamed I was performing in a play with the King's Men, only I was stark bollock naked and I'd forgotten all my lines.'

She hissed and drew back, folding her claws beneath her. *'In darker days I dreamed of the future, morsel, and such a dream is this. The moon's life rests in thy hands.'*

'The moon? The moon *god*, you mean.' Eric knew he'd heard something about that, back in Smiler's Fair. He couldn't for the life of him remember what or where. He'd left the business of gods to the Worshippers, who were better equipped to handle them.

'The moon god indeed, the enemy of those that thou art being taken to serve.'

'So you're saying I'm gonna betray the people what bought me? That don't seem sensible.'

'Sense or not, it is thy fate.'

So, a future she wouldn't elaborate on, ending in a betrayal of his unknown masters in service of a god he couldn't recall.

'I understand thy sorrow,' she said unexpectedly. *'I am taking thee away from all that thou knowest. But my dream has told me this: thou wilt return to the lands that thou hast left.'*

'When?'

Her eyes blinked shut again and her wings wrapped tighter round her. Her voice sounded slurred with sleep or drunk on blood. *'When the moon rises.'*

18

Nethmi didn't know if she was more afraid of what hid inside the cave or the men waiting outside it. The rock wall was cold and damp against her back, but it was the thought of the creatures that might emerge from it that made her shiver. Jinn and Vordanna seemed equally afraid. His teeth were chattering so hard she could hear them. The first time she'd ever seen him, he'd told her that the worm men were the moon's servants and the moon was his god, but that didn't look to be much comfort to him now.

Only In Su didn't seem to worry about the darkness in the depths of the cave. His entire attention was focused outside. His bow was in his hand, an arrow nocked, and there was a fine quiver in his arms as he held the string drawn. Five Seonu warriors had tracked them to this stony valley. Nethmi thought In Su might be able to kill two of them before they got within axe range, but *would* he? They were his tribesmen, maybe even his friends, men who had been sent to hunt them from Winter's Hammer. His face was calm but sweat beaded on his forehead.

The men outside were talking in their own language. In Su must understand them, but she couldn't. One of them looked towards the cave and she shrank back as Jinn's hand reached for hers. She took it and squeezed, probably too hard. In Su's arm was beginning to shake in earnest now. Her father had let her hold his bow once and she'd been astonished at the tension in the string. In Su wouldn't be able to keep it drawn much longer.

It was a beautiful day outside, the sky pretty with white puffs of cloud and the air filled with the twittering of birds. Spring had come as they'd made their cautious, hunted way down from the Black Heights. She'd seen her first yellow bell this morning, a flower Jinn told her grew only near the plains. She didn't want to die before she reached them.

There was a muttering to her left and for a terrible second she thought the worm men had come. But it was Vordanna. Her eyes were closed and her lips were moving. Maybe it was a prayer to her moon god, but Nethmi wished she'd stop. In the silence of the cave it seemed terribly loud.

Perhaps the moon god heard, though. The Seonu hunters took one final look at the cave, then turned their backs on it and jogged away.

'Are they really gone?' she whispered, when they were lost to sight among the rocks.

'They think we go south,' In Su whispered back as he finally released the tension in his bow. 'One says: look in the cave? But the others say they will look if he will look first and he says no. They fear the ash men.'

'So do I,' Nethmi hissed. 'This place has never seen the sun. Surely we can leave it now?'

He slid his arrow back into its quiver. 'A thousand heartbeats more.'

Her heart seemed to take a very long time to beat. She eased away from the wall and Jinn came with her. She realised she was still clasping his hand.

'The worm men don't come so quick,' he said. 'They ain't everywhere in the earth, that's what Olufemi told me.'

'Olufemi?'

He glanced at Vordanna. 'She's Mamma's particular friend, a mage out of Mirror Town. She says the worm men can sense the warm blood inside us and it draws them, but they got to make their way to us from wherever they're lurking. We'll be safe here another few hours at least.'

'You're welcome to wait here if you like.'

He grinned at her in that disarming way of his she still hadn't learned to resist, despite more than a month in his company. 'Oh,

I reckon I'll stroll outside when In Su says it's safe. Just to stretch my legs, mind.'

They couldn't risk pausing for breakfast. The hunters from Winter's Hammer had headed south, so they went north, through a disappointingly familiar landscape. Low hills merged into each other without the startling cliffs and sheer drops of the Black Heights, and if there were no fields marked out on them, in every other way they looked like Ashanesland. After crossing the spine of the world to the land of the tribes, she'd expected something more impressive.

'Are we safe here?' she asked In Su as they walked. 'You said Seonu warriors wouldn't hunt on another tribe's land.'

'Yes, on the land of the Four Together. These hills were Dae. The Dae are dead, so any may come here.'

A bush shook to their left and Nethmi felt a stab of fear, but it was just a rabbit with peculiar black-and-white stripes in its fur. It turned to watch them a moment, twitched its ears and then bounded away over the young spring grass, flashing them its tail.

They followed its path, surrounded by the soothing smell of crushed grass. The sun was high in the sky and the fear of the morning seemed far behind. Then they crested another in the sequence of dull round hills and Nethmi saw what the plains truly were.

She understood the word, of course, but she hadn't truly visualised it. They were so *flat*. Flat and empty and endless. Her father had taken her to visit her cousins at Delta's Strength once. They lived at the great mouth of the Opal River, beyond which lay the sea. She'd marvelled at the width and power of the ocean, but this was stranger still. She'd never seen a horizon so distant. She hadn't known the world was so large.

In Su seemed equally stunned. He paused beside her to stare.

'I take it *these* are the plains,' she said.

He nodded, not moving his gaze. 'Yes, lady. I think.'

'You don't know?'

'I have never left Seonu lands. I have only heard.'

'Those *are* the plains,' Jinn said. He frowned. 'We'd better hope In Su here's right that the hunters went south. A person ain't exactly hard to find out there.'

Some of the tension that had eased from her shoulders returned to them. In the moment when she'd . . . when Thilak had died, it had felt like an end. When she'd fled the shipfort she'd foolishly believed her troubles over. Why hadn't it occurred to her that they'd be followed? She'd – she had to think of it, face it – she'd murdered a shipborn lord. Of course they'd try to bring her back.

'We'll be safe on the plains,' she said, and decided to believe it. Even terror became tedious when you experienced it for too long. She began walking again, and smiled when she saw more yellow bells sprinkled through the grass.

The plains looked near but she soon realised it was because they were so vast. Once past the brow of the hill the grasslands were lost to sight again and only the sun helped to draw them westward as it set. It was staining the hills red when they found the abandoned wagon. It sat beside a small, stagnant pool, its canvas hood slashed along one side, but otherwise whole.

In Su gestured her back, drawing his axe and placing himself in front of her. They waited in tense silence, but heard only the sound of the horse cropping the ragged grass around the pool. A bird landed on its back and its flank twitched to dislodge it. In Su slowly lowered his axe, and Nethmi waited a moment longer and then walked towards the wagon.

There was no one in it. There was a little food inside, a few scattered clothes, but it had clearly been ransacked and anything of value taken. It wasn't hard to see why the thieves had left the wagon itself, which was a shabby, ill-put-together thing. The horse looked almost as decrepit, sway-backed and evil-eyed.

'What happened here?' Nethmi asked.

'Raiders,' In Su said. 'Thieves.'

'But where are the owners? They didn't kill them.' There were no bodies. There wasn't even any blood.

'It was the Brotherband,' Vordanna said unexpectedly. She

spoke little and seemed to get more ill with every day of their journey, but she nodded firmly when Nethmi looked at her. 'The Chun did this.'

'Mamma's probably right,' Jinn said. 'Last time we passed through here the Brotherband were all the folk of the plains could talk about.'

In Su was making a slow circuit of the wagon, examining the ground all around. 'Four men attacked, and two people taken. Women. There are no men's clothes here.'

'I've never heard of the Brotherband,' Nethmi admitted. 'Are they another tribe?'

'No,' In Su said. 'Not a whole tribe. Part of the Chun.'

'The Brotherband *were* Chun raiders,' Jinn agreed. 'That's how they started. Then they attacked the Dae and killed the whole lot of 'em. Now you might as well say the Brotherband *are* the Chun. Any who wouldn't follow their new way of doing business were killed alongside the Dae and the rest moved to the Rune Waste two years back. Everyone thought they'd seen the last of them. The Rune Waste ain't no place to live. It ain't even a place to visit if you value your life. But last summer the Brotherband came out stronger than ever and started raiding the Four Together. Now there's thousands of 'em and they're the scourge of the plains.'

Nethmi reached out to stroke the horse, which snorted with disdain. 'But how do you know it was the Brotherband who did this? I can't see anything they left behind apart from a few muddy footprints.'

'They took the women,' In Su said. 'No other tribe would take women and leave a horse behind.'

Jinn nodded. 'He's right. The Brotherband *hate* women, that's what people say. These poor folk that've been took, they won't be for wives, like it is with raiders from any other tribe. They'll use them like the whores of Smiler's Fair, willing or not.'

Nethmi looked again at the muddy footprints. Their outlines were as clear as if they'd just been made, and when she felt beneath the horse's harness there were no sores. In Su saw her expression and nodded. 'They're close, lady. We must go.'

'But where? Seonu hunters, Brotherband raiders. There's nowhere we can go to be safe.'

'The moon will protect us,' Jinn said. 'He meant for all this to happen, I know it.'

'He meant for me to – to kill my husband? He meant for these women to be raped?'

'Yes,' he said, but his eyes slid away to look at his mother. She was staring at the ground, her arms wrapped round herself as hard shivers racked her too-thin body.

'We go on,' In Su said with unusual decisiveness. 'Behind we know what waits. Ahead?' He shrugged.

The wagon creaked as it moved and the horse balked at the slightest obstacle. It was barely quicker than walking and certainly more conspicuous, but the wooden walls gave Nethmi the illusion of protection and of home.

The first day they journeyed across the plain they saw nothing but rabbits. In Su said that a fire was too great a risk, even in daytime. Jinn set his traps all the same, and when he started a blaze to cook the meat the tribesman stared disapprovingly but didn't try to stop him. Nethmi hadn't realised how ravenous she was until he handed her a roasted haunch. The fat scalded her fingers as it trickled through them but it didn't slow down her eating. She tore the flesh from the small bones and smiled at Jinn when she was done.

He didn't smile back. He'd barely spoken all day and he quickly disappeared with a second rabbit to take to his mother, who'd stayed wrapped up in the back of the wagon since dawn.

The next day they passed a copse of apple trees and Jinn made them halt so he could shinny up the broadest. She thought he might be looking for fruit, though it was too early in the season, but when he came down he was clutching only a narrow branch. He whittled it as he walked, his small fingers skilful. She assumed he meant to make more arrows for In Su, but gradually she recognised the figure he was carving into the wood.

'The rune of safety,' she said.

He smiled for the first time all day. 'That's right. Olufemi taught me how to shape it. She's a mage, like I said. Reckon it can't do any harm to get us a little extra help.'

'The runes don't work,' she told him.

'Of course the runes have power. Why else would the mages use them?'

'My father thought the same, back when he was fighting his campaign in the Black Heights. He thought the rune of warmth might help to keep his soldiers safe, but he wasn't a man to take anything on trust.' She smiled, remembering the way he'd held her in his arms as he'd carved the runes himself. 'He ordered knives marked with the rune of sharpness and compared them with the rest. They all cut just the same. Then he tested a storebox marked with freshness against an unmarked one and the food rotted in both. There was no difference.'

'That's because your papa made the runes. He didn't know how to put the power in them. What the mages do is different.'

'He thought that too, so he tested mage-made knives and tinderboxes and clothes against his own smith's, and the result was just the same. The runes have no power. No doubt the mages claim they do to gain a higher price for their goods.'

When he slapped her, it was such a shock she laughed, and so he slapped her again. 'You're lying! You're a liar!' He glared at her for a moment and then turned and ran until his small form was lost in the tall grass.

She looked in consternation at In Su, hoping to understand what she'd said that was so wrong.

'The moon made the runes,' the tribesman said gravely. 'You insult his god.'

'*His* god? I thought you worshipped the moon too. If he's not your god now, why did you come with us and leave your people behind?'

He looked away, a delicate red colouring his cheeks. 'You needed me, lady. You would die without me.'

★

The boy returned later in the day and slipped straight into the wagon to sit beside his mother. The next morning, neither of them emerged. Nethmi was unsure what to do, but In Su hitched the decrepit horse to the shabby wagon as if nothing was amiss, and when he led the beast on she followed.

She wasn't sure at first what she was hearing, but after a while she could no longer deny that the sound emerging from the wagon was sobs. In Su looked across at her, but why was their sorrow her problem? What did she know about crying children? She owed Jinn nothing – if it weren't for him, she'd still be safe in Winter's Hammer. In Su kept on looking at her, though, and after a while she gave in and pulled herself inside the wagon.

Jinn was turned away from her, his back hunched, round raised knees as he sat beside his mother. Her face was waxy pale and sheened with a sick sweat. It tangled her brown hair into knots and her body shivered convulsively with every breath. When Nethmi felt her forehead she expected heat and instead found icy cold. There was the residue of vomit around Vordanna's mouth and the whites of her eyes were yellow.

Nethmi touched Jinn's shoulder and his eyes met hers for a moment before flicking away. 'Get out,' he said, his voice hoarse from crying. 'I didn't invite you in.'

'I don't need your invitation. This is no more your wagon than mine.' He glared at her, but she shook her head impatiently at him. 'There's no use trying to keep secrets among us. We're bound too tightly to each other by what we've done. Tell me what's wrong with her.'

His expression was mulish and she wasn't sure her words had impressed him, but finally he said, 'It's not her fault. The Rah do like the mages, they feed their slaves bliss to keep them happy and obliging. When her master planted me inside her she still had enough will left to escape before he turned me into another slave. She couldn't escape the bliss, though. Olufemi gives us a yellow powder that makes the craving go away, but since we got taken prisoner it's all gone. Now Mamma's dying for lack of it.'

'I'm sorry.'

He shrugged. 'Ain't no point dwelling on the past.'

'I'm also sorry that I offended you yesterday. I know the moon god is important to you. What I said about the runes . . . I'm probably wrong.'

'But you ain't,' he said with sudden vehemence. 'It's all a crock. The runes have got no power, and the moon ain't nothing but a light in the sky. Everything I was ever told and everything I ever told anyone else is a lie.'

'Did you lie to me?' she asked, not sure she wanted to hear the answer.

His eyes slid away from hers to rest on his mother's pale face. 'People want to believe and I tell 'em what they want to hear.'

'But you spoke about Yron's heir, and he's real enough. He's been found, or at least the lost prince of Ashanesland has.'

'But I never knew it. I never felt it. All my life, Olufemi and Mamma told me I had some special link to him and I believed them. They played me for a cully and I didn't even see it.'

'Why would your mother deceive you?'

'The greatest liar is the one who believes his own lies. I was so sure the moon god needed me, it didn't matter what I said to get my own way. I told you things would get better because I could see your husband didn't treat you right. We needed help escaping, so I told poor In Su that the moon god wanted him to help you. Any idiot could see what stirred in him when he looked at you. I sold you both a gilded coin and now I need it to be true gold. Because if the moon god ain't real, who'll save Mamma?'

'She will not die,' In Su said and they both turned, startled, to see him standing in the entrance.

'How long . . .?' Nethmi began, but his face had always been open and it showed that he'd heard everything that mattered. 'How can she be saved?' she asked instead.

He crouched beside the sick woman, stroking her filthy hair back from her face and cupping her cheek in his palm. 'She is very sick, but Eom medicine can help. It is like bliss, but not so wicked. It will keep her well if she takes it every day.'

'The Eom?' Jinn asked. 'They don't let strangers into their lands. Not even Smiler's Fair.'

'The Spiral, north by the Moon Forest. The Eom go to trade there with the tribes and the folk. You will find the medicine there.'

'But how do you know about this?' Nethmi asked.

In Su looked down at his nails, suddenly bashful. 'Before I was called to Winter's Hammer, I wished to be a healer. My sister taught me these things.'

'We'll go to the Spiral then,' Jinn said. 'It's a good long way from Ashanesland, as safe as you can get on the plains. Maybe you can go and live in the Moon Forest among the folk and the monsters. Thank you, In Su.'

The tribesman nodded, unsmiling, and left the wagon as quietly as he'd entered it.

They turned north. Jinn stayed inside the wagon with his mother, and Nethmi walked beside In Su as he led the horse. It was strange. She'd always known that he felt more for her than her husband's guardsman should. She'd used it herself, just as Jinn had, to get what she wanted. But hearing it spoken aloud and not denied changed things. She had begun to find her eyes drawn to him, to the shape of him, in a way that made her flush. They travelled in an awkward silence.

The plains yielded little in the way of landmarks to distract them. They crossed a shallow stream, wound through a copse of willows drinking the water with their roots and crested a small rise, the only break in the flatness of the landscape. Its sides were so perfectly smooth and its top so flat she wondered if men had made it.

As the sun crested its own midday rise, she noticed something building in the west. At first she thought it was another mountain range, its top lost in clouds. But she soon realised that no mountain moved closer so quickly. And the colour, that pale yellow . . .

'It's sand,' she said to In Su. 'A cloud of sand.'

'Yes, lady. West lies the Rune Waste. I think it reaches out for us.'

She shivered, even though it was an absurd thought. 'Can we

outrun it?' But that was an absurd question. It had already crossed half the distance between them.

'We must shelter in the wagon.' He eyed it uneasily and she shared his doubts. The power required to move that much sand would surely overwhelm the half-wrecked thing. She could feel the wind reaching out for her now, stroking her cheek with rough, grit-filled fingers. The storm filled the entire sky to their left.

'Jinn!' she called, already having to shout over the howling air.

His head poked through the wagon's door, looking puzzled for a second and then horrified. 'We have to –' he began, but she never knew what he meant to say next. The horse had also seen the storm and, with an animal's blind instinct, it bolted.

Nethmi sprinted in pursuit but, old and sway-backed as it was, the horse was terrified and terror made it fast. A few more paces and she tripped and fell to her knees. As In Su hauled her upright, she realised that she could no longer see the wagon. She could barely see her own feet. She had no idea what had tripped her and if she ran on she knew she'd fall again. Besides, there was nowhere to run *to*. The sandstorm had already reached them.

The sand cut like knives. She felt it score her face before In Su threw his arms round her and pressed her cheek against his chest. The wind was too strong to resist. They ceased trying and fell to their knees, clinging to each other as the storm raged.

19

When he was a young boy, Seonu Sang Ki had still been thin enough to ride a horse. He remembered the way it had felt between his thighs, the painful jarring at the trot and the terror of a full gallop. At this moment, though, he'd have spent all the gold his father Thilak hadn't quite left him for that skittish white gelding. The hill mammoth smelled appalling, and that was the best thing about it. On even ground, it walked as if each leg was controlled by an entirely different animal. Descending the foothills of the White Heights as it now was, it seemed absolutely intent on shaking its riders from their palanquin. Sang Ki's men, to his shame, had roped his ungainly body in place, and the thick cords bit into his thighs and chafed the rolls of fat at his waist. Only the reddening sun gave him hope that this day might finally end.

Beside him, his mother seemed supremely unconcerned, sitting upright and unsmiling as if the noble blood ran in her veins and not his. This journey had been her idea. After the mourning period for Lord Thilak had ended and he'd been sent to the bottom of the lake with a ceremonial anchor roped to his foot as befitted a shipborn lord, she'd told her son that if he wanted to hold his father's lands, he must act and not wait for them to be handed to him. He must petition King Nayan in person.

Sang Ki had never surrendered to false modesty, but he couldn't help doubting his capacity to charm such a great concession out of a man who would surely rather award the shipfort and its lands to a loyal minion than promote the mixed-blood son of a savage. Still, for the cost of a few bruises it seemed a gamble worth taking. And the search for his father's murderers had led nowhere. His mother had forbidden him to join the hunt; now at least he might stumble across the trail himself. He'd schooled himself to feel few things strongly, but he burned with the desire to see Lady Nethmi brought to justice. He'd liked her, that was the problem. He'd failed to see what she truly was, for all his trust in his own judgement, and his father had died because of it.

They were only a few hours' journey now from the pass that led through the mountains, from the grasslands of the tribes to the hills and fields of the Ashane. Sang Ki had never visited his father's homeland. There had been plans, but the larger he'd grown, the harder he'd resisted making the journey. He liked his comforts – Winter's Hammer and its library had been all he wanted – but now, to keep his home it seemed he had to leave it. The air was warmer down here, the snow just a dusting like sugar on the cinnamon cakes he loved so much, and his furs were sticky with sweat.

'It will be worth it,' his mother said suddenly. She always knew what he was thinking. It had blighted his childhood.

'Oh, I'm sure it will,' Sang Ki said breezily. 'For the moment, however, my poor posterior would beg to differ.'

She didn't smile. She had little sense of humour, though his father had been able to make her laugh. Sang Ki had often wondered what his father saw in her that made him so devoted, but he'd not had the courage to ask and now he never could.

He'd wanted to bring only a few of their people with him, his closest friends among the Seonu youths of his own age and a few Ashane retainers and armsmen. Here again his mother had overruled him. She'd forbidden him all Seonu followers, though Winter's Hammer was filled with them. Thilak had long since come to trust them above his own countrymen, but San Ki's mother felt there was no need to remind the King of his foreign roots. If she'd trusted Sang Ki to handle matters, he was sure she herself would also have remained behind. Instead she'd gathered 200 Ashane armsmen and retainers from the scattered corners of their holding: a suitable retinue for the lord of one of the great shipforts.

The mountains hulked at their back but the path, such as it was, was beginning to level and broaden. It seemed they were finally approaching the pass. A few days' further riding and they'd be in Ashanesland proper. Sang Ki had heard the country was a riot of green, a garden kingdom, but he couldn't imagine it. All his life, he'd known only black rocks and white snow and, when it melted, black ash and greyish moss growing above it. Even the hill mammoths lacked the colour of their lowland kin.

He was trying to call to mind the exact text of Canut's *Bestiary of the Mountains* when he became aware of the noise ahead of him. His mother rose in the palanquin, gesturing to the leader of Sang Ki's guard, who drew his men's mammoths and mules protectively around. The sound, now Sang Ki paid attention to it, was clearly the clatter of a large group of men.

He looked a question to his mother but she shrugged and gestured on. The King's peace extended the length of the pass and there should be no enemies here. Sang Ki's heart beat fast all the same and a cold sweat soaked those few areas of his clothing still dry. He'd never cultivated courage as a virtue and it was too late to start now.

When the gulley they were following turned sharply left, the soldiers were suddenly ahead of him and there was no possible escape.

It seemed almost a small army that was gathered between the rock walls of the pass. They were Ashane; that was immediately clear. Most looked like landborn levies, unarmoured and clutching flint knives or hardwood scythes, but a few were shipfort men armed with metal. They outnumbered Sang Ki's followers by two to one and their expressions were more curious than hostile as the groups drew closer to one another.

When they were only twenty paces apart, a thin old man stepped forward from among the Ashane, a ragged carrion mount pacing beside him. Sang Ki had never seen one of the creatures in the flesh before – they couldn't thrive at the altitude of Winter's Hammer – but he'd studied enough pictures to know this was no bird in its prime. Its beady black eyes looked unlovingly at Sang Ki as he urged his own mount forward.

'Well met, fellow traveller,' Sang Ki said expansively. His mother stiffened. She understood politics but not people. One never impressed the powerful with one's humility. At least, not until after one had firmly established one's own strength.

The carrion rider raised an eyebrow, making no gesture of respect but signalling his men to no violence, either. 'Greetings, in King Nayan's name.'

Neither group moved. There was only the jingle of harness, the huffing of the horses and the strange high hoots of the mammoths. Clearly, more would be required. 'I am Seonu Sang Ki, son of Lord Thilak of Winter's Hammer, may the Five remember him kindly. And you, sir?'

The carrion rider's tension seemed little abated, but at least now he bowed. His cloak swirled behind him in blue and green waves. 'I am Gurjot, formerly of Ashfall. Our king's carrion rider once, and now his justice.'

Well, that explained the state of his bird, retired from active service. It didn't, however, explain Gurjot's presence here with a small army at his back. There had been no major conflict in Ashanesland since the Fool's War of 185, and that had been against the Eternal Empire. The kingdom had skirmished with the Seonu before their conquest but had always kept a wary peace with the rest of the Fourteen Tribes.

'Two forces of Ashane on the lonely road, the sun near setting,' Sang Ki said. 'What say we make camp and share a drink and our stories?'

For a moment it seemed Gurjot would refuse him. Then the justice bowed a little more deeply and turned to shout orders at his men.

The camp threatened to be a ramshackle and somewhat ill-humoured thing. Sang Ki's men refused to give precedence to the peasant soldiers, and the lowlanders would be cursed if they'd allow themselves to be trampled by the troops of a man who was clearly half mountain savage. In the end, Gurjot and his small group of shipfort men proved their competence and organised a neat encampment with latrines downwind and pickets all round. The vibrant young grass of the pass was soon trampled to mud beneath the boots of the conjoined forces, but here and there bright red and orange poppies dotted the ground.

Sang Ki invited the justice to share his fire, knowing that etiquette would forbid Gurjot to refuse. He'd ensured there were ample rations for his journey and the other man was offered a goblet of fine wine from the vineyards of the Five Stars and a platter of spiced lamb on a bed of spinach and blue mushrooms. The effect pleasingly mimicked Gurjot's cloak of office, but he seemed oblivious as he spooned the meat into his mouth and washed it down with a vintage that should have been savoured sip by sip.

His bird perched on the ground beside him, its half-bald head resting close to his thigh, and Gurjot's hand paused from its spooning of food to mouth only to stroke it. The carrion mount made a sound almost like a cat's purr. Its smell in no way enhanced Sang Ki's enjoyment of the meal.

'Lord Thilak has left this land, then?' Gurjot said when his rate of feeding finally slowed. 'A terrible thing to lose a father.'

'And especially to murder.'

Gurjot's expression of startlement was quickly hidden. 'Murder? Do you require my services, then? Wherever I am, there is the King's justice. So says my oath of office.'

'Would that I could use your services, sir. Alas, the culprit has not yet been caught.'

'But you know his identity?'

'*Her* identity, though she wasn't unaided. It was my father's wife, Lady Nethmi, daughter of Lord Shaan of Whitewood.'

That produced a slightly longer silence. 'Is that why you've come to the lowlands?' Gurjot asked eventually. 'On the hunt for Lady Nethmi?'

'It's one of the reasons, yes. And your reasons for crossing the pass to the grasslands? I'd heard of no threat from the Fourteen Tribes.'

'The Fourteen Tribes.' Gurjot's look said he considered Sang Ki one of their number. 'No, we have no business with them, unless they harbour our fugitive.'

'A fugitive from the King's justice?'

'Indeed,' Gurjot said.

It was a clear end to their discussion. Sang Ki could have probed for more, but he knew the way this game was played. The one who seemed most desperate to know lost power. So they talked casually of minor things: the twin sisters Nimrit and Nimrat who ruled Leviathan had fallen out over a horse. The fisherfolk had fared poorly this season at Delta's Strength but the farmers had a bumper harvest. Wanderers who traded with the Eternal Empire had brought a new spice north, so hot it burned going in and coming out. Sang Ki listened politely and only withdrew to his tent when the moon had sunk beneath the horizon.

What Sang Ki hated most about sleeping on the ground was the undignified process of getting up from it. But after a sleepless hour spent staring at the roof of his mammoth-hide tent he rolled to his side and pushed himself to his knees with a grunt of effort.

The fat of his belly slapped against the furs beneath him and he felt a familiar moment of disgust at the vast, useless lump he was forced to inhabit. Another grunt and he was on his feet and pulling his robe around him. His hair was so fine there was no need to comb it; it floated around his head in a pale cloud. His mother had often begged him to dye it dark as Seonu tradition demanded. But even with black hair no one would confuse him for a pure-blood Ashane or a pure-blood Seonu, so what was the point?

When Sang Ki pushed open the tent's flap, a chill wind greeted him and he heard the distant hooting of owls. From nearer at hand came the low murmur of voices. He soon found the source: a redly glowing campfire with a huddled group of Gurjot's men around it, most landborn and a couple of shipfort guards. Exactly the people he needed.

They didn't notice his approach from the darkness until the

stale smell of his sweat hit them. He saw a wool-swathed peasant sniff, then look around, and fought not to blush as he went to warm his hands at their fire. They didn't give him a welcome but they didn't tell him to leave either. It was a good enough start.

'You're a long way from home, friends,' Sang Ki said.

One of the men grunted, another spat. Most were sneaking looks at him. He was used to their expressions: a combination of disgust and fascination that his mother too sometimes wore. His father had been different. Lord Thilak had asked the tribe's elders for concoctions to help his son shuck off the growing layer of fat and had only frowned thoughtfully as each failed, as if the medicines and not his son were at fault for his immensity.

'And is your journey nearly at its end?' Sang Ki asked after the silence had lingered a while.

A round-faced shipfort man with an ugly scar across his cheek shrugged. 'Who knows?'

'You don't know this fugitive's location?'

'The plains,' the soldier conceded. 'There was a party close on his tail, but he killed 'em, they say. They disappeared in the Black Heights, anyhow.'

His tail. It was a little more information, a drip of it. 'And what has he done for such a force to be sent in his wake?'

There was another silence, but he sensed that this arose more from puzzlement than reluctance to speak. These men didn't know the fugitive's crime. And suddenly Sang Ki had a very good idea who they were chasing, and perhaps why Gurjot chose to play with his cards clutched close to his chest. 'So it's Yron's heir you pursue – as some villains call him – our King's ill-omened son.'

'A criminal is all we were told,' one of the landborn said. 'A wanted man.'

'And a valuable one.' The expressions that statement elicited were even more carefully blank and Sang Ki smiled. 'Fifty thousand gold wheels for his capture, or so I heard.'

The blank faces melted not into shock, as he'd expected, but chagrin, and he realised they'd already known the full sum.

Interesting. He'd expected Gurjot to lie to his hirelings and pocket the bulk of the coin himself.

'A hundred wheels for each man and a thousand for the officers with the rest for Justice Gurjot,' a peasant said.

'A great deal of coin,' Sang Ki agreed. 'But enough to lure a man away from his fields for weeks, maybe a full season? Who knows how long you'll be gone when the man you seek could be anywhere.'

'I've no fields,' a youth with a pitifully thin moustache told him. 'They went to my brother.'

'And mine,' another said and Sang Ki nodded.

'I see. Gurjot has brought an army of second sons on his quest.'

The shipfort man scowled. 'There's no shame in being a second son.'

'Indeed not,' Sang Ki said. 'Our ancestors were led to these lands by the fifth son of an emperor, or so the legend goes. Not every man is given his due – some must earn or fight for it.' He smiled at the soldiers and left them to their fire, ready for his sleeping furs at last.

He woke stiff and cold as the morning mist crept through the tent flap he'd failed to shut the night before. When he emerged, rubbing crumbs of sleep from his eyes, his mother was already up and cradling a steaming mug of tea in her hands. She jerked her head sharply when she saw him and he knew she meant for him to approach. He stooped to kiss her cheek before scooping a ladleful of tea for himself.

'You wandered last night,' she said. 'You spoke to the soldiers.'

He could ask how she knew but what was the point? 'I found out what this little gathering is all about. It's Yron's heir. They're hunting the King's prodigal son and the fifty thousand gold wheels he carries with him, in a metaphorical manner of speaking.'

'Thilak had enough gold.' There was a hitch in her voice when she said his father's name.

'I'm not interested in the gold. And neither, I think, is Gurjot. I don't believe his mission is fully sanctioned by our King, who would surely have sent either all his strength or only spies. I think Gurjot hopes to capture the fugitive himself and so win back the favour of one who long ago discarded him. And if the mission isn't official – ah, Justice Gurjot, a good morning to you.'

The old man approached their fire, looking more weary after his night's rest than he had before it.

'Your men tell me you're seeking a rich prize indeed,' Sang Ki said, handing him a mug of tea.

The other man's sagging face looked gratifyingly chagrined, but Sang Ki didn't want to leave him with the impression he was seeking coin. 'I've no need of gold, but I've a mind to help you, if help is needed,' he said. 'And given how wide the plains are, how lost your fugitive and how few your numbers, I can't see how my assistance might be unwelcome.'

'The coin's already been promised and divided between my men,' Gurjot said carefully.

'I'll make sure my men are equally recompensed from my father's coffers, so there'll be no ill-feelings when the prodigal is apprehended.'

'We could use the extra blades.' Gurjot was still studying him untrustingly. 'But you told me you were heading into Ashanesland. Why would you interrupt your journey for no reward?'

Sang Ki's mother was watching him carefully, clearly seeking the same answer. *Because I'm a fat half-breed who wants to inherit from a full Ashane lord,* he thought, *and what are the chances of that unless my reputation with the Oak Wheel is increased? Because I believe Lady Nethmi most likely fled this way and I'd give almost anything to find her? Because I've read a great deal about Yron's heir and I think it would be fascinating to meet him?*

But all he said was, 'Assisting the Oak Wheel will be reward enough.'

20

Krish didn't like the sky. There was too much of it, stretching miles towards the horizon in every direction. He'd been walking south for nearly two weeks now, and only the temperature had changed, growing a little warmer with every mile and every day. The same grass surrounded him, silver or green as the wind took it. Every so often there'd be a tree, and once or twice he'd found streams meandering aimlessly over the endless plain.

He'd had a lot of time to think about his ma's last words to him. The shipborn were constantly fighting, that's what he'd heard. There'd been the War of the Sons, he didn't know how many years ago, and the Fool's War later on. The lords seemed always to be battling each other or fighting against the Oak Wheel. There'd be people in Ashanesland who'd fight for him, like she'd said, but plenty more who'd sell him to his father the King for what it would buy them. The men of his village had done as much, and they'd known him his whole life.

Here on the plains he was safer. No one would know what his strange eyes meant, but no one would know why he was worth fighting for, either. If he wanted to raise an army, he'd need to offer them something. He could offer the tribes part of Ashanesland, but then his own people wouldn't be too happy with him, would they? And was it more important to have the warriors of the tribes or the loyalty of his own landborn?

He didn't know enough, that was the problem. When he'd wanted to understand how Snowy could have a brown kid, he'd spent a long time studying the goats and their breeding. That's what he needed to do now. He couldn't be rash. He needed to know more about King Nayan if he meant to overthrow him. He needed a plan.

Of course, it was hard to find out anything here on this vast, empty plain. And he could hardly raise an army out of thin air. His ma had seen a map once, but he never had. He didn't know where he was going except west, which the village men had always used as a word to mean far away and foreign. At least each stride took him further from the King's men and the bitter cold of the mountains. His lungs cleared a little more every day and he felt stronger.

The plains teemed with wildlife: ponies and birds and deer and small, stripey rabbits and rats bigger than the rabbits. The ponies he couldn't catch and the birds and deer he couldn't shoot, having no bow. The rats alarmed him, but he'd caught a few of the rabbits. It was probably time to inspect his traps now. He turned in a slow circle, trying to remember where he'd laid them. To the left, he thought, beyond the tree that reminded him of the one outside his old home, gnarled and near death.

But the tree wasn't the only thing he could see in that direction. There were two black smudges on the horizon he was sure hadn't been there before. As he watched they grew larger, resolving into the figures of men on horseback. He felt a cold knot of dread in his stomach. These were the first people he'd seen since he descended from the mountains and all his brave thoughts of building an army vanished. His instinct was to hide, but he knew it was pointless. The silver-green grass was only waist-high and he must be as obvious to them as they were to him. He judged that he had a little time before they reached him. He couldn't think of anything better to do with it than check his traps.

The first two were empty but the third contained a creature he didn't recognise. It was long and sinuous with a banded, bushy tail and the sharp teeth of a predator. The snare had tightened round its leg rather than its neck and it was mewling pitifully. It turned big brown eyes on Krish as he approached, pleading rather than fearful. Krish wondered if he'd worn the same expression when the village men had chained him up.

The creature's leg was a little bloody where the noose had

tightened, but Krish didn't think it was broken. He sighed and reached for it. 'Don't bite me now.'

It snarled and hissed but didn't attack as he loosened the cord and set it free. It looked at him for a moment, teeth bared, then turned and slunk into the grass, its silver fur rendering it instantly invisible.

'You're welcome,' Krish said.

He wasn't hungry anyway. It was clear now that the two horse riders were heading towards him. As they drew closer he could see that their dark red shirts were covered in fine beadwork. Their skin looked very pale against the cloth, the colour of curdled milk. These weren't the king's carrion riders. They must be of the Fourteen Tribes. That should have been reassuring, but their swords were drawn and their expressions weren't friendly. Krish had always been taught to fear the savages of the plains, who sometimes raided mountain villages.

When the men reached him they slowed their mounts. The horses were beautiful beasts, one brown with a white diamond on its forehead and the other a solid and shiny black. The men were less appealing. The first, little older than Krish, had a permanent squint that narrowed his eyes to untrusting slits beneath his turban, and the other's face was cross-hatched with thin white marks that suggested a deliberate scarring rather than the wounds of battle.

The two men circled their horses round him, one in front and one behind, never quite stopping, so that he had to keep turning if he wanted to keep one in sight. He chose to watch the older man.

That man smiled, but when he spoke it was in a language Krish didn't know.

'I'm sorry,' Krish said. 'I don't understand.'

The man spoke again, maybe repeating himself. He spoke more slowly, but it was still a nasal-sounding gibberish.

Krish just shook his head this time. He was sure his own words would be nonsense to them and he doubted they much cared what he had to say.

The tribesman's smile widened as he slid from his horse. His sword was still in his hand and as he approached Krish he swung it in lazy arcs. Behind him, Krish could hear the younger man dismounting. His shoulder blades itched but he stopped himself turning round. He remembered the thieves who'd ambushed him outside Frogsing village. He'd outwitted them, but they'd only been half-witted. And they'd threatened him with flint knives where these men carried steel.

The older man spoke again, his sneer evident even if his meaning wasn't, and the younger man laughed. He was only two paces from Krish now, close enough for Krish to see the rust-coloured stains on the sword's single edge. He made a gesture with the weapon, nodding towards the ground and then looking at Krish.

Krish shrugged, not understanding, and the man did it again, more sharply this time. Then, when Krish still looked uncomprehending, he stepped forward and struck him hard across the face before gesturing at the ground and pushing down on his shoulders.

He wants me to kneel, Krish thought, as blood dribbled from his nose to his lip. He knew he should obey. Even armed, he'd stand no chance against the tribesmen in a fight. But he'd done nothing to provoke them, just like his ma had never done anything to provoke his da. And he was a king's son. He looked the man in his eye and shook his head.

For a moment the tribesman looked surprised. Then his expression changed to anger. He stepped back a pace and raised the sword above his head, where the metal glinted in the sun and the rust-red bloodstain stood out plainly.

The man remained with his sword raised, unmoving, and Krish wondered if he was savouring the moment. But as the moment stretched, he saw the tribesman teeter – and then he saw the bloom of blood on his chest. Krish stumbled back as his attacker fell on his face to reveal the yellow-fletched arrow protruding from his back. The air was suddenly thick with the stink of shit.

The younger tribesman yelled in outrage and Krish instinctively flung himself to the ground as a sword cut through the air where his chest had been. Listening for it this time, he heard the dull thud of an arrow striking, and the second tribesman toppled to the ground.

The arrow had found his throat, not quite killing him outright. Krish watched a moment as the young man's hands clawed at the wood, trying vainly to pull it free while the blood leaked out of him. It was a pitiful sight and his whimpers drove Krish to grasp the arrow, twisting it until the tribesman shuddered and was still.

He could see the bowman now, standing fifty paces away admiring his handiwork. By the look of his planed face and pale skin he was another tribesman, but he was dressed like a man of Ashanesland in green and blue checked trousers and shirt below a leather jerkin. Krish remained still as he approached. The newcomer hadn't lowered his bow. There was an arrow nocked and it was pointed at Krish's heart.

When the tribesman reached the gnarled tree, his eyes scanned Krish and seemed to dismiss him. He released the tension in the bowstring and slipped the arrow back into his quiver. He grinned wolfishly as he moved to the older man and unsheathed a metal knife to cut the arrow from his back.

'Thank you,' Krish said. 'You saved my life.'

'Did I? Then you're welcome.' The newcomer looked at him briefly, then back down at his gory work. 'You can pay me if you want. I'm short of gold and metal would be good.' He was wobbling a little as he crouched by the corpse. A gust of wind blew past him and Krish caught the strong scent of alcohol.

'I don't have any gold or metal,' Krish said. 'I don't have anything. I'm a stranger here.'

The man had finished extracting the arrow. He braced his elbows on his knees as he studied Krish in turn. 'A stranger? I'd never have guessed. Well, you can help yourself to that one's knife.' He nodded over at the other body. 'You know what, take whatever he's got except his sword. I need that.'

Krish didn't like the idea of touching the corpse he'd helped to kill, but he'd be crazy to let anything useful in this endless wilderness go to waste. He knelt beside the young man, gingerly pulling aside his embroidered shirt to see what lay beneath. There was a metal knife far better than any Krish had ever seen in a sheath at his belt, and Krish took both. There was also a money pouch. He looked up to see what he should do with it.

'Keep it,' his rescuer said.

'Thank you. I'm Krishanjit. Just Krish, if you want.'

He didn't think the other man would answer as he stood and stretched. But after he'd pulled out a flask from beneath his jerkin and taken a long swallow, he said, 'Dae Hyo.'

'If you didn't come to help me,' Krish said, 'then why did you kill these men?'

Dae Hyo seemed to think about that for a while. Then he spat out a slimy gob that landed on the dead man's cheek and dribbled into his greying hair. 'Because this is Dae land, and they aren't Dae.'

'But I'm not Dae either.'

Krish regretted it as soon as he said it. Dae Hyo scowled at him and his hand tightened on the haft of his axe. 'I took you for a knife woman. Are you a knife woman?'

'No.'

'Want me to correct my mistake?'

Krish backed away a step. 'No!'

Dae Hyo laughed and slapped him on the back. 'You've got a woman's mercy in you, I'll grant you that. I would have let this one bleed to death slowly after what they tried to do to you.' He kicked the young man's corpse. 'Tribeless scum, poaching on other men's grass.'

The two mounts had bolted when the killing began, but they'd eased their way back until they were just beyond the tree, warily eyeing the standing men and the dead ones.

Dae Hyo approached the nearest, the black stallion. He stooped to pick some grass and then held it on his outstretched hand, humming softly. The horse snuffled the grass and Dae Hyo swung himself into the saddle while it was still chewing, grasping the mane and laughing as the creature tried to buck him off. He hummed at it again and it settled down, only prancing sideways a little in irritation.

'I tell you what, you can take the other,' Dae Hyo said to Krish, waving at the handsome brown gelding. He looked pleased with himself for his generosity and Krish smiled his thanks, though he'd never ridden a horse in his life. It was larger and much more intimidating than the mule he'd been forced to abandon in the mountains when it couldn't climb down the cliff.

'Well,' Dae Hyo said, 'try not to get killed.' Then he tightened his knees on the black stallion's sides, shook its reins and took off towards the horizon at a trot.

'Wait!' Krish shouted, but Dae Hyo either didn't hear or chose to ignore him.

The only person he'd spoken to in a month – the only man who'd actually helped him – was disappearing into the distance. An army had to start somewhere, didn't it? Even with someone as unfriendly as Dae Hyo. Krish considered running after him, but the horse was already a hundred paces away and he knew he'd never catch it.

He eyed the brown gelding instead, which was cropping the grass around the corpse of the man who'd once ridden it. At least it was smaller than the stallion, and the crooked white diamond on its forehead gave its face a cheerful cast. Krish stooped to pluck some grass and held it out on his palm towards the animal, trying to imitate Dae Hyo's low humming.

The horse raised its head, blinked its soft eyes, then returned to the grass at its feet. Krish dropped his own handful but took another step nearer, still humming. The gelding remained placidly eating, clearly not afraid of him, and why should it be? Only the rabbits had reason to fear him. Another pace and he was close enough to rest a hand against the animal's withers. The skin beneath his hand shuddered a little and then stilled. Up close, he could see the size of the horse's teeth and the heavy muscles in its legs and flanks.

'Right,' he said. 'Right.' There was nothing left for it but to mount. Dae Hyo had made it seem easy, but then Dae Hyo had shot two men at fifty paces while falling-down drunk. Krish looked around for a stone to boost himself, but of course there was nothing but earth and grass for miles in every direction. There was only the single, stunted tree.

He took the horse's reins in his hand and gently tugged until it raised its head. It blinked when its eyes met Krish's, as if their oddness surprised the gelding as much as it did most people. Krish stroked the horse's cheek and pulled on the reins, leading it towards the tree.

The tree was harder to climb than Krish had expected, but at least it had rained yesterday; the ground was soft and the grass would probably stop him breaking anything when the gelding bucked him off. He slid his legs forward until both hung from one side of the branch and then dropped.

The horse raised its head to peer back over its shoulder for a minute before dropping it again to the grass. Krish laughed. 'Not that different from a donkey, are you?' He gently kicked his legs against its sides. It whickered and began to walk in the same direction as Dae Hyo, who was now little more than a speck on the horizon.

By the time Krish caught up with the tribesman, the day was nearly over and the clouds were smeared with pink and orange. Dae Hyo must have heard him coming, but he didn't look round as Krish's gelding trotted up beside the taller stallion. The two animals breathed into each other's noses and then walked companionably side by side.

'I don't know anyone here. I don't even know where here is,' Krish said.

Dae Hyo grunted.

'But I can cook and catch rabbits and four eyes are better than two, aren't they?'

The other man didn't bother to respond to that at all. He was sitting low in his saddle, his back slouched and his head nodding towards his chest. His eyes, which had seemed a little hazy before, were now visibly bloodshot. Krish wondered if he'd found more drink in the dead man's saddlebags.

They were heading almost directly towards the setting sun. When Krish looked behind him he saw their long shadows stretching over the grass, giants where they were mere men. He wondered if Dae Hyo would ride through the night. He'd become accustomed to the gelding's rolling gait by now, but his buttocks felt like one large bruise and the muscles in his thighs were so tight he wasn't sure he'd be able to walk once he dismounted. His chest was tightening too, fatigue letting the illness regain its hold on his body.

After his third hacking cough, Dae Hyo turned to look at him. 'Are you dying, boy?'

Krish shook his head. 'I'd like to rest, though.'

'Nothing's stopping you.'

He didn't complain again and they rode on as the sun touched and then sank beneath the horizon. The sharp sounds of day faded and the murmurings of twilight replaced them. Finally, when Krish thought they really were going to travel all night, Dae Hyo pulled his stallion to a stop. He slid from the saddle with the same grace with which he'd mounted and bent to tie a hobble round the animal's front legs.

Krish groaned as he dropped from his own saddle. His legs buckled and he sprawled on the ground, not sure he was capable of rising. His calves were knotted with cramp and it was very tempting to close his eyes and fall asleep where he lay. He looked at the stars above him and the sliver of moon in their midst.

Dae Hyo paid him no mind, somehow finding enough wood to build a fire and a few rocks to contain it. He whistled tunefully while he scavenged.

When Krish felt his eyelids drooping, he made himself sit up. 'Can I help?'

Dae Hyo grunted again, which Krish took to mean no. There wasn't much he could do, anyway. It was too dark to lay his snares and he didn't have Dae Hyo's skill with camp-making. He had some food though, a few strips of rabbit he'd smoked over the fire. He pulled them from his pack and passed all but one of them to Dae Hyo. He stared at the meat as if Krish had handed him one of his own turds.

'It's rabbit,' Krish said. 'It's good.' He took a bite of his own and chewed, trying to look like he was enjoying the tough stuff.

Dae Hyo watched him until he swallowed and then took a careful bite of the meat. When he'd finished the first mouthful he nodded and gobbled the rest, polishing it off before Krish had finished his single strip. He wiped his hands clean on his trousers, took two deep gulps from his hip flask and then wrapped a grubby blanket round himself, turned his back on the fire and closed his eyes. A few seconds later he was snoring.

Krish pulled his own blanket from his pack and then lay on the opposite side of the fire. The wind sweeping from the mountains was icy, the air smelled of horseshit and wild mint and he could hear the screams of hunting cats from somewhere in the night. Even so, exhaustion quickly overcame his unease and he drifted into sleep, wondering if Dae Hyo would be there when he woke.

21

They were lost. Nethmi knew it and In Su must too, though he denied it every time she said the words. The walls of the ravine were sheer on either side, but not solid. In Su had made several attempts to climb them, and each time had fallen to the ground in an avalanche of loose sand. Only a thin strip of sky showed above, a cheerful and cloudless blue. It forked ahead as they came to yet another junction. Left, right, it made no difference – the maze seemed endless.

They'd drunk the last of their water that morning. There was none here. There was nothing but the sand.

The storm had brought them to this place. It seemed right to think of it that way. It was as if the storm had wanted to strand them here, or as if the Rune Waste itself had sent out its sands on the wind to draw them in. They'd survived the initial, monstrous blast huddled together on the ground. The sand had nearly covered them but when the winds had eased they'd been able to pull themselves clear of it.

The air had remained choked with dust, though, and the sky hidden. The ground was yellow in every direction and the wagon utterly gone. Nethmi hoped the horse had taken Jinn and Vordanna to safety. Its animal panic might have been wiser than their human hesitancy. She and In Su had no choice then but to move on. They'd both feared the storm would return and headed off in the direction they guessed was north.

They'd been deceived. With sand dunes everywhere, they'd barely noticed as the sloping mounds on either side grew taller until they were sheer cliffs. One ravine had led to another and then another, and by the time the sky had finally cleared it was too late. They'd been heading west, not north, and they'd entered the true Rune Waste.

Perhaps it was what she deserved. She'd done her best not to think about her killing of Thilak in the weeks since, but she couldn't escape the fact of it. And she'd begun to think of In Su . . . She'd begun to have thoughts no widow should, especially about a mountain savage. When they'd huddled together against the storm she'd been more conscious of his lean arms round her than of the howling of the wind. In Su told her the tribes believed the Rune Waste judged those who entered it. She thought she might believe it too.

The day wore on as they kept walking but travelled nowhere. At midday, the sun finally showed itself in the narrow strip of sky. The heat of it beat down at her and she knew she needed to rest. The sand had worked its way into her throat and with no water to wash it away it was a constant torment.

'Stop,' she croaked.

In Su turned to look at her. His gentle face was scored with scratch marks from his fall and she fought the urge to soothe them with her touch. 'We must go on, lady. We must get out.'

She shook her head. 'There is no way out, and we'll die quicker if we walk in the sun. Here –' she began to dig out a hollow in the soft sand of the walls '– this will shelter us.'

He bowed his head and moved to dig beside her. He never argued with her for long. When they finished digging and huddled together in the cool hollow, she looked at him and wondered.

He didn't catch her eye – he seldom did – but she often felt his regard on her. And now he was holding himself stiffly against her, a light flush in his cheeks. She was intensely aware of his breathing, the way it shifted his body against hers with every inhalation. Was he drawn to her in the same way she was drawn to him? Jinn had seemed to think he was. If she asked him, he might lie with her. If there was no hope left, where was the harm in doing what she wanted? She wondered if she might enjoy it.

Not now, though. She was sticky with sweat and itchy from the sand that had stuck to it. In Su was no better. He'd shed his furs when they descended the mountains, but his wool jerkin and trousers were still far too hot and his hair hung greasy around his face. She stared at it, noticing for the first time that its colour was changing, blond roots showing through the black.

'You dye your hair,' she said, reaching out to rub one of the locks between her fingers. 'I didn't know the tribes did that.'

He held very still as she touched him, only breathing out when she drew her hand back. 'Not all tribes. Just Seonu. It is shameful for the pale hair to show. I'm sorry.'

'Just the Seonu? I thought all the tribes were the same.'

'No, lady, the tribes are different. That is why we are tribes and not one people like the Ashane.'

'But you all came here together, didn't you? I read it in . . . in Lord Thilak's library.'

'Yes, true. We came because the tribes made war. We were not free in the old land, in Mazdan. Strangers ruled us, but they could not stop the war. The emperor, he ordered peace and even his word wasn't followed.' He trailed into silence, looking suddenly bashful. 'You want to know this, lady?'

She smiled at him. 'I do. I'm in the land of the tribes now. I need to understand them. And besides, it passes the time.'

He smiled tentatively back. 'Good, then. So our story is, the emperor killed all the men who made war – every man of the tribe and every boy who'd lived more than five years. Then he gave the women of the fourteen tribes fourteen ships. He told them they must leave Mazdan in exile and taught them how to sail across the wide sea. But the emperor was clever. He taught the women of each tribe a different secret: one how to fish in the salt sea, one how to sail with the wind, one how to find their way by the stars. He made the tribes need each other so they must cross the ocean together. When we came to this land, the women chose to keep their secrets. So the men need the women and the women need each other and there is no war.'

'And what are the Seonu's secrets? Or do only the women know?'

'No. The Maeng, the Dae, the Four Together, they all say women are wiser than men, so only women can know. The Seonu say women are wiser *with* men and both can know. But for me, not yet. The other tribes say a boy is a man in his thirteenth summer. The Seonu say no: twenty-eight is a good number. At twenty-eight a man is a man, a woman a woman and both are told the tribe's secrets. Until then we are children in the elders' eyes.'

His voice was soothing and she let her eyes drift shut, resting her head against the soft sand. 'I suppose it makes sense that the Seonu are quite different from the other tribes. You were separated from them for a long time, weren't you?'

'Yes. When we first came here, our ships landed on the desert coast. The mages of Mirror Town told us the way to the grasslands, but on the journey the Geun died and the Seonu were lost. We were alone many years before we saw the other tribes again.'

'And where were you all those years? Not in Ashanesland or the Moon Forest.' There was a long silence and she fumbled at his side until she could take his hand, twining her fingers with his. 'I understand: that's one of the secrets you're too young to know. Doesn't it bother you, to live in unnecessary ignorance?'

When there was another silence she opened one eye and cocked her head to look at him. His face was pained, as if struggling with a thought he wasn't sure he should articulate.

'It doesn't matter what you say to me,' she told him. 'We're both going to die here, aren't we?'

'No. Jinn said you would live. He said you will meet Yron's heir.'

'But Jinn's a liar – he told us so himself. He tricked you into helping him.'

In Su looked away. 'Perhaps he spoke truth and didn't know it.'

She let her eyes drift shut again, comforted by the warmth of In Su's body, the clasp of his hand in hers. She didn't realise she'd fallen asleep until she snapped awake again with In Su clutching her shoulder. When she opened her mouth to speak he pressed a finger against her lips. 'Listen,' he whispered.

At first all she could hear was the *shush* of wind through sand. Then, slowly, she realised what it was In Su had heard: a soft musical twitter running in counterpoint to the wind. It was the sound of birds, and it was near. It wasn't much to offer hope, but those without took table scraps where they could.

In Su pointed left and she nodded and let him draw her to her feet. The sun had passed from overhead, leaving the ravine in gloom. She stumbled on a hidden rock but kept moving, left and then right and then right again. The maze wasn't easy to navigate and twice they took the wrong turn until the sound was almost lost. Then suddenly it was much louder and the smell of water joined it.

Nethmi ran round the last curve and found herself in a far wider gulf, at least fifty paces across. In its centre sat a bowl of rock and a brackish pool within it, where the birds they'd heard pecked and drank. She fell to her knees, frightening them into flight, and gulped the water from her palms. The taste was stagnant and another time it might have nauseated her. Now she filled her belly until it could take no more. Beside her, In Su did the same.

She turned to him as she lowered her waterskin into the pool to fill it. 'It would appear you were right. Yron's heir doesn't mean for us to die quite yet.'

It was strange to feel a little disappointment as well as relief. But their coming death had broken down what walls remained between them and she'd felt that she finally knew the young man who'd been her companion for weeks. She remembered her father had once said the same: that the sharing of mortal peril bonded men in ways nothing else could.

She studied In Su's face, but it was as hard to read as it had ever been. She sighed and watched his hand dip his waterskin into the pool. She watched the spreading ripples in the water's surface – and realised just a moment too late what they meant as the snake surfaced and sank its fangs into In Su's palm.

In Su screamed and flung the creature away from him. It smashed against a rock, writhed a moment and was still, but the damage had been done. Within seconds his palm was puffy and weeping a clear fluid and only moments later ominous red threads began to spread from the wound. In Su keened as he held his wrist in his other hand and rocked. His eyes were dazed with pain and shock.

Nethmi felt paralysed too. She couldn't believe how quickly everything had changed. She'd thought she was ready for death, but now she saw that she'd been fooling herself. Secretly she'd always believed that both of them would come through this unharmed, that they'd have time to understand what lay between them. But she'd seen a snakebite such as this before. It was how her father had died.

Her shock lasted a moment longer and then she tore a strip of fabric from the bottom of her skirt and bound it round In Su's arm, pulling tight. The venom mustn't be allowed to spread to the heart.

In Su screamed as she tightened the tourniquet and clawed weakly at her hands, but she was unrelenting. The next stage, she knew, would be to cut off his hand and cauterise the stump. Fewer than one in three survived that treatment. His eyes pleaded with her and she made herself smile.

'This will help,' she said. 'But I need to cut the wound and see if I can get the poison out.'

He flinched but nodded and she drew the knife from his belt and held it above his hand. 'Ready?' she asked, and in the moment when he was listening and not attending she slashed his palm.

This time he only whimpered and she jumped back as a spurt of vile discharge came out of the wound. It smelled like decay and she could already see a tinge of green to the surrounding flesh. She feared there'd be no saving his hand, but she'd done all she could. Walking would be dangerous for him, she knew that. It would pump more blood round his body and hasten the spread of the poison. But they couldn't stay here, where there might be more serpents.

'We need to move,' she told In Su and he only hesitated a moment before nodding his understanding.

She sheathed his knife and led the way. The harsh rasp of his breathing told her he kept pace at first, but he soon dropped behind. When she turned to watch him, she saw that his face was fiercely flushed. She strode back and wrapped an arm round his waist to urge him on. His flesh was hot beneath hers and close to she could hear the gurgle of liquid in his lungs. She brushed his sweat-soaked hair from his eyes as tears filled hers.

Before long he couldn't walk even with her aid, and he was too heavy for her to carry. The gloom in the ravine had grown and she guessed the sun must be near setting. The sky above was a deep and beautiful violet. She gently lowered In Su to the ground and sank down beside him.

His face was drawn with pain and she reached out to cup his cheek but he flinched away from her. His eyes were hazy and she wasn't sure how much he could see. Still, she carefully arranged his head so that he was looking not at the imprisoning walls of the gulley but at the freedom of the sky and the stars appearing one by one in it. His body was too hot to hold, so she rested her head against his shoulder and closed her eyes, trying to shut out the sound of his desperate, wheezing breath.

She woke to the sound of groaning and the smell of rot. In Su had moved away from her in the night, but she could feel the heat of his body even without touching him. He was burning with fever and she could see red veins where the poison had spread up his arm despite her efforts. Foul-smelling gangrene had followed it, gnarling his fingers and turning them black and their nails a sickly green. When he rolled towards her the arm hung limp and useless from his shoulder. She thought briefly of trying to cut it from him, until she saw the red lines rising up his neck towards his flushed cheeks. Then she knew he was doomed.

She'd already drunk a quarter of the water she'd taken from the stagnant pool, but she used most of what remained to soak her skirt. She tore another strip and used it to mop his forehead. His eyes stuttered for a moment and then fixed on her.

'I feel bad, Nethmi.'

She stroked his cheek to remove a bead of moisture. 'I know. The poison's spread, I'm afraid.'

'I am dying?'

She nodded.

'I hurt.'

'I know.'

It was her fault. Everyone close to her died. In Su would have lived out his whole life in Winter's Hammer if she hadn't come along and tempted him away. And her father . . . She remembered the way he'd looked as the poison ate him up. He'd begged for purple sorghum tea to end the pain. He'd asked her to be the one to give it to him.

'I can make the pain stop, if you want,' she told In Su. Her words came out thickly through a throat clogged with tears.

His eyes when they met hers were feverish but not uncomprehending. Her right hand was clutched tight round the hilt of his knife, but the left was shaking. She could feel her own heartbeat in her ears, and she found that a perverse part of her longed for him to say yes. She felt so *close* to In Su in this moment. Coupling with Thilak had been a cold thing. It had bridged not an inch of the gap between them. Only in his death had she known him. There was no act more intimate than the taking of another's life.

'Thank you,' he said. 'Please, make it stop.'

'Look at me, then,' she whispered. 'Just look at me. There's no need to be afraid. There's peace at the end of this. I'll end your pain quickly.'

He nodded weakly and his eyes scanned her face but didn't slide lower to where she pressed her knife against the pulsing vein in his throat. There were threads of virulent red around it and she knew if she didn't end him soon, the poison would.

'Goodbye, In Su' she said, and slashed the knife across his flesh.

His blood sprayed all over her, warm and sticky. His body convulsed and, despite her promise, she saw a moment of pure agony in his eyes. His hand clutched hers and she held his back just as tightly.

She studied every inch of his face, memorising it: the tilt of his eyebrows, the little mole above his lip, the thin white scar on one cheek. She felt she knew him then completely, and as his dying eyes looked into hers, she felt he knew her. She smiled at him and he smiled back, but it turned into a rictus as his back arched and his life left him.

She couldn't bear to see that harsh expression on his gentle face and she reached out to smooth it away. But the touch of his dead flesh sickened her and she quickly dropped her hand. In Su was gone and what remained was only a shell.

She stayed by his body as long as she could, but the stench of decay was strong and she knew it would draw predators she was ill-equipped to fight. There was no lake to sink him in or cairn to raise in the manner of the landborn, but she heaped sand over his body and said the same prayers to the Five she'd recited over her father. She wished she could have prayed to In Su's own gods, but she'd never asked him their names and now she never could.

When she left his grave, she found a gulley wider than the others and followed her own shadow down it, heading north, where the exit from the Waste must surely lie. She didn't care if she found it, but In Su had wanted her to live. He'd believed she would and suddenly it felt very important to prove him right.

She drank her waterskin dry as she walked, until the walls of the ravine began to lower and its floor widen. Stalks of grass poked through the sand and at sunset she realised that, almost without noticing, she'd returned to the plains. The smell of vegetation was rich all around her.

She turned for a last look at the desolation that held In Su's corpse, but some trick of perspective hid it from her so that the plains seemed to stretch to infinity in all directions.

22

After a week of travel, Eric had grown used to the motion of Rii's muscles beneath his legs and the unpredictable swoops and dives as she navigated the currents of air. He'd taken to dozing on her back, though the cold made his sleep restless and he often dreamed, but never of the moon. He was dreaming of Lahiru when Rii's voice woke him.

'*Wilt thou look ahead, morsel?*' she said. '*Our destination approaches.*'

The endless water and endless sky had become so monotonous to him that he'd ceased to really see them. Now the sun was rising to the east, casting a pinkish glow over the restless waves, but the brightest glow was ahead of him. For a disorientated moment he thought it was a second sun. Then he realised that he was looking at snow, a vast great stretch of it. The entire land was frozen.

'People *live* there?' he said as they drew closer and still all he could see was white.

'*The Servants do. This is their home and soon it will be thine.*'

They were flying over the snow now, low enough that Eric began to see features in it, dips and drifts and bright lakes of ice. Even wrapped in his furs he felt the lancing cold and he realised that spring was over for him before it had really begun. Rii had flown him back to a permanent winter.

They flew another half an hour into growing darkness before he saw the city. There was a strange jolt, the sun seemed to jump back upwards as if in an eye-blink he'd lost hours of time and then there it was, its spires breaking the smooth line of the horizon ahead. When they were closer he realised that it was made entirely of ice, pure and clear. *No bloody secrets there,* he thought. *Everyone knows just what everyone else is getting up to.*

Insect-tiny figures crawled through the city's chambers and there was another group closer at hand, waiting on the ground and looking up at Rii and Eric as they approached. They stood among an ordered copse of golden-leaved trees, which were the only splash of colour in the white land.

Rii landed inelegantly, ploughing a furrow through the ice so that Eric was surrounded by a temporary snowstorm as the figures approached. He blinked the flakes from his eyelashes and sat where he was, all the fear he'd managed to hide from himself over the long journey rapidly reappearing.

'Dismount, *morsel,*' Rii said. '*My task is done and I would away.*'

Her shoulders shrugged impatiently and he did as she asked, untying his baggage and throwing it down before him.

The instant his feet touched the ground he was knocked off them and to his knees by the powerful beat of her wings. She was airborne and receding before he could say goodbye, though he doubted she cared. He watched her retreating form for a long time. She hadn't been friendly or at all reassuring, but she'd become familiar. And she'd promised him that he'd return home one day. If she'd left him already, what was her promise worth?

He shifted his gaze to the people approaching. They were swaddled in white furs so that when tears of cold blurred his eyes they became just another part of the landscape. Their faces were hidden, only a narrow slit of skin visible around their eyes. He made himself smile and nod and clasped his hands together so their shaking wouldn't be visible.

'Eric!' one of the swaddled figures said.

Eric frowned. He was sure he recognised that voice. Then the figure threw back its hood and he blinked, then blinked again, but it was still a face he knew very well. Bolli had been at Madam Aeronwen's when Eric had first arrived, the only other man there with his unusual pale colouring and the one who'd taught Eric all a sellcock's tricks. He'd been mates with Eric for two years until one day he'd just disappeared.

'Well, ain't this a surprise?' Eric said, moving to embrace the other man. 'You're looking as pretty as ever, Bolli.'

Bolli returned the hug, then held him by his shoulders as he examined his face. 'You're looking well too, Eric. The years have been kind.'

Eric didn't remember the other man's voice ever being so posh. His face looked more refined as well. All the boyish roundness had gone and there was a new knowingness in his eyes that was more than just a whore's cynicism. 'What *are* you doing here, Bolli? We're off the edge of the bloody world!'

Bolli flicked his blond fringe from his forehead. 'I'm doing the same thing you are.'

'And what am *I* doing here?'

The other man glanced at his companions, still swaddled in their furs, and smiled. 'You're getting hitched, of course.'

There were no gates to the city, just a vast open arch in the ice, its rim carved with circles and spirals that drew the eye into infinite loops. It was no warmer on the inside and Eric wondered how he'd cope with living here, but the others seemed glad to be indoors and pulled back their hoods. They were all men, he saw, some almost as young as him, none looking much older than thirty, a round dozen of them. And they were all of them fair and pale like him, though the cast of their faces said they came from different lands and peoples.

'Welcome to Salvation,' said a green-eyed man with a sharp nose. 'It may not look the warmest hearth you've ever huddled by, but we call it home.'

Eric gave him the smile he saved for strangers he hoped to charm. He always set out to make friends, though he seemed to have lost his touch at it recently. 'It ain't exactly enticing, but Salvation's a hopeful name. And any home's better than none.'

Another of the men nodded. He was the oldest looking, with a few strands of silver in his golden hair. 'Indeed. We've found it so.'

'But you don't come from here, do you? You ain't those

Servants what Rii was talking about. I know your accent; you're an awful long way from home, if home's the savannah, and I reckon it is. And Green Eyes here is Jorlith same as me. That I'm sure about.'

'You're right on both counts,' Green Eyes said.

'We're not the Servants of Mizhara,' Bolli said. 'We're wed to them. It's all right, lads, you've done your duty now. I'll take Eric from here.'

The men all smiled and nodded to him and went their separate ways at a crossroads in the icy corridor. The material had looked see-through from the air, but inside it foxed the eyes so that you only got a tantalising glimpse of what lay within it. As Bolli led Eric down corridors that turned at sharp angles and through halls with curved walls he spotted glimpses of what might have been the Servants, but it was impossible to make out anything about them. Would they be hideous like Rii? Eric had slept with many an ugly man that made him feel handsome, but a boy had his limits.

'So they brought me here to marry me?' he asked Bolli.

The other man nodded. 'It's the same for all of us.'

'But who'd want to marry a whore?'

'Shh!' Bolli took Eric's arm and shook him. 'I thought you'd have been told. The Servants don't know what you were, and they don't need to. Radek takes their gold to bring them the finest men the world has to offer, so that's what we have to be.' He saw Eric's expression and loosened his grip, smiling reassuringly. 'Don't worry, they won't ask any questions. They're not an inquisitive bunch. All they do is talk and talk about Mizhara, trying to learn us her ways. They don't care about the world outside Salvation, but don't go volunteering anything that'll get you into trouble. Just make up some simple story – you're the son of a rich thegn, whatever you like – and stick to it. We're on to a good thing here and you're not to spoil it for the rest of us, you hear?'

He started walking again and Eric was forced to trot to keep up with him. The ice crunched beneath his heels. 'But why? I mean, don't they have no decent men of their own?'

'They don't have any men at all. They all died, or they're all gone anyway. There's no need for me to explain – they'll tell you about it themselves. By the Smiler, they'll tell you more than you want to know, not that you should name the Smiler here, or any of the prow gods, nor the Hunter neither. Especially not her. The only goddess here is Mizhara and she don't abide any others. But no, they've got no men, or none but us.'

'So I'm to have a wife.' Eric's mouth twisted. Babi's revenge was more subtle than he'd imagined. 'Might as well have stayed in the Moon Forest. I just hope I can do my manly duty when the time comes.'

'You'd better. And you're not marrying one of the Servants – you're marrying all of them. No, don't panic, you won't be wearing your cock thin servicing them.' Bolli's accent was slipping, Eric noticed. It must be the bad company he was keeping. 'We're all married to all of them, see. The thirteen husbands, they call us, and we're each to serve for thirteen years. The first husband finished his duties twelve days ago and you're to replace him. The wedding's tomorrow, because that's your day on duty.

'Each of us has one day in the oroborus – no, don't ask, they'll tell you all about that too. This is all you've got to know right now: there's thirteen husbands, thirteen days and one thirteenth of the Servants what's looking to use your manhood on yours. They're big on thirteen, in case you hadn't noticed. Oh, and if they mention Mizhara, you just say something respectful and reverent and drop your eyes, got it? They're big on piety, too.'

Eric's head was spinning, filled with visions of a future like nothing he'd ever imagined. He stopped and after a few paces Bolli turned to face him. 'Are you all right, mate?'

'I'm to marry a whole bloody nation of women?'

Bolli laughed. 'Don't worry. It isn't as bad as it sounds.'

His room was made of ice, of course. The bed – a solid slab of the stuff – was piled with furs. He stripped and crawled inside them, shivering. His own body warmed the nest eventually, but sleep wouldn't come. As the day drew on, the sun crawled towards the horizon, the way it was meant to do. Except when it reached it, it just crawled back up again. Its golden light seemed to fill the walls and floors and they pulsed with an energy that made the hairs on the nape of his neck stand on end. Or maybe that was just the thought of what awaited him tomorrow, whatever tomorrow meant in a place without any night.

He was to get married. He was to get married to a bunch of *women* who were scary enough to frighten Rii, and Bolli too, though the other man hadn't said it. But Eric had seen it in the tense set of his shoulders whenever he talked about the Servants. And he was destined to betray these women too, or so Rii had dreamed. The thought kept him tossing and turning in his furs, slipping into a half-daze but never quite sleeping the long hours away.

He'd thought Bolli would come for him, but as the sun rose higher to send rainbow slivers of colour bursting from the ice all around him it was two of the other husbands who entered the room. Each had a pile of clothing in his arms and Eric raised an eyebrow.

'I'm supposed to wear all that?'

The two men were so alike they might have been twins: blond and handsome and thin. Only their eyes distinguished them. Blue Eyes dropped a pile of silk on the bed, while Green Eyes laid out a row of shoes and stockings and looked down his sharp nose at Eric. 'We thought you'd like to choose,' he said.

Eric felt his loins reacting, though he usually preferred his men darker and older. But beggars couldn't be choosers and it seemed the Servants had a taste for blonds. 'Are there any other lads here?' he asked Green Eyes. 'Or is it just us husbands?'

'Just the husbands,' Blue Eyes said. Although he was as white as a lily, he had the musical accent of the mages of Mirror Town. Eric wondered what his story was. He supposed he'd have a long time to find out.

Eric picked out a beautiful turquoise shirt that he knew would set off his eyes, and there was a sapphire brooch to go with it. White silk hose and soft calfskin boots completed the outfit, with a big, fur-lined cape over it to keep out the chill. There was no mirror, so he turned to the other two men.

'You look very handsome,' Green Eyes said with a smile as Blue Eyes gave him a solemn nod.

'So what have I got to do?' Eric asked. 'Stand there and look pretty?'

Green Eyes laughed. 'That's about it. It'll be in their tongue, so you won't understand it. Just look obliging and bow if you hear them say Mizhara's name. They'll like that. Honestly, there's nothing to it, is there, Abejide?'

Blue Eyes – Abejide – mustered a small smile. 'They know you don't know their ways and they won't blame you for your ignorance. They'll start to teach you afterwards.'

Eric swallowed nervously. He'd been called on to service a woman from time to time, and he'd done all right by them, but he still didn't know what these Servants were.

Green Eyes seemed to understand his anxiety. 'Don't worry, there's a drink they give you, they call it the Tears of Mizhara. Don't ask what's in it, but they could sell it for all the gold in Smiler's Fair back home. A few sips of that and you won't have any trouble performing. It's the next day that'll be harder, when they start your lessons in Mizhara's law, the Perfect Law they call it and they take it dead seriously. They're very set in their ways, the Servants.'

'I ain't what you'd call a good student,' Eric said.

'Don't worry, you've plenty of time to learn.'

Yes, Eric thought. *Thirteen years.*

They led him down a narrow corridor and then into a broader one, its walls carved with more circles and swirls and spirals but never any living thing.

Fifty paces ahead, the corridor ended in a wide space lit with the same golden glow that had kept Eric awake last night, as if they'd trapped the sun inside. His pace faltered and he ran a hand over his curls. 'They really want to marry *me*?' he asked Green Eyes. 'Are they sure?'

Green Eyes squeezed Eric's shoulder. 'You've been chosen, Eric. Maybe not exactly the way the Servants thought, but they believe you're special. They do want you and you'll be everything they want, I promise. We all felt like you did when we got here, but it's the best thing that ever happened to us. Did you want to die a – well, doing what you were doing? When Sarv left a week before you came, they loaded him down with jewels. Rii could barely carry it all. I know it seems like it'll last an eternity. I thought that too, but I've already been here nine years. It's worth it. Just do what they say – you're used to that, aren't you?'

He couldn't argue with that. He ran his hand over his hair one last time, and then squared his shoulders and marched towards the golden hall.

The Servants were waiting within, lined up in ranks along the walkway that led towards a big block of ice at the far end. He'd expected . . . he'd expected something monstrous, he could admit that to himself now: a sort of two-legged version of Rii. He'd noticed the way the other husbands never said anything about how the Servants looked, and he'd assumed that was because they wanted to hide the horrible truth from him. Now he saw the way Green Eyes was grinning at him and realised it was the complete opposite. They'd meant it to be a pleasant surprise.

He knew the Servants. Well, not them, but someone like them. They were the spit of the pictures of the Hunter that had hung around the village of his birth. He couldn't think what that meant. Like her they were almost human, but their skin and eyes looked like pure molten gold and their ears were too sharp to be quite right. Some of them even had the Hunter's tight-curled hair and broad noses, the same as the mages of Mirror Town, though most looked more like his own folk, if his own folk had been painted all over the colour of the sun. They were beautiful, if you liked that kind of thing. He could do his duty with a woman like this, though there really were an awful lot of them: hundreds packed into this vast chamber.

Green Eyes took his arm as he hesitated and led him onward, past the ranks of solemn golden women. It felt like a very long way on very wobbly legs, but eventually he reached the front and the great lump of ice, which he guessed must be holy to them, because it certainly wasn't pretty. There were just a handful of the Servants here – no, thirteen of course, when he counted them – in a circle round the ice. For one horrible instant Eric wondered if they meant to sacrifice him on it. But there didn't seem to be any bloodstains, only a flat surface and two indentations that after a moment he realised were footprints, delicate and long-toed.

'Kneel,' Green Eyes whispered, and then he and Abejide backed away, leaving Eric alone with all those women. He bowed his head to the floor and did as Green Eyes had said.

After they'd finished their long, long ceremony and said all the words in their strange, clipped tongue, and bowed to him and watched him bow to them and never smiled, the Servants led him through a back door from the hall. It was here they gave him a golden flask and told him to drink its contents down. It must be the stuff Green Eyes had told him about, the Tears of Mizhara. It lit a fire in his loins that burned so strong his cock was immediately pushing out his hose. He felt a little ashamed in front of the Servants, who seemed awfully serious about everything, but they never even looked at him down there. He wasn't sure if he pleased them or what they thought of him. Their faces were beautiful but blank.

His groin ached so badly it was almost a relief to know he'd need to service all these women, though he wasn't entirely confident of his ability to spend into all of them. Did that matter to them? Was he here for their pleasure or just for making babies? It would explain why the Servants chose their husbands fair and pale, so the children they got on them would look the same. But maybe they wanted to enjoy the process too. Though he was proud of his bedplay, he wasn't too sure he knew how best to please a woman. Kiss their cunny, he'd heard once. It wasn't an appealing prospect, but he could do it if he must.

His head was terribly fuzzy, though. The same fire that had ignited in his cock seemed to be burning all sense out of his brain. The Servants led him through a low arch into a chamber that was nothing but bed.

He was naked and lying on his back without quite realising how he'd got there. And the Servants were . . . They were still chanting those bloody mantras that had made the wedding itself last an age, as if this was just another part of the ceremony. One of them was on him now. He felt he should be doing more than lying back, but his body seemed entirely out of his control. He watched her rise and fall, in rhythm with the chanting. She was chanting too, and he wondered what it meant and if they'd ever tell him.

He reached up to touch her breasts, which he'd also heard women liked, but she gently pushed his hands down. And then it seemed to be over, though he felt nothing, nothing at all, and the next one was on him and then the next. It wasn't pleasant exactly, or unpleasant either. It was almost like a dream. The part of him that thought and wanted drifted away and left the animal body behind to perform its duty.

23

The stew was terrible, but Nethmi was ravenous and she only had a few coins. She spooned the lumpy liquid into her mouth and tried not to wonder what had gone into it. Two days wandering the featureless plain with no food had left her desperate. When she'd seen the black blot on the horizon, she hadn't cared what it was. It could have been guardsmen from Winter's Hammer and she would have thrown herself gladly into their arms. But it had been Smiler's Fair.

She'd re-entered the place dazed with hunger and disbelief. It was strange that what had seemed frightening when she'd first visited now felt like a haven. She'd given a false name at the gate and no one had questioned it. The jostling crowds would hide her from pursuit and the shopkeepers and barmen would take her money until it was all gone. After that, she didn't know what she'd do, but worrying about the future seemed futile. Everything she had ever believed about it had proven to be wrong.

When the stew was gone she leaned back in her chair and looked around. The table was outside, on the perimeter of a large square. It reminded her a little of the place where she'd first heard Jinn speak, but she knew it wasn't the same. That had been surrounded by houses of ill-repute, whereas this was ringed by gambling dens. Banners showing dice and spinning tops; a hand splayed for luck flapped above doorways and the clatter of the games was all around.

It was said that you could never return to Smiler's Fair. When she was a child, she thought it was because the fair somehow magically disappeared after you'd visited it. Her father had laughed and explained that the saying meant both you and the

Rebecca Levene

Smiler's Fair would change, so that you'd be a different person and it would be a different place.

The fair certainly did seem to have changed. The streets were crowded with almond-eyed tribespeople, not darker-skinned Ashane. The beaded clothes on the stalls catered to their new hosts' tastes and the food was flavoured with herbs Nethmi had never tasted before. Some of the buildings had clearly been repainted since the mountain crossing and the babble of voices spoke an entirely different mix of tongues.

In its essence, though, Nethmi wasn't sure Smiler's Fair had changed at all. It still wanted its visitors' coin – and maybe their virtue – and proposed to give as little as possible in return. And the tribespeople wore the same amazed and often scandalised expressions as the Ashane had three months past. Last time she'd seen two fist-fights and one duel. Now a wrestling match was getting under way in the centre of the square, drawing an interested crowd.

As for herself, she *did* feel that something had altered inside her, something fundamental, but she didn't know what it was and she wasn't sure if she liked it.

The fair had found its pitch only two days ago and Marvan was already restless. His house was near the outskirts this time, just off Maidenhead Alley. His window faced the plains and he looked out over the grass and sighed. Now that they'd passed through Ashanesland, the circle was complete. Every view he saw would be a view he'd seen before. He remembered this land and he knew that it stretched for leagues upon leagues south and north. He'd better get used to the sight of blue sky and silvery grass and the unlovely faces of the Fourteen Tribes who lived on it.

His axes would be the right weapons for this place. He hooked two into his belt, slid a stiletto into his boot and turned to examine himself in the mirror. He didn't very much like what he saw: the usual long, beaky nose, smiling mouth and messy brown hair; but his eyes had a feverish glint that, had he seen it in another man, would have led Marvan to avoid him.

The hunger was gnawing at him. He hadn't fed it for two months now, not since the fuss after Jaquim disappeared. The fair had been in an uproar. Some hysterics thought the worm men had taken him, though everyone knew they never struck when Smiler's Fair was in motion. Others had cried murder, and although interest had soon refocused on the far larger scandal of Jinn and Vordanna's kidnapping, Marvan had seen doubting eyes on him. And everywhere he turned, there was that bloody clerk Lucan, watching him with eyes that held no doubt. Lucan knew full well what he'd done. Marvan could swear the man had actually taken to following him about the fair. It was enough to spoil anyone's appetite, no matter how strong.

There was another reason to stop, too. He'd wanted to prove to himself that his peculiar hunger wasn't his master, but his experiment had forced him to the opposite conclusion. Today he *had* to satisfy it. His cat, Stalker, slid between his legs and he bent to stroke her head and then left the house to hunt.

Smiler's Fair was a different place here in the plains. The Four Together loved to gamble and some of them liked to drink, but they mostly stayed away from the whores, except the few who fancied themselves in love with the floozies and tried to lure them away, to a life on horseback.

The dollies and sellcocks seemed to cope well enough. The Fine Fellows had chosen their pitch near the Drovers this time, and when Marvan crossed the boundary he saw that the houses of ill-repute had transformed themselves into dens of a different vice, their pictures of blowsy women and fresh-faced lads replaced with images of dice and spinning tops. The whores served drinks to the gamblers lounging around the outside tables and smiled at being treated with respect for once.

Marvan knew those men would be no good to him, too caught up in their games to let him provoke them. He passed through the narrow alley between two erstwhile whorehouses and found himself in Cockermouth Square, where the cheapest sellcocks usually plied their trade. The sagging buildings lining the open space, filled with dingy rooms that hired out by the hour, usually drew in the cullies. Today, though, the crowd was in the centre of the square, on the brown-green slush that had once been fresh grass.

Marvan recognised beaded shirts belonging to many different bands and hearths of the Four Together. The tribes must be gathering nearby for their spring festival, else the men wouldn't have left their herds even for the pleasures of Smiler's Fair. The elder mothers had stayed in their camps, but long-haired girls and knife women in colourful scarves rubbed shoulders with warriors made taller by their turbans and prouder by the battle scars they wore from skirmishes between the bands.

It was a sweeter-smelling group than usually inhabited Smiler's Fair. Where normally such a crowd would be rank with the odours of piss and old sweat, here Marvan scented only a confusion of flowers from the oils they rubbed into their hair. The tribespeople were tightly packed, but parted amicably enough as he pushed his way through until he found himself at the rim of a clear circle.

Now he understood. The Four Together loved to wrestle almost as much as they liked to gamble their winnings on the dice. It let the bands compete without a cost in blood. It was said an elder mother of the Dogko had learned the sport from a Wanderer and taught it to her tribe after her son was killed in a raid. When her son's murderer had been captured, he'd expected death, but instead the elder's other son had wrestled him into the mud and forced him to eat his pride. He'd walked away with his life, greater wisdom and a bad back. It was a pretty story, and maybe even true.

Today, they'd marked out the edge of the arena with white rocks and the crowd was pressed close, watching the fight. The two men in the ring looked like they'd done this often before. One was wiry rather than muscular and quick as a ferret. The other seemed nothing *but* muscle, as immovable as the first was lithe. It hardly seemed an even match, but Marvan was no expert.

The thinner man circled the larger, his eyes darting as he searched for an opening in defences that looked impenetrable. The thickset wrestler stood with a slight smile and a gaze that seemed focused on the horizon, as if the man in front of him was barely worth bothering with. But when the small man moved he responded quickly enough, blocking the grab for his groin and returning a jab to the gut that left his opponent on his back and gasping for air.

Some of the crowd roared and others groaned and Marvan saw coins changing hands as a group of warriors detached from the onlookers to carry the smaller opponent away. The big man laughed and shouted out a challenge, but no one answered it and after a few moments he shrugged and left the ring.

The man who replaced him looked considerably less intimidating. He was taller but slightly stooped and there were threads of silver in his long hair, which he wore loose over his shoulders rather than in the topknot most tribesmen preferred beneath their turbans. That was a mistake, Marvan thought, a potential handhold for his opponent. The man moved a little stiffly too, and he favoured his right leg. He went to the centre of the ring, raised his arms over his head and shouted the same challenge to the crowd.

There was a stirring among the throng opposite Marvan and he thought an opponent was about to emerge. He pushed aside the man in front of him and stepped out before they could. 'I answer you,' he said in the language of the tribes. 'I'll fight you.'

There was a murmur from the crowd, not entirely happy.

'You, Ashaneman?' the warrior said. 'What tribe are you? What band?'

'No tribe,' Marvan said, 'and Ashane no longer. I'm just a man of Smiler's Fair, as you can see. Why – are we too much for you to face? Will the tribes only play their little games with each other, or would you take on a real warrior?'

The man's face darkened with anger as there were whoops of derision from the onlookers, though it wasn't clear if they were aimed at Marvan or the tribesman. Probably both. There were a dozen different bands here, and each liked to think itself the best. The man he'd challenged would have more enemies than friends in the crowd, or so Marvan hoped. He eyed them speculatively and found his gaze caught by a woman: petite and very pretty and clearly Ashane. She held his gaze with a confidence that sent a jolt up his spine.

He watched her a moment longer and then pulled out the two axes from his belt and turned to the elderly man beside him. 'Will you look after these for me, friend?' One glance at the muddy ground and he shucked off his shirt and jacket and handed them over, too. His movements felt a little jerky, the blood already pumping faster through his body and his head buzzing with the hunger about to be sated.

The elderly man sized him up as he took the weapons and the clothes. As Marvan stepped further into the ring he heard him offering two to one on his opponent to win. Well, Marvan didn't look like much, he knew that: tall and skinny with a pigeon chest and an odd twist to his walk that made him seem as if one leg was shorter than the other. He liked to be underestimated; he just hoped he hadn't done the same with his opponent.

The other man eyed him as he approached. 'Think you can defeat me, Ashaneman?'

Marvan grinned. 'I'll certainly give it a try.'

If only Smiler's Fair wouldn't keep bloody changing. Marvan was gasping for breath, his pursuers were only a few score paces behind him and he'd just turned in to a dead end where he'd expected to find himself in Tailors' Row. He spun to face the mouth of the alley and his hands reached for the axes at his belt – only to remember he'd left them with the old man before the fight. He pulled the stiletto from its sheath in his boot, knowing it would be close to useless against so many.

The crack of his opponent's back breaking echoed in his mind, but rather than pleasing him it filled him with self-disgust. Now that his hunger had been satisfied, he knew he'd been a fool. The wrestling wasn't to the death, that was the whole point. Only the shock and confusion following his victory had allowed him to escape the square at all. He'd broken a trust along with the man's back and now the tribesmen would settle for nothing but blood.

The warriors shouted in their nasal tongue as they approached the blind alley that had trapped him. They had no need to be stealthy when they so outnumbered him. Marvan realised that his hand was shaking. What a stupid way to die, and what a horrible place to die in. The alley stank of piss and there were fish-heads and animal guts in the soup of mud at his feet.

He tightened a hand round his knife and resolved to die with more dignity than most of his victims when another voice joined the tribesmen's, a woman's soft tones. Marvan couldn't quite make out the words, though he didn't think it was any of the plains dialects. The tribesmen grumbled a reply and then she spoke again, for longer. And then . . . when the tribesmen next spoke their voices were fainter. They were walking *away* from the mouth of the alley.

He sagged against the rotten wood behind him, the stiletto hanging limp in suddenly nerveless fingers. The rush of relief was almost as intense as the thrill of a kill. Death had walked past him and looked aside.

He was still shaking when the woman appeared. She stopped about ten paces away and stood studying him. She was an Ashanewoman with the darker skin and straighter hair of the south, and the proud bearing of the shipborn. Her familiarity nagged at him until he realised that he'd seen her in the crowd at the wrestling match. He smiled uncertainly at her. 'I think you just saved my life. Did you?'

'I told them I'd seen you back at that last crossroads.'

'Thank you.'

She shook her head, denying the thanks as if she'd helped him only by mistake. He thought she meant to move away, but he didn't want her to go. He sheathed his blade and held out his elbow to her. She looked at it, startled.

'Let me buy you a drink,' he said. 'It's the very least I can do.'

The man took her to a dingy parlour with the sign of the fat, smiling cook swinging on a rotted rope outside it. Nethmi didn't think it was wise to go out in public with so many people after his blood, but her companion seemed confident. He climbed through the trapdoor to the upper floor, offering a hand to help her after him. Her skin prickled with fear but no one spared him a glance as he led her to a corner table.

She studied him as he raised an arm to order a flagon of wine from the barmaid. He wasn't a handsome man. His nose was *huge*. And he wasn't a good man; that was clear. She still didn't understand why she'd helped him. But she'd seen his face as he killed the tribesman in that duel. There had been something in his expression she'd recognised.

'I'm Marvan, by the way,' he said as he threw back a mouthful of the wine.

She sipped at hers. It was rougher than any she'd tasted before, but the heat of it erased the cold terror she'd felt when she'd directed the warriors away from their quarry and wondered if they could tell she was lying.

'I'm Nethmi,' she told him. 'Are you sure it's safe here? Anyone could recognise you.'

'In Smiler's Fair we look out for our own. Well, some of the time. Besides, this place belongs to the Merry Cooks and they won't betray a Drover. Don't worry, I simply need to wait until the Jorlith have had their chance to calm things down. I'll tell them it was all a terrible mistake and they'll pretend to believe me, especially once I've paid the blood price and a little extra for the clerks' coffers.' He grinned, but she didn't smile back. She didn't see how he could be so calm when he'd just killed a man. She'd thought about In Su every day since she'd taken his life, and Thilak's dying gasps haunted her nights. She wondered if this man could teach her how to stop caring so painfully much.

Marvan studied her with disquieting thoroughness. Then he leaned back and rested his forefingers against his lips. 'You've come a long way from Ashanesland. From Whitewood, unless I miss my guess.'

She started, and then knew her surprise betrayed her, making denial pointless. 'How do you know that?'

'I'd recognise those eyebrows anywhere. I hail from Fell's End myself, third son of the lord of nowhere in particular. And you must be . . . Of course, you're old Lord Shaan's daughter, aren't you? Little Blade, they used to call you. We met at a banquet once when your father was newly elevated, though you were probably too young to remember. Oh, don't worry, I abandoned Ashanesland long ago, and whatever's caused you to leave it is of no interest to me. Well, that's not entirely true – I'd love to know what's made you seek out the delights of Smiler's Fair. But I'm not planning to turn you in to the clerks, if that's what you're worried about. And even if I did, they'd just turn you back out again. A person leaves their past behind when they enter the fair.'

Was that possible – to leave your past behind? But something made her tell him, 'I was married to Lord Thilak of Winter's Hammer.'

'And you didn't like it, so you ran away.'

She looked down into her cup, stirring the wine with her finger. 'Yes. Yes, I ran away.'

'Then you're without a home and in need of a friend.'

'I can take care of myself,' she said stiffly. She didn't think it wise to take favours from any resident of Smiler's Fair, even a shipborn Ashane.

He seemed to understand her doubt. 'I'm in your debt,' he said. 'I can't repay it, as I place a very high value on my life and I'm short of coin. But if nothing else, I can be your guide around this place. I remember what a maze I found it when I first came. We'll need to wait a few hours for my trouble to calm itself down, but once the clerks have done their work, will you let me show you Smiler's Fair?'

The crowds pushed Nethmi against Marvan and she found she didn't mind. His body was warm and his scent clean and she was weary after the hours they'd spent walking the streets of the fair. She rested her hand against his arm and turned her attention to the stage.

Half the dancers wore wooden masks, carved to resemble

horses' heads. The long jaws that looked pleasing on the animals seemed sinister on the men. The other performers were dressed as men of the tribes in beaded vests and high turbans. They were singing to the horse-masked figures as they danced. In front of the stage, a row of men sat cross-legged with drums in their laps and did their best to drown out the singing. The crowd seemed to enjoy it, but she had no idea what it meant.

'I don't understand the words,' she told Marvan. 'I don't speak the tribes' tongue.'

'And why would you? It's a nasty-sounding thing.'

When he said no more she cut her eyes to him and saw that he was grinning. She realised he was teasing her and felt an odd mix of warmth and melancholy. The last person to do that had been Lahiru. In Su had been gentle and kind, but he hadn't been a merry man. She hadn't realised how much she missed it.

'So what *does* it mean?' she asked Marvan.

'Well, they're composing poems in praise of the horses.'

'Really?'

'Truly. These men are Snow Dancers, the first company of Smiler's Fair to come from among the tribes. This is a thing the plainsmen do, you know. The women run their affairs instead of the men, and the men sing the praises of the horses instead of the women. They're an odd people.'

'Not all one people,' she corrected him. 'The different tribes have different ways.'

'Indeed. You've studied them, I gather.'

She looked back at the stage. 'A friend told me.'

They watched a little longer, but it was more intriguing than entertaining.

'How would you like to see some real animals?' Marvan asked during a break in the drumming.

'Whatever you'd like to show me.'

He led her through a warren of alleys and streets that she thought led deeper into the fair. At least he was helping her develop some slight sense of the geography of this maddening place. 'Much of Smiler's Fair is subject to change,' he told her as they walked. 'But a few places always take the same pitch. Ah – and here's the first of them.'

They'd spilled from a shadowed avenue into a wide square. An enormous building sat in its centre, the largest she'd yet seen. It dwarfed even Whitewood but was far less elegant. Like the shipfort, it seemed to have been built of wood, but it had since been patched with cloth and here and there faced with stone, which had in turn begun to crumble away. There were decorations everywhere, carvings of flowers and trees and paintings of people and animals, but none of them seemed to bear any relation to each other.

'This is the Temple,' Marvan said.

'To which god?'

'Oh, all of them. The Worshippers aren't fussy that way. Pay them their coin and they'll pray to whomever you choose. It saves you the effort of showing any piety yourself. Would you like to go inside?'

She nodded, and he slipped two clay anchors to a child standing by one of the many doorways and led her in. She stopped to gasp and Marvan laughed. 'More gods than you expected? The world is full of them. Over there are our Ashane prow gods.' He pointed at wooden statues of the Lady and the rest. 'Except for the Smiler, of course. This being his home, the god of pleasure and revel gets pride of place. See?' The Smiler's statue sat at the centre of the room, easily thirty feet high and gilded all over. It made his rolls of fat and unsafe smile seem overwhelming.

'And those are the gods of the tribes.' Marvan gestured at a large cluster of statues, human-sized and human-shaped but dyed all colours of the rainbow. 'They're an easy-going lot, always adopting new gods into their families and hiring the spirits of the tribesmen's ancestors to serve them as their clerks. And the rather striking lady over there with the strange ears is the Hunter of the Moon Forest folk.'

'And where's the moon god?' she asked, obviously not as casually as she'd hoped, since Marvan turned to regard her thoughtfully.

'You didn't tell me you'd been to Smiler's Fair before. You must have done, to hear Jinn preach. There's no statue of his moon god here. Apparently there's no need of it, as the god himself is walking this earth. Have you ever thought that we Ashane are rather hard done-by in that department? There's the Moon Forest folk with their goddess protecting them in person, the tribes due to join their gods when they die, and all we have are five statues in Ashfall. They say the five prow gods sat at the front of the five ships that brought our people here, with the Lady making the weather fair and the Smiler keeping them all happy through the long journey, but I wonder if that's true. I sometimes think our forebears left them behind in the old land when they sailed and came here godless.'

'But there are the god-dreams,' she said, a little scandalised. Her father would have had a man whipped for such talk. 'And our personal prow gods too.'

'Yes – I had a handsome fellow myself, called him the Sun-summoner, but he never seemed to do me much good and I left him behind in Fell's End.'

'I had to leave my Peacebringer in Winter's Hammer,' she admitted.

'There, you see – and yet you fetched up here and fell into my company. I'd say you're doing very well without him.' He smiled charmingly and she couldn't help smiling back.

They spent a little longer wandering between the statues, but after a while Nethmi began to feel their painted eyes following her, and she shivered and asked to leave the Temple.

'The Menagerie, then,' Marvan said and led her down another alley, lined with shops selling nuts and squares of glistening red meat. She frowned as he bought a packet of raw chunks.

'For the beasts,' he said.

The Menagerie lay at the end of the alley. It was a little smaller than the Temple, but ten times noisier and a hundred times more malodorous.

'Keep a hand on your coins,' he instructed. 'The Fierce Children run this place, but they've a deal with the cutpurses of the Queen's Men: a share of all they steal from the gawping cullies.'

She understood why visitors might be distracted. The first cage held a creature she'd never seen before or even imagined. Its body was the size and shape of a cow's, but entirely covered in bright scarlet scales. There was a ruff of feathers round its neck and its teeth were as sharp as needles. She might have thought it a curiosity sewn together from the corpses of five different animals until a golden eye blinked open and stared at her.

Marvan threw it a gobbet of meat, which it swallowed whole. 'A desert creature,' he told her. 'A reptile of some sort. But not quite as impressive as this fellow.'

The next cage held a snake. Marvan was right: it was impressive, its coils as thick as her torso and its head little smaller than hers. She'd never seen a serpent so large, but she'd seen its smaller cousins and she knew its species: a yellow viper, the creature sacred to the Fierce Child. She couldn't move her eyes from it. Marvan was speaking, but his words were just noise until he put himself between her and the tank, hiding her view of the snake.

'What is it?' he asked. 'There's no need to be afraid – it can't escape its cage.'

'I'm not afraid,' she said, but her voice cracked. 'I'm *not* afraid. We had a shrine to the Fierce Child in Whitewood. I saw the snakes in their tank there every day.'

She saw the moment he understood. 'Of course, I'd forgotten. Your father was killed by a serpent, wasn't he? Murdered by your uncle.'

A wave of unexpected tears washed over her and Marvan stared at her in alarm for a moment, then cautiously put his arms round her while she sobbed. Eventually shame overcame her grief and she pulled away, wiping roughly at her face to clean her cheeks and nose.

'It *was* murder,' she said. 'Puneet cracked the glass to free the serpent on purpose, I'm sure of it.'

'So the rumours said.' He looked a little puzzled at her vehemence and she laughed moistly. He couldn't know what it meant to finally hear her own suspicions voiced by someone else. She'd been so young when her father had died. In the small hours of the night she'd sometimes doubted her own interpretation of events. But now it seemed every shipborn lord in Ashesland believed the same thing.

'I gave him the purple sorghum tea to ease his passing,' she told Marvan.

'I would have done the same,' he said. His voice shook a little, as if her emotions were infecting him.

Suddenly, she wanted to confide everything 'In the Rune Waste, before I came to Smiler's Fair, I had another friend bitten by a snake. I had to kill him too.' At that his face froze and she felt tears start in her eyes again. 'You think I did wrong,' she said.

'No. No, Nethmi, I think you did absolutely the right thing. Tell me, where are you staying?'

The sudden change of topic confused her, but she answered, 'In a room I've rented above one of the taverns. The One-Legged Stool.'

'I know that place,' Marvan said. 'It's cramped and noisy. You deserve better and I can provide it. Why don't you come and stay with me? I've a room and a bed that's big enough for two –' he held up a hand before she could protest '– where we two can sleep chastely with a sword between us if that makes you feel safer. I'm told that's how the maids liked to do things in the old tales.'

'You're very kind,' she began, and he laughed.

'I'm never kind, but I won't hurt you, I swear it. Smiler's Fair is a chancy place if you don't know the rules, or when there aren't any. Let me teach you a thing or two, just enough so you can make your own way here. I think I can be a good friend to you, Nethmi of Whitewood.'

She wasn't sure how good he was, but she *did* need a friend. In Su had tried to help her and had died for his generosity. Marvan of Fell's End seemed like a man who could survive her company.

'Very well,' she said. 'Just for a little while.'

24

On the second day they came to the end of the pass as the rocks
of the valley floor melted into soft soil beneath the feet of their
horses and mammoths. Here, it was far easier for Sang Ki to see
the trail Gurjot and his men had been following. The grass had
been trampled to mud in a swathe nearly five hundred paces
wide.

Their own force seemed dwarfed by the one they were
following. If their quarry marched with an army this size, what
chance did they stand? But after a while, Sang Ki began to notice
objects scattered in the mud, scraps of clothing clinging to piles
of dung and then, finally, a ragged pennant caught beneath a
clod of dirt. He'd never visited Smiler's Fair, but he recognised
the rayed sun that was the symbol of Journey's End, the company
of traders.

Gurjot rode beside him, his horse in the shadow of Sang Ki's
mammoth. The carrion mount strode at his side, its scraggly feathers
a sorry contrast to the glossy black hair of its master's stallion.

'Smiler's Fair?' Sang Ki asked, pointing to the pennant. 'You
think to find our fugitive there?'

'The prince is just a boy, and an uneducated goatherd at that.
You forget that I've met him. There's nowhere else for him to
go. Smiler's Fair is like a beach after a storm: everything washes
up there eventually.'

Sang Ki couldn't fault his reasoning. He'd thought the same
of Nethmi. He'd sent a man to the fair to demand the return of
the murderers if they were present, but he didn't imagine his
demand would be heeded. The fair cared for its own and Thilak's
kidnapping of Jinn and Vordanna would not have been forgiven.

So for three nights they camped in the mud Smiler's Fair had left in its wake and sent outriders into the grasslands to hunt game and ensure no other trail led away from the one they followed. But it was clear the fair had passed many days ago, and if they were catching up to it, they weren't doing it fast enough.

'Shouldn't they be stopping?' one of Sang Ki's armsmen asked him in frustration on the fourth day. 'When will they turn back from a caravan into a town?'

Sang Ki caught Gurjot glancing his way and realised the other man was interested in the answer too. It always astonished him, the aversion most people had to the knowledge to be found in books. 'Smiler's Fair won't make its pitch here,' he told both his questioner and his surreptitious listener. 'We're crossing Dae lands now – have you not observed the distinctive rabbits? – and the Dae are dead. There are no customers here for the fair and its pleasures. They'll travel to the territory of the Four Together before they stop, I'd lay money on it.'

The trail led onward with no end in sight, confirming his prediction, and Gurjot seemed content for them to follow it. Then, on the third day, it veered left. Sang Ki knew why, of course. Every tribesman did. He turned his mount to follow the fair's path, but he hadn't gone many paces before he realised Gurjot and his men weren't doing the same.

It was a ponderous thing to turn a mammoth around. The palanquin swayed alarmingly and Sang Ki's checked shirt flapped in the breeze as he rode back to Gurjot.

'What happened?' Gurjot asked. 'Why veer from their course after so many days?'

Sang Ki smiled, glad that once again he knew something Gurjot didn't. 'Their course still lies straight ahead,' he told the other man, 'but so does the Rune Waste. They'll have skirted its edges and then returned to their north-western path.'

'Hmm . . . Well, we don't need to do the same. We can carry enough food and drink to cross it safely, surely?'

'It's not the lack of water that keeps travellers from the Rune Waste.'

'Superstition, then?' Gurjot smiled thinly. 'But we're Ashane, aren't we? What do we care for the fears of the tribes? If we cut through the waste we might finally catch our quarry, or have your men become as credulous as those you rule? Would they refuse an order to travel here?'

Before Sang Ki could reply, his mother snapped, 'My son's men will follow him anywhere, even the Rune Waste.'

Gurjot looked surprised that she'd spoken. Among the Ashane, Sang Ki knew, a woman's words carried little weight. But the tribes respected the wisdom of women, and Sang Ki couldn't ignore his mother's veiled order, however much he might wish to. He hesitated only a second, then clicked his tongue and used the thin willow switch to turn his mammoth towards the bleak and forbidden waste.

The place didn't have a clear beginning. They travelled for hours and only gradually saw the grass under their mounts' feet wither away to reveal the sandy ground beneath. Sang Ki's men hid their feelings, but most had lived among the Seonu long enough to know the tales and he sensed their fear in the way they touched the hilts of their weapons as they glanced around. The day was hot, far hotter than any spring day had a right to be, and the sky above had the same sullen and lowering cast as his men.

All the vegetation had gone before they saw the first rune. Even Gurjot's troops shifted uneasily at the sight of it. A black line, unnatural in its straightness, crossed the landscape ahead, cutting brutally through the yellow. It continued until lost to sight in either direction, thousands of paces long. Within half an hour, the blackness was beneath their hooves and Sang Ki realised that it was ash. It sucked in the sunlight and gave only a few crystalline glitters back while the whiff of soot hung over everything.

All speech ceased as they crossed the blackness. No animals lived in this desolation and no birds overflew it. The ash muffled their steps so that the silence was absolute. And then a line of yellow appeared on the horizon and shortly they were back in the ordinary desert. It almost seemed comforting by contrast.

Sang Ki wondered which stroke of which huge rune it was that they'd just traversed. It was impossible to know. No one at their level could comprehend them, any more than an ant could read the letters of a scroll no matter how often it crawled across the parchment. Indeed, the runes' very existence hadn't been known in Ashanesland until a hundred years ago, when King Jagraj's regent, Gurman of High Water Fastness, had sent a division of carrion riders to scout the plains and the runes had become suddenly and startlingly clear to the airborne men.

The Chun blamed the Dae for the runes and the desolation around them. They said the neighbouring tribe had once struck a bargain with a powerful mage of Mirror Town, only to renege on their end of the deal. The Waste had been the mage's terrible revenge, rendering uninhabitable the Dae's old hunting grounds so that the tribe had moved to the south to steal the Chun lands. The Dae, before their destruction, had told exactly the same tale about the Chun.

The mages themselves were silent on the matter, but when had they ever shared their knowledge with anyone? The folk of the Moon Forest gave their Hunter credit for the ruination. They claimed it had come in retaliation for a great wrong once done to her Wanderers. Sang Ki had read all the accounts and concluded that none of them was to be trusted. In his judgement, the Rune Waste had been present long before the tribes began their exile and the Ashane crossed the great sea. And now that he could see it for himself, he imagined it would outlast them all. When the lands were empty the runes would remain, immutable and incomprehensible. It wasn't a very comfortable thought and he shivered in his palanquin.

It was late in the day when they saw their first sign of habitation. At first it looked like a small building on the horizon, lonely in the midst of the sand, but when they drew nearer, Sang Ki saw that it was a gateway: the stone-built mouth to a broad tunnel leading down. Its entrance gaped wide and threatening and the light seemed shy of entering it. It was impossible to say how deep

the tunnel delved or how far it went. There was no similar structure marking an exit in sight.

'The Night Roads!' Sang Ki said with sudden inspiration, then
cursed himself as he saw the wave of fear that passed through
the company in the wake of his words. 'A legend only,' he added,
but the legends said that the subterranean tunnels were the domain
of the worm men, the means by which they travelled the world.
He allowed the men to march until the crumbling stone structure
was lost to sight before calling for them to make camp.

The tents went up more quickly than usual, as if the men were
keen to put something between them and the view of the wasteland. Sang Ki found he felt the same.

While the day had been subdued, the evening turned into a
raucous letting-off of tension. It started harmlessly enough, with
drinking and singing, but the atmosphere soon soured. As Sang
Ki tried to enjoy his supper of cured venison and spring greens,
he heard the sound of a loud-voiced argument and prayed it
wouldn't end in violence.

His prayers were naturally futile. He sighed as his lieutenant
approached, knowing the news wouldn't be good, and five minutes
later he was standing above the body of one of his armsmen as
he whimpered out his life in a pool of his own urine. The knife
was still sticking out of his kidney, bobbing up and down with
every laboured breath until it stopped moving entirely.

'Who's responsible for this outrage?' Sang Ki asked, rather
hoping that no one would know.

'The lowland scum,' one of his men told him and, alas, there'd
been sufficient witnesses for the culprit to soon be named.
That left him no choice but to summon Gurjot to deal with the
matter.

'One of my men has been murdered,' Sang Ki told him. 'I'm
afraid there's no question of this man's guilt.'

The killer was shaking, but it was impossible to tell if it was
with fear or rage. Sang Ki certainly felt the anger all around
him. With blood spilt, there was little chance of the two groups
forgetting their enmity now. He looked to Gurjot, wondering how

the other man intended to handle it, but the justice said, 'I think it's only fitting that you choose the punishment.'

He made it sound like a favour; Sang Ki knew it was quite the opposite. Harshness would alienate Gurjot's troops and mercy would sit ill with his own men. Gurjot could clearly see no right answer and was glad to pass on the responsibility for making a wrong one to someone else. He half-smiled as he watched Sang Ki, no doubt enjoying his dilemma.

Sang Ki smiled too, because he understood his own people better than Gurjot could. Like his father, most had gone native during their time in the mountains. That was why his mother had chosen them. They were Ashane enough on the outside to satisfy the king, but Seonu on the inside where it mattered.

'The Rune Waste is to blame,' Sang Ki said. 'It spreads its destruction inside men's heads and they lose their senses and their self-control. Your soldier wasn't himself when he struck mine; it would be wrong to kill him for it.'

He could see Gurjot's men sniggering behind their hands. No doubt they were delighted that the tribe's foolish superstitions would spare their comrade. His own people nodded, though, pleased with his words.

'Let the land be his punishment, then,' he told them. 'Send him from us without food or water. If the Waste lets him leave it then his life is his. If not, his bones will bleach and become a part of it.'

The killer smiled, pleased at his reprieve. His mates slapped his back and laughed and made plans to reunite with him back in Ashanesland. Sang Ki's own men said nothing, but their eyes glittered as they looked at the soldier, and he knew they saw a man marked for death.

Gurjot nodded curtly to confirm the sentence. His expression when he turned to Sang Ki was a mix of annoyance and grudging respect. Sang Ki had never mastered the Seonu habit of controlling his expressions, but he managed not to show his self-satisfaction as he turned and made his way to his tent.

★

It was shortly after sunset the next morning when they saw the first evidence that the waste was changing. At first Sang Ki thought it was snow, a scattering of ice across the black stroke of the rune ahead. But when their mounts were crossing the ash he realised that the white pinpricks were blossoms.

'Moonflowers,' he said, stopping the mammoth to gaze down at them. He would have liked to dismount and examine them more closely, but his ungainly flop from the beast's back was too humiliating to undertake more often than absolutely necessary.

His mother felt no such constraint. She clicked her fingers at one of her personal guard, then climbed deftly down the ladder rested against the mammoth's hairy flank. The guard held her arm as she squatted to examine the flowers more closely. When she reached out to pluck one bloom, Sang Ki was startled to see her smile. It happened so seldom that he always forgot how the expression transformed her. It made her face look almost pretty.

Gurjot dismounted too, tramping the blossoms beneath his boots as he approached. 'I thought nothing grew here.'

'It was always said that nothing did,' Sang Ki agreed. 'And these flowers aren't native to the plains. They grow only in the great northern forest.'

'Clearly not,' Gurjot said, and stomped back to his horse, gesturing for the column to proceed.

The white grew thicker on the ground as they moved forward, and Sang Ki began to see droplets of red, bloodbells from the far east of Ashanesland, and then a rainbow of colours strewn across green as grasses and flowers from around the continent changed the waste to a meadow.

When they came across the spring, rising from the once-blasted earth to trickle a bubbling stream through the greenery, all order broke down. The men had been on short rations for two days and they broke from their ranks to fling themselves down at the stream's bank and lap up its water.

It was while they were scattered and inattentive that the other force arrived. The thunder of their hooves announced them seconds before they crested the hill on the stream's far bank. The

Ashane force leapt towards their mounts or to draw their weapons, but the intruders already had recurve bows at the ready and arrows nocked.

'Hold your arrows!' Sang Ki shouted, panicked and in Seonu first and then more firmly in Ashane.

Despite his words, a handful of arrows flew from his own side, one finding its mark in a screaming horse. But nothing came towards them from the other and when Gurjot realised it he repeated the order and the threat of violence retreated one short pace.

Sang Ki realised that the newcomers were quite few in number. There were no more than a hundred of them to the near half a thousand he and Gurjot had mustered between them. They were tribesmen, that much was clear from their pale faces and almond eyes, but he didn't recognise their clothing. No tribe of the Fourteen wore black robes and silver turbans.

'Come no closer!' Gurjot shouted to the newcomers. His men had formed themselves into something resembling ranks by then, swords and scythes and a few bows at the ready, and his voice reflected the new confidence this gave him. 'Lower your weapons and state your purpose.'

A ripple moved through the facing line and a horse stepped forward. Sang Ki admired the rider's courage. He saw more than one Ashane hand tighten on its weapon, but none was raised and the tribesman smiled and touched his forehead in salute.

'It's strange you challenge me,' he said, 'when you're in my lands. I'm Chun Cheol.'

Chun. But the Chun had recently become something else entirely. 'The Brotherband,' Sang Ki replied. 'How delightful. And I'm Seonu Sang Ki, and this is Justice Gurjot. It's wonderful to meet you here, of all places. What an astonishing coincidence. Or am I mistaken in calling it that?'

Gurjot was frowning at him, uneasy with his light tone. His frown deepened when Cheol shook his head and dismounted.

'Chance didn't bring us here,' the tribesman said. He snapped his fingers and the ranks of horsemen parted for another figure to stumble through, bloody and bruised. 'He did.'

It was the soldier Sang Ki had passed judgement on the previous night. The man's eyes were almost swollen shut but a narrow slit of white showed as he glanced up at his fellows. His smile was ghastly, full of broken teeth.

'He was slow to speak,' Cheol said. 'We encouraged him.'

'You had no right to questions my man!' Gurjot snapped. Around him, his soldiers shifted and muttered.

'He wasn't your man. He told us he was dismissed from your army.' Cheol shrugged. 'No matter. We'll pay blood gold for his injury if you wish it. Our purpose here isn't war.'

'Then why come armed?' Sang Ki asked. 'You certainly don't look *peaceful.*'

'We brought our arms to offer you their aid. We've come to join you.'

Sang Ki couldn't help smiling at Gurjot's sour expression, so like the one he'd worn when Sang Ki had offered his own assistance. 'Why would you help us?' Gurjot asked. 'Our mission is nothing to you.'

'Your fugitive is nothing to us, but you follow him to Smiler's Fair. If there's to be a sack, we want a part of it. You take your man, and we'll pick through the riches of the fair. What say you?'

Gurjot said a lot, and Cheol much in reply, but Sang Ki already knew what the decision would be. Gurjot needed more men and, more importantly, he couldn't risk a conflict with the Brotherband. Cheol's men were only a fragment of a far larger force too dangerous to be alienated. And so they finished the day's journey an increased party, if not a more unified one.

Sang Ki wasn't entirely surprised when Cheol came to his fire that night. It was late, his mother had already retired to her tent, and the moon was bright and full over the camp. The air was filled with the smell of crushed grass. There should have been nothing but sand, and the unnaturalness of the scent made him uneasy.

Cheol stood for a moment, studying him. Sang Ki wondered if the other man expected him to rise. He was comfortable on his cushions, though, and merely watched the other man with a quirked eyebrow until Cheol settled cross-legged in the grass opposite.

Sang Ki nudged a half-empty wineskin with his foot. 'Please, share my drink. We're brothers now, aren't we? Or is membership in the Brotherband not won so easily?'

'Membership is open to all,' Cheol said. 'Why? Do you wish to join?'

'I wish to know why *you*'ve joined *us*.' Sang Ki smiled and picked up the skin to take a swig of his own wine, his eyes never leaving the tribesman's.

Cheol was a hard-faced man, difficult to read. But the long scar on his left cheek twitched as he said, 'That's been discussed. And why has a half-breed Seonu joined the hunt? That *hasn't* been discussed.'

'I dare say my reasons are as good as your own.'

'Perhaps. The other tribes have always taken the Seonu at their word. When we first came to these lands, the Seonu wandered in the Silent Sands and were lost. We thought them as dead as the Geun, but many years later another people came from the mountains and told us they were the Seonu. Some might have asked where they'd wandered for so long. Some might have asked why their hair was so pale now beneath their dark dye. We didn't ask. We knew our questions wouldn't be welcome.'

Sang Ki found himself, for the first time, bereft of a swift answer. These were the same doubts he'd secretly nursed, after he'd first read the history of his people, but he'd never heard anyone else express them. He'd always assumed he'd learn the answer when he reached his twenty-eighth year.

'You know,' Sang Ki said at last. 'I've always hoped to meet a man of the Brotherband. Your history has yet to be written – perhaps I can be the one to pen it, if you'll share it with me.'

'What is there to know?'

'You were Chun once.'

'We were many things once. Aren't men allowed to change?'

'Of course, but in my experience they seldom do.'

Cheol's regard made Sang Ki uneasy. But finally the other man said, 'The messenger makes no matter if the message is true. We'd already defeated the Dae after they condemned us to starvation. We'd shown that men are wiser than women and we'd taught our women their place. We were ready to hear the truth, even from a child.'

The other man's mouth clamped abruptly shut, and Sang Ki was instantly and absolutely certain that he was referring to Jinn, the dangerous young preacher. He had no reason for his certainty, except the expression on Cheol's face. It was the tense look of a man who knew he'd said too much, who was perhaps a little more drunk than he'd intended.

'Indeed?' Sang Ki said pleasantly. He kept his own expression friendly as he clicked his fingers for two of his men to help lift him to his feet. 'Well, perhaps we can continue this conversation tomorrow. I believe there's a lot I might learn from you.'

He smiled and turned round and ignored the prickle of his shoulder blades, knowing that the other man's eyes followed him all the way to his tent.

The next morning he sought out Gurjot, allowing his mammoth to drift towards the other man's stallion as if it was pure coincidence.

'I mislike our new allies,' he said, as soon as he was sure none of the Brotherband could overhear him.

Gurjot didn't quite roll his eyes, but his thoughts were easy to read.

'Yes, I know,' Sang Ki said, 'and the fox accused the wolf of raiding the henhouse. But look at their clothing: it's black and silver, the colours of the moon.'

Gurjot frowned, not understanding the point.

'There are those who say our King's missing son is the moon reborn. We had two such heretics in our dungeon, until they conspired in my father's murder and escaped. The moon's men aren't to be trusted, and they're most certainly not on our side.'

'You want me to dismiss a fifth of our fighting strength –

and let's not fool ourselves, probably the best trained of it –
because you dislike the colour of their clothing? Forgive me if
I'm hesitant.'

'It's more than that. Cheol said something that led me to believe
that he's been taken in by the very boy who killed Lord Thilak.
They're serving their own interests here, can't you see it?'

'And you aren't?'

'Perhaps. But mine happen to align with yours. The Brotherband
. . . I'm not so sure.'

Gurjot shook his head, a sharp gesture that Sang Ki understood
meant an end to the discussion. 'They're useful and they're
controllable. When they cease to be either, we'll part ways. Until
then, you'll follow my leadership, or *we'll* part ways.'

'Of course,' Sang Ki said blandly, and he smiled and left the
other man.

He sat beside his mother in silence for a while, watching their
force's progress through the waste that had become a garden.
Insects filled the air with a comforting hum but the hot sun was
a pressure on his neck. Sweat slicked between the folds of his
flesh and his head pounded. He saw Cheol glance his way, the
other man's eyes unreadable, and resolved to set his own watch
that night, and every night the Brotherband remained with them.

25

Eric had begun to imagine a life of leisure from the moment his duties were explained to him. But the second morning in Salvation, and every morning after that, he was woken well before he was ready. With no darkness it was hard to judge the length of his sleep, but he reckoned they never let him laze in bed for a full night's worth.

It was always Bolli who came to rouse him. He'd been pleased at first, until he discovered that the other man was only interested in giving him his lessons: reading and writing and history and even mathematics, which couldn't serve any purpose in the world that Eric could see. He was, at that very moment, staring at a triangle. Bolli had scratched it into the ice tray he used instead of paper, its surface cleaned by pouring water over it and letting it freeze.

'I don't know, do I?' Eric said sulkily. 'One side's longer and two are short – what else matters? I don't need to figure out the angle of a man's cock to slide it in me.'

Bolli sighed. 'You won't be sliding a cock inside you at all if you know what's good for you. The Servants don't like that sort of thing – they say it isn't in Mizhara's Law. Which you'd know if you attended more to their lessons, but I hear you were snoring loud enough to wake the dead yesterday when they were trying to learn you the proper ways to behave.'

It was true. The lessons with the Servants were even worse than the lessons with Bolli. They took him to their library under a huge dome of ice. It was stacked with books of pure white vellum written in their goddess's own hand, or so they said. They told him the books held all the rules and regulations that should govern any person's life.

The Servants were very big on rules, as it turned out. Their time passed in cycles of thirteen days: what they called the 'oroboros,' beginning from the day they were born. The first day they were supposed to spend sitting around thinking about how they could improve themselves. The second they prayed, which Eric had never seen the point of when you could pay the Worshippers to do it for you. Days three to six they worked, and day seven was when they called upon Eric to do his manly duty.

Each husband had a different day out of thirteen. Since the Servants all began their oroboros the moment they were born, they were out of time with each other, some working on days others prayed, or shagged, or sat around. But that way there was always a husband available to see to their needs, no matter when their seventh day fell. Days eight to eleven they studied this Perfect Law of their goddess, which they seemed to know by heart already, and wrote down their thoughts about it to store away in their great library. The twelfth day they were at their praying again, and then on the thirteenth they thought about everything they'd done wrong and how much better they were going to be next time round. Eric couldn't imagine what their idea of a wrongdoing was. It all seemed a sort of madness to him, but they never asked his opinion.

In time, they told him, he'd be expected to start his own oroboros. The longer he could put that off the better. In the meantime, they wanted to educate him, and if it was be educated or be stuck in that endless routine of theirs, he supposed his knowledge could stand a little increasing. So when they'd recite Mizhara's words to him, boring sentence after boring sentence, he learned he was to recite them back and moon monsters take him if he got just one word out of place. Then the whole lesson would have to begin over.

Not that they ever got angry with him. He was never sure if it was the same Servant who taught him each day or different ones. He asked her name when they first met, and she told him she had none. Without names, the tall, gold-skinned women were hard to tell apart. But she – or they – never treated him with anything but an endless, wearying patience. They were big on rules but not too big on feelings, as far as he could tell. The most emotion he'd ever seen out of them was when they talked about their goddess, Mizhara. A bright light shone from their eyes then, but it wasn't one he altogether liked.

It was a rum set-up all round. Housed in ice, made to learn to be a gentleman when he didn't ever claim or want to be one, and taught a bunch of rules that served no good purpose he could see. And when he wasn't learning, there was nothing to do but wander the ice corridors of the city or talk to the other husbands, who were pleasant enough but not the company he'd have chosen. They were much too concerned with what the Servants thought, too careful of everything they said. And most of all, they weren't his type: too pale and blond and just like what he saw when he looked in the mirror, which had never put iron in his pecker. He thought of Lahiru, but the other man's face seemed to get bleached out in his mind as if the endless whiteness of this place leeched the colour even out of memory.

Anyway, Lahiru was gone and less-than-perfect was better than nothing at all, wasn't it? Bolli had always been a game lad, ready for a tumble with a fellow sellcock if there were no johns around to please.

Eric relaxed back on to one elbow and lifted the other hand to rest it against Bolli's forearm. It wasn't quite a caress, but definitely the promise of one. 'So,' he said, 'you've been here a while, ain't you? What can a boy do to pass the time beside learn about triangles?'

Bolli brushed his hand off and leaned back. 'Not that, that's for certain.'

Eric pouted, an expression he knew made his lips look especially plump. He put his hand back on Bolli's knee this time. 'Don't act the maiden with me, Bolli. You liked a bit of meat with your vegetables back in the day.'

But that hand was brushed off too, and Bolli stood. 'That was then – I had no other way to buy my membership in the company. Why would I want it now when we have all the cunny a man could wish for? We're not all of us mollies like you, Eric. And you'd better heed me: there'll be none of that here, not if you know what's good for you. I told you, the Servants don't like it. And if they don't like it, we don't neither. We'll keep you in line if they won't, and we can hurt you in ways they won't be able to see.'

Eric was so shocked by the coldness in Bolli's eyes that he just lay without a sound and watched the other man walk from the room. But he'd seen a stirring in Bolli's britches, despite all his words. Bolli had always been a hypocrite, Eric recalled now. But the threat in his eyes had been real. Eric shivered and turned back to the ice tablet, trying to figure out just how long the longest side of that triangle was.

The afternoons were his own, whatever that was worth. He'd been slowly exploring Salvation, though many a time when he'd approached something interesting one of the Servants had floated into view to forbid him to go on. It was against the rules, of course. He'd seen some beautiful things all the same. In one vast room he'd found hundreds and hundreds of statues, all of the same figure – their Mizhara, he was sure – but clearly carved by different hands. The icy, stern face was never quite perfect. He liked that. The Servants tried to pretend they were all identical, without even names to tell them apart, but they couldn't stop their individual natures coming out.

Another day he'd found a room with a giant ice sculpture hanging from the ceiling: great globes and rings and jagged lumps all rotating round each other like a baby's mobile. A Servant had told him it was a map of the universe, but hadn't explained how that could be.

He'd even gone back to the hall where he'd been wed and looked at the cube of ice with the two footprints in it. He now knew it showed Mizhara's last steps on this world before she'd departed it for ever, leaving only her endless books of instructions behind.

Today he decided to go down rather than up. From the outside,

Salvation seemed only interested in reaching skyward with its huge octagonal towers and needle-sharp spires, but the city was built on snow and the snow went many levels down, with hundreds of rooms carved into it.

He half expected to be stopped at the top of the spiral stairs, but there was no one there and he paused a moment to admire the rainbows flung every which way by the clear ice. The footing looked treacherous. The Servants had their methods, though, and they'd scored the surface of the steps with diagonal grooves to provide grip for his soft-soled fur boots. His cape trailed behind him as he descended, picking up no moisture. The ice here never seemed to melt, no matter how bright the sun.

There was a landing after one rotation of the stairs, but he'd explored this level already. It seemed to be where the Servants had their quarters. Their rooms were even smaller than his and each was decorated with nothing but a golden sunburst on the far wall. He glanced around to see if he was being watched, then took the next flight down and then, on a whim, the next two after that as well.

The fourth level beneath the ground looked more interesting. It was darker here, the sunlight filtered through multiple layers of ice that turned it a pale blue so that the whole area had the feeling of being underwater. Bizarrely, it was also warmer. Some of the ice had even sweated a few droplets of water, which had carved runnels in the walls as they trickled down. The corridors seemed entirely empty, but there was a noise, a booming sort of roar that was also like the sea.

The sound was oddly directionless. Eric tried to find its source, following corridors curving right and left in the half-dark like the innards of some fabulous sea creature. The roaring never seemed to get louder, but after a while he realised he could feel it as well as hear it. It was a vibration that hummed deep in his chest and scattered the tiny droplets of water from the walls to splash his face. And then, with no warning, he turned one more corner and the source of all the noise was ahead of him.

It was vast, filling not just this level but what must have been

at least ten more below. It was beautiful too. Cogs of crystalline
ice turned within cogs, white pistons that might have been
compacted snow rose and fell, and all of it hung without visible
means of support within the enormous void it inhabited. His eyes
kept getting caught by different bits of the mechanism, but the
longer he looked, the more impossible it seemed. A cog that had
been circling upwards suddenly seemed to be moving down. A
sphere became a cube and a straight line twisted into a spiral,
then back into a line again.

He stared at it open-mouthed until he heard the soft crunch
of a footfall behind him and turned to find one of the Servants
approaching. He expected to be sent away, but she just smiled.
Her face radiated the nearest thing to joy he'd seen from one of
them.

'Beautiful, is it not?' she said.

'I suppose. What does it do?'

Her hand reached towards the nearest cog, her long, elegant
fingers stopping just short of its furious rotation. 'Mizhara, may
her name be exalted, made it many seasons past, in the days
when she still dwelt among us and the world was a better place.
It keeps the light shining here in the days that would otherwise
be night.'

'It controls the *sun*?'

The Servant shook her head, her long blonde hair swishing
around her white robe. 'Better to say that it controls us. Salvation
follows the sun between the poles of the earth. Such was the
power of our mistress's magics.'

Eric stared at the whirring cog. He saw that it was engraved
with a long, curved stroke like a fragment of a huge letter. There
were other strokes on other cogs and on levers and wheels too.
As he watched the mechanism spin and turn, the strokes came
into brief alignment. He caught the suggestion of some important
word that he had no time to understand before they'd moved on
and a new alignment was reached, a new word written by the
goddess's machine.

'Is there more you wish to know?' the Servant asked, sounding eager to impart it, but Eric shook his head. He didn't like the thought of staying within reach of a power that immense.

It took him a long time to find his way back to the staircase, and then he fled up and away to the familiarity of his room and the other husbands.

The next day, though, he found himself exploring the bowels of Salvation once again.

Now that he was ready for it, he could feel the deep vibration of the machine as soon as he descended below ground. He passed the fourth level where he'd first seen it, then the fifth, then some impulse made him continue down twenty-three more levels until the spiral staircase ended. The sound of the machine was more profound here, rattling his teeth. He thought this might be the bottom of the city at last, but when he walked a little further along the icy floor he found another staircase, this one carved into stone.

His foot hesitated above the first tread. There was still light below, he could see it shining softly up, but all his life he'd been taught to stay within the sun's reach. At Madam Aeronwen's he'd chosen a room on the second floor, because everyone knew the First Death came from below. Still, the Servants had built their city here and the staircase was part of it. They'd have warned him if there was any danger, wouldn't they?

Then again, none of the other husbands seemed inclined to explore, content with their comfortable existence. Maybe the Servants hadn't warned him of what lay below because they didn't think it necessary. And the existence here *was* comfortable. It was boring but not filled with any risks a boy shouldn't take just to entertain himself of an afternoon.

He was still hesitating, one foot on stone and one on ice, when the voice boomed up from below. *'Come then, morsel, if thy will is to come.'*

'Rii!' He was more pleased to hear her than really made sense. But she was familiar and, if not friendly, then at least more interesting than the Servants with their endless lessons and rules.

The stairs were smoothly polished, ornamented only with patterns of lead hammered across the rock. The patterns were quite unlike the writing he'd seen in the many books of Salvation's library. They were curved where those letters had clean lines, twisted and hard to follow. He could almost sense the mind behind the markings, though he wasn't sure it seemed a very friendly one.

After fifty steps or so he found himself in a network of corridors very like the maze of ice above, only a little darker. There was still light though, a diffuse golden glow, and he shivered to think Mizhara's machine could bring sunshine even where there was no sun.

'*Lower,*' Rii's voice echoed up to him.

He wasn't keen on descending further, but it was clear Rii couldn't squeeze her immense body into these narrow corridors. Eric wandered them a while, sometimes reaching out to trace the complex patterns of metal fixed to the rock walls, before he found the next stairs down. The light was weaker here and he couldn't see the bottom. It wasn't pleasant to think about walking into that unknown space. He swallowed and made himself do it, step after step downward and no sign of an end.

He couldn't judge how long it had been when he finally reached the bottom. The ceiling was hidden in the darkness above him, and the walls – if there *were* walls – were lost to distance. He could see only a score of yards along the floor in each direction. Ahead of him and running into the distance to right and left was a row of statues, some dressed as warriors and others as sages in long robes, but none of them human. They looked, Eric realised, like the missing males of the Servants, tall and thin with misshapen ears. They were carved from stone, but their hair and large round eyes had been faced with silver. It wasn't an altogether pleasing effect.

He heard a sudden rustling in the darkness behind him and spun to face it, heart pounding. A shadow approached and he would have run for the stairs if his legs hadn't turned to water, but then he saw that it was only Rii. Her hulking form moved further into the light, leathery wings folded against her back and her claws skittering on the rock. The smell of mouldy cinnamon wafted ahead of her.

'*Well, morsel, thou art bolder than thy brethren,*' she said.

Eric forced a smile. 'No one ever said I ain't game.'

'*And what makest thou of this city, so much less fair than that above?*'

He might not be educated, but he knew a loaded question when he heard one. There was a proprietary air in the way she studied the space around them, her small black eyes perhaps piercing the darkness better than his. She opened her mouth wide, revealing her fangs, and let out a horrible series of chirps. The echoes flew back from a very long way away.

'It's good down here,' Eric said. 'More like a real home. It weren't built by the Servants, was it? This place is solid. It takes a different kind of person to make a whole bleeding castle out of ice, with no privacy and light everywhere. It's like they're afraid of what hides in the shadows.'

Rii let out a thin, yipping laugh. '*Thou speakest true. The Servants of cursed Mizhara fashioned their Salvation on the ruins of this, my home.*'

'*Your* people made this place?' He eyed her long, curved claws, wondering how they'd ever held the tools.

'*Not we, but our brethren. At the moonrise of the world, our master Yron bade them build here, where he would ensure for us an endless night. It was he who fashioned the great machine that kept us ever in darkness, though the Servants who corrupted its purpose now claim it for their own.*'

'That thing up there used to make it dark, not light?' Eric looked at the glow that had followed him down the stairs and died in the folds of her dark skin and fur. 'Don't tell me – Mizhara took exception to it.'

'*She wished all to be light and beautiful. There was no room in her world for ugliness or doubt, and so she quarrelled with her brother, who was master of the moon and all its mysteries. They fought a great war, the greatest the world has yet known.*'

'And she won. I heard this story already. Well, I suppose the sun's stronger than the moon.' Which made it even more unlikely that he'd betray the one for the other, as her dream had predicted. But he didn't think he'd tell her that.

Rii growled, a sound a little like the vibrations of the machine above. *'The sun hath no greater strength. Yron was the god of secrets, which are always more powerful than that which is known.'*

'But he *did* lose. It's the winners what get to build their cities on top of the losers, ain't it?'

She reared up above him, her wings beating so close to his face that one of her claws scratched his cheek. *'My master's forces were defeated, it is true,'* she hissed. *'Lord Yron was killed and his servants driven to madness and to life beneath the ground. My own people were slain, every last one but I, and I have been made to linger on in this bright age of the world, a slave to those who conquered me.'*

'I'm sorry,' Eric said. But after a moment, he couldn't stop himself asking, 'Why did they spare you when they killed everyone else?'

'My brethren fought to their last breaths. I chose surrender.'

'But why? It don't take a genius to see how much you hate the Servants.'

'Ah . . .' Rii said. Her long black tongue flicked out to wet her lips. *'My reasons are my own, morsel. Perhaps if thou shouldst return, I will share them with thee.'*

There was a leathery flap of wings, a mustier, more rank stench than her breath, and then she was gone into the vast darkness.

26

When Krish woke there was water in his mouth and nose and his heart thumped with unreasoning panic. Then the sound of laughter penetrated the sleepy fog and he rolled on to his back to see Dae Hyo standing over him with a bowl in his hand.

Krish half rose to his feet, angry enough to attack the other man, before good sense returned and he fell back to his knees and shook himself like a dog. There was still a last chill of departed winter in the air and he shivered even as the sun began to dry him. They'd camped beneath an apple tree where the petals floated in the air, fragrant freckles of colour across the blue sky.

'Awake now, boy?' Dae Hyo asked.

Krish nodded, still nervous around the other man and his changeable moods, though it was too early for even Dae Hyo to have started drinking.

'Get up, then. It's time you learned to be useful.' He threw something at Krish's feet: a wooden sword, crudely carved. Krish wondered if Dae Hyo had made it himself that morning. There was another in Dae Hyo's hand, equally crude. He twirled it casually, then rested the long, blunt blade against his shoulder.

Krish stayed kneeling on the ground and didn't reach for the sword. 'I can't use that.'

'I know. That's why I'm going to teach you. It's all right, you can leave the sword for now. We're going to run first. I've seen you panting for breath whenever you have to walk. You've got no stamina. You wouldn't last five minutes in a fight.'

'I don't *want* to fight.' Krish intended to find people to fight for him – he'd meant Dae Hyo to be the first – but maybe a leader needed to know how to do the things he ordered of his men.

'What, I'm to do all the bleeding for you?' Dae Hyo asked, as if to confirm it. 'You can spit a rabbit so it isn't burnt and you know how to shut your mouth when a man wants some quiet. Apart from that, you're fucking useless. So if you want to stay with me, follow me.'

He'd dropped his own wooden sword and set off running before Krish could respond. There was nothing he could do but jump up and follow after.

Krish knew that Dae Hyo was slowing his pace for him, and yet he struggled to keep up. His lungs had cleared in the warmer, richer lowland air, but now he felt the breath catch in them with every step and his muscles burned. The grass felt like it was pulling at his legs to hold him back and he was soon going at little more than a stumbling walk. And still Dae Hyo ran on. Krish would have begged him to stop, but he couldn't spare the breath.

Each step had become an agony when his legs suddenly gave beneath him, tumbling him to the ground. It must have taken Dae Hyo a little while to realise he'd lost his follower, because Krish lay gasping miserably for a long moment before he felt the other man's boot in his ribs. He curled round the blow and gasped some more.

'What's wrong with you, boy?' Dae Hyo asked. He bent at the waist to peer into Krish's face. His expression was halfway between annoyance and concern.

'Tired,' Krish gasped. 'Hurt.'

Dae Hyo rested a hand against Krish's sweating brow. 'You're hot.'

'You made me run ten miles!' Krish gritted.

'Not even two.' Dae Hyo rose, his spine cracking. 'Well, it takes time. You'll get better. I tell you what, a bit of swordwork will loosen you up.'

He strode away. Krish had just about enough strength to rise to his feet and follow. 'What about breakfast?' he said. 'There's rabbit left, and those boiled roots.'

Dae Hyo cast a jaundiced eye back at him and sighed.

'Breakfast, and swordwork after. But hurry. You'll never be a warrior if you slouch along like that.'

The sword felt like stone in Krish's hands. 'Again,' Dae Hyo yelled and he swung it at the tree to watch it clatter against the bark. It barely broke off a splinter.

'Again,' Dae Hyo said, and ten more times, before he sniffed and stepped forward to inspect Krish's work. 'Useless. You haven't even dented it.'

'The sword's made of wood!'

'So's the tree. Try again.'

But Krish's arm refused to obey him and the sword wilted at the end of it, its tip drooping towards the ground.

'Fine. Rest, then,' Dae Hyo said, but after ten minutes he had him up and at it again, to even less visible effect.

When Krish's arms were as exhausted and weak as his legs, Dae Hyo finally told him to mount up, and they set off again on their trek through the plains. It was an aimless wandering whose purpose Krish had yet to fathom. He knew that soon he'd need to start directing the other man where *he* wanted to go, but he thought there was currently little chance of being listened to. Maybe if he learned to fight as Dae Hyo wanted the other man would be more willing to follow his cause once Krish explained it to him.

The plains, he'd learned over the weeks on his own and the days in Dae Hyo's company, weren't entirely featureless. After an hour's ride they saw something black swell on the horizon until they drew close and found themselves passing a huge round rock. It rested on the grass as if a giant had dropped it there. No vegetation clung to it, not even moss, and Krish wondered at the mystery, but Dae Hyo just shrugged at his questions.

He'd been equally uninterested when they'd passed the crumbled remains of a huge stone structure, listing to one side and nibbled away by time and rain. 'Not a Dae place,' was all he said. He'd only once said more, when from the top of a small hill, Krish had seen a yellow stain on the horizon. He'd turned to

Dae Hyo to find the other man scowling. 'The Rune Waste,' he'd said. 'Men who go there get sick. All except the Chun.' He'd walked fast in the other direction and Krish had been happy to follow.

There were hills sometimes too, and meandering rivers. Once they'd even skirted the lily-fringed shore of a great lake. The air had been filled with the high, forlorn cries of the stilt-legged white birds that waded in it. Krish thought he might come to love this land, if he could only get used to the wide sweep of the sky above him.

They ate their lunch after a few hours, some unnameable creature Krish had caught in his traps. It was plump and the meat juices dribbled down Dae Hyo's chin as he carefully stripped the fat from its skin, then hung the hide on his saddlebags, maybe for later trade. For once, he didn't swig the foul vodka in his flask to wash down his meal, and Krish guessed it was for his sake Dae Hyo remained sober. He knew he should feel honoured, but the other man was at least jollier when he was drunk. When Dae Hyo had finished, he took out his bow and handed it to Krish.

'I've loosened the string,' Dae Hyo said, 'but we'll make you your own when I'm sure you won't accidentally stick me in the back with an arrow.'

Krish was a little more confident with the bow. He'd grown up using a sling to scare the hunter birds from the goats and he had a good eye. His first few shots went wide of the target Dae Hyo had carved in one of the lonely sentinel trees that scattered the plain. Then two shots landed inside the ring and Dae Hyo smiled and clapped him on the back. The next was true as well, but then the arrows started to fall short until Krish found he didn't have the strength to pull the bow at all. His shoulders had failed him along with the rest of his body.

'Well,' Dae Hyo said. 'You show some promise there, at least.'

Krish thought that, surely, must be the end of it. But when the sun was touching the horizon and they'd started to make camp, he saw Dae Hyo clearing a square of grass, stamping the long stalks and the blue spring flowers among them flat with his boots.

'Gods of my hearth,' Krish said. 'What now?'

Dae Hyo shrugged out of his shirt, revealing a chest thick with both scars and muscle. 'A warrior fights with hand as well as sword. Strip, boy, and come and face me.'

Krish was so tired it made him reckless. He folded his arms, pulling against the burn in his shoulders. 'That's crazy. You'll crush me.'

'I'll go easy.'

'You'll still crush me. I'm half your size. Don't worry: if I'm disarmed and facing someone like you, I'll surrender.'

'Surrender?' Dae Hyo looked so baffled Krish wondered if he genuinely didn't understand the word. 'Come here, boy. Or are you a coward as well as a weakling?'

Krish knew the flare of rage was exactly what Dae Hyo wanted. He tamped it down and kept his place. 'I'm not stupid. I'll never beat a man in that sort of fight, and I'm not going to try.'

He turned without waiting for an answer and went to their packs, where the fire needed feeding and another rabbit skinning. After a few moments Dae Hyo stomped over to join him and they ate supper in a frosty silence.

Once tiredness had crept into every part of Krish, including his spirit, he began to regret his words. But he didn't need Dae Hyo, not really. He could trap his own food and keep a better eye out for enemies now he knew they were there. And there must be other possible allies on the plains besides him.

Krish was too exhausted to worry about it overmuch. He wrapped his aching body in his blankets, turned his back on the fire and almost instantly fell asleep.

In the morning, he was woken by another splash of water in his face.

'What?' Dae Hyo said when Krish glared at him. 'Not giving up already, are you? Or did you think I had? I'm made of stronger metal than that, boy, and you don't want to test it. Now get up.'

Running was, if anything, even more painful this morning. His legs had stiffened in the night and his stomach felt like he'd swallowed splinters, though it had seemed the one part of his body he hadn't exercised to exhaustion yesterday. He barely managed fifty paces at a run and then he was forced to stumble after Dae Hyo's disappearing figure like a cripple chasing the man who'd stolen his crutches.

Then, without warning, Dae Hyo stopped. Instinct sent Krish to his knees before he knew the reason. It was an ambush. Three men leapt from the long grass towards them and the sword thrust meant for his throat passed through air to be knocked aside by Dae Hyo's blade. Another weapon came for him, a hunting knife. Krish couldn't avoid it, but Dae Hyo was there, stabbing his own knife into the attacker's guts and ripping upwards so that blood and intestines tumbled on to the grass in a steaming heap beside him.

The two remaining men didn't bother with Krish after that. The fight had at first seemed like it would last only a moment, but now they stepped back, one with two hand axes hefted and the other with a curved sword, keen only on one side. Their clothing was black and their turbans were silver. Their eyes were hard when they looked at Dae Hyo and his were full of venom.

'Chun scum,' Dae Hyo grated. 'These are Dae lands.'

'Not any longer,' the swordsman said, smiling. 'We killed the Dae. They screamed as they died.'

'You fought women and children,' Dae Hyo said. 'I tell you what – now see how much you like fighting a man.'

The swordsman spat his contempt at Dae Hyo's feet and the two Chun warriors moved to flank him, the axe-wielder standing in his shadow. Krish's mouth was dry with fear and he hated his helplessness, but when the tribesman swung his axes at Dae Hyo's undefended back, Dae Hyo twisted and blocked so smoothly it left his attacker with one weapon on the ground and a thick welling slash on his arm. After that the pair were more cautious, circling and circling and never attacking.

Dae Hyo stood in the centre of their circle, almost negligently at ease. 'Afraid of me?' he asked. 'Rat-fucking cowards.'

The taunt worked better on the men than it had on Krish, perhaps because it was less true. The two must have fought together often. They moved almost as one. One axe rose and fell towards Dae Hyo's neck as a knife hacked at his hamstrings, while the single-edged sword swung in an arc meant to take off his head.

It didn't seem possible to escape the suddenly sprung trap. Krish leapt forward determined to do – he didn't know what. But he leapt into the empty space where Dae Hyo had been. His clumsy lunge took him into the path of the axe and only luck let the haft rather than the blade strike him.

His head was still ringing as he watched Dae Hyo dance away from the triple blow, leaving only a lock of his dark hair for the sword and nothing but air for the knife. His own blades were slashing at the same time, his shorter sword somehow finding an opening through the arc of the longer and cutting open his opponent from groin to neck. For a moment, Krish thought Dae Hyo had forgotten the axe-wielder, but then the man grunted and dropped to his knees beside him, hands clasped to his gut where Dae Hyo's knife was buried deep inside.

The world seemed to draw a breath, release it and continue. Birdsong and the soft whisper of wind through the grass restarted all around them. Those sounds were shortly joined by the buzzing of flies as they descended on the three corpses that Dae Hyo was now calmly looting.

The warrior smiled when he found a leather flask tucked inside a black jerkin, downed the contents, burped thunderously and stuffed the flask inside his own shirt. Next he examined two belt knives, their blades made of sharpened flint, and threw them aside. He took the axes, the sword and a necklace of amber beads from round the neck of one of the dead men along with a silver ring from another.

'The Chun always were showy fuckers,' he said. Who needs a pretty necklace to tempt thieves when there's no one to admire it but the rabbits?'

'You're taking it,' Krish pointed out, standing upright on wobbly legs.

Dae Hyo frowned, then flicked the necklace to him. 'Put it on, then. The Jorlith say amber's lucky.'

'It wasn't very lucky for him.'

'Well, let's hope it'll serve you better.'

Krish wasn't sure he believed in luck, but the stones glowed pleasingly gold in the sunlight and he shrugged and tied the leather cord at the back of his neck. 'Shouldn't we leave? There might be more of them.'

'If there were more they'd be here already. The Chun – the Brotherband, they call themselves now, the ignorant scum. What's a brother without a mother or a sister? Anyway, I was told they've moved north, out of their own lands and the Rune Waste, to raid the Four Together. They've broken the Poppy Peace for the first time in fifty years. I don't know why these three stayed behind. Maybe they didn't like the way Brother Yong was running things.'

Dae Hyo finished his work. He stripped the black silk shirt from the man he'd gutted, though it was dripping with blood, and then they walked together back to camp. Over and over in Krish's mind, the fight kept following its lethal course. Dae Hyo had been so *quick*. He hadn't even seemed afraid. When they'd finished their breakfast and Dae Hyo called him to his feet for sword practice, he didn't complain.

There was more enthusiasm in Krish's strokes this time and he could see that the wooden sword was sinking a little deeper into the bark. Dae Hyo offered no praise, though, and after five minutes Krish was already tiring despite his new-found determination.

'No no!' Dae Hyo shouted after a blow so wild it missed the trunk entirely. 'You're not doing it right.'

Krish swallowed down his impatience and nodded. 'I know. When you moved it seemed easier.'

'I've been doing it longer.'

'But it's not just that. I saw you. You were swinging differently and the way you moved your feet . . . You never lost your balance. I think if you teach me how you stand, I'll get better.'

'How I stand? I stand like I stand. Like a man.'

'Show me.'

Dae Hyo moved reluctantly to raise his wooden sword. He looked ill at ease, with his shoulders hunched in discomfort.

'No,' Krish said, 'use your real weapon.' He hardly noticed that he was giving the older man orders.

Dae Hyo sighed theatrically, then dropped the wooden blade and pulled out the metal from its sheath on his hip. Instantly, his posture altered. His spine straightened as his knees bent, one foot shifting in front of the other. He was rooted, Krish now saw, precisely over the midpoint of his body.

'That's it, stay just like that.'

Dae Hyo tensed and almost moved, but he looked at Krish and waited until he'd put himself into the same position. His eyebrows rose as Krish lifted the point of the wooden sword, which now felt much lighter in his hand.

'You look almost like a warrior,' Dae Hyo said. 'Take a swing.'

Krish did, and instantly lost his balance, falling forward on to his front foot so the sword once again clattered uselessly against the trunk.

Dae Hyo's face fell. 'Oh well, it was a good idea.'

'It *is* a good idea. I just need to learn how to move first. Show me how you go forward holding the sword.'

Dae Hyo looked doubtful but did as Krish asked and then watched, half-amused but gradually more impressed, as Krish spent the next hour practising what he'd been shown.

They travelled on a little after that. Krish's horse hugged the side of a small stream as he led Dae Hyo's beast and the other man scouted ahead for danger. He found nothing but two large fish, which he presented to Krish for cooking. Their silver scales gleamed in the sunlight and flaked against his palms.

When they'd eaten, Dae Hyo brought out his bow and they repeated the morning's exercise. He showed Krish how he drew the weapon, its string kissing his lips as his shoulders expanded to draw it, and then Krish took it and spent another hour imitating the move until his shoulders were in agony. But the bow had begun to feel a little more natural in his hands.

Supper was more cheerful that night, though Krish once again refused to wrestle, this time with the excuse that he'd do better when he was stronger. After they'd eaten the smoked remains of the fish he lay back on his elbows and watched the animals of the plain slinking through the twilight while the stream burbled to their left. He held still as a tiny rabbit emerged from the grass to sniff at his feet. Its liquid brown eyes met his in complete trust for a moment. Then Dae Hyo came trudging back through the grass with a filled water pot and the baby rabbit hopped away, its white tail bobbing as it retreated into the mouth of its burrow.

Krish frowned. 'I never thought before, but it must just be men they hunt.'

'What?' Dae Hyo crushed some aromatic leaves in the water and set it over the fire to boil.

'The . . .' Krish was reluctant to give them the name he'd heard in children's stories, afraid the other man would mock him. 'There are ash-skinned people, monsters, living below the ground.'

'Oh, the worm men. No, they take horses too. I've seen them in the mines. And they ate Jasper the Nose's best hunting dog.'

Krish digested the information that others knew the creatures were more than legend. 'But the rabbits live in the dark, underground.'

'Mmm . . .' Dae Hyo frowned as he poured the tea. 'I tell you what, you're right. And it's not just rabbits. Foxes too, and badgers and moles.'

'It must only be men and men's servants they hate.'

Dae Hyo sipped his tea. 'Can they hate? Can they think? They never seemed to have much on their minds except feasting on the nearest flesh.'

Krish remembered the attack in the ruined city. The creatures, the worm men, had seemed mindless in their violence, but they'd chosen to spare him. There must have been some intelligence behind the decision. He didn't want to share that experience with the other man, though. He was afraid of what Dae Hyo would think. His fingers played with the amber beads of his necklace as he thought, soothed by their smooth coolness.

'It suits you, boy,' Dae Hyo said. 'You Ashane aren't pretty, no one could accuse you of that. A man can't love skin so dark or noses so like a hook. And as for those eyes of yours – just like the worm men. As I'm sure you know.' He smiled at Krish's startled look and Krish was reminded that the other man had a sharp mind when he wasn't drowning it in alcohol. 'At least with the necklace you look civilised. Better than those ugly bracelets round your wrists, anyhow.'

'They're not bracelets,' Krish said, worrying at one of the manacles, which had chafed the skin raw beneath.

'No?' Something in Dae Hyo's expression suggested he'd already guessed this.

'I was . . . chained,' Krish admitted.

'A slave? Well, good for you for escaping. No man should own another. They say the Janggok sell their captives to the Rah, but what else can you expect of men who cut off other men's cocks and a people who'd rather weave than hunt? You weren't taken in a raid, were you?'

'I wasn't a slave. I was a prisoner. They arrested me for . . .' He'd been about to say *a crime I didn't commit*, but if he was ever going to tell Dae Hyo the truth, now was a good time for it. 'I didn't do anything wrong,' Krish said. 'I'm the Ashane king's son. There was a prophecy I'd kill my father, so he'd planned to kill me first, but someone got me away to safety when I was a baby. I didn't know who I was until the King's justice found me this winter. He recognised me by my eyes.'

Dae Hyo's delighted guffaw wasn't the reaction he'd expected. 'Really, boy? And there I thought you looked like that because your mother let some worm man have his wicked way with her.'

'It's true!' Krish protested. 'I'm going to build an army and kill my father. I'll be a king myself and you can be the general of my army.'

Dae Hyo shook his head, still laughing. 'I'm honoured,' he said, and Krish realised he didn't believe a single word of it. It did sound absurd, he knew that. He wouldn't have believed it himself if his ma hadn't told him. He twisted the manacle on his left wrist and wished he had some way to get it off his arm. Maybe then he'd seem less like a common criminal.

'Leave it,' Dae Hyo said. 'A man should have something to remember his enemies by, whoever they are.'

'Who are yours?' Krish asked. 'You seem to have a lot of them. The men today, and those ones when we first met – and you don't seem to like any of the other tribes very much.'

'Each tribe likes its own best. The others have their own ways; it doesn't have to make them enemies. And those men I killed when we first met, they were like a wolf or a flash flood: a natural thing a man battles against because he has to. There's no hate in it.'

'But you hated those men today.'

Dae Hyo's face twisted and he looked away. 'The fucking Chun. We'd always fought, us and them. A blood feud here, a raid there – you know, nothing out of the ordinary. Their land was poor, just scrubby grass and giant rats the uncivilised scum bred to eat. They envied us our deer and rabbits and sometimes they tried to steal them. The first time I wetted my blade it was in Chun blood.

'Then came the year of the great murrain. The disease struck their rats and our deer. The creatures' eyes gummed up and they moved slower and slower until they ended their lives bleeding from every hole. I remember the stink of it. It was worse from the ones who were still alive, a mix of pus and shit, and the crying they made was like a baby that needs feeding. Nearly all the deer died and all the Chun rats too. But the sickness spared our rabbits, so we still had a little food. The young and the old suffered, but most of the Dae lived. It was different for the Chun. They had nothing. Their elder mothers sent to beg us for some of our stock, but what could we do? We didn't have enough to feed our own and they'd never been our friends.'

He was quiet for a long time, watching the stick he used to stir the spitting embers of the fire. 'The Chun men came in force from their lands and fell on our winter camp where the women and the children were,' he said finally. 'That bastard Chun Yong led them. The Dae warriors were hunting in the hills for what game we could find. Only a few were left to defend the camp. The Chun killed the elder mothers and our wives and knife wives and sisters. They killed our children. And when we returned, a band at a time, they killed us too.'

'But you survived,' Krish said softly.

'My band was high in the foothills of the Black Heights, hoping to steal game from Seonu lands. We found nothing, and when we returned the Chun were gone. I wanted to hunt them down but we were only seven, and the others said we needed to bury our dead. We spent days at it, until the rot was too great and we had to leave them for the wolves.' There were tears in Dae Hyo's eyes and Krish looked away. 'No man should take his blade to a woman or a child, but the Chun had stopped caring what a man should do.'

'All your people were killed?' Krish asked after a moment.

Dae Hyo dashed away his tears and coughed to clear his voice. 'Near enough. A few were taken as slaves. And there were those in my hunting band, my brothers. I thought we were the seed of a new Dae nation. I thought they felt the same.' He spat on the grass. 'They've all forgotten who they are. Not me, though. So when I heard the Chun had moved on, I came home where I belong.'

He stared into the fire for a long while, as the sunlight faded and the sounds of night crept in to fill the silence. 'But the land's just dirt without the tribe. And the Chun still haven't paid for what they did. They will, though. I'll take a sword to all their futures, the way they took one to mine.'

The training continued: running in the morning, swordwork after that and the bow before supper. Once Krish had realised he needed to tell Dae Hyo what to teach him, he could see the point to the lessons. It was slow, but he could feel himself getting better. On the fourth day, he ran for almost twenty minutes before he tired. On the fifth day his wooden sword finally bit through the bark and released the sap beneath. His bow work was best of all.

He rarely missed the target now, though he could still loose fewer than a dozen arrows before his shoulders tired and locked.

On the eighth day, he felt the fluid dance of the sword movements for the first time. And for the first time he was facing Dae Hyo himself, rather than the chestnut in whose shade they'd made camp.

The other man attacked and Krish parried, slapping the wooden sword aside then lunging in to put the point of his own blade against Dae Hyo's heart. He grinned and backed away, raising his sword again as Dae Hyo had taught him, never letting his guard down. But Dae Hyo just sighed and dropped his own sword to the grass. There'd been rain in the night and it fell into a puddle, splashing his trousers with mud.

'What's the matter?' Krish asked, still not lowering his own sword. He wondered if this was a test. 'That was better, wasn't it?'

'Much better,' Dae Hyo agreed. 'You're a fast learner. With a mind like that, good reflexes, you could be a great warrior.'

Krish smiled.

'But you never will be. You haven't the strength for it. Look at those arms.' He clasped Krish's shoulder, then moved the grip downward, testing the muscles. 'As thin as twigs and that's after seven days' work. But the problem's all here.' His hand moved to Krish's chest, pressing in and expelling all the air. 'There's not enough breath. You can train all you want, but you'll never have the wind to keep going long enough. I wouldn't fight with you at my back now and I wouldn't do it in a year's time. This body's only fit for herding goats.'

Krish glared at him. 'There's nothing wrong with being a goatherd. The goats had more kindness than most of the people I've met since I left them.' Without thinking, he raised his sword to press the tip against Dae Hyo's throat.

The other man laughed. 'Now there's the heart. You've got heart enough for ten men, but it isn't enough. '

Krish wanted to be angry but felt only a kind of dull despair. Dae Hyo spent half the day and all of the night drunk, and he seemed to attract trouble like shit attracted flies, but he was the only person Krish knew in the thousand miles of the plains. 'You want me to leave?'

'Leave? Don't be ridiculous!'

'But . . . You said I was no use to you if I didn't fight.'

'Did I?' Dae Hyo frowned. 'Well, not everyone's a warrior. If you'd been born in the tribe we'd have raised you right and you'd have been fighting like a true Dae since your balls dropped. But it's no use lamenting the arrow that missed. You've got a mind, boy. You think. As for me – I'm a man of action. But I see now that I need someone like you, someone who'll ask the right questions. If I'm to get my revenge, I'll need a thinker as well as all of the fighters.'

Krish's chest felt hollowed out with relief, but he couldn't help asking, 'What fighters? I thought it was just you.'

'Well, at the moment. I've been considering paying others to join me, since my own brothers won't. I need weapons for them first – I was working for iron when those rat-fuckers at the mines kicked me out.'

'But wouldn't a real warrior already have his own weapons? If you're planning to train the men yourself you'll end up with an army like me.'

'There you go, you see: your mind's nearly as sharp as a woman's. If you'd been born in the tribe they'd have seen that straight away. When you reached your twelfth summer they'd have made you a knife woman and one day you could have joined the elder mothers instead of sweating to swing a sword you can barely lift.'

'A knife woman?'

Dae Hyo made a horrifying snipping gesture at his privates. 'A gelding, you know, so you never grow into a man and lose the brains you were born with.'

Krish took a step back. 'But I *wasn't* born in the tribe.'

'No.' Dae Hyo kicked his wooden sword back into his hand and twirled it, then rested the blade against his shoulder. 'Tell me, how do I get men to fight for my cause and women to lead it?'

Krish dropped his own sword to the ground and sat down

beside it. It hadn't occurred to him that Dae Hyo had the same problem as him. They both needed an army. Dae Hyo didn't believe Krish's reason for wanting one, but did that matter? If they could raise an army together, it could fight for him as easily as for Dae Hyo. And he knew that Dae Hyo would make a far better battle leader than he would. He could use the other man's cause to further his own, because Dae Hyo's cause was a far better rallying cry here on the plains. If the Chun really behaved the way Dae Hyo said they did, they must have thousands of enemies.

But was revenge a good enough motivation? It didn't seem to have got Dae Hyo very far. He'd been content to wander aimlessly as long as it led to the occasional bloodletting. People needed something to fight for as well as against – and Krish realised suddenly what it could be. There was a reward he could offer his soldiers that wouldn't mean giving up any Ashane land.

'You need people who fight for the same reasons as you do,' he told Dae Hyo. 'People who hate the Chun as much as you do. These Dae hunting grounds are empty now. I've seen it myself – there's no one here. You say your old brothers have stopped being Dae – then find men who'll take their place. You should offer to share the land with whoever fights beside you. That way they get a reward for risking their lives.'

'I tell you what,' Dae Hyo said, 'you're absolutely right. This place will be home again if it has a tribe on it. The Dae need to live again. Will you become Dae, boy? Will you be the first?'

He knelt beside Krish, a light burning in his eyes a little like the warmth of alcohol. This was more than Krish could have hoped for. By binding Krish to him Dae Hyo would also be binding himself to Krish. Krish's battles would become his, even if he didn't realise it yet. The army they raised would belong to both of them.

'Yes,' Krish said. 'I'd be honoured to join the Dae.'

Dae Hyo grinned and rocked back on his heels. 'Good. Now drop your trousers.'

'*What?*'

Dae Hyo pulled out his hunting knife. 'Drop your trousers, I need to be able to reach your cock.'

Krish was too shocked to move for a moment. Then he made a desperate scramble to escape, but Dae Hyo was quicker and he grabbed Krish's leg and held him back. 'What's the matter, boy? I didn't take you for a coward.'

'I'm not a coward,' Krish gasped, still struggling. 'But I don't want – I want to stay a man.'

'Well of course you do, idiot. No need to piss your pants. It's far too late to turn you into a knife woman; you've grown all the parts.'

Krish relaxed a little, then tensed again as the other man began to work at the tie of his trousers. 'Then I don't – What?'

Dae Hyo sighed and released him to open his own trousers and pull out his member. It was thankfully flaccid but Krish still turned away from it.

'Look,' Dae Hyo said impatiently. 'See how the head's bare, not wearing a hood like yours? I'll just take off the hood and you'll be done. There's nothing to worry about: they did the same thing to me in my twelfth spring. Well, there was all sorts of ceremony and chanting as well, but I can't remember it, so we'll just have to make do with cutting you and hope the gods understand the meaning. They say they're wise; I'm sure they will.'

Krish looked down at his own manhood, hanging limp and very shrivelled. 'You want to cut my penis.'

'Just the skin around the top. I swear to you it won't hurt. Not much, anyway. And then you'll be a proper man: a Dae man and my brother. What do you say?'

Krish turned his head to look at the grassy plains all around, which had so far yielded only rabbits and men intent on killing him. He looked back at Dae Hyo. This would bind them for ever: their lives, their causes, permanently intertwined. His heart felt like a stone and his guts so liquid he was afraid he'd embarrass himself. 'All right,' he said. 'Do it.'

Dae Hyo hesitated, suddenly looking far less sure of himself. Then, just as Krish would have pulled away, his cold hand reached out to grasp his member and the knife moved in a viciously quick circle around it.

He'd lied. The pain was astonishing. Krish screamed and fell on to his back and tried to clasp his hands over his groin as Dae Hyo forced them to the ground. He could feel blood running wet and warm down his thigh and the agony just went on and on, seeming only to get keener.

Then Dae Hyo drew him to his feet and clasped him in his arms, though it only made the pain worse. There was dampness on his face and he thought he might be bleeding there too, but he wasn't. Dae Hyo was crying. As the blood dripped down Krish's legs the other man whispered, 'I greet you as my brother, Dae Krish.'

27

Olufemi moved faster than the army, but they couldn't be more than a day behind her. Smiler's Fair had settled in a basin within the great plain, with low hills ringing it on every side. She looked down from one of those hills and sighed as Adofo chattered in her ear. Her bones ached from the unforgiving ride that had brought her here just in front of the Ashane force.

Storm clouds were building around the rising sun; she thought she might use it as a metaphor when she told the congress and its consul what awaited them. If she timed it right, the lightning would strike and the thunder rumble ominously as a counterpoint to her words. She clicked at her horse to urge it down the hill and towards the entrance to Rotgut Avenue, the nearest of the Roads to Ruin. Whatever layout the fair fell into at each pitch, those four roads always led from its outer reaches to its corrupt heart.

Her own heart felt lighter than she'd imagined. The fair had always occupied an ambiguous place in her affections. It was the site of her failure and exile but also the place where she'd met Vordanna. And her failure seemed less absolute now that news of Yron's heir was sweeping through the plains.

Two Jorlith lounged against the great wooden gateway that led to Smiler's Fair. Above them, the banner of the Snow Dancers snapped in the breeze. Olufemi's robe did too, the moon god's rune flexing and stretching on its back. If the Ashane understood who they were truly hunting that rune might soon become dangerous to wear, but she refused to forsake it.

'Halt, stranger, and speak your name,' the right-hand guard commanded, bored by his own words. The other waited, his stylus poised above the wax tablet that would record her presence in Smiler's Fair. She could see that the pair were too hot in their skintight yellow wrappings and too proud to show it.

'I'm Olufemi of the Worshippers,' she told them. 'I'm no stranger here.'

If she'd expected surprise or even respect, she would have been disappointed, but she knew the Jorlith of old.

'Pass then, Olufemi,' the second said, 'and keep the Smiler's peace.'

Peace was far from what she brought, but she saw no benefit in telling them that.

Every morning, Nethmi was woken by the dawn sun shining through Marvan's window. He told her he'd been late to set up his home this pitch and had found himself with an exposed, east-facing room, the least desirable in the fair except for those on the ground floor.

She didn't mind. The light allowed her to study her companion while he still slept. Marvan had kept his word to her like the shipborn lord he'd once been, but as they lay in his bed together every night it had been she who found herself drawn to him. She studied his body with a fascination that would once have made her blush. Clothed, he seemed slender, almost scrawny; with his chest and arms bare she could see the tight muscles beneath the smooth skin, the dips and hollows intriguingly shadowed by the low sun.

He stirred and she rose quickly so that he wouldn't see her scrutiny or her half-clothed state. By the time he'd rolled out of bed she was already wearing the plain blue dress she'd bought from a street vendor. It was far less conspicuous than the finery she'd taken with her from Winter's Hammer and she liked the feeling of anonymity it gave her. All her life she'd been known, noticed wherever she went. There was unexpected freedom in being one stranger among so many.

'Where to today?' she asked Marvan.

He was shaving carefully in his small mirror, delicate swipes of the blade across his skin. 'I have a task to perform, I'm afraid. I'll have to leave you to your own devices.'

She tried to hide her disappointment. So far, they hadn't spent a day apart. 'Of course. I've been taking too much of your time.'

'Not at all.' He turned to look at her, wiping the soap from his face. 'You could come with me, if you liked.'

'To help with the task?'

'To watch me perform it.' He smiled crookedly. 'You might enjoy it. I certainly do.'

She thought he'd shown her all that Smiler's Fair had to offer after the days she'd spent in his company, but when they left his house, he led her somewhere new. It was a field at the far western edge of the fair, flush against the high wooden walls that ringed the whole place. Jorlith guarded it, more of them than she'd ever seen in one place. They stepped aside to let Marvan pass, though their expressions weren't welcoming.

'Here for the testing, Marvan?' one of them asked, a young man with a thin moustache and a thick red welt dividing his face nearly in two. 'Perhaps you'll get some scars of your own today.'

'Perhaps,' Marvan said, but he didn't sound as if he believed it. He nodded to the other men as he passed and walked on to the centre of the field. The man who greeted them there did look a little more pleased by Marvan's presence. He smiled and clapped him on the back.

'You're here, good. I'd heard you were entertaining a lady of late – you know how Rah Bae talks – and I thought you might not make it.'

'Piyuma is a friend, nothing more,' Marvan said reprovingly. Nethmi had told him she preferred to go by that name while her husband's men might be searching for her and he'd seemed to understand. She didn't think he was a stranger to subterfuge. 'Piyuma, this is Agnar, captain of the Rotgut Division of the outer circle Jorlith.'

'Of course, yes,' Agnar said, glancing only briefly at her before returning his attention to Marvan. 'Just one for you today, but I warn you, he's good. You won't find Otkel so easy as poor Skoedir.'

'A slip of the blade,' Marvan said, with what Nethmi immediately recognised as complete insincerity. 'I didn't mean to cut him so deep.'

'No matter,' Agnar told him. 'He's recovered, as you saw, and he'll know not to be fooled by that feint again. I'll fetch Otkel – he's sharpening his weapon.'

He strode away and Nethmi turned to Marvan. 'You've come here to duel?' The idea both fascinated and frightened her. She didn't know what she'd do if Marvan came to harm.

'Not to duel,' he said. 'A test.'

'They're testing you? Why?'

'Oh no, the test isn't for me. It's their half-warriors, the young men trained to join the Jorlith guard but not yet granted the spear. Each division needs to ensure its men are fit for duty and Agnar prefers to put his candidates through a true-steel fight. It's a fine idea, but there's a problem setting his own men as their opponents. There's a danger they won't fight hard enough – they wouldn't want to hurt the youngsters too much and the youngsters would know it and nothing would be tested. Or if they did hurt them, they'd be serving beside them afterwards and ill will never did any company of soldiers any good. You saw how Skoedir loves me for the scar I gave him.'

'So you fight them instead?' Nethmi asked.

'Yes. And they know I *will* hurt them, if I can. Nothing maiming, of course, but if they're too slow they'll end the fight less pretty. And they might not pass the test.'

She could see the reasoning of it, from the Jorlith's end. 'But what's the benefit for you?' she asked Marvan.

'A little coin, practice at keeping my blade swift and the chance to hurt them if I can.' He smiled his mocking smile and she didn't know how much of what he'd said to believe. 'And look, here comes Otkel now. He certainly is a large fellow.'

He was more than large. He was one of the tallest men Nethmi had ever seen, and not gawky with it as tall men sometimes were. He moved with a fluid grace as he drew his sword and took up position opposite Marvan.

She could see the flutter of the pulse in Marvan's throat, though his face betrayed no fear. *She* was afraid. Her stomach was knotted with it and she had to fight the impulse to grab Marvan's arm and pull him away from the danger.

'Are you ready?' Agnar asked, and both men nodded. 'Then in the name of the Lion of the Forest, make the fight worthy, and may the greater man triumph.'

Otkel wasn't just tall, he was quick too. The moment Agnar finished speaking, his sword slashed, Marvan's intercepted, it slashed again and this time Marvan wasn't fast enough. He fell back with a line of red scored along his left arm.

Otkel grinned fiercely and Nethmi's heart pounded but Marvan wasn't done. He danced in, flicked his blade upward, danced out when Otkel moved to parry and somehow Marvan's sword was under his, past his guard and now Otkel was the one with blood dripping from his thigh.

She hadn't realised that Marvan was so skilled, but in Otkel it was clear he'd met his equal, if not his better. Their blades probed, tested, slashed but never truly hurt. Otkel was younger than Marvan, though, and a warrior who trained every day. Marvan would tire and then Otkel would have him.

Otkel knew it too; he sensed when the older man began to weaken and substituted cautious flicks of his sword for a full swing. Caught off guard, Marvan was too close to escape the tall man's reach. He fell to his knees instead, a move of desperation, and Nethmi knew it was over and that Marvan had lost, but at least he had his life. Only Marvan wasn't finished. Kneeling on the ground, he grabbed a handful of mud and flung it upward, into Otkel's face.

The other man swore and stumbled back, and that moment's loss of control was all Marvan had needed. He lashed out with his sword, laying open Otkel's sword arm; the sword fell out of it and then Marvan's blade was at Otkel's throat and it was all over.

A ring of men had gathered to watch and they groaned to see their man defeated.

'The fight to Marvan,' Agnar said.

Otkel's eyes glared at him from his mud-streaked face. 'It was an unfair move,' he said, but Agnar only laughed and told him, 'If there are rules to the kind of fighting we do, I'd like to know them. Thank you, Marvan: a good testing, as always. Yes, Otkel, it's over – but have no fear, you fought well enough to win your spear. Now go and get that cut bandaged.'

No one offered to tend Marvan's wound. He looked a little unsteady on his feet now the fight was over; Nethmi took his arm to guide him from the field and support him on the way back to his room. He leaned against her as they walked and she put her arm round his waist to steady him. His body smelled less clean now: the scent of his sweat was strong but she didn't dislike it. It was a man's smell, a fighter's smell. She remembered it from her father's war-camp.

Back in his room, he sat on the bed and allowed her to strip off his shirt. She remembered this from her childhood too and was careful to clean each cut thoroughly. None was too deep and he had clean-flower ointment for rubbing into them.

'That's a foolish risk to take,' she said when the last of the wounds was bandaged. 'Why do you do it?'

'There are no better weaponmasters in the fair than the Jorlith. I need to fight well and the best training for a brawl is a brawl. Everything else is just play-acting.'

'And why do you need to fight at all? You told me you were a Drover. You don't need a sword to tend your mammoth.'

He leaned back on his arms to look at her. 'The world's a dangerous place, Nethmi, and Smiler's Fair is as perilous as any part of it. I need to be able to protect myself.' He paused a long moment while she watched his pulse, quivering in the soft skin of his throat, and the rise and fall of his chest with each breath. 'And I need to be able to protect you,' he said softly.

His voice was more sincere than she'd ever heard it and his eyes wouldn't let hers go. She realised she hadn't moved away when she'd finished tending him. She was standing between his knees, the heat of his body palpable. She let him see her study it in a way she'd never before allowed and the strong muscles in his arms tightened and flexed. His skin was pale where it hid from the sun, roughened where it saw it. She wanted to touch it. She wanted that very much. In Su had slipped away from her before she could explore what was growing between them. She wouldn't make the same mistake with Marvan. 'Would you like to make love to me?' she asked him.

His breath hitched. 'Most men would, I fancy. But are you sure this is what you want? If you regret this tomorrow then so shall I.'

'I'm no virgin,' she said. 'Thilak took my maidenhead, despite my wishes. But he's . . . he no longer has control of me. I don't owe a duty to anyone any longer and I have no reputation to ruin. Why shouldn't I do this?'

She was a little afraid, but the tightness in her chest was mostly excitement. The pain had already happened. Thilak had taken that too. Maybe now she could find some pleasure.

Marvan's chest dipped in the middle, a strange little hollow. She'd seen it before; now she ran her fingers over it and he shivered. 'Take all your clothes off,' she said daringly.

'I see you *do* know what you want,' he said. He was trying for his usual light tone, but his husky voice betrayed him.

'Undress!' she ordered.

He couldn't seem to bring himself to hold her eye as he undid the ribbons tying his breeches and dropped them to the floor. His member stood out stiffly from his body: a strange round-headed rod. She realised suddenly what the banner of the Fine Fellows was. 'I never saw Thilak's,' she told Marvan. 'He kept the lights out when he . . . when we were together. It's an odd-looking thing, isn't it?'

He smiled uncertainly. 'It doesn't please you? I'm afraid I haven't another.'

'It will do its job, I'm sure. Now lie on the bed.'

Her heart was pounding as he obeyed, a pulse she felt both high and low. She was shipborn, raised to be obeyed. It had never occurred to her that she craved the same obedience in this act, or that she'd ever have the opportunity to demand it.

Marvan lay back, spreading his arms wide in a gesture of surrender. 'I'm yours, Lady Nethmi, every part of me – even the less pleasing ones. Do with me as you wish.'

The fair was as ever both familiar and unfamiliar. The map changed but its essence remained the same. Olufemi's journey inward took her through the clustered houses of the Snow Dancers and the broader squares where the wine vendors sold their wares to the tribespeople come to watch the Dancers dance. After that it was Journey's End, the company once founded by Rhinanish traders.

A Jorlith guard struck her name from one census and added it to another as she crossed the border between quarters and then she was in streets filled with goods from across the wide continent. Diamonds shone outside one store and there was the clash of many perfumes at another, while above them all the banner of a rayed sun flew. Next were the Fine Fellows, with pleasures on offer that a younger Olufemi might once have paused to sample, and beyond that she reached the heart of the fair.

The first thing she smelled was the menagerie: the musk of the animals and the sweat of the people who crowded round their cages. Three quarters were cullies and the rest those who meant to prey on them. A clever-handed lad brushed against her, but she clutched her purse and he went in search of easier marks when Adofo screeched at him from her shoulder.

The Blue Hall loomed ahead of her, the second largest building in the fair. The thunderclouds had gathered above it so that the colours of the world seemed reversed, the hall as bright as the sky and the sky as grim as the rain-struck fair. It was pouring down now, rivulets running through her tight-curled hair to drip from her nose. Adofo snuggled against her, seeking shelter. His wet scales chafed her skin.

The Blue Hall was ringed by Jorlith, these men alert, unlike their brethren on the fair's borders. Four snapped to attention as she approached, and spears crossed in front of her to block her way.

'Clerks only, stranger,' one of them said. 'There's no entertainment inside.'

'It's the clerks I seek,' Olufemi told them. 'I need to call a meeting of the congress.'

The spears didn't move. 'Congress meets at pitch-start. No meeting now till the next pitch.'

'It meets for emergencies, too. And it will meet for me.'

The Jorlith eyed her, their thin, pale faces unimpressed beneath close-cropped blond hair.

'Let me in, at least,' she said. 'Let me speak to the clerks – to the consul if he's here. Let them judge.'

She thought they might deny her even that, but then there was the shuffle of footsteps behind them and their spears parted to let a man out. His face lightened with recognition when he saw Olufemi, though she knew she'd changed since they last met. He looked older too: what hadn't fallen out was sagging and his whole skin had a yellowish tinge that showed a liver on the point of expiration.

'Ethelred,' she said. 'You've been promoted, I see. An arbitrator. Well deserved, there's no doubt of it.'

'And you look more ragged than ever, Olufemi.' He stepped back and waved her through into the interior of the hall, which glowed with candlelight and the gold leaf coating every wall. 'You should never have left the fair. If you hadn't, Vordanna and Jinn wouldn't . . . Well.'

His expression was ominous and her stomach clenched. 'What about them?'

'You haven't heard?'

'I haven't been to see them yet. My business here is too urgent.'

'Oh. Oh, well, they were taken, snatched away in the night when we were camped in the Blade Pass.' He looked uncomfortable, clearly unhappy to be the one breaking this news to her. 'We believe it was Seonu who did it, but the lord of Winter's Hammer didn't answer our demands for their return.'

'And the congress did nothing?' she asked furiously.

He shrugged. 'What was there to do?'

'I need you to summon the congress. You have the authority to do that, don't you?'

'Don't be absurd, Olufemi. You know as well as I do that this is not enough to merit an emergency session. Why, there have only been seven in the fair's whole history. They can't meet just because you want your lover returned.'

'I'll have words with them about that, never fear, but that's not why I've come. The congress needs to hear what I have to say. Oh, for the love of the gods!' she snapped at the continued doubt on his face. 'An army is coming – hours behind me. Your own people will see it soon enough, but by then it may be too late to do anything. Convene the congress and let me tell them what I know.'

It took far longer than she would have liked to summon the congress to the hall, close to two hours. None of them looked pleased to be dragged from their daily quest for profit, the fair's true god. The sour-faced delegate of the Merry Cooks scowled as he took his place at the table, but the painted boy the Fine Fellows had chosen for their representative grinned as he sat cross-legged on his chair and Rah Bae of the Drovers made at least one familiar face. He nodded thoughtfully at her as he took his seat.

The consul was the last to arrive. Stanhild Thedlefsdochter of the clerks had been nothing but a lowly apprentice when Olufemi first visited the fair. Now she was grey-haired and stooped with age. Adofo observed them all from his place on the table beside Olufemi. Those who didn't know her of old eyed the lizard monkey uneasily. His strange eyes shone silver and troubling in the dim room.

'So, Olufemi,' Stanhild said when everyone was settled. 'You have us here, at much inconvenience. If this is about Vordanna –'

'It's not! Though your cowardice in that regard certainly merits discussion.'

'Then just what do you want?'

She took the time to circle the table with her gaze, catching

each set of eyes for a moment so that they could see the serious-
ness of her intent. 'I want nothing of you but what you'd want
for yourselves: your safety and that of the fair. I came to warn
of the army that's poised to descend on you.'

'An army, you say?' That was the very unmerry cook. 'Why
comes it here? And how come you to know of it?'

'It's here in search of the Ashane King's lost son.'

Harnoor of the Worshippers, a broad and usually jolly woman,
half rose out of her chair in anger. 'This is nonsense, Olufemi
– peddle it to the cullies if you like, but don't bring it here, and
don't drag us from our business for it.'

'It's true!' Olufemi shouted over the sudden hubbub and again,
when they'd quietened, 'It's true, and you know very well that
the King of Ashanesland did lose his son. Whether he's what I
claimed isn't really important. What's important is that the lost
boy has been found, against all expectations, and an army comes
in pursuit of him.'

Harnoor slowly settled back in her seat, only a little mollified.
'Maybe it's so, but why come here?'

Olufemi laughed and Adofo echoed her with a high screech.
'Where else to look for a fugitive with no place else to go? They
believe the prince has found his way here, and they may well be
right. But it hardly matters if they are. They'll sack the fair in
their search for him and if you're not ready you'll be powerless
to stop them.'

'What's his name?' Stanhild asked.

Olufemi hesitated, but she needed their help. 'Krishanjit, they
say. He grew up a goatherd in one of the nowhere mountain villages
at the border of Ashanesland. It's why he was never found.'

Stanhild nodded. 'Krishanjit. Not a common name.' She turned
to the junior clerk taking notes at her side. 'Search all of the
censuses for him and bring him to me if he's found. If not, tell
the Jorlith to watch for his arrival at the gates. We can't have him
wandering loose in the fair.'

'Good,' Olufemi said. 'Now, I have some thoughts about your
defences.'

'Defences?' Stanhild stared at her. 'An Ashane *army* is heading our way. There is no defence against that.'

'Well, it's not truly an army, just an armed force, four hundred or so strong. It's not the full might of the kingdom and there are no carrion riders among them. Most are simple farmers, few are trained and many are ill-armed. The Jorlith are a match for them.'

'Perhaps, but why should we put it to the test? We have no business crossing King Nayan. In all our years we've never sought conflict with those who host us. We'll simply hand over the boy and the fair will continue on its way.'

There were mutters of agreement and not a single voice of dissent. Olufemi felt a panicked sweat start between her shoulders. She couldn't allow Yron's heir to be handed over now, not when he was so nearly within her grasp.

'The force isn't solely Ashane,' she said. 'They've recruited Brotherband raiders to their cause. Do you really want to let those murderers through the gates of Smiler's Fair?'

She could see that gave some of them pause, but Stanhild shook her head. 'No. All the more reason to give them their prince and be on our way.'

'You think it will be so easy? Do you really believe the Brotherband will come to our door and turn away without the chance to pillage and rape? It's the promise of rape and pillage that bought their loyalty to the Ashane cause!'

'I think they're more likely to leave us be if we give them no reason to harm us. Smiler's Fair has always had safe passage. The Brotherband are still part of the Fourteen Tribes, and they know there's no better way to unite the rest against them than to attack us. We benefit everyone, harm no one. That's the way of the fair.' Stanhild smiled patronisingly at Olufemi. 'You've been wandering the outside world too long, mage. It's no wonder you've forgotten it.'

Rage built inside her, made mostly out of fear. 'I've forgotten nothing. My people never forget. We were here when the Fourteen Tribes wrecked their ships on our shore at the beginning of their exile. We remember when there *were* fourteen tribes, before the

Geun perished and the Seonu were lost. We were here when the Four Together were still the Five Together and when Ashane was just a man and not the land he named for himself in his pride.

'We remember when Smiler's Fair began at the Five Stars, when it was nothing but a few wagons and candied apples on a stick. We were there when King Balkar summoned the fair to Ashfall and began its travels, and when the War of the Sons drove it from Ashanesland to cross the Blade Pass and meet the tribes for the very first time.

'We were here before all the other peoples of the land, before the Moon Forest folk and the Ashane and the tribes. We were here before you brought your gods with you and we remember the gods who came before. We witnessed the war fought by Yron and Mizhara so vast it broke the land itself. Why do you think you found it near empty when you came? Mizhara killed her brother then but now he's been reborn. Yron's power is back in the world and you would dare to oppose it?

'We saw Smiler's Fair burn to ash in the Star Fire and again on the borders of the Moon Forest. And if you don't listen to me – if you don't heed my warning – the fair will burn once more. Turning the Ashane king's son over to his pursuers won't save you. Only he can save you, but you have to align yourselves with him. Yron's heir is your only hope.'

A long silence followed her words. Some of the delegates looked frightened. Harnoor seemed both impressed and a little amused, as if she'd watched someone perform a very clever trick. But Stanhild was blank-faced. She rested her chin on her knuckles and regarded Olufemi through narrowed eyes.

'When you lived among us, you were a Worshipper,' Stanhild said. 'You gave your prayers to every god and your heart to none. When you left to travel the world, I thought it was just another way to rob the cullies of their coin. It's clear I was wrong. You've fallen into the worst error a citizen of the fair can – you've started to believe your own lies. But I won't make the same mistake. The Ashane king's son is nothing to us. I won't risk a single street of Smiler's Fair for his safety.'

Despair settled over Olufemi like a shroud. They'd been too cowardly to save Vordanna and now they were too foolish to save themselves. 'Then you're doomed,' she told them. 'And all the Worshippers' prayers won't save you.'

Stanhild smiled. 'When this is over, you may remind us you said so. In the meantime, the congress has spoken. The Ashane will have their fugitive, and we will keep our peace.'

Marvan woke before Nethmi. The day was ending but enough light still shone through his one window for him to study her. She was very pretty: a perfect mouth, small nose and rich brown skin. Even her hair, unwashed as it was, still somehow contrived to be lustrous. It shouldn't surprise him the pleasure he'd found in lying with her, and yet it did. For months now, the only time his prick had hardened was over a cooling corpse.

She'd enjoyed their fucking too, he was sure of it. Fat Vera of Smiler's Mile had taught him a trick or two to please women and he'd deployed them to the best of his ability. But it was more than her body: he enjoyed her company. He looked forward to speaking with her, to showing her his world. He'd never felt that way about anyone else. They were all less than him, that was the thing. They moved and talked and smelled like people, but in truth they were little more than puppets. You could pull their strings. You didn't mourn when they were cut. Nethmi was different; he'd known that the moment she told him about killing her father. There was so much he wanted to tell her too, but he hadn't yet found the courage.

She stirred and opened her eyes a crack.

'Hungry?' he asked.

She murmured something unintelligible and he took it for a yes. But he had no food in the room, nothing fit for her. 'I'll be back in a moment,' he said, bending to kiss her brow before throwing on his breeches and shirt. He'd find her something sweet to end her day.

He went to Damith's place, thankfully only three streets away and always the best for honey pastries. It had been set up next to a cobbler, and the smell of leather mingled pleasantly with the scent of fresh bread as Marvan leaned against the counter and clicked his fingers for attention.

Damith was a remarkably slim man for his job, only his cheeks looking rounded and well fed. 'Did you hear the chatter?' he asked, as he always did.

Marvan shook his head, impatient to return to Nethmi, but Damith wasn't to be deterred.

'An army descending on the fair,' he whispered. 'What do you say to that?'

'I say it's nonsense. What cully told you that?'

Damith looked affronted. 'No cully. It was Olufemi of the Worshippers told the whole congress not but an hour past.'

'Your news is fresh.'

'Hot off the stove, just like my cakes. It seems the Ashane king's missing a son and wants him back.'

'Then let King Nayan have him.'

'Aye, but is that our way? Seems to me the bloody Ashane have been demanding a lot from us of late.' Damith's face twisted with contempt. Though pure Ashane blood ran through his veins, he was a Smiler's Fair man in his bones.

'I don't recall them asking us much,' Marvan said. 'No more than any other host.'

'Oh, you don't listen, Marvan, that's your problem. Nalin Nine Eggs tried to demand five thousand gold wheels for the trade lost when the congress chose not to pass his way. The taking of Jinn and Vordanna, snatched from their beds in the Blade Pass, surely you remember that? And then those messengers came from Winter's Hammer insisting we turn over Lord Thilak's murderers. Accused Jinn and Vordanna themselves of the crime – the cheek of it! Said they'd conspired with his own wife or some such nonsense and offered a thousand gold wheels for her return.'

The words hit Marvan like a lance. He clutched a sudden hollow in his chest and asked, 'Thilak was killed?'

'Aye, and the high-and-mighty shipborn lord thought the culprits were sheltering here. So what if they are? Smiler's Fair is a refuge, always has been. If they're here, good luck to them and the Ashane lord can keep his money.'

'Won't you excuse me,' Marvan said, 'I have a lady waiting.'

Nethmi had dressed herself while he was gone. She perched on the edge of his one chair, running her fingers through her tangled hair. Her expression when she saw him was hard to read. He thought there might be a little shame in it, but also some triumph. 'Where did you go?' she asked.

'To get pastries.' He nodded to her and then moved quickly to his arms chest.

'Well, where are they?' she demanded after a moment.

'I forgot them. Come here.'

There was a tense edge to his voice and he could see she sensed it and it made her uneasy. But after a moment she crossed to the chest as he raised its lid. His fingers closed round the scabbard of a fine, jewelled sabre. She backed away a step when she saw it, but he handed it to her still sheathed. 'I had that from the Ahn warrior I killed in a duel three years back, when Smiler's Fair skirted the Silent Sands.'

She ran her fingers round the largest ruby in the hilt. 'It's beautiful.'

Next he passed her a serrated knife. 'That was a Moon Forest man. I took the blade from him in the fight and slit his throat with it. This axe here belonged to a Maeng. You see that scar to the left of my ear? He gave me that before I gutted him. The trident I had from Ishan of Fellview. And this one . . .'

His hand shook as he took out the final trident from its velvet nest. He saw that she was shaking too as he gave it to her. 'This I had from my brother. He was the first man I killed. Like you, I started with my family.'

She backed away another step. 'It's not the same. My father was *dying*. I'm not a murderer.'

'That's not the news I heard. I heard you killed Lord Thilak.'

'He was dying too!'

'Really? And what was he dying *of?*'

She had no answer to that. Her cheeks paled but she raised her head haughtily to stare him down. His chest clenched like a fist, so tight he wasn't sure he could breathe.

'What do you intend to do?' she asked. 'I'd rather you kill me than send me back.'

'I don't want to kill you. The first time I saw you, I knew there was some bond between us. I know you felt it too. Why else would you save me?'

She didn't reply but her face told him he'd struck his mark.

'Listen,' he said, 'I know what this is. When I was a child, my father took us to read the omens at the Feathered Lake. There were so many birds there, more than a man could count, and a thousand different kinds. Some were tiny, no bigger than my thumb, with wings that moved so fast you couldn't see them. Others had beaks sharper than a dagger, or throats deeper than a sack. There were long legs and short legs and blue and green and red and every colour you could imagine.

'It was spring then, the mating season, and I didn't see how it was possible the birds could find their proper partners, not in all that confusion. But then I realised they were singing, each bird a different song. And that was how they found each other: like called to like. Do you understand what I'm saying?'

'Yes.' She rubbed her hands down her arms, as if to comfort herself. 'But I never killed from choice.'

'Not *yet*. Look me in the eye and tell me you didn't like it.'

She looked away. There was a moment of silence and then she whispered, 'I felt close to them. When I killed them. I felt so close to both of them.'

'And you had all the power. A third son and a woman aren't so different in Ashanesland. I know what it's like to be weak, to be at someone else's mercy. People tell us that's how it's meant to be, but it isn't. You and I are meant to be strong. I saw how you were when we lay together – how it made you feel. You think killing those people was an accident? It wasn't. It's who you are, who we both are. Don't run away from it. Embrace it.'

'The way you have?'

'Yes. We can be even stronger together than we are apart. We belong together, don't you feel it? No one else will ever understand you the way that I do. I only want us to do together what we've already done apart.'

Her face was like a mask, impossible to read. 'And if I refuse?'

But he couldn't let her refuse. He knew that he was right, and he would make her see it too. 'You murdered Lord Thilak,' he said. 'You're a fugitive from the King's justice with a price on your head. A thousand gold wheels – that money would keep me for my whole life. And why shouldn't I take it, if you're going to be foolish? What do I care about a woman too weak to accept what she is? But a woman who killed by my side, my true partner: her I would never betray.'

28

Eric was sleeping when Bolli shook him awake and told him he was to be a father. He blinked stupidly at the other man, noticing the way the sun shone through his white shirt to outline his muscles and failing to understand what he'd just been told.

Bolli shook him again and when that didn't work he rolled Eric until he fell on to the cold floor. 'You've done it, you lucky sod,' Bolli said. 'You've only gone and got one of them in the family way.'

'Pregnant?' Eric said. 'But how?'

Bolli just raised an eyebrow at him.

'Pregnant.' Eric didn't know why he was finding it so hard to take in. He'd been told all along that this was what the husbands were for. But in all his time in Salvation he hadn't seen a single child. He'd managed to put the thought of them from his mind. It wasn't as though he was used to fathering children being a possible consequence of his bed-sports.

'Well?' Bolli said. 'Will you ever get up? You're late for your classes and there's to be a celebration tonight.'

Eric's heart, which had sunk at the mention of learning, rose a little at the mention of a party. The Servants weren't the most joyful bunch, but surely even they would drink a glass or two at the happy news. He rose to his feet and faced Bolli, allowing his furs to fall away so that he was bollock naked in front of the other man.

'We could start the celebration right now,' he suggested, looking meaningfully down at his prick, which obliged him by stirring to half-mast.

Bolli's face hardened. 'I've told you to stop that, Eric. I mean it.'

'If a boy can't enjoy a roll in the hay with another boy on a day like this, when can he?' He stepped up to the other man and pressed a hand against his pale chest. 'It ain't as if anyone has to know. It's just a bit of fun between friends.'

Bolli stared at him a moment and Eric's pulse sped. Then Bolli turned on his heel without a word and left the room.

Eric sighed and sank back to the hard block of his bed. It was worth a try, wasn't it? But now he knew he ought to be getting to his lessons. Today he was due to learn Mizhara's teachings on orchard-planting, about which she'd apparently had very strong opinions. He couldn't summon the energy, though. The Servants would let him off this one day, wouldn't they?

He sighed again and rifled through his clothes. The Servants *wouldn't* let him off. That wasn't the way they were. He picked a blue shirt that had started to soften pleasantly with use and was just pulling it on when Bolli returned. He'd brought Abejide and Gwyn with him, the two so alike with their blue eyes and tightly curled hair they might have been twins.

'Now that's more like it,' Eric said. 'Why wait till later to start the party?'

Bolli didn't smile. 'I warned you, Eric,' he growled. Then, before Eric really understood what was going on, the other two had grabbed his shoulders and forced him to the bed while Bolli took firm hold of his legs. Eric's guts clenched in sudden terror as he saw that Bolli's other hand held a cane.

'Try not to scream too loud,' Bolli said. 'You don't want us telling the Servants what this is about.'

He couldn't help screaming, though. The agony was searing as Bolli brought the cane down across the soles of his feet. He did it again and a third time and then Eric lost count as he screamed and sobbed and struggled uselessly to get free. The pain was so all-consuming that when it ended, he didn't realise for a moment. Then he just curled into a ball and hugged himself, shivering and wondering what came next. Bolli touched his shoulder and he flinched away.

'It's over, Eric,' Bolli said. 'Don't make us do it again.'

Eric stayed curled up and weeping for a long time after the other men left.

He kept away from his morning classes and no one came looking for him, but at lunchtime hunger and a sort of wounded pride made him limp to the long hall for his food. The place was hushed beneath its dome of crystalline ice. Outside a snowstorm was raging, turning the sunlight a strange muffled white, but long hearths filled with sweet-smelling pear-tree wood kept it warm inside. It was warm enough to melt any ice, yet the walls stayed as solid as ever. If Eric had cared enough, he would have asked one of the Servants how that could be.

The husbands all sat together at one bench. He thought of eating with the Servants, but they had their set places and he was forced to take his too, at the end of the long table beside Oskar. The other man looked questioningly at him and Eric looked away. He didn't know how many of the husbands had been involved in what was done to him, but he answered Oskar's attempts at conversation with grunts and was soon left to eat his reindeer and red berries in peace.

He would have gone back to his room afterwards, but one of the Servants approached him. The other husbands melted away as she drew him aside. Though he'd given up trying to tell the women apart, he thought this might be one of his particular wives. She had a small black spot above her right eyebrow and a very thin nose.

'You're to be congratulated,' she said.

He managed a weak smile. 'Thanks. I did my best.'

She looked momentarily puzzled. It was more expression than any of the Servants normally wore. 'You're to be congratulated,' she repeated slowly, 'tonight. There will be a ceremony in the hall of Mizhara's departure where you will thank her for the gift of fertility. Hours of prayer will give voice to our devotion.'

'Yeah,' Eric muttered. 'Of course they will.'

★

He should have guessed that the Servants' idea of a celebration didn't involve anything resembling fun. They filled the great cold room, rank after rank of them, their faces showing nothing but love for their goddess, and Eric had to stand in the middle of them and pretend to be pleased. His feet were in agony and the pain screamed louder with every second he spent standing. The other husbands watched from the sidelines. Eric couldn't bear to look at them.

As the long hours of the ceremony dragged on, he found himself thinking about Lahiru. Lahiru had been a molly every bit as much as Eric, but he'd taken a wife and she'd had children and then he'd been trapped. Eric almost smiled as he remembered Yo-Yo and the way only she in all of Smallwood hadn't seemed to judge him. But she might as well have been an iron shackle round Lahiru's wrist. She and her brothers were what had bound Eric's lover to a life he hated. Without them, he would have been free to give up that life and join Eric at Smiler's Fair.

Children were a shackle and now Eric was to have his own. Maybe the Servants were right: that wasn't something to sing and dance about.

When the ceremony was finally over he limped back to his room. The sun hadn't set, of course, but it rested at its lowest point, red and swollen on the horizon, and Salvation would be sleeping.

Eric still had the backpack Radek had given him. Once he'd stuffed his sleeping fur inside there wasn't room for much else, but it wasn't as if he'd be needing to change his clothes. He had some jewellery, though: a gold chain set with small emeralds and two diamond-studded rings. They'd be worth a pretty penny when he returned to civilisation and he stuffed them at the bottom of his pack. Now all he needed was food.

The corridors were deserted as he crept through them. The Servants slept when they were told and woke when Mizhara said they should, but the husbands might still be about. Eric could hear his own heartbeat in his ears as he paused at every junction to listen. He heard nothing, though, except the deep hum of the machine beneath their feet.

He'd found the kitchens on one of his wanderings. The pans

hung neatly on their hooks, more metal than he'd ever seen in one place, and the fire was tamped down to a soft glow. The red of the slaughtered meat looked stark against the white ice. The golden sun pears were more tempting, but they wouldn't last long. He'd gone hungry often enough to know that meat was what his body needed most. He chose some big, fatty cuts of it, but then realised he had nothing to wrap them in. The one spare shirt he'd packed would have to do.

Then he was ready to leave. Was he really going to do it? His feet hurt from the caning and he hadn't even started walking yet. But he'd be walking through snow and that was soft, wasn't it? He tried not to think about how long he'd have to walk *for*. Rii had flown a terrible great distance to get here. But Rii had also promised him that he'd return home. She'd said that he'd betray the Servants and it seemed likely this was what she'd meant. She might have been able to fly him back herself, but he didn't dare ask her. When he imagined taking a ride on her back that no one knew about he couldn't help thinking it would end with his blood in her belly and his corpse dropped in the sea.

It didn't matter – he was going to do it. He'd always managed before. He'd walked away from the Moon Forest and found Smiler's Fair. And he'd walked away from Smiler's Fair to find Lahiru. He was like a cat. He'd always twist to land on his feet.

He crept to Salvation's gate, as tense as he'd ever been. He could smell the fresh meat in his pack and little droplets of blood fell from it to the pristine ice. Anyone he came across couldn't help but wonder what he was doing. But he saw no one, and then he was at the entrance. He hesitated only a moment before taking a step through it to the vast and cold emptiness beyond.

It took an awfully long time for Salvation to disappear from the horizon behind him. He hadn't realised how big the place was until he was trying to escape it. He'd walked through the pear-tree orchard two hours ago and now there was only the ice.

From inside the city the ice had seemed featureless. He hadn't realised it was a landscape all its own, riven by deep crevasses and shaped into tall and twisted peaks. The snow wasn't as easy on his injured feet as he'd hoped. It pulled at his legs, tiring them almost beyond enduring, and the maze-like gulleys forced him to take a step back for every two steps forward.

It was beautiful, though. The ice wasn't white; it was every shade of blue. And there were birds here where he hadn't thought anything could live: squat flightless things that honked indignantly as he walked past. He'd brought his warmest gloves and a thick fur scarf to wrap round his face, but he found that he didn't need it; the constant sun blazed down and it was almost pleasant. He realised he was smiling. It felt good to be free.

The fall of night was so abrupt and shocking that for a moment he could only stand and gasp. The sun hadn't moved across the horizon and set; it was simply gone from the sky. All the heat went with it and Eric clutched his furs round him and shivered. In the sudden darkness he could see nothing but the brilliance of the stars above, clearer than they'd ever been.

A hard shudder racked his body but his mind sharpened. He'd seen the machine that kept the sun always in the sky; he should have realised that its magic only extended so far, or the whole world would have been in perpetual sunlight. He'd felt the same strange transition when he came to Salvation, only he hadn't understood it then. To find the light again, he only needed to turn round. But if he turned round he'd never escape.

He had his sleeping furs in his pack. He wrapped himself in them, then wound his scarf twice round his face and put on a pair of mittens over his gloves. He was still colder than he'd ever been, but perhaps moving would warm him up. At least it had numbed the pain in his feet; he could barely feel them. He drew in a deep, painful breath and walked on. The night could only last so long, and then the sun would rise in its natural way and he'd be warm again.

In the darkness, time ceased to have meaning. The stars remained constant above him and the snow beneath his feet never changed. Beyond that, he could see nothing. The cold seeped into every bone and sinew and deeper still, into his mind itself. Thinking was as much of an effort as walking, but eventually he remembered his food and stopped to pull the raw lump of meat from his pack. It was solid ice and he'd brought no way to make fire. There was nothing to burn, anyway, but he couldn't afford to be fussy. As he walked, he tore off chunks of frozen meat and allowed them to melt in his mouth before forcing himself to swallow them down half-chewed. The flavour might have made him gag, but the cold had killed everything except a faint smell of blood.

The frozen meat quickly became unbearable. He felt that one more bite might shatter his teeth. He meant to put the remains of the steak back in his pack, but his fingers fumbled inside their mittens and he found himself dropping it to the ice. He knew he should pick it up, yet his feet kept on walking and he didn't have the will to stop them. He could no longer entirely remember where he was going, only that it was important for him to get there.

An uncounted number of steps later he realised that it was growing warmer. He tried to smile, and managed to twitch his lips through the stiffness of his face. The sun must be rising. He knew that was a good thing. But as he walked on, step after step, the dark remained as stubbornly impenetrable as ever while the warmth increased.

He stopped and forced himself to think. It was very hard. His mind kept wandering to more pleasant things. He remembered the first time he'd met Lahiru, when his Ashane lover had spotted him across Winelake Square. He felt the heat of Lahiru's arms around him, the wet press of his lips against Eric's cheek. But that wasn't a kiss, was it? It was a snowflake. It was snowing – so why did he feel warm?

He'd turned round before his mind made the decision to do it. Some small part of him knew that the warmth was a bad thing and his growing sleepiness even worse. And the sun *hadn't* risen. He didn't know how long he'd been walking but it felt like a hundred hours. Dawn should surely have come. He couldn't go on into endless darkness. He'd never find what he was looking for, whatever it was. He could no longer quite remember.

The journey back felt easy. He was almost running, each step as effortless as flying on Rii's back. Except, why was he on his knees? And now the snow was all around him, as soft and welcoming as down. He let himself sink into it and closed his eyes. There was nothing to see, anyway. The world behind his eyelids was pleasanter.

It was the smell of mouldy cinnamon that woke him: overpowering and rank. His eyes opened to darkness. There was no light. Or perhaps a vast shape was blotting out the stars above. Something touched his forehead and he flinched away, but it was only a hand. It swept his hair from his eyes and a voice kept saying his name, but his mouth wouldn't move to reply. He closed his eyes again and sighed, letting himself sink back into the restful warmth.

It took him a long time to return to consciousness. In the end, it was the pain that banished his exhaustion. His fingers and toes burned with an evil fire and his head throbbed in time to the beat of his heart. He saw light through his closed lids, though, and felt a sweaty heat very different from the drowsy warmth that, he now realised, had taken him close to death.

When he opened his eyes, he knew at once that he was back in Salvation. He was in his own room, on his own bed. He groaned and tried to wipe the sweat from his brow but his hand was too big and clumsy. There were bandages wound round it. He stared at them stupidly, trying to remember when he'd injured himself. It was as he pulled the furs aside to see more bandages covering his feet that he realised he wasn't alone.

The Servant sat quietly by his bed, watching him with what looked almost like an expression of sympathy. She wore the plain white robes of all her kind, but her long hair was tied back from her face and there was a darkness beneath her eyes, as if she needed rest. Did the Servants ever suffer sleepless nights? It didn't seem possible.

'I just went for a walk,' he said. 'I got lost, didn't I?'

She nodded gravely and he wasn't sure if she believed him.

He didn't know what else to say to her, so he looked back down at his bandaged hands. They felt *wrong*: numb where they weren't agonising and too full of blood.

'You needn't fear,' she said. 'We were able to save nearly all of them, and most of your toes.'

'You saved *nearly* all of them?!' He began tearing at the bandages with his teeth, horrified, but she reached out to stop him. Her grip was far stronger than his.

'You lost the tips of three fingers,' she said. 'You'll lose more if you remove the bandages too soon.'

He swallowed thickly as he felt tears sting his eyes. 'And my toes?'

'Two on one foot and none on the other. You'll walk without a problem, though it may take you a little while to relearn. Half of your left ear is also gone.'

He lifted a hand to feel it, but the bandages made it impossible to sense what was missing.

'Can I have a mirror?' he whispered.

It was the first time he'd seen anything like uncertainty from a Servant. 'Your face is . . .' She shook her head. 'It will heal, and your nose should remain whole. But it's best you don't see it yet. It would only alarm you.'

He lay back on his furs and concentrated on slowing his breathing and holding back the tears. It was his own fault, wasn't it? He needed to learn to think things through. When he looked back at her, he noticed for the first time the small mole above the perfect golden arch of her eyebrow. She was one of his particular wives. It occurred to him that she might be the mother of his child.

'Did you rescue me?' he asked her.

'I searched for you. It was another who found you.'

'But you're . . .' He didn't know how to ask. He didn't even know if he was allowed to ask.

She nodded. 'Through Mizhara's blessing, I carry a child.'

'*My* child?'

She looked as if she meant to deny it, as if she'd prefer to remove his part entirely from the baby-making and give all the credit to her goddess, but she nodded again.

He studied her closely. The Servants' robes were loose, but he didn't think a woman showed much so early in her pregnancy anyway. A few of Madam Aeronwen's girls had forgotten to take their virgin-flower tea and ended up with something unwanted cooking in their ovens. They'd been able to hide it from their clients for a good long time. And then, of course, there'd been the johns who preferred it when the girl was good and round.

'My sisters were undecided what to do with you,' she said after a short silence.

'Because of me – because of me getting lost?'

'Because you're no longer perfect. Mizhara's laws tells us our husbands must be whole, but she left no words on what to do with those who cease to be so.'

'You mean you're thinking of letting me go – I mean, sending me home?' What should have made him joyful filled him with sudden dread. Would Madam Aeronwen take him back after he'd fled Smiler's Fair and his debt bond to her? Would anyone else want him, so mutilated?

'We debated,' she said. 'I spoke for you. What happened to you was no different from the marks of age, and we don't forsake our husbands when their hair turns grey or their skin wrinkles. You're human and these are human things. We shouldn't punish you for being weaker than we.'

'Thank you,' he whispered.

'I've never borne a child before.' Her eyes were unfocused and he couldn't tell what strange inner track her mind was following.

'How old are you?' he asked.

'A hundred and seventy-three years, in the world of the sun's true circuit.'

Eric stared at her, briefly dumbstruck. 'And you've never had a child before?'

'Children among us are rare. The last was born twenty-six years ago.'

'So none of the rest of them, the other husbands, they ain't never fathered a child.'

She smiled at him suddenly. 'Only you.'

He reached out tentatively to rest his bandaged hand against her middle. His daughter lay beneath his palm, but he couldn't feel her. She might as well not exist.

'The baby hasn't quickened yet,' his wife said.

'How long before she moves?'

'Three months, and longer before you'll be able to feel her.'

That was a long time while his baby was nothing more than an idea, and ideas didn't much matter, did they? He'd had the idea that Bolli was his friend, and look where that had led him.

'There will be a great celebration at the birth,' she said.

When he tried to smile, his face didn't move the way it was meant to. He turned his head aside and stared at his pillow. After a short silence his wife left the room, only to return a few minutes later with broth. She held it up to him, but he closed his mouth. He refused the water she offered him too. He'd been a fool to think he could escape alive, but there was one last way he could defy the Servants and all their neat little plans for him. Without food or drink, he'd be gone long before his child was any more than an idea.

29

Krish could see the smoke of Smiler's Fair ahead, and the circle of scavenger birds above it. The last time he'd been close to the place, he'd been too cautious to enter it. Things were different now and he was eager to see what he'd denied himself before. The sun was near setting, though, and Dae Hyo decided to make camp and travel the last distance with the dawn.

'That place isn't going anywhere,' he said. 'At least not right now.'

Krish sat gingerly beside the fire. His member was still tender, though thankfully no infection had set in, and he was awkward in the leather jerkin that Dae Hyo had stolen for him from a corpse. The other man had insisted they must both dress like true warriors of the Fourteen Tribes now. The turban on Krish's head felt absurd, but the weight of the twin knives was comforting at his waist and his muscles ached pleasantly rather than unendurably from the last hour's sparring. Dae Hyo was sure that, with those weapons at least, Krish could learn not to disgrace himself.

The fire snapped and danced and for the first time since he'd begun to travel with the other man he felt confident enough of his place – that this was *his* hearth as well as Dae Hyo's – to pull out the stone figure of his prow god and place her in the flames. The blood had flaked off long ago, and she shone white and pure.

'Funny-looking rock,' Dae Hyo said, thumping to the ground beside him with a string of small silver fish on a line. 'Planning to use it to warm your arse as you sleep?'

'She's my prow god.'

'A *god?*' Dae Hyo leaned forward to squint into the fire. 'Looks like a stone to me. What's her name?'

'I don't know. I haven't dreamed it yet.'

'Fuck me, brother! What sort of god is that? How many worshippers does she have?'

'Just me. You too, if you want. The Five are there for the important things but they're too busy with the affairs of the ship-born to care for the landborn most of the time. Our own prow gods protect us and our families. Don't the Dae have gods?'

'Of course. Well, it's no surprise you're so ignorant. You were brought up by barbarians, but it's time you learned the real way of things.' Dae Hyo reached into one of his saddlebags, rooting through hemp shirts and bottles of rough spirits until he drew out a leather parchment case. The scroll within was brown with age and crackled as he gently unrolled it. 'I saved this from the camp. It was with the elder mothers' . . . with their corpses.'

Krish saw a collection of miniature portraits scattered across the page. Green lines linked some, red lines others and there were black scrawls beneath each, which he guessed might be writing. 'It's very pretty,' he said. It was. The faces were full of character, despite being so small. The frowning, red-crowned woman could have been his father's cousin, soured by years as a widow, while the haughty man looking down the length of his long nose reminded Krish of the headman of the neighbouring village.

'Now these are the true gods,' Dae Hyo said. 'See, here are Belbog and Volog, the fathers of the universe.' He pointed at the topmost portraits of identical men with broad, smiling faces. 'Volog pissed out the oceans and Belbog shat out the earth. But then the all-mother Bogdana came along –' a red-faced woman with golden hair '– and she cried because the world the brothers made was so ugly. Her tears became rain and the rain ran into rivers. Fish swam in them and trees grew on the banks, the way trees do. She made the world beautiful, like only a woman can.'

There was a lot more after this. Krish tried to attend to it. He needed to be convincing as a Dae if he was going to hook his army using the Dae lands as bait. But the Dae gods had left them to their slaughter, while his prow god had seen him safe through the mountains and into Dae Hyo's company. So he listened and he tried to learn the strange foreign names, but when they broke camp the next morning he waited until Dae Hyo's back was turned, then lifted his goddess out of the ashes and stowed her in his saddle pack.

Smiler's Fair was vast. Dae Hyo told him that it was packed up and moved every month or so, but Krish couldn't imagine how. They approached it over the brow of the hills surrounding it, so that he was able to look down on the whole shambolic, crowded place and marvel. It was even more astonishing from close up than it had been from a distance. How many people lived here? He hadn't known there were so many people in the world.

The buildings were mostly three and four storeys high, many painted, most faded, all in some more or less advanced state of decay. Higher structures rose here and there. Krish saw a windowless blue hall and beside it a collection of tall, improbable spires topped with figures depicting animals Krish didn't recognise. They seemed unstable, wobbling in the slight breeze that blew in across the plains. And everywhere there were flags: pictures of snowflakes and men and women waving in the same wind.

'Those flags are what we need to follow,' Dae Hyo said. 'That's how to find your way around. Smiler's Fair moves, you see, not just all of it over the land but its own streets inside itself. When they rebuild it's always changed, but the banners show the different companies: the whores, the traders, the cooks, more whores.'

'Which company do we want? Who'd want to follow us?'

'Well . . . No need to get ahead of ourselves. Let's feel out the lie of the land first. We're looking for men who'll fight for honour rather than gold. Not everyone in Smiler's Fair is worthy to join the Dae.'

'They'll probably be more keen to join if you don't insist on cutting off pieces of their penises,' Krish said, not for the first time.

'But then they won't be Dae. Don't worry, we'll ford that stream when our feet are damp. Ah, here we are – this is what we need.'

Krish realised they'd reached the stables, a cluster of stalls outside the gates of the fair that reeked of manure. He dismounted and Dae Hyo led their horses towards the light-skinned, hunch-backed man who seemed to be running the place. There was a brief negotiation and then coins were exchanged and Dae Hyo slung his arm round Krish's shoulder and turned him towards the fair.

'Look, you see that tower to the left, the one with the raven flag on it? I say we separate, find out what we can and meet there at sunset.'

'Separate?' Krish's suspicion that Dae Hyo didn't really have a plan started to harden into certainty. He was afraid the other man had insisted they come here because of the entertainment on offer, not for the warriors they might find. But before Krish could question him Dae Hyo was striding towards the open maw of Smiler's Fair, and by the time he'd caught up they were at the gates.

Two guards blocked them, hard-muscled men with spears. Their hair was an unnatural yellow and their skin was as pale as fungus. They stared at Krish and Dae Hyo as they approached, then lowered the spears to block their way.

'Halt, strangers, and speak your names,' one of them said.

Krish had almost managed to forget he was a hunted man; now the careful gaze of the guards sharply reminded him. His wasn't a name he wanted said aloud, and he grasped Dae Hyo's arm, but the other man spoke first.

'I'm Dae Hyo and this is my brother, Dae Krish.'

'Your brother?' Both guards studied them sceptically. Krish knew that no two men looked less like brothers: one thin and dark and big-nosed and the other huge and pale and flat-faced.

Dae Hyo laughed. 'You work in Smiler's Fair – don't tell me we're the strangest thing you've ever seen.'

One of the guards scowled, but the other relaxed and waved

them through. As Krish felt a weakening rush of relief, he knew that it was Dae Hyo who'd saved him. It hadn't even occurred to the other man that this might be a problem, and his unfeigned calm made them seem guiltless in a way Krish knew he'd never have been able to pull off.

'Pass then,' the guard said, 'and keep the Smiler's peace.'

The stink of the place was astonishing. The source of it was no mystery. The ways between the buildings were more liquid than solid, full of turds and spoiled food and the occasional rat or chicken corpse. Krish saw that many of the residents wore wooden overshoes tall enough to hold their clothes above the muck. He had nothing similar and his sandals and trousers were soon soaked through with the unbelievable filth.

Dae Hyo had told him that Smiler's Fair was filled with those driven from their own homes by famine, or greed, or boredom, or a crime for which they didn't want to pay the price. It had sounded like a hopeful place to find recruits, but Krish saw little to encourage him in the faces he passed. They were all clenched like fists, holding everything important in and threatening the world to keep out. Only the visiting tribesmen who wandered among them met his eye and sometimes smiled, but they had a place in the world already – they wouldn't want to become Dae. They certainly wouldn't fight for an Ashane king's son.

And would the Ashane themselves follow him now he'd made himself a tribesman? His manhood had almost recovered from the cutting, but every time he pulled it out to void his bladder he was shocked to see its strange baldness. The hemp-cloth trousers felt too rough and tight against his skin and Dae Hyo had told him he had to grow his hair like a man. At the moment it was still too short to wind beneath his turban and hung ragged into his eyes. He was pretending to be Dae to further his cause, but was he changing too much? He mustn't *become* Dae.

A red-haired, bone-thin man passed him and Krish tried to catch his eye but got only a glare and a shove for his trouble. Clearly the street was no place to go recruiting. Dae Hyo had told him about the fair's taverns, which sold spirits and ale. Drink had driven his da to violence but it made Dae Hyo friendlier. Krish hoped a tavern's customers might at least be willing to listen.

He'd noticed that the ground floors of many of the wooden buildings were open to the street. Most had signs hanging outside, but it wasn't always easy to guess what they meant. The dice he knew – some of the men in the village had liked to gamble away their scant earnings – but was the sheep a livestock market or a butcher's?

It took him nearly an hour to figure out that the bunch of round red fruit meant a place where drink was served. Dae Hyo had given him a little of the coin he'd pilfered from those he'd killed. There were a few clay anchors and one glass feather but the rest were foreign to him. It was strange to think that he might be carrying more than his da had ever earned in his life. He hid the coins away in a purse tucked close to his skin and stepped through the open door of the tavern.

The inside was crowded with people of every race and nation. Voices were loud, faces were red and swords and axes hung on many belts. There was an edge of suppressed violence that made Krish want to turn and flee, but he went to the long bar instead, where he saw others exchanging coin for drink.

'What's your pleasure?' a woman asked him. Her bosom bulged above the low neck of her dress and her skirt barely reached her knee.

Krish tried not to look at her breasts as he passed over the glass feather and said, 'Whatever this will buy.'

She bit the coin and then smiled. 'Take a seat, my lovely. I'll keep the ale coming till your money's spent.'

There was a chair wedged into a far corner. He sat in it and eyed the room, too ill at ease to do more. Most of the customers were in groups. There were rowdy collections of laughing friends and the occasional pair, a coy woman and a man with lechery in his eyes. The few lone drinkers were deep in their cups, staring sullenly into the distance. None of them looked like they'd want him to interrupt.

'A motley collection, friend, and that's the truth.' The man was suddenly there, sitting opposite him, though Krish hadn't noticed him approach. Krish smiled awkwardly and the man smiled back far more naturally and offered his hand. 'Marvan son of Parmvir, formerly of Fell's End, latterly the proud company of Drovers. And you would be?'

'I'm Krish,' he said, then winced and wished he'd thought to lie. He needed to be careful around other Ashane, but Marvan showed no recognition at Krish's name and there was a comfort in his familiarity.

'A stranger here, I'll hazard a guess.' Marvan's grin was wide beneath a pointed nose. All of his features seemed a little exaggerated, as if they'd been drawn larger than life for comic effect.

'Yes, I'm a visitor,' Krish admitted.

'But an intriguing one. A native of Ashanesland dressed like a man of the plains. Were you kidnapped as a young boy? Or perhaps you simply aspire to the warrior way. I remember being impressed with tales of the tribes in my youth.'

There was a mocking edge to the man's tone that Krish didn't like. He bristled but kept his silence. Anything he said could only betray him.

'Not much of a talker, I see. Don't worry, I've been told I speak enough for four men. But what brings you to our fair? Surely you can tell me that?'

'I'm . . .' Krish realised he should have been better prepared, but Dac Hyo had a way of rushing him into things before he'd had a chance to think them through. 'I'm looking for some good men to join our cause,' he said finally.

'*Good* men? You may have come to the wrong place. But what's this cause of yours?'

'We – we're rebuilding the Dae tribe. We're recruiting warriors to take back the Dae lands.'

'It's a noble aim. But the Dae are dead and buried, aren't they?'

'Not all of them.'

'No? How many survived? How great is this army you're building?'

Krish held the other man's gaze defiantly. 'It's growing. But you're not really interested in joining, are you?'

'No, I'm no soldier,' Marvan said, though Krish could see the axes hanging from his belt. 'I wish you luck in your quest, friend. I'm afraid you might need it.'

And as suddenly as he'd arrived, Marvan was going. Krish stared at his departing back as he weaved his way to the door. Several times, Marvan stopped to exchange words or handclaps with other patrons, but none of them looked keen to be in his company, as if he made them all a little uneasy.

He made Krish uneasy too. There was something too watchful in his eyes and too knowing in his smile. His questions had seemed innocent enough but Krish had sensed a meaning beneath them that he couldn't decipher. Marvan hadn't seemed to recognise him, but there'd been something more troubling than mere mockery in his gaze. The other man turned for a moment at the door, his dark eyes locking with Krish's. When he turned back, Krish kept watching until he was sure Marvan was really gone.

By the end of the day, Krish had spoken to four more men and two women. But only one – a scrawny, black-skinned youth – had agreed to meet with him and Dae Hyo the next morning. He didn't think he could call his mission a success, and his head felt light and his body heavy from all the ale he'd drunk. He placed his feet with extra care as he navigated the winding streets towards the tower with the raven flag. It loomed ahead of him, now to the left, now to the right, the ochre tiles shaded crimson by the setting sun. Finally it was directly ahead of him, across a square filled with music and dancing.

A tall tribesman elbowed Krish as he passed and three women dancing in a circle cursed as he forced his way through. For a brief moment he thought he glimpsed Marvan through the crowd, his crafty eyes watching Krish over his long nose. Then the dancers moved and the other man was gone.

The music was deafening and not quite tuneful. The bass beat of a drum underlay a tortured wailing and low, musical farts from what looked like a hollow log. Everyone seemed to be drunk or angry or filled with lust or all three. A woman tried to draw Krish into the dance, pressing him against her sweating chest, but he blushed and pulled away.

Finally he saw Dae Hyo waving to him. The other man was leaning at his ease against one of the slender pillars supporting the raven tower. As Krish approached, he realised his companion had been drinking – and when he was right beside him he knew he'd been drinking a lot. Dae Hyo's face was flushed along his planed cheeks and his hair, normally secure in its topknot, was loose and tangled round his shoulders. His shirt had slipped to reveal a collection of red bruises on his neck.

'I think I've found one,' Krish said.

Dae Hyo frowned as he breathed spirits fumes into Krish's face. 'One what?'

'Someone to join the Dae.'

'Oh, yes. That's very good, but Svarog's cock, brother, we're in Smiler's Fair! A man only gets to see the place a few times in his life, so stop being so serious and think about having some fun.' He slung an arm over Krish's shoulders and drew him away from the tower towards one of the buildings on the left. It was one of those with a board showing a naked woman on the outside and many barely clad women on the inside. Krish dragged his heels as they drew close and Dae Hyo raised an eyebrow at him. 'What's the matter?'

'What *is* that place?'

'It's a whorehouse. Women sell their bodies to men who have the coin.'

Krish thought suddenly of his mother, her face blank as she gave herself to buy his freedom.

Dae Hyo noticed his expression and frowned. 'I tell you what, no Dae woman would do it, but these are foreigners with foreign ways. And when a man has needs and coin in his pocket, why not?'

They were among the women now. Their half-dressed bodies brushed against his as Dae Hyo led him through. His manhood couldn't help stirring at the sight of those breasts and thighs, the silky hair and the red, pouting lips. The village girls had always scorned him. If his odd eyes hadn't driven them away his reserve would have. He'd had nothing to offer them but a small herd he would inherit from a father who seemed healthier than he was. And none of them had ever shown as much flesh as was on display here. Krish wanted to avert his eyes – he knew he should – but instead he found them tracing the swell of a bosom or the curve of a plump young cheek.

'See anything that takes your fancy?' Dae Hyo asked.

'I don't . . . I can't . . . '

'I knew it!' Dae Hyo crowed. 'A virgin! Well, don't worry, I've paid for you already and she's a fine-looking woman, hair the colour of a well-seasoned bow and lips as ripe as cherries. It's painted on, of course, but why should a man complain when a woman's willing to share herself with him for less than the price of a dagger? I call that generosity.'

Krish struggled to find something to say; he felt it should be a refusal, but it just wouldn't come.

Dae Hyo peered at him in concern. 'You do like women, don't you? There are pretty boys here who look like knife women but they still have their balls. I've made that mistake myself once.'

'No. No. I like women,' Krish stuttered. He couldn't imagine how a man could lie with another man, with balls or without. 'I just . . . isn't our mission more important?'

'So speaks someone who's never experienced the joy of joining. Don't worry, brother, I'll give you instructions if you need them but your body will know what to do.' He looked down at the growing bulge in Krish's trousers. 'It's strung and aimed already.'

They squeezed past groups of women who hoisted up their skirts to show their legs whenever someone looked their way and girlish boys who smiled falsely as they snuggled up to older men. Several reached out for Krish, but Dae Hyo pushed them amiably aside until they were climbing the narrow wooden stairs to the rooms above.

Krish knew what a man and a woman did together. He'd seen

Dapple mount the nannies in the herd a thousand times and he'd heard the sound of his parents coupling as he tried to sleep. He knew what to do, but the thought of actually doing it filled him with terror, and his manhood wilted as his anxiety grew. What if it stayed like that and he could do nothing but stare at the woman? Would Dae Hyo laugh at him? Would she?

She was waiting for them in a small room at the far end of the corridor, lying on the bed. The room's walls had been painted a dark red almost exactly the colour of the intestines that tumbled out of the man Dae Hyo had killed a week ago.

The woman herself was barely older than Krish. That made him feel a little better. Her face was thick with make-up, scarlet on her cheeks and lips and a lurid green above her eyes. It lent her an exotic look, but underneath her features were very ordinary. Her skin was only a little paler than an Ashane's, her nose was too bulbous and her ears unusually large. That made Krish feel better too. She smiled at him and he managed to smile back.

'Both you gentlemen together?' she asked.

'No no,' Dae Hyo said. 'Just my brother to be shown the ways of love.'

'His first time?'

Krish blushed as Dae Hyo slapped him on the back and nodded. 'As virgin as the new-fallen snow. You'll be gentle with him, won't you?'

'If gentle's what the gentleman wants.' She was speaking Ashane, following Dae Hyo's lead, but her accent said it wasn't her native tongue.

'What's your name?' Krish asked.

'What would you like it to be?' She sat up to let the sheet fall and expose her breasts, but laughed and settled back when she saw his expression. 'It's Kim. And yours, my fine lad?'

'I'm . . . Dae Krish'

'Well, Krish, they say I'm good, but even I can't deflower you from ten paces. Come nearer and let's get better acquainted.'

Krish took one uneasy step closer, then looked at Dae Hyo. Was the other man planning to leave? He hoped he was, but no,

Dae Hyo sat in the room's solitary chair, crossing his legs and taking a pull from the bottle of spirits he'd brought with him. He looked like he was settling in for the evening's entertainment.

'Come here, lover,' Kim said. 'Don't mind him. Give me a few minutes and a bit of skin and I'll make you forget he's here.'

Krish crept closer until he was standing beside the bed. When he made no further move, Kim sat up again and the sheet fell entirely away to expose every inch of her flesh. It was loose on her bones, with red creases round her middle that he guessed came from bearing a child. The hair between her legs surprised him by being like his: wiry and dark. He tore his eyes away from it as she unbuckled his leather jerkin and cast it aside, and then began to unbutton his shirt. Her fingers grazed his chest with the motion and his manhood sprang fully upright again. He didn't know how he could be so terrified and so aroused at the same time.

'Try touching her, brother,' Dae Hyo said. 'That's generally how it goes.'

Krish reached out a tentative hand, looked to Dae Hyo for approval and saw that the other man's eyes were no longer on him. They'd drooped shut and Dae Hyo began to snore, the nearly empty bottle slipping from between his slack fingers.

Then Kim's fingers were at the ties of Krish's trousers and his breath caught as they brushed against his member once, then again, and for a third time until he realised she was doing it on purpose. He wondered what she thought of his body, with its almost hairless, narrow chest. There were muscles in his arms that hadn't been there weeks before, but he knew he wasn't pleasing to the eye, or at least no girl in the village had ever thought he was.

'Well, ain't you a handsome one?' Kim said. Her nails were long. He stared at them as she ran them up and down his chest, a feeling so ticklish it almost made him laugh. Then she ran them along his manhood and he shuddered and fell on top of her, pressing her down into the bed and putting his mouth against hers.

He'd never kissed before and it was awkward and messy, all tongues and teeth and his lips not quite knowing what to do, but exciting all the same. She hadn't moved her hand from his member and now she used it to guide him towards her, the way he'd sometimes had to guide Dapple when the billy had been unwilling to mate with a nanny.

Krish wasn't unwilling. He wasn't thinking about much of anything, except how good it felt and how very soon it was going to be over. Kim urged him on, her hands against his buttocks. Her nails dug into him and he moved the way she wanted because it was what his body wanted as well. She made little moaning sounds and so did he.

He was very close. The room darkened and he thought it was the approach of his climax. But then he felt a waft of air against him and realised that someone else had entered. He turned his head to see a rough linen jacket, a feathered mask and an upraised arm, and then something struck the back of his head with agonising force and everything went black.

30

Eric's stomach was hollow with hunger and his mouth like a desert from thirst. When he'd made his big decision, he'd imagined just slipping away. He hadn't quite considered how unpleasant it would be to starve himself to death. He was contemplating allowing himself just one sip of water when he saw a shadow through the ice walls of his room and Bolli walked in.

The other man flinched very slightly at the sight of Eric's bandages and then stuck a determined smile on his face. 'What's this, Eric? Not eating? We can't have that, can we?'

His forced cheerfulness made Eric's teeth ache. 'I'm fine. No need to concern yourself.'

Bolli held out a ginger biscuit that he'd kept tucked behind his back and waggled it in front of Eric's face. It smelled good, but he turned his head aside. He didn't imagine eating would be too comfortable anyway, not with his face still swollen and half-numb. They'd told him he could take the dressings off, but he hadn't yet. He was afraid to see what lay beneath.

'Please, Eric,' Bolli said. He perched on the end of the bed. 'Look, I'm sorry for what we did. It was just the kind of prank a fellow plays on his mate. It didn't mean anything, not enough for you to get yourself worked up into this sort of state. You can't go not eating for days. It isn't healthy.'

Eric looked him in the eye and only smiled when Bolli dropped his gaze. 'I tell you what, *mate*. If all's forgiven and forgotten, why don't you give me a kiss just to show there ain't no hard feelings. Then I'll eat that biscuit you brought.'

'Eric . . . ' Bolli reached a tentative hand towards Eric's bandaged one but he slapped it away.

'I ain't your mate. I ain't a nob, I ain't a husband and I ain't a father. You can pretend to be whatever you want, Bolli, and I won't make trouble for you. But I know what I am. I'm a molly and a whore of Smiler's Fair. I'd rather die as that than live as anything else.'

Bolli looked down at his own hands for a long moment. Then he rose and left the room.

Later, Eric's wife came to see him, the one he'd knocked up. At least she didn't try to smile and look all cheerful the way Bolli had, but she was after the same thing.

'You have refused food,' she said.

Eric nodded.

'Drink as well, even water.'

He nodded again.

'A human such as you can only survive three days without food or water, and you're already weak.'

'Then I should be out of your hair pretty soon.'

She tilted her head, puzzled. He wasn't sure if she didn't understand his meaning, or understood and didn't grasp why he could mean it.

'Just leave me be,' he said. 'I done my duty by you. You don't need me no more. It's not like I can put a second baby inside you on top of the first.'

'I don't wish you to die,' she said. 'If I had wished that, I would have left you on the ice.'

'Might have been better if you had.'

'Why are you unhappy?' She looked, in as far as a Servant's calm face was capable of showing it, like the idea made *her* unhappy. 'We have been blessed by Mizhara. We should give thanks.'

'Yeah? Give thanks for my new face? What does it look like, anyway?' When she didn't answer he banged his hand down on his bedclothes with an anger than startled him as much as her. 'Give me a mirror, then, if you ain't gonna tell me. I want to see.'

She watched him carefully for a moment and then nodded and left the room.

While she was gone, he unwound the dressings from his hands. It was awkward and he had to use his teeth, wincing at the bitter taste of whatever ointment the Servants had used on him. But finally they came free and he looked down at what was left of him.

His wife had lied. She'd said only the tips of his fingers were gone, but the littlest had been chopped off near to the knuckle, and his middle finger had lost almost two whole joints. He stared at the stumps, not quite able to believe it. It seemed like one of the magic tricks the Snow Dancers favoured. Someone should wave a cloth over them and then the missing fingers would reappear, only that was never going to happen.

He'd ripped the remaining bandages from his face by the time his wife returned. She made the beginning of a disapproving noise, but he snatched the mirror from her hand before it could turn into words and held the glass in front of him.

At least she hadn't lied about his nose being whole, even if half of it was black. His left ear was a different matter. It looked ripped off, as if the ice had teeth that had chewed away the top of it. The rest of him was red and swollen in places, bruised in others.

'It will look far better when it's healed,' she told him.

'Will my ear grow back?'

She sighed and sat in the same spot on the bed Bolli had chosen. 'This is hard, I know, husband. It will grow easier with time. We cannot permit you to die before you have accepted the fate Mizhara has chosen for you.'

'What're you gonna do – force food down my gullet?'

She didn't answer and he shoved the covers away and rose to his feet, though walking was still difficult on his mutilated toes. He'd shuffled like an old man every time he went to relieve himself. He pulled his furs out of the chest at the foot of his bed, and then some spare ones just in case. He might want to die, but he didn't want to die cold. He'd had enough of that.

'Where are you going?' his wife asked.

'Going for some air, ain't I? It's close in here.'

★

There were Servants labouring in their pear orchards, but he gave them a wide berth. The sun was at its highest point in the sky and he frowned up at it. What did the Servants love so much about it anyway? You couldn't even look straight at it without going blind. Rii was right: the moon was prettier.

As if in answer to his thoughts, a shadow on the snow ahead suddenly took wing and the smell of mouldy cinnamon enveloped him as Rii dropped heavily to the ground beside him, half-burying him in snow.

'Watch it!' he said, no longer caring if she took his tone amiss. But despite his irritation at getting his warm furs iced, he was glad to see her. At least she never smiled and tried to be comforting.

Her small black eyes studied him as blood dripped from one of her fangs on to the white snow. *'Thou hast lost thine ear, morsel, and also thy fingers,'* she said, sounding so matter-of-fact that he choked out a helpless laugh.

'Yeah, I seem to have misplaced them.'

'If I had found thee sooner, perhaps thou wouldst be more whole.'

'It was you what saved me?'

'Yes.'

'Why?'

She shifted her massive furred shoulders in a gesture he realised was meant to be a shrug. *'The Servants of Mizhara demanded it of me.'*

'Well, sorry to put you to any trouble.'

'It did not trouble me. Come, morsel, mount. There is something I would show thee.'

He took an uncertain step back. Even if he wanted to end things, he didn't very much want to end them in her stomach. 'I ain't in the mood for sightseeing.'

'Mount,' she said again. *'Thy mood is not my concern.'*

She held out one of her crooked legs, offering a route up to her back. In the pear orchard he saw that the Servants had turned to watch and it was the disapproval on their faces that had him grasping her dirty fur and pulling himself up to the saddle.

She gave him no more warning than before when she took off and he yelped as her powerful wings lifted him up. Salvation was a marvel from the air, glittering with rainbows, but it soon fell away to the size of a toy. The ground looked flat from this height, though he knew better now what it was actually like. He wanted to ask her where they were going, but the wind was fierce enough to carry away any words he might have spoken. It cut through his thick furs and he clutched them round his chest and kept silent.

The change to night was so sudden it shocked him even now, the third time he'd experienced it. The sun was gone and so were they. Between one wingbeat and the next they'd travelled somewhere else.

Rii didn't seem to notice the change. She flew on into the night until Eric wondered if she ever meant to stop. Finally he felt her wings dip. The filling dropped out of his stomach as his ears cleared with a painful pop and then they were on the ground. He didn't wait for her order to dismount, and she held out her leg to ease his descent. It was lighter than he'd expected, the snow holding an uncanny glow.

'I don't understand it,' he said. 'Where are we? Where did the sun go?'

'The sun is where it has always been, at the southern pole of the globe. My master's magic keeps Salvation in his sister's light, but when we escaped the reach of his machine, we returned to our true location.'

'Right you are,' he said, not comprehending a word of it. 'And that's what you wanted to show me?'

'No, morsel. Turn thy face about.'

He did as she asked and saw nothing, until she reached out a claw and delicately tipped his face up. Then he could only stare.

The sky was filled with light: green and blue and purple streaks of it like someone had taken paint cans and splashed them all about. The moon was in the centre of it all, seeming like a solid rock floating in a sea of fantastic vapours. The lights shifted as he watched, as if the same wind that chilled him could somehow move them too.

He tore his gaze away from them to glance at Rii, and saw that she was also mesmerised. The lights reflected in her eyes but died in her black fur. She watched a moment longer and then turned to him. *'Beautiful, is it not?'*

'It's bloody amazing is what it is.'

He knew her well enough now to know he'd pleased her.

'What is it?' he asked. 'Did the moon god make it?'

'Why wouldst thou wish an answer? Is the mystery not more wonderful than any certainty could be? The Servants deny themselves this sight, for the light they choose to live in is so bright it hides all others. They fear the darkness, but the night may hold more beauty than the day.'

They turned back to watch the display together, and when he shivered from the bitter cold, she draped her wing around him. The smell was worse beneath it, but a comforting warmth came from her body and he leaned against her greasy fur and relaxed.

'Why did you bring me here?' he asked when the lights had calmed to rolling ribbons of green and blue.

'I desired to speak to thee about thy child.'

He twisted beneath her wing to stare at her in surprise. 'I thought you hated the Servants. What do you care about another one?'

'I have heard his heart within the belly of thy wife.'

'*His* heart? All the Servants are women.'

'Thy son is not a Servant of Mizhara. The moon hath returned to the world and a new race of Servants will be born to serve him. Thy son will be the first.'

This, he realised, was her dream. This was what she'd predicted. 'But why would the son of a Servant be one of their worst enemies? It don't make no sense.'

'Thy wives do not tell you all the truth, but only those parts of it which it pleases them to relate. Hast thou not asked thyself why the Servants are all made as they are, without any males among them? Hast thou not asked why thou art needed?'

'It's just the way they are. They ain't exactly people, in case you hadn't noticed.'

She huffed out an annoyed breath, wafting the smell of blood all round him. *'Attend to this lesson, morsel. My master and his sister loved each the other until the day of her betrayal, and they made their Servants in their images and as one race. The Servants of Mizhara and the Servants of Yron were once the same people, wed to each other and born of the same wombs. When their masters sundered so did they. And when Mizhara killed her brother, his Servants were crazed with grief for want of him. They crept beneath the ground to hide from the sun's cruel face, and they sought to feed upon the life which my master created them to study.'*

'The worm men – they're Yron's Servants.' Eric realised that he'd heard this before, back in Smiler's Fair. Only he hadn't been paying attention, because what could all that talk of gods possibly have to do with him?

'So thy people have named them,' Rii said. *'It was not their choice to crawl under the earth, rising only to be slaughtered by thy brethren, so that but few of them remain despite how they are feared.'*

And then what she was really saying came clear to Eric. 'You're saying my child – my son – he's gonna be a worm man.' Back in Smiler's Fair, when the worm men crawled up from the ground and caused the First Death of a pitch, they sometimes left scraps of flesh and bone behind. He'd seen them once and lost his lunch. Rii was telling him that he was to be father to a monster. He stepped out of the shadow of her wing and backed away.

She shuffled forward, leaning down to peer into his face. Her own wasn't capable of much expression and he couldn't tell if she was angry, but he backed away another step just in case.

'Thou hast misunderstood. My master's Servants became those beings you call the worm men in my master's absence. But the moon has been reborn. Yron is in the world again, and thy son shall be the first of a new race made to serve him. Thy child will be not mad, nor need he shun the sun with Yron's power to protect him.'

'If you say so. I don't know, I suppose it's better for my boy to be something new than another bloody Servant. But it ain't no concern of mine. The babe ain't in my body, and I don't plan to be around to see it come out of hers. Though I would like to see their faces when it does. That'll be one in the eye for them, I reckon.'

'*Thou hast not heard me, morsel. The sun is the most bitter enemy of the moon. Her Servants love not his: they will not suffer thy child to live.*'

They'd kill his boy? His wife would murder her own son? It didn't seem possible she could do it, and yet he'd seen how one-minded the Servants were about what they believed in and their goddess most of all. If they decided it was Mizhara's will . . .

It was a terrible thought, a mother killing her baby. When he'd believed the child would be cared for, it had seemed just fine to leave. But how could he abandon his son to die? His heart twisted as he realised that he couldn't. He had to stay. It felt like the boy had reached out a tiny hand from within the womb and clasped it round Eric's wrist.

'*Thou shalt save him,*' Rii said. '*Thou shalt remain in Salvation until thy son is born, and then I will carry thee to safety, back to the land of thy birth.*'

'You'll take me home?'

'*I will return thee and thy son to where thou art needed most.*' She reached round her own back, picking awkwardly at the saddlebags hanging from her harness. Eventually, her claw tore through the material and the contents spilled to the ground. She scooped up a round of bread and held it out towards him. '*Eat, morsel. Thou wilt need thy strength, for a grave task lies ahead of thee.*'

31

Sang Ki could see Smiler's Fair like a blight on the horizon ahead of them. Their army had grown since leaving the Rune Waste. More warriors of the Brotherband had trickled in to join them by twos and threes until their force almost outnumbered his own. He wondered if that had been Chun Cheol's plan all along. Even Gurjot might have balked at adding so many strangers to his army, but like a canker that turns into a killing tumour, the growth had been too slow to alarm him.

As they approached, Sang Ki saw the fair's gates open to disgorge a small group of people accompanied by only a few yellow-clothed Jorlith. It didn't surprise him that the fair's masters had seen them coming. That they'd chosen to send out a welcoming committee rather than a sortie didn't surprise him either. The citizens of Smiler's Fair were famed for many things, but bravery wasn't one of them.

He could have dismounted his mammoth as they approached. It would have been the courteous thing to do, but he saw no harm in looking as threatening as possible. All his reading had taught him that people bargained more obligingly under the shadow of a blade.

The group was within hailing distance now, and their spokes-woman stepped forward. She was a Rhinanish matron in the rich silk robes of a senior clerk of the fair.

'Sorry to show up unannounced,' Sang Ki said. 'I hope the arrival of such a large force hasn't alarmed you.'

Gurjot shifted on his horse but remained silent, apparently happy to let Sang Ki be the one making veiled threats.

'Unannounced but not unexpected,' the clerk said, seemingly

unrattled. 'We know why you're here – you're looking for the boy called Krishanjit. Our gatekeepers have watched for him and our clerks have checked the census, but he's not in the fair.'

The woman's knowledge startled Sang Ki, but he did his best not to show it. 'Forgive me if I don't take your word for it.'

'I would hardly expect you to. You have a picture of the fugitive as well as his name?'

Sang Ki nodded. Gurjot, who'd actually met Krishanjit, had made a sketch of his face and had a scribe copy it for each company of men. At his gesture, one of the parchments was handed over to the clerk.

'This is the boy we seek. I'm sure you won't mind if we search the fair for him ourselves.' Sang Ki smiled falsely at the clerk.

'Of course.' The woman's answering smile was chilly. 'We're as keen to make sure the boy isn't among us as you are to find him. We want no trouble with the Ashane. The gates of Smiler's Fair are open to you, but your men must either submit to the census or be gone by sunset.'

The sun was barely rising above the horizon and once they were inside the fair, the Jorlith would be fools to try to remove them if they outstayed their welcome. Sang Ki nodded. 'Sunset, then. I thank you for your hospitality.' He looked across at Gurjot, who nodded too, pleased at the outcome.

Their army lay stretched out behind him: some he trusted, more he didn't. Well, such was the nature of the world. He gave the signal to march towards Smiler's Fair.

Marvan had told Nethmi the stables were the best place to do it. The enclosure that held his mammoth was within earshot of the Drovers' slaughter yard. He'd said that the screams of one dying animal would be drowned out by the screams of many others.

He'd tethered the mammoth itself in one corner of the enclosure, where it stamped its feet uneasily, as if it sensed what they intended and didn't like it.

Marvan was staking their captive out on the floor. The boy was still unconscious, though he was whimpering softly, so would probably come round after not much longer. He wasn't much to look at: Ashane, but clearly landborn. His naked body was too thin and his face gaunt, as if he'd recently suffered a wasting disease. He was neither ugly nor handsome, just ordinary. It seemed impossible that they were going to kill him. Dread churned her guts and covered her in a cold sweat. Or was it excitement? Marvan had told her she enjoyed killing. She didn't think he could be right, but she didn't see what choice she had. It would cost her own life if he betrayed her location to the people of Winter's Hammer.

'Wait until he opens his eyes,' Marvan said. 'They're the oddest things I've ever seen. No wonder he made his way to Smiler's Fair. Something as freakish as him doesn't belong anywhere else.'

'Where did you find him?' Nethmi asked. Her voice was shaking, but Marvan didn't seem to care. He smiled as if they were talking about the choice of food for supper.

'In a tavern, of course. The poor lad tried to *recruit* me.'

'For what?'

'To join the Dae.'

'I though you said he had no friends? Wasn't that why you chose him? What if they come after him and catch us?' What if she was forced to murder him for nothing?

'It was precisely why I chose him,' Marvan said. 'There *are* no Dac. The whole tribe was wiped out a few years ago. Besides, I followed him all day and the only person he seemed to know in the whole fair was that drunken tribesman we found passed out in his room. I've met the fellow before and believe me, he has no problem with one man wanting to kill another. If we asked, he'd probably offer to help us bury the body. There, all done.' He took the rope between his teeth to tighten the last knot, then backed away.

His face still wore the expression of sardonic amusement Nethmi had come to recognise as habitual over the days she'd known him, but his eyes gleamed with excitement. She saw him clench and unclench his fist, as if his hands were longing to close round their captive's throat.

Nethmi looked down at her own hands and realised they were doing the same. The moment was here. The boy's eyelashes were beginning to flutter as his head tossed from side to side. She tried to tell herself she was giving him a gift. She'd ended In Su's pain and he'd been grateful. Their captive looked sick and half-starved – maybe he'd be grateful to escape his life too. Maybe she was doing the right thing.

Marvan drew his knife and moved it towards the boy's throat, but Nethmi pushed his hand aside. She couldn't do it while his eyes were closed. It didn't seem fair that he wouldn't even know.

'Wait till he wakes up,' she said.

Marvan looked like he might argue, but she clasped his hand, caressing his palm with her thumb. It was easy to do, almost as if she did feel something for him.

'I want him to know his death is coming,' she said, and Marvan smiled delightedly.

The Ashane had taken over the entire Blue Hall, to the clerks' impotent displeasure. A few of them remained at the back of the room, muttering mutinously while the most junior among them carried trays of spiced wine and fire-fern cakes for their unwanted guests.

Gurjot and his commanders occupied the left side of the hall, and Sang Ki and his men the right. The Brotherband had chosen to roam throughout the fair, apparently keen to be the ones to lay hands on the fugitive. Sang Ki wasn't sure if their absence made him feel safer or more anxious.

The dim light of the hall was intermittently brightened by a shaft of sunlight as the doors were thrown open and another candidate was dragged in. There were two this time, one brought by Gurjot's own men and the other, bruised and cowed, held between two warriors of the Brotherband.

Gurjot strode over to inspect the captives. The youth his own men had brought looked very much like the picture: he was hollow-faced and lank-haired, but his eyes were as ordinary as Gurjot's own. The justice sighed and gestured for his men to take their captive outside. 'Close, but not close enough,' he told them.

The man being held between the Brotherband warriors barely merited his glance. 'Don't be ridiculous,' Gurjot said. 'Get him out of here.'

'But he's Ashane,' one of the warriors protested. His face was so blank, it was impossible to tell if he was in earnest.

'He's got nearly as much flesh on him as me,' Sang Ki pointed out. 'Our quarry is half-starved.'

Now the warrior was definitely smirking. 'He could have eaten something since he got here.'

'A whole mammoth, perhaps? Go away and stop wasting our time.' Sang Ki dismissed them with a wave and returned his eyes to the page in front of him, though his attention was only half on it. He'd insisted on checking the fair's census for himself, but in truth he doubted there was much point. If the clerks were trying to hide the boy from them, they'd hardly have been stupid enough to leave his name on the list. For a similar reason he didn't expect to find Nethmi's. She wasn't a fool; she wouldn't have revealed her real identity, though every instinct told him she was here.

He was so certain he would find nothing that he almost missed the name as his eyes passed over it. He blinked, moved his finger back and looked again. The chair toppled as he stood. 'I've found him, Gurjot!'

The other man looked around, as if expecting the fugitive to have been dragged in.

'In the census,' Sang Ki said. His knees creaked as he heaved his bulk over to the other man. 'His name was on the list all along.'

Gurjot grabbed the parchment from his hand. 'Where?'

'There. Dae Krish.'

'That's not him – the boy isn't a tribesman. He's as Ashane as I am.'

'And Krish is an Ashane name; the tribes don't use it. Not to mention that the Dae are as dead as the Geun, which is to say very dead indeed. I'm telling you, this is the boy we seek. And now, thanks to our hosts' careful record-keeping, we know where he is.'

When Dae Hyo woke his mouth felt full of earth and his head full of rocks. There was a moment of disorientation when he couldn't understand why the sky was so dark and the smell so cloyingly sweet. He shifted, sank deeper into the armchair and remembered: the whorehouse.

He looked around, expecting to see his new brother on his back snoring, as the gods had decreed a man must do when he'd had his pleasure. But although the bed was mussed enough and the smell of sex lurked beneath the cheap perfumes, the room was empty.

Where had the boy gone? He was a strange one – Dae Hyo wasn't so blind that he couldn't see that – but he knew no one in Smiler's Fair. As far as Dae Hyo could tell, he knew no one in the whole of the grasslands, which was why he'd stuck to Dae Hyo like moss to a stone since he'd found him.

Could he have run away? Dae Hyo had to admit that Krish hadn't been too keen on the circumcision. He hadn't taken it quite as much like a warrior as Dae Hyo would have wanted, but then he was still learning the Dae ways. And Dae Hyo didn't believe he'd run. It didn't seem to be in his nature. He was a tryer, Dae Hyo knew that about him. It was one of the things that had drawn him to the boy, despite the weak arms and the annoying cough that woke him up in the night, and those very strange eyes.

So where had Krish gone? Dac Hyo levered himself out of the chair, groaning at the ache in both his back and his head. His foot kicked the spirits bottle on the floor and he realised it was empty. He contemplated going down to the bar to refill it. A few drops would definitely help steady his hand.

No. He had to find Krish first. He stumbled over to the bed, and then had to sit on it until his head stopped spinning. The smell of sex was stronger here, so at least thc woman had done what he'd paid her for. But he realised that there was another smell too, coppery and less pleasant, and then he saw the blood-stain. It wasn't enough to fill a body, thank the gods, but there was a good red splash of it on the pillow and the sheets around. There didn't seem to be any bone fragments in it, nor any of the spongy grey stuff that filled up a man's head, but it had clearly been a hard blow.

Dae Hyo felt the first swell of panic. What had happened here? Had the woman robbed Krish and run? But then – he fumbled at his own purse – his money was still all here and he'd been so deeply asleep he hadn't heard the fight. If she'd robbed Krish, why hadn't she robbed him too?

Guilt, an emotion he'd grown good at banishing, began to gnaw unpleasantly at him. It never sat quite right with him, to pay a woman for what should only be given freely. A man was meant to woo a woman with his songs and impress her with his exploits and earn the right to ride her share of her mother's horses. The bile rising in his throat drowned out the lingering aftertaste of the alcohol. This was his fault for forgetting the Dae ways and acting like one of the sit-still people, whose women knew no secrets and whose men therefore thought they knew best.

Well, it didn't matter whose tent the guilt should live in; he wouldn't find any answers here. He shouldered open the door, his sword drawn, but there was no assassin waiting outside, only a drunken man lurching down the corridor towards a welcoming smile at the far end.

Downstairs, Dae Hyo pushed his way through to the bar. 'Who's in charge here?' he asked the barman and when he shook his head, not understanding or pretending not to hear, Dae Hyo grabbed him by the throat and asked him again.

'I'm Madam Aeronwen,' a voice said behind him, 'and I'll thank you to keep your hands off my boys.'

Her wolf-grey hair was cut short and her face was an almost perfect rectangle, the skin over it sagging and pale. There'd be no mistaking Madam Aeronwen for one of her whores.

Dae Hyo released the barman and turned to glare at her. 'You've taken my brother. Where is he?'

'I've taken no one – no one who doesn't want to be taken. What are you talking about?'

'He was with one of your girls, now he's gone and there's blood on the sheets. I tell you what, I'm not a suspicious man, but that looks bloody suspicious to me.'

She scowled at him. 'My hospitality's the best in Smiler's Fair. Which girl was your brother with?'

Dae Hyo fumbled in his memory. Krish had asked her name, hadn't he? 'Kit? Ko?'

'Kim?' the barman asked. Dae Hyo felt slightly ashamed to see the red bruising round his throat. 'She left here near an hour ago. Ran out like the monsters of the forest were after her.'

'Did she now?' Madam Aeronwen turned her fierce expression on the barman. 'And did no one think to stop her?'

The barman flushed and looked away. 'There wasn't time, honest. She was out of here like shit off a hot shovel.'

Madam Aeronwen looked back at Dae Hyo, less hostile now and more worried. 'Did your brother do something to my girl?'

'Krish? No. He was so shy he could barely pull his cock out of his pants. And he's Dae; Dae don't hurt women. Someone hurt *him*.'

'Well, maybe they did. If you find out who, you let me know. No one lays a hand on my girls without my say-so.'

And that, Dae Hyo realised in frustration, was as much help as he was going to get. He tried asking others if they'd seen anyone go upstairs after him and Krish, but who'd remember a thing like that? Men went upstairs in a whorehouse all the time. It was the purpose of the place. And the only people who thought they'd seen anything were those deepest in their cups. He slammed the door behind him and wondered where to go next. Smiler's Fair was falling asleep as the sun rose, but many remained at their revels. The dancers in the square outside the brothel still danced, though some had forgotten the steps. They moved in time to the music but in strange configurations of their own, winding through the formal squares and rings of the others. The scene looked to be teetering on the brink of chaos. Already Dae

Hyo could hear angry shouts as toes were trodden on and part-nerings disrupted. The eyes that turned to him were smudged with shadows and hot with the dangerous energy that allowed them to push themselves beyond exhaustion.

There was a commotion at one edge of the square. Dae Hyo turned to watch it, expecting a drunken fight and instead seeing a group of soldiers, armed and Ashane, shouldering their way through the crowd. A solitary Jorlith accompanied them, making no attempt to rein them in as they pulled each dancer towards them and held them captive while they looked them over. One of the Ashane had a piece of parchment in his hand and seemed to be comparing the men in the square against it.

That wasn't right. Smiler's Fair didn't allow the soldiers of other nations inside its gates, and it didn't harass its visitors. It didn't care who anyone was, as long as they paid for their pleasures.

The Ashane were drawing closer. Dae Hyo was torn between avoiding them and asking them if they'd seen Krish. He'd made up his mind to approach when a hand touched his shoulder.

He turned, startled, and the man put a finger to his lips. 'I'm here to help,' he hissed as he drew Dae Hyo away from the square into a dark side alley. Dae Hyo thought of resisting, but the man was too slight to be a threat. His thin face, pale like those of the Moon Forest folk, was tight with tension.

'Well?' Dae Hyo said, when they were out of sight of the soldiers. 'Who the fuck are you and what do you want?'

'I'm Lucan, a clerk of the fair,' the man replied. 'I heard you talking to Madam Aeronwen. You're looking for your friend and I think I know who took him.'

'Do you? And why would you help me?'

'Because I want him stopped and you look like someone who might be able to do it. His name's Marvan. I saw him go up the stairs of the whorehouse minutes after you and your brother, even though he had no whore with him.'

Dae Hyo sucked his teeth. His instinct was distrust. 'And why would this Marvan take my brother? Krish did him no wrong.

Well I'll be honest, I wasn't with him all day, but Krish wasn't the sort to make enemies.'

'Marvan enjoys killing; he's never needed a reason. He's like a fox. He craves the taste of blood on his tongue even when his belly's full.'

Dae Hyo's own belly roiled with dread. 'You think he's killed my brother.'

'I think he means to. But I can tell you where he lives.'

32

The clerk Lucan led Dae Hyo through the warren of Smiler's Fair, taking him down narrow alleys filled with filth and across broader roads crammed with the dregs of humanity. Where before Dae Hyo had seen possible brothers, or probable entertainment, now he saw potential enemies in every face and scowled at those who caught his eye. The Ashane soldiers seemed to be everywhere and the mood darkened wherever they went. Dae Hyo felt the threat of violence hanging like a bad smell in the air.

Finally, Lucan led him to a quieter area, where the streets were more crowded with livestock than people. Dae Hyo shoved aside a pig rooting in the mud and kicked his way through a squawking clutch of chickens before they stopped in front of the door of a tall and narrow building. The place leant drunkenly over the street as if it planned to vomit up its occupants on to the muck below.

Lucan looked at Dae Hyo as he bared his blade, but made no move to reach for his own weapon. In fact, he didn't seem to possess one.

'So,' Lucan said. 'This is where I leave you. Marvan's put his home on the third floor this pitch, but it may be best to check all of them.'

Dae Hyo let the tip of his sword fall. 'I thought you were coming with me.'

'And face Marvan myself? I'm not such a fool.'

'But you think I am? I'll tell you what, it's hard to see that as a compliment.'

Lucan took a step back as Dae Hyo took a step towards him, his sword once more raised and threatening. 'No,' the clerk said.

'I think you're a match for him, which I'm clearly not. Besides, I can't be seen to be involved in this. He's broken no laws of the fair and my colleagues forbade me to pursue him. They won't listen to me. They don't see how dangerous he is.'

'So you've loosed this arrow and you'll leave it to hit the mark on its own.'

Lucan beamed. 'Exactly.'

Dae Hyo spat and turned his back on him. 'Go, then. If you've led me to my brother and he's alive, I'll find you to thank you. And if he's dead . . . I'll find you.'

He heard the other man's footsteps squelching hurriedly away as he raised his own foot and kicked open the door. It was even darker inside and filled with the scent of Rah spices from a bubbling pot of stew. The cook crouched over his broth, his eyes startled as he stared at Dae Hyo.

'Marvan?' Dae Hyo asked

The cook raised a trembling hand and pointed up.

The second floor was filled with cages, rabbits snuffling through their bars. There was no one else present, and Dae Hyo hurried to climb the next flight of rickety stairs.

A figure stood facing away from him in the last room. The room itself was a mess, clothes thrown about and books on every surface. A wooden chest had been opened and the armoury of weapons within scattered over the floor. Dae Hyo raised his sword but stayed his hand. He wasn't entirely keen on the idea of stabbing a man in the back. Besides, there was no sign of Krish. This Marvan needed to talk before he died.

'Show me your face,' Dae Hyo said.

The figure spun, robes whirling and dust motes swirling in the sunlight pouring through the window behind. The first thing Dae Hyo noticed was the symbol of the moon in all its phases sewn in silver across the cloth beneath the curves of an unknown rune. The second was that this was a woman, and an old one at that, with tight-curled silver hair and skin as dark as obsidian. She held a book in one hand and a boot in the other and looked very much as if she'd been caught ransacking the room.

There was a strange, high-pitched chittering, and for a startled second Dae Hyo thought it was the old woman's speech, until he saw the creature clinging to her shoulder with its tail wrapped round her waist. It looked at Dae Hyo and, without really meaning to, he took a step back. The little scaled monster had exactly the same eyes as the worm men – exactly the same as Krish.

'You're not Marvan,' Dae Hyo said.

'No.'

'You're a mage of Mirror Town.'

'I am.'

The mage stared at him, seemingly uncaring of the sword pointed at her, until Dae Hyo said, 'Well, I'm looking for Marvan. Where is he?'

'The same question I'm trying to answer.'

'Why?'

She shrugged. 'Do my reasons matter?' But when Dae Hyo waggled his sword she continued, 'I believe he may be in possession of something that I want.'

'What sort of something?'

'A living, breathing something,' the old woman said. 'A person.'

'You're looking for Krish,' Dae Hyo guessed, his gaze darting to the creature on her shoulder.

His words seemed to freeze the woman in place. 'You know Krishanjit?'

'Do you?'

He saw the mage struggle to regain her composure. She stroked her finger against the long, scaled nose of her pet and it chittered appreciatively. 'I don't, but I'd very much like to. And why do you want him?'

'He's my brother.'

She arched a disbelieving eyebrow, but said only, 'He's not here.'

'But how did you know he was with Marvan? Did you speak to that Lucan?'

'The clerk? No. That would hardly be wise; the clerks have allied themselves with the Ashane.'

'The Ashane?' Dae Hyo's head ached with fear and the poisonous remnants of last night's drinking, but light began to penetrate the murk. 'Those soldiers are looking for Krish.'

'You didn't know?'

'No . . . Well, there were those manacles round his wrists. I thought he must be a thief, but there are hundreds of Ashane soldiers out there. All for Krish? That doesn't sound like my brother. What did he do to call down an army on him?'

'It's not what he did, but who he is: the son of the King of Ashanesland.'

'You mean he was telling me the truth about that?' Dae Hyo studied her as carefully as his bleary eyes would allow, but she definitely didn't seem to be joking. And, now he came to think of it, Krish wasn't really the type to make jokes either.

'You've seen his eyes,' she said. 'I saw you looking at Adofo's. It's him. He was lost and raised a landborn goatherd until one of the King's justices found him. That's why he fled here, I suppose. But now the Ashane have tracked him down and they want him dead.'

Dae Hyo's head ached and he didn't know how to understand what the mage had told him. But whoever he'd been born, Krish had chosen to become his brother. If people wanted his brother dead, it was Dae Hyo's job to stop them.

Krish had thought it might be less frightening when his captors took off their masks, but somehow it was worse when they became a man and a woman, ordinary people who meant him harm. The man he recognised: it was Marvan, who'd sat with him in the tavern at the start of the day. The woman was a stranger, an Ashane like him and Marvan but far more beautiful than either of them. They'd stripped Krish of all his clothes before staking him down and Marvan had ripped the amber necklace from his neck and handed it to the woman. Krish realised that that loss bothered him most of all. Dae Hyo had said the necklace would bring him luck.

Why had they brought him here? Had they recognised him? But if they had, weren't they meant to take him to face his father the King?

'I don't know who you think I am,' he said. His voice only trembled a little. 'I haven't done anything wrong.'

'Everyone's done something wrong, friend,' Marvan said. His expression was bland and hard to read: amused, maybe. 'Only a fool or a liar claims to be innocent.'

'I'm just a stranger here,' Krish insisted. 'Let me go and I won't look for revenge. All I want is my life.'

The woman had been hanging back but Marvan gestured to her and she moved forward to kneel beside him. For a moment she seemed sad, maybe even scared – and then she looked at Krish's face.

'His eyes!' she said, shocked.

'I know, I told you. Just like the moon.'

Krish tried to shut them, knowing they would always give him away, but of course it was too late.

'Like the worm men,' she said. 'Marvan, this is . . . I think this is King Nayan's son.'

Marvan moved his knife closer to Krish's throat. He tried to squirm away from it across the muddy floor, but the ropes at his wrists and ankles held him spreadeagled. They'd used the manacles Justice Gurjot had put on him to bind his hands. 'I'm not who you think,' he gasped. 'I'm nobody!'

Marvan nodded. 'Which is precisely why we chose you. Killing somebodies has drawn unwanted attention to my activities. Nobodies are far more disposable. This can't be King Nayan's son, Nethmi. The lad died at birth, everyone knows it. He's just some landborn boy with peculiar eyes.'

'No,' the woman – Nethmi – said. 'It's him. He survived. Did you never hear the preacher Jinn talk about him?'

Marvan looked taken aback. He started to make a quick reply, then stopped himself and studied Krish more closely. 'This is really who he was talking about? Amazing. But King Nayan wanted him killed, as I recall.'

'Yes,' Nethmi said. 'I heard he'd been found when I was in Winter's Hammer. Half of Ashanesland was chasing after him.'

'And we have him.' Marvan laughed with sudden delight and

kissed his companion full on the lips. 'It's perfect, don't you see? We'll be doing our *duty* by killing him. We'll take his corpse to the authorities and it will buy your pardon. There's nothing King Nayan wants more than this boy dead.'

'I'd be pardoned? I'd be free of – of everything?' Hope blossomed on her face. Krish realised she'd been doubtful about killing him. That doubt looked banished now.

Marvan held out the knife towards her. 'You could return to Ashanesland if you chose. And this boy is marked for death already. You're simply carrying out the sentence.'

She hesitated for a long moment while Marvan watched her with a terrible intensity and Krish willed her not to take the weapon. But she did. Her fingers closed round the hilt and she moved it to his throat as his stomach heaved with terror.

'No!' Marvan said, and grabbed her arm before she could strike. Krish saw that he was shaking with suppressed excitement and, horribly, the front of his trousers bulged with his erection. 'That's too quick. Now we've got him here we can take our time. I was never able to really linger over it before.' He rested his hand on top of Nethmi's. 'I suggest the wide veins in his legs. Acwell the clerk once fell through a pane of glass and took a very long time dying that way.'

Krish was still looking at the other man's mocking smile when he felt a slash of fire across his thigh and then the gentler warmth of his blood flowing. He bit his lip to stop from crying out but couldn't contain a whimper when another vein was opened. His heart beat hard, pumping blood out of the wounds to soak into the mud.

Olufemi watched the Dae man as he searched the room. He reeked of cheap spirits and his hands were shaking, but his attention seemed focused on his task. He was thorough, if not methodical. It felt strange to be sharing space with a man who actually knew Yron's heir, who'd breathed the same air as him. She wanted to savour her success, but fear dug out the foundations of her triumph. Krishanjit was in the hands of a murderer, and they had no idea where he'd been taken.

It was Adofo who'd brought her here. She'd been fruitlessly walking the quarter of the Queen's Men when the lizard monkey leapt from her shoulder. He'd held her gaze as no normal animal would, ran a few paces, then turned to catch her eyes again. With no better lead to follow, she'd followed her pet – but it seemed he'd brought her to a dead end.

'There's nothing to find here,' she told Dae Hyo. 'We can only guess where Krishanjit's been taken. What do we know?'

'This Marvan's a killer,' Dae Hyo said. 'Not a fighter – a man who likes to kill for sport. That's what the clerk said. I tell you what, if I killed for pleasure, I'd want to do it somewhere quiet. Neighbours don't take kindly to that sort of thing.'

'Or somewhere noisy,' Olufemi said, straightening from her own search so abruptly that she felt the bones in her spine click. 'Marvan's a Drover. Their stables are near here.'

Dae Hyo nodded. 'Animals make a lot of noise.'

'Animals being slaughtered even more.' She didn't need to tell him to follow as she swept from the room.

Adofo chittered loudly as he clung to her, but it was impossible to say if there was encouragement or annoyance in his voice. He seemed unwilling to offer any more guidance. She could only hope that meant she was on the right path.

The house swayed as they descended the stairs and she was reminded again of the impermanence of Smiler's Fair, its fragility. She'd enjoyed that when she lived here – such a contrast to the weighty age of Mirror Town – but now it felt dangerous. There was no safety here.

No safety at all. When they exited the building they found a group of Ashane soldiers gathered outside the door. Olufemi realised a part of her had been expecting it. Encountering Dae Hyo had been too much good fortune and here was the ill-luck to balance it. There were ten Ashane and, in their midst, a grossly fat man. Even standing still he was gasping for breath and dripping with sweat. The air around him was rank with the stale smell of it.

She felt Dae Hyo shift beside her and grabbed his arm before it could reach for a weapon. She didn't know how adept a warrior he was, but none could be skilled enough to overcome these odds. She didn't intend to die in a fight he started.

The fat man was eyeing her speculatively. She didn't like the sharp intelligence in his round face. 'Have you perchance been visiting the Drover Marvan?' he asked. His accent was that of a shipborn Ashane, though his almond eyes and fair hair spoke of a more mixed heritage.

'He's not there,' Dae Hyo said before Olufemi could frame a more politic answer.

'And why were you seeking him?' the fat man asked.

'Why are you asking?' Dae Hyo's tone was belligerent and his arm resisted Olufemi's grip, creeping towards the sword at his belt.

'We believe he may be in possession of information that is of interest to us,' the fat man said with the easy politeness of someone who held all the power. 'Perhaps it's the same information you were seeking: the whereabouts of an Ashane lad going by the name of Krishanjit, or Dae Krish. And what would your name be?'

He knew, Olufemi realised, or at least he guessed, that they were friends of his fugitive. She could have tried to dazzle or deceive him, but he didn't seem the type to be impressed with tricks.

'My name's no business of yours,' Dae Hyo said.

'My name is Olufemi, a mage of Mirror Town, and it's not your place to question me,' she added, striding towards the Ashane troops with a confidence she didn't feel.

They at least seemed a little in awe of her people's reputation and parted to let her through. But the fat man smiled as she approached, entirely unmoved. And none of them expected her to sweep her arm in a wide arc, to jerk her wrist just so to release the mechanism hidden beneath her robe and scatter fire-dust over all the men around her.

She was already running as the first of them screamed at the particles scorching his skin. Others, wiser, fell to the mud and rolled to put out the fires the powder had sparked in their clothing. None of them was inclined to try to stop her.

'Belbog's balls!' Dae Hyo said as she grabbed his arm to pull him after her. The warrior hadn't proven to be much use, but she couldn't afford for him to fall into Ashane hands. He knew far too much about Yron's heir.

At the end of the alley, she risked turning to assess her pursuit.

There was none. One of the men she'd sprayed with fire powder had run straight into the tenement that held Marvan's home. The wood was old and dry and the powder ate through it with relish. As she watched, there was a sharp crack and the upper storey toppled sideways on to the house next door and set it alight too. The Ashane who weren't aflame themselves were already fleeing, the fat man panting in their midst. The whole street would be burning soon. The houses were packed too close together to escape the conflagration.

'Did you mean to do that?' Dae Hyo asked, horrified.

'I meant for us to get away. Let's do so.'

Krish didn't know how much longer he had left. He felt weaker than he had in the depths of his worst winter fever. He was as near to death as the day he'd killed his father. His legs were numb and he could no longer feel the blood leaking down his thighs. His head felt crowded with sensation: pain, the distant clamour of the fair, the dense, musky smell of the mammoth whose stable he'd die in, and fear.

'I killed my da,' he whispered. These people were killers. They'd like that, wouldn't they?

'You already told us,' Nethmi said softly.

Had he? 'He deserved it.'

'Most people do.' Marvan leaned into Krish's field of vision, which had shrunk and darkened. 'There's not much spirit left in him,' he said to Nethmi. 'Shall we end it now?'

'I suppose we should.' She sounded reluctant, but in Krish's hazy vision her face seemed to wear the same expression of dreadful eagerness as her companion's. She raised the knife, its blade crusted with blood from the times Marvan had already opened and reopened Krish's veins.

Terror brought Krish a moment of clarity. 'You'll regret it,' he forced himself to say. 'When I'm dead you'll have to find someone else. And then again and again until you're caught. You can't kill people for no reason.'

'I think we've proven you wrong,' Marvan said.

'No. You'll get caught. You will. You can't kill people for no reason. I can give you a reason.'

'What reason can you possibly give us?' Marvan asked, but Krish thought he was genuinely interested in the answer.

The jolt of fear gone, Krish's mind felt foggy and slow again. 'The reason . . . A fight. My cause. Soldiers can kill as often as they like. They're expected to.'

Marvan shook his head. 'No, that won't do. Soldiers are also expected to die, usually in large numbers. That isn't my intention.'

Krish thought of telling him that he could torture prisoners instead, if that pleased him. But he found that he didn't want to die with those words on his lips. The army he'd intended to build to fight his father had no place for monsters like Marvan. 'You're cowards,' he whispered. 'I couldn't beat you in a fair fight, but you haven't even given me that.'

'We're not cowards,' Marvan said in sudden earnest. 'I don't think there's a word for what we are. Now, I believe we've said all that needs to be said. Nethmi, are you ready? If we don't finish it soon, blood loss will end him before we can.'

He reached across to join his hand with hers on the knife. For a second they both stared at Krish. They seemed to be enjoying his knowledge of what was to come.

His dazed mind thought the scream that followed was his own. But Marvan and Nethmi's heads whipped round, the knife lowered and in the second before the beast was on them he realised it was the mammoth he'd heard.

The monster screamed again as it charged and Marvan and Nethmi flung themselves to either side seconds before it could crush them. Krish, trapped and helpless, watched its great feet descend towards him and wished for the clean death the knife could have given him.

The feet missed him by inches and then the beast was past. It flung itself against the far wall of the stable, trumpeting its distress.

'Five save us!' Marvan said. 'Something's on fire!'

Krish had thought his vision was failing. It wasn't. The air was filled with smoke. He could smell the burning too, and understood the mammoth's desperation. All creatures feared fire.

'Quick, kill him and let's get out!' Nethmi said, her voice high and panicked.

The flames were visible now, yellow above the stable walls. The fire must be vast. The heat of it was already causing sweat to start on Krish's body, banishing the chill of blood loss and fear.

Marvan stooped to retrieve the knife. The mammoth, mindless with its own terror, trumpeted and charged again. This time its foot caught Krish a glancing blow, bruising flesh almost too numb to feel. Marvan stumbled against the wall, dragging Nethmi with him. 'No time,' he gasped. 'The fire will finish him. Don't let it finish us.'

Without so much as a backward glance at him, Krish's tormentors turned and fled from the stable, leaving him with the panicked mammoth and the rising flames.

33

Outside the stables, the extent of the fire was terrifyingly evident. It appeared that all of Smiler's Fair had caught alight. The sky was choked with smoke and the air was ripe with the stink of charred flesh. Nethmi and Marvan had barely run two paces before they were swept up in the crowd fleeing the inferno.

The force of the mob was irresistible. It was like being caught in a flash flood, as they were tossed in the eddies and currents of its panic. Nethmi's heart thudded hard when the flow tried to tear her from Marvan, but she grabbed his wrist and kept him with her.

Everyone wanted to flee the flames, but no one seemed to know in which direction the fire lay. Perhaps it was in more than one. The air was thick with smoke and ash, almost unbreathable. Nethmi could see nothing but the people closest to her and the occasional wall of a building as she was crushed against it by others stronger or more desperate than she. The orange glow of the fire seemed to surround them on all sides. Maybe there was no escape.

'What happened?' Marvan repeated to everyone he passed. He looked frantic. She supposed it was his home that was burning, but she wished he'd stop. No one would answer. No one seemed to know.

They stumbled out of the narrow passage between two stables and into another mob fleeing in the opposite direction. All vestiges of order disintegrated. The fire was in sight now, even through the smoke. It was consuming the buildings around them at a terrifying rate. And they *had* been going in the wrong direction. They were deeper into the fair now.

The crowd surged, as mindless in its fear as the mammoth

had been, and no will or grip on Marvan's arm could hold him to her. He was swept one way and she another – even closer to the flames. She gasped as a man staggered out of them towards her. He was screaming: a harsh, desperate sound.

She tried to dodge the walking corpse, its melting flesh falling from blackened bones even as it staggered forward. Then it was on her, grasping her in flaming arms so that the flames caught her too. At first it was only a red glow, a few tiny patches barely alight. She should be able to quench it – she must. But when she beat the fire with her hands it seemed to leap beneath her palms, scorching them and spreading outward. One moment her dress was whole, and then it was alight: a torch that burned all around her. The heat was so intense she felt the material fusing with her flesh. It brought a bone-deep agony like nothing she'd ever experienced and she lost all reason, screaming and trying to flee the fire she carried with her.

People screamed when they saw her too. She reached for them in desperation but they pushed her away. One man jabbed a knife towards her and she felt the sting as it penetrated, so much less than the pain of the fire that was chewing through her clothes and into the flesh beneath.

She didn't know where she was going. She didn't know what she was doing. She wished that Marvan was still beside her. She wished for her father. The fire was everywhere. She was caught in a maze of it, in the death throes of a place she barely knew. Her father had always said the Five would judge Smiler's Fair for its offences against the gods. Were they judging her for her own? Was this her due for killing her husband and for trying to kill Yron's heir? She couldn't say it wasn't just.

She found herself in the centre of a square. The moist mud sucking at her feet was a baffle against the relentless fire. She fell into it and rolled, putting out the flames that still burned on her. The pressure was agony and the cool of the mud only the slightest relief. She barely had the energy to rise. No part of her felt untouched by the flames.

The fire was on every side. There was no escaping it, but

perhaps she could wait it out here. Smiler's Fair was dying; she didn't have to. She smiled and looked up, towards a sun she couldn't see through clouds of smoke and ash. She didn't see the tower falling towards her either, not until it was a moment away from impact and by then it was too late.

The masonry collapsed over her, pushing her down into the mud. She felt bones snap beneath its weight. The harsh wood tore the ragged, burnt skin from her arms and pierced her leg. For a single moment she felt every particle of the pain, the burnt flesh, the crushed bones and bleeding wounds; her lungs aching from the choking smoke and the weight pressing against her body.

And then she felt nothing.

The mage was crazed. That was the only explanation for it. Dae Hyo hadn't been too keen on talking to those Ashanemen either, but he hadn't thought to set the whole fucking fair on fire just to get out of the conversation. He'd liked to have abandoned her, but she was the only one who knew where to go.

They were running towards the outer edge of Smiler's Fair, where Olufemi said the Drovers' stables were. They were running away from the flames, but the flames were outpacing them. Dae Hyo wasn't ashamed to admit he was afraid. No one wanted to die by fire; it was a nasty way to go. The mage was sweating too, and not just from the heat. Her face was twisted with panic and she'd forced her old legs to a pace even he found hard to keep up. Only her pet was calm. It clung to her robe and glanced at the destruction all around with slitted, untroubled eyes.

Smiler's Fair was finished, that was plain. In the distance, its towers were aflame. The Merry Cooks' pennant was half singed away, its smile turned grotesque. The gambler's dice of Smiler's Mile had rolled their last and he could hear the terrible screams as the Fierce Children's trapped menagerie burned alive at the heart of the fair. The cacophony of smells that normally accompanied the fair had been reduced to just two: ash and cooked flesh.

Still, it almost seemed that Dae Hyo and Olufemi might make

it out of the destruction alive. The horizon ahead was dark with smoke and no hint of orange or red. But sparks flew overhead, carried on an unkind wind, and fell on the waiting wood. There'd been no rain for a week and the fire caught in seconds. The flames danced their way across the street and took the other side too until there was no route through. There was no way back either. The fire was everywhere.

Olufemi stopped and Dae Hyo skidded to a halt beside her. There was no point running. There was nowhere to run to. Voices floated through the smoke, raised in pain or panic, but they had this corner of the inferno to themselves. They'd reached the stables, he realised. High-pitched howls pierced the walls to either side. Hooves beat against the door to their left in a desperation that wouldn't find any answer.

'Well?' Dae Hyo said to Olufemi. 'You're a mage – do something!'

She tried to laugh and ended up coughing, leaning over and drooling sooty spit into the mud.

'There must be a spell. A rune! Come on – what use are you?'

She straightened, wiping her mouth. 'I'm no use at all. We're going to die. Yron's heir lives and I die.' She laughed again. There was a dangerous edge of hysteria in it.

The flames leaned inward, reaching for them. Dae Hyo looked around frantically, as if an escape route might somehow appear. He didn't want to die here. His life hadn't amounted to enough for it to be over. He'd achieved nothing he'd set out to do. He hadn't even found his brother so they could die together.

He realised he was crying. The tears evaporated as they fell and he snapped a look at Olufemi to see if she'd noticed his weakness. She wasn't looking at him, though. She was stroking her pet and muttering to it, as if that was the most important thing she could be doing as the flames closed in and the end drew near.

Except, Dae Hyo realised, it wasn't ending. Olufemi *was* doing something. All around her, the flames were dying. When they reached towards her they faltered and the few that licked her robe melted away into smoke. On the material of her robe, the strange rune was burning a bright silver, brighter than the fire.

The flames didn't touch her but they burned Dae Hyo. He felt the scorch of one at his back and leapt forward to fling his arms round the mage.

She gave him a look of mingled shock and disdain. 'This is not how I want to die,' she hissed.

'Good. It's not how I want to die either, so keep doing whatever you're doing.'

'What I'm –' Then she saw the way the fire held back from them. Her eyes widened.

'Your rune stopped it. I tell you what, you might have tried it a bit sooner. Not that I mean to complain,' he added, tightening his arm round her shoulders. 'You've saved my life. I'm grateful.'

'The rune stopped it,' she whispered, looking at her own robe. 'Yron's rune killed the fire.'

He and Olufemi stood in a tunnel of light, orange and red and yellow flames arching above them. The crack and spit of destruction was all around. If they didn't move soon, the fire would be the least of their worries. The fair would fall on top of them, and that would be that.

'We have to go,' he said. 'The stables haven't all burned yet. If Krish is there, we can still find him.'

'Yes, yes we can.' She laughed again and he wished she wouldn't. He didn't like relying for his safety on someone whose mind seemed a little cracked.

'You'll have to lead me,' he told her with careful patience. 'I don't know the way.'

'I don't either,' she said, still smiling. She stroked her pet's muzzle and asked: 'Adofo?'

The little creature cocked its head at her, exactly as if it understood, then leapt from her arms and scurried two steps before turning back to face them, chittering impatiently.

'Apparently he does,' Olufemi said, striding unafraid into the fire.

★

Sang Ki sat on a hill and watched the destruction of Smiler's Fair. His breath was still rasping and his legs ached from their desperate flight to get here. Barely more than a third of his men sprawled on the grass around him, soot-smudged and shocked by the enormity of the fair's demise. There would have been far fewer of them if he hadn't left a group of forty in their camp outside the gates. He'd told Gurjot they were to guard his mother, but in truth they'd been insurance against an internal betrayal.

Even in his most anxious imaginings, though, he'd never pictured *this*. What had possessed that mage to start the blaze? He could only assume she was an ally of the prodigal prince's, but what she'd done could hardly have helped him. Of course, it hadn't much helped Sang Ki either. The most likely outcome was that the prince had died in the inferno, his bones blackened and nothing left of him to prove he'd been disposed of. There was unlikely to be anything Sang Ki could take back to King Nayan as evidence of his success. And then again, the boy could have escaped among the streams of fugitives fleeing the fair from all sides.

Sang Ki could have set his men to ring the fair and attempt to search them. Perhaps he should have. Here and there he could see members of the Brotherband or a few of Gurjot's men doing precisely that. But he preferred to keep his force intact. The citizens of Smiler's Fair couldn't possibly be happy with the destruction the Ashane had brought in their wake. He'd rather show them enough strength to discourage any thoughts of revenge.

Every now and then, a few more of his soldiers would flee the fair and make their way to his encampment, but the numbers grew fewer as time progressed. There weren't many living things left inside Smiler's Fair. The desperate screaming of the animals trapped in its stables had ended, but the smell of scorched flesh that filled the air was a terrible thing. A column of black smoke nearly a mile wide and countless miles high rose into the air and blotted out the sun. All the tribes of the plain must be able to see the fair's pyre.

Sang Ki was watching the black column and wondering just

how many bodies had been reduced to ash to make it when he became aware of the approach of another force. The thunder of their hooves was his first warning. Their forms were vague in the smoke and they were closer than he would have liked before he recognised Chun Cheol with a good thirty men of the Brotherband around him.

They had no weapons drawn and they made no threats. Sang Ki nearly let them come. They were fleeing the fire too – why shouldn't they take refuge with the Ashane? But there was something fixed and dangerous in Cheol's expression and instead Sang Ki shouted at his own men, 'Up! Up! To arms!'

They were almost too slow to react. Several remained lying on the grass and those who reached for swords and bows did it with clear reluctance. One of his lieutenants shot him a puzzled look and opened his mouth on what was clearly going to be a protest. Sang Ki didn't give him time. 'Ready your arrows,' he yelled at his men, then forced himself to his feet with a groan of effort and shouted, 'Halt! No closer!' to the Brotherband.

The Brotherband kept riding and now his own men looked alarmed. They held their weapons with greater intent, a few arrows flew and finally he saw Cheol's horse rear as the other man reined it in savagely. One by one his men did the same. The horses whinnied in protest and stamped their feet restlessly. The Brotherband looked equally frustrated and Sang Ki knew he'd saved his own life and that of his men, though he'd never be able to prove it.

Only twenty paces separated the two forces. Sang Ki could see Cheol's expression clearly as they eyed each other for a long moment in silence. The other man seemed angry at first, but then his expression calmed. It might almost have been a look of respect.

'Until we meet again,' Cheol said at last. He raised his sword – whether in salute or in threat, Sang Ki didn't know – then wheeled his horse and rode away.

★

Desperation had given new strength to Krish's weakened body. At the cost of a raw scrape all the way round his wrist he'd dragged one hand free of its manacle. His fingers fumbled at the knot securing his other arm, but the rope wouldn't give and he'd nearly torn out a nail trying to pull it free.

The fire was very near. The air was heavy with smoke, thick and unbreathable. The mammoth had collapsed, gasping, and now lay still beside him. Krish choked on every breath. The thought that he'd suffocate before he burned was a bare comfort. He wasn't ready to give up.

The knot began to loosen and his aching throat tightened with hope. The fire was cruel, though. It chose that moment to reach the stable wall. The wood blackened and burned with incredible swiftness. The heat of it struck him like a blow and even as his right hand came free he knew he wouldn't have time to release his feet.

At first they seemed like nothing but swirls of smoke. It was only as a grey hand reached for his foot that he realised the worm men had come. There were scores of them crawling from the ground. He thought they meant to eat him and jerked away, yelling, but the needle-sharp teeth closed around the rope, not his leg, and severed it instantly. Another creature freed his right foot as three more surrounded him, as if they meant to ward off the flames with their bodies.

They did. When a spark caught in the pile of straw beside him one flung itself on the flames to smother them. It whimpered and writhed in pain but stayed in place until the fire was quenched.

Krish tried to rise, but his head swam the instant he raised it. The blood he'd lost made his limbs heavy, too heavy to lift. The creatures stared at him with their eyes so like his own. Then one grabbed him beneath his elbows, another two took a leg each and, heaving him to their shoulders, they began to run towards the stable door. The movement was agonising. Too much of the straw was burning now for the creatures to slow down. The stable would be gone within a minute.

The door itself was framed by fire. He heard the creatures'

skin sizzle like fat on a skillet as they carried him through it. His own skin reddened with the heat but they spared him the worst of it. There was no relief outside. Smoke obscured everything except the glow of flames all around. The creatures turned, finding some direction he couldn't see in the chaos, and began to carry him away from the stables.

One stumbled over the outflung arm of a corpse and another leapt to take its place at Krish's ankle, leaving the first to the flames. A woman's face loomed out of the smoke, wide-eyed with panic and even wider-eyed when she caught sight of the creatures carrying Krish. Then the woman was gone and Krish was alone again with his monstrous rescuers.

But the smoke was thinning. Held slung between the creatures, he gazed up as black-flecked grey lightened to the colour of grubby snow and then blew away altogether to reveal the perfect blue of the sky, which had been above the destruction all along.

In the moment the sky was revealed, the creatures caught fire. Krish fell to the ground as they released him. The flames ate through them like boiling water through ice, quicker than any natural fire. Krish dragged himself to his knees and reached a hand out to the nearest. The creature stared back at him, its eyes full moons. It screamed in its last moments and then it was gone, burnt away to a grey ash that sank into the mud until no evidence remained that his saviours had ever existed.

Krish stayed on his knees, gasping for breath as his head swam. He couldn't quite believe he'd survived. The most recent moments of his life felt like a dream, the most recent day a nightmare. He realised that he was kneeling in an open space with no houses on either side, while ahead of him stretched the open grasslands. The creatures had brought him clear of Smiler's Fair. He only needed to walk forward and he'd be free, but he didn't know if he could. He felt as if he there was nothing left in him.

He heard the crunch of footsteps through the ashes behind him. He wanted to call for help but he could only cough. Then someone shouted his name, the footsteps turned to a run – and Dae Hyo fell to his knees in front of him and pulled him into a crushing embrace. The scent of stale alcohol enveloped him, familiar and comforting.

'You're alive, brother,' Dae Hyo said. 'I knew you would be.'

Krish tried to smile. He probably wasn't very successful, because Dae Hyo grasped his head between calloused palms and turned it this way and that before running his hands over Krish's body. Krish cried out when they brushed against the still bleeding wounds on his thighs.

'My legs,' he managed to croak. 'They cut me.'

'Here, let me see,' said a new voice. He flinched away as an old, very dark-skinned woman also knelt in front of him.

'Don't worry, she's a friend,' Dae Hyo said. 'She saved my life. Mind you, she almost got me killed first, but I think we can put that behind us. Her name's Olufemi.'

Olufemi gently probed the wounds. She tssked and hurriedly tore strips of cloth from her robe to bind them. 'You'll live,' she said. 'When we're away I've a cream that will stop infection setting in. And you'll eat the liver of every beast your brother here kills, to regain the lost blood.' As their eyes met he felt an almost physical shock he didn't understand. There was recognition in her face and also something that seemed to hover between astonishment and joy.

'You really are him,' she whispered.

'I'm Dae Krish,' he rasped.

'You're a lot more than that, brother.' Dae Hyo slipped an arm round Krish's waist and hauled him to his feet with easy strength. His leather jerkin chafed against Krish's bare skin. 'I'm sorry I didn't believe you, but you have to admit you're not the most likely prince a man could meet. The important thing is, you are who you said you are – and your father's men are here for you. Well, those of them that survived our fire. We need to put some miles between us and Smiler's Fair, but we'll have to walk. Our horses burned up with the rest of the place, the poor fuckers.'

Krish looked behind him. A thick column of smoke rose into the air above the ash and ruin, and yellow flickers showed where the fire still burned. He turned his head away and allowed

Dae Hyo to half carry, half lead him towards the refuge of the grasslands. He was beyond feeling more fear. He just wanted this day to end.

Olufemi walked at his other side. His vision was blurred with fatigue but each time he glanced at her he caught her looking at him. She was carrying a creature with her, a strange thing that looked almost like a miniature man, but scaled like a snake. It leaned towards him, chittering, and he saw its eyes for the first time: silver moons exactly like his. The creature reached out a thin hand to stroke his cheek. Its expressive face looked almost as startled by their resemblance as he was.

'Just a little further, brother,' Dae Hyo coaxed as Krish stumbled. 'Just over the hill and we can make camp. They'll be too busy dealing with the fire to send out search parties. For all they know, you're already dead.'

The walk felt endless. His vision darkened and he returned to consciousness to find himself being carried in Dae Hyo's arms. Even the big warrior was panting with the effort. The sun was bright in the sky, adding to the heat of the inferno at their backs. He could hear no insects or birds and see no rabbits or deer. With the wisdom of beasts, they'd fled the flames. When the top of the hill finally came in reach, he told Dae Hyo to set him down. The other man kept an arm round his waist and together they crested the rise.

The warriors were waiting for them on the other side: a dozen of them as heavily armed as Dae Hyo and not shaking with exhaustion. They were tribesmen, their turbans and shirts black and silver.

'Chun bastards!' Dae Hyo hissed. He released Krish and drew his sword, his teeth bared. Olufemi blanched beside him but Krish found himself laughing weakly, astounded that the day could continue to worsen.

'Show us your eyes!' the lead warrior demanded.

'Ignore him, brother,' Dae Hyo said, circling to the left as the man approached.

Krish raised his head to meet the Chun warrior's gaze. There was no need for anyone but him to die here. 'I'm Krishanjit,' he said. 'You've found me.'

The warrior's expression was almost a mirror of Olufemi's when she'd first seen Krish. His broad face froze and his eyes flared in shock. Then, inexplicably, he bowed.

'A trick,' Dae Hyo said.

'The Rune Waste sent us visions of your coming, lord,' the warrior said to Krish. 'We followed the Ashane on their hunt for you. If they found you, we could protect you.' His accent was strong, but he spoke Ashane well.

Olufemi hobbled forward. The climb had been almost as hard on the old woman as it had on Krish. She looked as weary as he felt, but her gaze was keen on the Chun man. 'What vision did the Rune Waste send?' she asked.

'The moon rising. The boy prophet told us, and so it has. The moon has risen.'

'The moon has risen!' the rest shouted and they all bowed.

'They're yours,' Olufemi told Krish. 'It's no trick. You *are* the risen moon. The runes have woken to prove it.'

'We're yours,' the warrior said. 'Command us.'

'They're Chun,' Dae Hyo said. 'These are the men who killed our people, brother. They raped my sister before they killed her. They cut off her breasts. They're beasts.' His face was drawn and horrified, and Krish realised that it was the look of a man who knew he was already defeated. These men were promising to obey Krish in a world full of people who wanted him dead. He'd thought he needed to build an army to fight his father and this one had been waiting for him all along.

'You're mine to command?' he asked.

The warrior nodded. 'We want to protect you, lord. We will summon our warriors to guard you on the journey. Most hearths of the Brotherband are north. We will meet with them there and Chun Yong will pledge us all to you.'

Krish turned to Dae Hyo. 'These are the people who killed the Dae?'

Dae Hyo pointed at one of the warriors, a scarred man with

streaks of grey in the fringe of hair beneath his turban. 'That one killed my cousin. He ripped the baby from her arms and killed it too.' He pointed at another. 'He took his axe to the elder mothers as they slept.' Another. 'He raped a girl not five years old. I found her body nearly split in two.'

Dae Hyo had told Krish that he'd returned to the camp too late to prevent the slaughter. He'd returned after the killing was over and never seen the men responsible. His accusations couldn't be true. But looking at Dae Hyo's face, Krish understood that it didn't really matter to him. *Someone* had done those things and it might have been these men.

He turned to Olufemi. 'What does it mean when they say I'm the risen moon?'

'You're the son of King Nayan of Ashanesland,' she told him.

'I know. They said I'd kill my da, so my da tried to kill me. Why do the Chun care about an Ashane prince?'

'Because you're more than that. The prophecy didn't say that you'd kill your father. They all misunderstood. You were destined to eclipse the King, not destroy him. You'll outshine him because Yron is reborn in you, the moon god who's been gone from the world for a thousand years.'

'Yron returns,' the Chun warriors echoed.

Krish felt a flare of rage. Gods, prophecies, lust, gold. Everyone had their reasons and none of them were any good. One father had tried to kill him and another had driven him to murder. The magistrate Gurjot had meant to send him to his death. His ma had offered her virtue to free him and Rahul had taken it as if it meant nothing. Marvan and Nethmi had tried to kill him just for the joy of it, the way boys caught flies in sport. All these people, who thought they could do anything and never be punished for it.

'That's enough,' Krish said. 'I don't want to hear any more. You think you know who I am? I'll tell you who I am. I'm Dae. And the Chun killed the Dae.'

He turned from Dae Hyo's incredulous expression to face the Chun leader. The man looked agonised, as if the contempt in

Krish's voice gave him physical pain. 'But lord,' he said, 'it was you who ordered us to slaughter the woman-loving Dae. Chun Yong told us so.'

'Chun Yong was wrong. I'd never have ordered that.'

The leader bowed his head. 'I'm sorry, lord.'

'You've failed me,' Krish told him, 'but you can make it right. You promised you'll obey me. Will you do anything I say?'

New hope bloomed in the man's face. 'We will obey any order. Our lives are yours.'

'Then I order you to let Dae Hyo take them. If that's what you want, Dae Hyo. Do you want to kill them for what they did? Then kill them. Kill them, Dae Hyo. I command them to allow it.'

Olufemi made a strangled sound of protest, cut off when she saw Krish's expression. His head was light with blood loss, but the feeling was almost like joy. He'd meant to use Dae Hyo. It felt so much better just to be his brother.

Dae Hyo didn't seem to quite believe it. He approached the first of the warriors on light feet, his sword poised for a fight. His gaze flicked between the warrior and Krish, but Krish only nodded and the warrior lowered his eyes and held his hands away from his weapons. Dae Hyo hesitated a moment longer and then swung his sword in a savage slash across the warrior's throat.

The man gargled as blood spurted on the silvery grass and across Dae Hyo's face. Some of it caught on his companions' black shirts. The blood soaked invisibly into the fabric and the men tensed and shifted, but none of them tried to run.

Dae Hyo took more time over the next man. He pulled out his knife and cut through the man's right ear and then his left. Krish was appalled by the Chun warrior's resolve. He struggled only a little before allowing Dae Hyo to gouge out his eye. After that, Dae Hyo tore through his stomach and his guts and then left him to sink to the ground, moaning. He'd be a long while dying.

'Have we proved we obey?' their leader asked Krish in a choked voice. 'Is this enough?'

'Is it enough?' Krish asked Dae Hyo.

Dae Hyo didn't answer. He just killed another, then another, more quickly now but with the same fierce joy, until only the leader was left standing.

'Leave me alive, lord, to fetch my brothers,' he begged. He was sweating now and shaking, but his hand still hadn't moved to his weapon. Krish marvelled that he could believe in something more powerfully than his own instinct to survive. These men would form the most devoted army he could possibly have. They wouldn't drink themselves into oblivion and leave him to be taken by Marvan and Nethmi. They'd protect him from his father. But they'd be an army of men just like his da.

'Finish it,' he said to Dae Hyo, and watched as his brother struck a knife straight through the other man's heart.

Olufemi looked horrified. Krish only felt weary. But Dae Hyo was grinning as he wiped the blood from his face, and Krish was certain he'd done the right thing. He accepted the other man's arm for support and offered his own to Olufemi as they walked past the sprawled corpses of the men who'd pledged to follow him, and away from the ruin of Smiler's Fair.

Epilogue

Vordanna lay shivering in the wagon, growing weaker with every mile. Jinn sat in the saddle of the sway-backed horse, shaking the reins and leaning forward as if he could somehow urge the decrepit creature to go faster. His mother was sick, she was nearly dead, and the moon god hadn't come to help them. Despite everything, though, a part of Jinn still kept expecting that he would.

His skin still itched from the grating the sandstorm had given it, and the wagon was now in ruins. Sometimes he thought about Nethmi and wondered if she'd survived. More often he thought about In Su, who'd told him there was a cure for his mother in the Spiral, if he could only get there in time.

The grasslands had turned to gentle hills this far north, scattered with trees. He knew that the trees were the outer groves of the great Moon Forest, and that should have given him hope, but nearly all his faith was gone. And then they eased through a valley between two slopes, and when they spilled out of the other end beside the river that divided it, the Spiral was in front of them.

There must have been a thousand wagons there. They'd been drawn up in the spiral pattern that gave the place its name, each wagon one wagon-length from its neighbour. Jinn knew that every day the pattern moved forward one length and the innermost wagon had to walk the spiral to the very outside and rejoin the formation there. More Wanderers would arrive as winter drew on, the days would pass and the Spiral would move, drawing them inexorably towards its centre.

There wasn't much more speed to be coaxed from their horse,

but Jinn did what he could. He forced it into a trot over the trampled grass that surrounded the Spiral until they'd reached its outer limit and he could leave the half-wrecked wagon as the last dot in the vast pattern. He barely waited for the horse to stop before he slid from its back. There was no need to hobble the idle animal. It dropped its head to crop the grass as he ran round the curve of the Spiral.

His chest was tight with tension as he hurried past a fat Ashanc trader with a wagonload of silks from the Eternal Empire, a Wanderer's heaps of brightly coloured spices, a cobbler, a smith, a jeweller. If In Su was wrong, if no Eom came here . . . Jinn passed a bird seller, a farrier and a fur merchant, and nearly missed it in his hurry. It was the bright figure of the trader herself who caught his eye and he skidded to a stop beside her stall.

The Eom woman had painted her face an extraordinary swirled mix of yellow and blue, while her hair was dyed violet and fell straight to her waist. Her wagon was just as gaudy, a patchwork of different shades of red with gold curlicues winding around them. The herbs and salts piled in front were lost in the riot of colour.

The trader looked up as Jinn approached. There was a pipe clenched between her teeth and the smoke that puffed out of it had a soporific smell. This didn't seem like a person Jinn wanted to trust with his mother's life, but according to In Su, the Eom knew the mixing of herbs better than anyone on the plains.

'How may I aid you, young master?' she asked.

'Medicine,' he said, and then paused awkwardly, not quite sure how to explain.

'Do you have an ague, child, a rash? Are your energies unbalanced or your joints misaligned? Do you have pains, or do you wish pleasure? What is your need?' Her expression was hard to fathom amidst the paint.

'It's – it's bliss pills.'

There was a shifting movement in the blue and yellow that resolved into a frown. 'Those are an evil thing, young master, a perversion of the plant's will. I do not sell them.'

'No. It's for my mother. She was – she was put on bliss. And now she's dying because she ain't got any. I heard you've got some medicine can make her well again. I've got the coin.'

'Ah.' She tipped her head to the side as if weighing up his truthfulness. She must have decided in his favour, because she turned to a shelf behind her and pulled down a jar full of white pills, different from the pale purple of bliss itself. 'Not cheap, young master. Very precious stuff, very rare. One glass feather for each tablet and your mother must take one every day. Every day, you understand? Or else her illness will be worse.'

It took half their remaining money to buy fifty, but he made the trade and hoped he'd find a way to earn more. As soon as the pills were in his hands he turned and sprinted back to their wagon.

It was almost too late; when he flung open the door and leapt inside it was to see his mother arched in agony, froth bubbling from her lips. His skin felt as if it had been coated in ice, but he made himself pry open her mouth and place one of the pills on the back of her tongue and then hold both her mouth and nose shut. He'd seen the Fierce Children do the same when they wanted to give medicine to one of the beasts in the menagerie.

Her back remained arched, her eyes shut. He wasn't even certain she'd swallowed it. He felt the last dregs of hope drain out of him – and then she let out a long sigh and fell back to the wagon's floor as all her muscles suddenly softened. After that, the working of the pill was so fast, it was almost like the rune magic he no longer believed in. The feverish flush faded from her cheeks, her shivers ended and finally she opened her eyes.

'Jinn?' she said. 'What happened?'

He smiled and held her hand, his chest too full of happiness for him to speak. They stayed that way as the sun set and the noises of the Spiral changed from trade to revelry. The smell of roasted pig drifted in and he almost laughed when his mother told him she was hungry. She'd barely eaten in weeks.

'I'll get you some, Mamma,' he said.

It was full dark outside and hard to pick his way, but off to one side he saw a bonfire and guessed that the local tribe, the Maeng, were holding a feast. They were known to be a generous bunch and he thought they'd spare him some. The sound of drums drew him towards the blaze.

It was only when he'd crossed half the distance that he realised the deep vibration in his bones came from elsewhere. He stopped, hovering between feast and Spiral as he heard yells coming from both. And then one word became clear, repeated over and over: 'stampede'. The sound was coming from the north, from the forest. He looked that way and gasped.

The moon was high and full. It made it easy to see the approaching animals – and to see that they were neither cattle nor horse. There were many shapes among them, many vast shapes. Jinn had spoken all his life about the monsters of the Moon Forest, Yron's creations banished to the dark beneath the trees by his treacherous sister. He'd made them sound something pleasant. What an idiot he'd been.

The monsters were approaching with terrible speed and the Maeng warriors rode out to meet them. A succession of bangs and bright flashes followed and he realised that they'd brought their famous fire javelins. The noise didn't seem to scare the beasts, though. Too late, Jinn thought of his mother, helpless in their wagon, and began to run back to her.

Before he could reach her, the beasts were upon him. They were all around. A winged horse twenty feet high nearly crushed him beneath its hooves, and when he flung himself aside it was into the path of a monster with ten eyes and a hundred jagged teeth. He heard screams and knew with dread that some had made it through to the Spiral. Wood snapped as they crushed the wagons beneath their huge feet. It was impossible to know what was happening. There were flashes of wing and claw and fang, and sometimes sword and axe as the Maeng warriors fought the beasts. There was blood as they died.

Then, clear and unexpected, he heard another noise: a hunting horn. And moments later another force joined the fight, riding in on beasts as monstrous as those they hunted. One galloped so close to him he could see its riders. They were monsters too, shaped like men but with heads like birds. But no, no – those were only masks. These were the hawks of the Hunter: the human servants of the goddess of the Moon Forest folk.

Their high-pitched hunting yelps joined the roars of the attackers. He saw a cluster of them bear one of the great beasts to the ground beneath their combined weight. Once it lay on its back their knives descended to hack its flesh apart. Another hawk was crushed beneath the claw foot of a thing half-mammoth, half-bird, but the death was avenged moments later as a spear the thickness of a man's arm took the monstrosity through its slitted yellow eye.

He couldn't quite believe when it was over. Blood streamed from a cut on his brow, and there was a deep ache in his flank from a wound he didn't remember receiving.

The beasts were all dead, huge humped shapes in the darkness. Jinn forced his shaky legs to carry him back to the Spiral. The dread was so awful he almost turned round again. It seemed better not to know. Hundreds of wagons lay shattered, their owners killed, the beautiful pattern entirely broken. But a few stood untouched by the damage and as he drew nearer he realised that theirs was one of them. He saw a flash of white in the moonlight as his mother's face peered out from the dark interior. They'd been saved. The Hunter had saved them.

Other survivors began to emerge. Some fled the carnage without a backward look, while others stopped to tend to the wounded. Jinn saw a figure striding through the darkness towards them. She held her own glow around her. Her hair was as bright as fire and she was taller than any of the hawks who formed up around her. They turned their masked faces towards her like flowers drinking in the sunlight.

She said nothing, but gradually others became aware of her presence until a crowd had gathered round her. Jinn found himself joining it.

The Hunter's face wasn't masked. Jinn had seen it before, painted on the sides of wagons, but she and her hawks hadn't once left the forest in the 200 years since she made the pact with her Wanderers.

One of the Maeng warriors stepped forward to meet her.

'First Hunter,' she said in a clear, hard voice. 'This is a dark night.'

'Lighter for your help,' the warrior replied. 'Thank you. But these creatures – they never leave the forest. We were told they were banished from sun-touched land.'

The Hunter moved closer and Jinn saw that her face, though once as beautiful as the paintings showed it, was now viciously scarred. Four long scores ran from brow to lip. They pulled down the lid of her left eye and twisted her mouth.

'The rules have changed,' she said. 'The moon has risen and his magic strengthens his creatures. There is a new force in the land, a dark one. We must fight it, or it will defeat us. The moon is rising, but there are powers greater than his. And if we unite, the people of the plains and the mountains and the farmlands of the east, then we can defeat him.'

Jinn looked around him at the dead beasts and the slaughtered people and the shattered wagons. She was talking about fighting the moon god, *his* god, who he'd been taught to worship all his life. But Yron had left his mother to die and then sent his beasts to kill them all. The Hunter had saved them. She was *here*.

Jinn stepped forward and bowed. 'I'm with you, my lady,' he said. 'I'll help you fight him. Just tell me what to do.'

Acknowledgements

Huge thanks to Matt Rowan, who gave me the idea for the book in the first place and then provided invaluable feedback on an early draft. Likewise to Matt Jones and Carrie O'Grady for helping me to pull the whole thing into shape. David Bryher, Peter Norgate and Naomi Alderman gave much-needed brainstorming assistance and my brilliant agent, James Wills, not only helped sell the book but also to make it much better. I'm grateful to you all. And finally a big thank you to my editor, Anne Perry, who knows what she's talking about.

WANT MORE?

If you enjoyed this and would like to find out about similar books we publish, we'd love you to join our online SF, Fantasy and Horror community, Hodderscape.

Visit our blog site
www.hodderscape.co.uk

Follow us on Twitter
 **@hodderscape**

Like our Facebook page
 **Hodderscape**

You'll find exclusive content from our authors, news, competitions and general musings, so feel free to comment, contribute or just keep an eye on what we are up to. See you there!